Fruit of the Poppy

a *novel* *by* ROBERT WILDER, 1901-

Fruit Of The Poppy

G. P. PUTNAM'S SONS
New York

42,678

To
WILLIAM POPE
This small return for your friendship

Fruit of the Poppy

1

THE summer rain which falls upon the plateau of Mexico from towering, black thunderheads split by an awesome play of lightning had spent itself. The streets glistened darkly now and water swirled through the gutters. *Libres* and private cars rolled in a showering procession along Juarez and the Paseo de la Reforma. At one o'clock in the morning the tempo of night life begins to accelerate.

He walked alone, feeling strangely alien in this city where he had been born. Earlier he had taken a cab to the *zócalo,* the vast, open quadrangle occupying what was once the central court of Tenochtitlán. It is now a district of shops, outdoor markets, pushcart vendors and small eating places. By day it is colorful and noisy; by night mysteriously somber and with the spell of history upon it. In the side streets are the *vecindades,* the tenements; gloomy, dank and a little frightening. Homeless children, old men and women huddle in the doorways, trying to find some small measure of warmth and shelter.

For awhile he had sat in the vast Cathedral dominating the plaza. Here was the deep silence of reverence, the brilliant scarlet and gold of the altar, the yellow cones of flame from the many candles unwavering in the breathless hush. When the rain stopped he went outside and started walking uptown along the Avenida Madero, turning

to stroll across Isabel la Católica to Tacuba and then in the direction
of the alameda. There was no purpose in the wandering beyond a
vague desire to recapture the feeling of the city he had known as a
boy. He was reaching back in an effort to hold on to something of
substance.

Lieutenant Carlos Mendoza. It had been so long since he had
been addressed by the title or the name that he could almost forget
they were his. He had come back on a two weeks' special leave from
an assignment which had kept him in Juarez for three years. His
mother wept at the sight of him, for she sensed he was somehow lost
to her and the world in which he rightly belonged. The family was an
old one in Mexico and the home was in the Churubusco district
where, it was said, Cortés first met Moctezuma on a stone causeway.
Nearby was the country club and he had played golf, sat at the bar
with old friends, taken *la comida* on the bright terrace outside. And,
nothing seemed real.

Tomorrow he would go to Chihuahua for instructions from Colonel Ortega and from there to Hermosillo, in the State of Sonora. In
Hermosillo he would again take up the name, the habits, the dress,
the role, the character, the life which had become his. He would forget he was Carlos Mendoza. It was necessary to erase from his mind
all the familiar things which gave a man pleasure. How it was to have
the company of a lovely, gently bred girl; the welcome of a gracious
hostess; the talk of horseracing, of music, of books, of sports and a
little of art. The memory of good brandy or wine from fine crystal
and a meal served on delicate china with snowy linen and gleaming
silver. These things he would efface.

There were others in the service. Only the Mexican Government
knew how many, who and where they were. They had all given over
their lives, sublimated their identities, merging themselves with their
surroundings, blending unobtrusively in the dedication to a task. So,
one might be a taxi driver in Tijuana, a bartender in Tampico, a porter in Vera Cruz, a hotel clerk in Juarez, a shiftless bum in Matamoros. These were the men who worked quietly under a broad variety
of covers in Mexico's effort to shut off the traffic in narcotics as they
moved into the United States. It was a life of loneliness, of devotion
to duty, in which there was no room for family or home. From the
information gathered in the half-world in which they lived an illegal

laboratory, where the raw opium underwent the transformation into heroin, was located and raided. Acting upon their tips the Customs and men of the Federal Bureau of Narcotics picked off a smuggler at a border crossing. A word here, a careless phrase there, were put together and the location of a poppy field in a hidden valley was given to the *Federales*. Soldiers went in to destroy the opium at its source. A peddler, coming from the hills, was arrested and searched. Raw opium was in his pack. He would not recall a drunken boast made in a remote village cantina of the money he was making while a peon quietly drank his mescal and listened without apparent interest. A taxi driver picked up a man at an airport and reported his presence and someone from the *sindacato* in the United States was taken into custody with the money he brought to make a buy.

These men rarely knew each other. So, it was quite possible for one agent to sit at a bar, order a tequila, and be served by another without either being aware of the situation's grim irony. But all of their information, the small threads, were spun through a central agency in the District Federal and they provided a pattern. With this the Government was able to follow, and sometimes even predict, the operation from the first flowering of a poppy to the heroin as it reached the border.

In the United States there were also men of single purpose who worked within the shadow of anonymity out of the Federal Bureau of Narcotics. Between the two countries there was a continual exchange of information and, often, personnel. Yet despite the combined efforts the traffic expanded. Drug addiction, the demand and supply, had become one of the great national problems.

Mendoza walked across the alameda, the park lying between the Avenidas Hidalgo and Juarez. There were puddles of water on the paths, and the leaves of the trees shone as though lacquered. When a light breeze riffled them a small shower fell upon his face. Opposite the park was the gleaming façade of the Hotel del Prado. This, to Mendoza, was always the fascination of his city where the new Mexico stood side by side with the old. For in the lower section of this park there had once been an arena, the *quemadero,* "the burning place" where those of the Inquisition put to death the stubborn heretics.

For a moment he thought about stopping in at the Del Prado bar and having one last drink; to sit among well-dressed men and beautifully gowned women, listen to laughter and music. Tomorrow, in Chihuahua, this would be impossible. Tomorrow he would be another man who called himself Jalisco; a panderer, one of small chicanery, a petty thief and sometime drunkard who was always in trouble with the police on minor offenses. After a moment's pause he decided against it. Too many Americans frequented the Del Prado and there was the danger someone would see and remember him at another place and at another time. Always the cover must be protected. Never for a moment could he forget this.

He hailed a cab and gave the driver the Churubusco address. They rolled swiftly through the traffic on Juarez, turned right on San Juan de Latran. Three quarters of a mile or so south this broad thoroughfare became El Nino Perdido.

Mendoza smiled to himself. "The Lost Child." It seemed fitting he should travel this street on his last night at home and before he went back again into the shadows.

* * * *

Fear gnawed at the little man in the gray suit, eating out his guts and leaving him as empty as a termite-ridden log. He tried to pull away from the monster, crouching back into the shallow corner of the taxicab but the thing remained with him. His small, almost dainty and expensively shod feet rested on soiled carpeting and he hunched against the worn cushions. Only the crown of his dove-colored Homburg hat showed above the window.

Outside, the sooted rumble of Chicago eddied and swirled. Heavy trucks lumbered noisily, charging into narrow spaces, clearing their own paths between slithering cabs and private cars. Swinging into Dearborn Street the driver of the taxi inched toward the curb of the Santa Fe depot. For the first time since he had given the original directions the man in gray spoke.

"Drive slowly. Don't stop. Go around the block and come back again."

The hackie turned questioningly. "It's late."

"Do as I say. That's what you're paid for." There was almost a startling rasp in the little man's voice and he didn't look at all like a person with a snarl. "There's time."

The driver muttered beneath his breath. The world was filled with bastards in gray, blue or brown suits and, somehow, he managed to get them. He loafed past the crowded entrance. Last-minute arrivals stood in nervous knots, superintending the transfer of their baggage from cabs to porters' trucks. They fumbled with checks and bills, consulting their watches and hurrying inside. The cab dragged past and from the security of his corner the little man's eyes darted from doorway to doorway, from group to group, with the twitching intensity of a panicked rabbit. He touched the back of his hand to dry lips and brushed the knuckles against a closely cropped mustache of reddish-brown.

The cab picked up speed as it rounded the corner, completed its run around the block and drew up again before the entrance.

"Suit you, Mac?" He was unsmilingly sarcastic.

The little man ignored him. He stepped to the sidewalk and waited while a porter hauled the heavy bag from the cab and then thrust out half a claim check.

The man in gray waved the pasteboard aside. "I want you to walk with me. Compartment C, Car 104. Super-Chief."

The porter hesitated. "Bag'll be all raight, suh. I put it on th' truck an' carry it raight in with the others."

The man held out a five-dollar bill. "I want you to go with me; right with me, understand?"

The redcap sighed with resignation born of long experience with travelers and money. He picked up the bag and waited while the man in gray paid the driver.

Walking over the narrow sidewalk the little man held close to the porter's side, brushing against him as they threaded their way through the eddying crowd, across the jammed vestibule and toward the gates.

It was late with only a few minutes left on the station clock. Last-minute passengers pushed impatiently through the entrance lane, their progress blocked every few feet as the gateman checked their tickets for space and train. The little man wedged himself into the line, keeping the apologetic porter at his back. His fingers opened and closed convulsively over the coupons in his hand and he kept his face averted as though in deep study of the slips of paper before turning them in for inspection.

The girl with the honey-colored hair had been standing by the baggage truck near the gates for almost half an hour, ever since they opened. As the minutes lengthened she seemed to be reading a copy of a news magazine, flicking through the pages slowly. Most of the time, though, her eyes had been on the entrance to the trains. As the man in gray passed through she closed the periodical, bent gracefully to pick up a small makeup case of polished alligator and joined the end of the line. Her movements were casual and unhurried. She was not unaware of the hungry, male eyes which took in each detail of her slender figure from the soft mass of hair to the small tips of her green shoes. She was as delicately exquisite as a rare orchid and the expensively simple suit of cream-colored silk flatteringly touched her hips and the contours of her long legs. Her oval face was as fresh as wood violets and she looked as though she were the perfectly poised and turned-out product of an exclusive finishing school. Without speaking she turned her tickets over to the gateman, received them back, nodded pleasantly and passed on.

Once past the barrier the man in gray moved in close company with the other travelers, making of them a phalanx within which he was shielded on all sides. The path led along the platform flanked by the rear cars of the shimmering Super-Chief and its less expensive and aristocratic brother, El Capitan. Earlier arrivals stared from behind the broad, plate-glass windows with smug complacency and there was an air of expectancy about them as they waited for departure time.

At the steps of her car, 103, the girl seemed to be having trouble with the clasp of her bag. It took her a few moments to adjust it and during the interval the man in gray had entered the car ahead. She fumbled with the catch but kept her eyes on the vestibule opening of 104.

"Bes' hurry, miss," the car porter urged and held out a hand to assist her to the steps.

Still she delayed until the porter of Car 104 swung his footstool up and she heard the clanging sound of the platform closing and the door slam. Then, without haste, she stepped lightly up, followed by the porter. He watched her disappear and shook his head bewilderedly. People were always doing funny things. She could have just as well fixed her bag inside. Dickty white people were an awful pain most of the time.

The Super-Chief moved out as slowly and as effortlessly as a breeze, snapping gently across yard switches and twisting its long, gleaming body through the short curves. Time enough later to stretch out and settle down for the run to Kansas City.

First-time travelers hurried a little self-consciously toward the rear car, ignoring the center club lounge which would be preempted by the Hollywood film and TV gin rummy addicts for which the Super-Chief was sort of a de-luxe commuter's train.

In Compartment C, Car 104, the man in gray locked the door and then bent to fumble with the straps of his bag. Taking out a bottle of Scotch he poured himself a large, straight drink in a paper cup and tossed it down his throat with hungry eagerness. Then he sat on the edge of the divan and pulled from the bag a large, thick envelope. He weighed it gently, pressing it with his fingers, fondling it as though the touch created a sexual excitement.

There was $250,000 in the packet. It made a bulky package. Two hundred and fifty thousand dollars. He said the words to himself. A man, a man his age, could live out the balance of his life comfortably with that amount. He could, he amended, live it out if Dano and a couple of others to whom it, more or less, legally belonged didn't rub him out before he had a chance to spend any of it. But the man in gray had no intention of just living comfortably. He wanted magnificence, every imaginable luxury: a villa in France, on the Riviera; a hilltop mansion overlooking the incredibly beautiful bay at Acapulco. He wanted servants and pliant women, exquisite food, the finest of wines. He also wanted, and needed, a bodyguard; two, three men whose loyalty could be bought. Properly handled this $250,000 represented only the beginning, for he knew every detail of the operation, the contacts, the methods, the distribution, which would turn a quarter of a million dollars into a tenfold sum. But, and this he somberly weighed, he must first stay alive.

He hadn't wanted to take the train but it had seemed the best choice. Only a fool would try to get away and out of Chicago on a train. No one but an idiot would shut himself up in a stainless-steel trap for thirty-six hours or so. Harvey Mitchell was no fool. Dano

and the others might have called him a number of things but not a
fool. So he, Harvey Mitchell, had bet his life on this slim margin of
error. He would do what no man in his right mind would attempt,
take the train because Dano would not believe him capable of such
idiocy. He had bought a couple of airline tickets under his own name
—one to Rio and the other to Miami. At this moment two slightly bewildered but gratified strangers, who saw no reason to turn down
five hundred dollars and a free round trip to Brazil and Florida, were
winging over the country as Harvey Mitchell. He had even bought a
bus ticket to Cleveland, changing his mind several times about the
schedule and departure time so he could be certain the harassed clerk
would remember and be able to describe him when questioned. None
of the things he had done was particularly clever or inventive but a
man in a hurry, a man who had stolen a quarter of a million dollars
from Dano, didn't have much time to plan elaborately. They would,
of course, find out the men on the Rio- and Miami-bound planes
were decoys and the bus ticket unused. But—again he walked the
high wire of danger—by that time he would have found a measure of
security. For years Harvey Mitchell had kept a finger on the pulse of
Dano's activities and he knew the potential defectors within the organization; the ones with small ambitions, the cheap punks and guns
who fancied themselves as masterminds if only they were given a
chance. They could be bought, enticed by a vision of an organization in which they were equal partners, shrewd and ruthless manipu-
lators who would give orders instead of taking them. They would
provide a temporary sanctuary for Harvey Mitchell and never suspect they were being used.

He took another drink. The stuff gagged him but he forced it
down. This wasn't smart but the alcohol had an assuasive effect. He
had a trip to sweat out and it wasn't going to be easy. The compartment could be a safe refuge or a coffin. His imagination began to
play. It could happen that in a few minutes someone would knock at
the door or sound the buzzer. He would have to answer because it
might be the porter or conductor, checking the occupancy. Again, it
might be someone he had never seen before. This was what chilled
him. Suppose it was a stranger, cold-eyed, impersonal, with a gun
and a job to do; someone who wouldn't give a damn about Harvey
Mitchell or how his belly would feel with three or four red-hot slugs

in it. He felt panic clot in his throat with the taste of clabbered milk. Suddenly, the compartment no longer seemed the safe refuge he had imagined it would be. He would be better off in the club car, surrounded by passengers and stewards. As long as he could keep other persons around him he had protection; nothing was going to happen in a crowded lounge.

He hefted the bulky envelope in his hand. It made an uncomfortable and obvious bulge in his inside coat pocket and Harvey Mitchell was a fastidious little man, fastidious and vain. Even now, when his life was balanced so precariously, he was concerned about his appearance. Almost absentmindedly he dropped the packet back into his bag. Persons who traveled on the Super-Chief didn't have to worry about their baggage being rifled. He locked the case and slid it beneath the seat. He felt better. It was foolish but the absence of any physical contact with the money made him feel safer.

Pausing briefly to straighten the neat isosceles triangle of his tie into his collar, he reached for the door, unsnapped the catch, swung it open and stepped out into the corridor. As he did, the door of the adjoining compartment clicked and he experienced a frantic horror that stopped his breath. His small, nervous eyes felt as though they actually popped, protruding like the pulp of a squeezed grape. There was the clammy, damp gathering of perspiration on his body. It almost had an odor. Mitchell backed with a cautious, crablike movement into his room, his gaze never leaving the stranger's face. He was dimly conscious of making small, gurgling sounds which were choking him.

"Something wrong? You all right, fella?" The man was concerned.

Mitchell could only shake his head with a negative gesture. He wanted to run screaming somewhere, anywhere. He wet his lips and continued backing until he was clear of the door. He tried to shut it but lacked the strength to put out a hand. This was the way it would come; unannounced, quickly and without preliminaries.

The man squinted narrowly at him for a moment and then nodded sympathetically.

"You've really tied one on, haven't you, brother? You ought to be careful with that stuff or you'll be climbing the wall." He laughed, a small, understanding chuckle reserved for drunks, and passed on down the carpeted lane.

Harvey Mitchell stood where he was until he heard the subdued roar of the train as the vestibule door opened and closed. Then he bolted, snatched open the folding washbasin and was sick. I've got to get off this train, he told himself. I was crazy to try it. I'm trapped. Unconnected fancies shaped themselves in his mind as he rinsed his mouth and wiped it with a towel. He would manage to get off somehow; sleep in the woods; let his beard grow; shave his mustache. He would become a tramp, a hobo with two hundred and fifty thousand dollars wrapped in a bandanna bundle. The illogical terror ebbed slowly. None of it was any good. The Super-Chief wouldn't make a stop until it reached Kansas City. His one hope of survival was to stay on the train and keep himself close to other persons and take a chance Dano would first have him hunted in Mexico City, Miami or Cleveland. He understood well enough the "family"—the *borgata,* as the organization called its units—could afford to take its time. It wouldn't have to exert itself. All Dano had to do was sit back in Chicago and pass the word. It would be transmitted through a hundred channels, the arteries and veins, until everyone in what was known as *Cosa Nostra,* "our thing," was aware of the defector. As money went the two hundred and fifty thousand dollars was unimportant but it represented a breach in discipline. This would have to be corrected as an example and the correction was the elimination of Harvey Mitchell. A moral lesson was needed. Besides, he told himself, he had not made this move for the purpose of hiding in some shabby town; hoarding the money which, then, would serve to do nothing more than feed, clothe and house him. It wasn't for this he had risked everything.

He wanted another drink. He wanted to get so drunk he could lie down and sleep but he didn't dare. Already he could feel the liquor he had taken creeping on him, clouding his faculties, lulling them into a false security. He drew up his narrow shoulders and walked into the corridor again. It was empty. He closed the door and automatically moved down its length through a second, third and fourth car to the lounge.

Swaying at the edge of the small, crescent-shaped bar he steadied himself with a hand and made a quick census of the occupants. The white-coated stewards shuttled back and forth with trays, glasses and the individual bottles of Scotch and bourbon. Highballs frosted, cards on the tables, fat cigars and cigarettes alight. Mr. Mitchell's fellow travelers barely glanced up as he passed. There was a vacant chair next to a girl with honey-colored hair. He teetered, slightly off-balance, and made for it with a quick lurch.

The girl was seated with an unaffected naturalness. A current magazine, in the Santa Fe's leather cover, lay on her lap. She was oblivious of the covert glances of the unattached males who scanned every detail of her breasts, legs and face; the figure so artfully molded in the tailored suit. When her eyes did meet an inquisitive and speculative stare they did so without the slightest trace of recognition but passed on and beyond.

Beside her sat a ruddy-faced man of sixty or so. His expression was one of interested benevolence for everyone and his white hair had the soft sheen of silver powder. He looked happily around, nodding his approval over the spectacle of so many well-dressed, well-fed and entertaining persons being with him on the same train. He was obviously enjoying himself and his attitude seemed to say this was all new and quietly exciting.

Harvey Mitchell hesitated in front of the vacant chair. The girl looked up and saw the question in his eyes.

"Certainly," she murmured. Her words were soft, tinged with a well-bred huskiness. "There is no one sitting in it."

"Thank you."

Harvey Mitchell breathed his gratitude and sank with an open sigh of relief into the cushion. For a moment or two he just sat there, conscious he was breathing heavily, as though he had been running. After a few seconds some of the nameless dread began to drain from him. He relaxed his slight body and pulled his feet and legs into a more comfortable position. He was safe here. Nothing could possibly happen in a car filled with passengers. If necessary he could have his dinner brought to the small table at his side and there would always be someone around, unaware that they were shielding him. He lit a cigarette and noticed with satisfaction his hands had all but ceased their trembling.

The elderly man with the pink cheeks and the frosty sparkle of a Santa Claus, somehow, leaned partly past the girl and spoke directly to Harvey Mitchell.

"Is it true," there was a bemused humor in the tone, "that they won't serve a drink on this train while it is in Kansas?"

Mitchell took a deep breath. He had been startled by the abruptness of the question and the approach. He forced himself to unbend and adopt a casual air. There was something so gentle and reassuring in the innocently beaming face.

"I don't know. It used to be that way. Local or state law."

The questioner mulled this information over with obvious wonder at the absurdity. "You," he spoke thoughtfully, "wouldn't think a little bit of whisky on a train going a hundred miles an hour would taint the morals of even a prohibitionist, would you now?" The silver head shook itself unbelievingly and then his eyes were bent upon the girl to include her in the conversation. "Not that I really care," he assured her. "I don't drink much. Sometimes it can be very soothing. I just heard about it and wondered if it was true."

The girl smiled with a pleasant impersonality but said nothing.

"This is the first time I have been west of Akron, you know." The gentle eyes sparkled with suppressed excitement. "Going to California to see my daughter and her children. Sent for me. Told me to come out." He seemed inordinately proud of this. "Said I would live twenty years longer in Santa Monica. Don't know whether that's a real advantage or not." He chuckled at the mild jest. Then, as an afterthought, he fished about in a breast pocket, removed an old wallet, extracted a creased photograph and tentatively extended it toward the girl. She took it with a small expression of patience. "That's my daughter and her children." A pleased smile creased his features. "Of course it isn't a very good picture." He laughed happily. "I guess everyone says that about a photograph."

The girl studied the group with forced interest. "Nice-looking children." She started to hand it back.

The man waved in the direction of Mitchell. "Would you like to look at it, sir?" he coaxed.

Because he couldn't reply with a flat no Harvey accepted the picture from the girl. Their eyes met briefly and she smiled a little resignedly. Gravely Harvey regarded the faded images and then passed it back.

"Nice-looking family." He made the comment with a friendly and approving nod. "Handsome."

"It was taken a long time ago." The man replaced the picture in his wallet. "I guess the boys are real young men by this time. It is going to be quite an experience to see them. They are the only grandchildren I have. A man," his eyes actually grew misty, "a man isn't much good without a family about him when he's my age, is he?"

He was prattling with such disarming innocence and goodwill that Harvey Mitchell found himself warming despite himself. The man was filled with an unabashed curiosity about everything. He asked the train's speed, the arrival time in Los Angeles, how much one was expected to tip the porter, would they really bring him breakfast in his compartment? The questions were directed impartially to Mitchell and the girl. Now and then she added a comment as though realizing that to remain silent would be unnecessarily rude. The conversation became easy, relaxed and completely trivial.

The old gentleman beckoned to a passing steward.

"I think I would like a lemonade, no sugar but with just a touch of bourbon in it." He spoke the words with a relish. "Would you join me?" His bright, birdlike eyes swept between Mitchell and the girl. "Of course," he added, "you may order something different."

"Lemonade and bourbon would suit me fine." Her fine eyes crinkled with laughter. "I don't think I have ever tried the combination."

"I'll have a Scotch and water." Harvey added his order and then, as the steward moved away, he added, "Perhaps"—he hesitated only briefly—"perhaps we three could have dinner together? I mean," he spoke directly to the girl, "I mean, if you haven't an engagement."

"Thank you." She gave him a smile which flooded over him like warm sunshine. "I think it would be pleasant."

The elderly gentleman was naïvely delighted. "Why, that would be just crackerjack! I always say the whole world could get along if people just acted like people to each other. You know. Be themselves, friendly like, talking things over. There wouldn't be any need for killing and bloodshed."

The final words jolted Harvey Mitchell with an almost nauseating abruptness and he experienced a sudden revulsion. What could this garrulous old fool know of killing and bloodshed? Had he ever, in his dull and placid existence, run for his life? Did he know what fear meant? He reached quickly for his drink as the steward brought the tray, emptied the tiny bottle into the glass and drank it quickly and without apology.

"I'll have another, Steward." He was aware of the girl's eyes turned upon him with shaded curiosity. "Nerves," he explained. "My stomach. Acts up sometimes."

She said nothing.

After a few moments Harvey could feel the lenitive effect of the alcohol and he found himself regarding the girl and the man with a feeling of superiority. What did either of them know of the life with which he was so familiar? He wondered what they would say if he told them he had stolen a quarter of a million dollars from the *Capo,* the boss of the Chicago *borgata,* and that at this minute the "family" was trying to follow his unpredictable movements with but one idea in mind: to kill him. That would make them sit up. He was no longer someone of unimportance. The knowledge made him smug.

The girl was watching him. "For a moment I thought you were not feeling well. Your face changed so quickly."

"I'm all right." Mitchell brushed away the concern almost rudely. "Nerves. I've been working too hard."

The elderly man nodded sympathetically. "You ought to try a little warm milk. I don't think whisky is good for indigestion."

Mitchell sought to divert the conversation. The dining car steward was standing near the bar. Harvey caught his eye and beckoned.

"Will eight o'clock be all right for dinner?" He spoke to the girl.

"That will be fine." Somehow, he thought, she managed to charge the simple words with an unexpected intimacy.

Giving the reservation to the steward Mitchell thought that this meeting was something in the nature of a providential miracle. These two were his shield. Without knowing it they were his protectors from unexpected violence, the intrusion of a stranger of whose presence he must be wary. When the steward asked in what name the reservation should be held, Mitchell hesitated only briefly.

"Cameron. Horace Cameron." Even as he spoke he wondered from what hidden corner of his mind the name had sprung. "There will be three of us."

"I have some neighbors in Akron by the name of Cameron." The old man regarded him with approving interest as though he had just discovered an old friend. "Fine people."

"It's a common name." Mitchell found he was growing impatient with the compulsive chatter. The fellow just didn't seem able to keep quiet. Who the hell cared if he knew a hundred Camerons in Akron? He forced himself to retreat from the edginess which might well alienate this small security. I have to be pleasant and agreeable, he warned himself, or I will lose them both. "I don't believe any of my family came from Ohio."

"By the way"—the old one again—"we haven't introduced ourselves. My name is Williamson, Charles Williamson." He all but forced Harvey to take his hand. "I always say people traveling together should be natural. We come together and we part. Then it is always nice to be able to say: I remember meeting a man named Smith or Mason or Cameron going to California one time. It makes for conversation when no one has anything to say."

"I am Judith Royal." The girl smiled at Williamson and then, again, all but secretly at Mitchell. "Now we all know each other."

"Well." Mr. Williamson stood up with apologetic regret. "I have some things to do in my compartment. And," he smiled, embarrassed, "if I am going to have supper—dinner, I guess they call it on a luxury train like this—with a beautiful young lady I ought to shave again and wash up. It takes me quite a time to work out the mechanics of those folding washbasins and all. I'll meet you both here later. It has been a most enjoyable interlude, most enjoyable."

"Until later, Mr. Williamson." The girl tucked in her slender, beautiful legs to give him room to pass.

Mitchell watched her veiled amusement as her glance followed the slightly waddling figure as it trundled down the car's length. His eyes studied her greedily. This is what you could buy with the money he would have someday. Maybe not this one. He wasn't able to catalog her. But the world was filled with girls, tall, slender and with high, hard breasts; perfume on their bodies, invitation in their eyes. They all wanted the luxury of furs, jewels, and were willing to trade for it. He could feel the excitement rising as he thought about it. Two hundred and fifty thousand. He would plant it in a poppy field. The notion tickled his fancy for he was not, ordinarily, a man given to such imagery. It would flourish in the fine, heavy blooms with their silken pods. From these, properly incised by skillful hands, first came the gumlike sap of opium to be transformed into the white crystals of heroin and the fortune. He knew exactly where he was going. What he would do. How he would do it. Only one thing. He must stay alive until he could buy the protection he needed. Mexico. The State of Sonora. A little village some kilometers away from Hermosillo. Batuc and a man named Francisco Pilar, a *pistolero,* who could be trusted so long as he was well paid.

"Mr. Williamson," the girl's voice snapped him back to the moment, "such a pleasant gentleman but," there was a light of subdued amusement in her glance, "I can imagine he could become something of a terrible bore on a desert island or," her laughter was soft, "even on the Super-Chief."

Harvey Mitchell wondered if there was an invitation behind the seemingly innocent words. Maybe after dinner, when the old fool had gone to bed, he could have some time alone with her. You could never tell about a girl, especially on a train or a ship. They did things. Or so he had heard. Things they wouldn't do in more familiar surroundings.

"He talks too much." Mitchell's words grated. "A little conversation is one thing. Monkey chatter is another."

"And you, Mr. Cameron," she studied him gravely, "you have said practically nothing. What business are you in?"

"Well . . ." Harvey thought this was going to be a fine joke. "I'm sort of a horticulturist."

"How interesting." She stood up and he rose quickly. Surprisingly, she offered her hand and its clasp was warm and firm. He was positive there was a slight squeeze. "Until eight o'clock then, Mr. Cameron?"

"That will be fine. I think I'll just stay here for awhile longer and maybe have another drink."

He watched as she moved away and was aware of the turning of heads as the eyes of every man in the car followed her. Her body, exquisitely outlined, was as graceful as a willow wand. As she passed from view the masculine heads turned to regard Harvey Mitchell with undisguised interest and envy. They seemed to be asking: How the hell did you catch that prize package?

The Super-Chief was a great silver needle threading its way through the gathering darkness. At the bar the attendant dialed a radio for a news broadcast. The world outside seemed comfortably rcmote. Without much cffort Mitchell could imagine he was aboard a spaceship bound for a distant planet. He resumed his seat and ordered another drink. I'm getting a little tight, he warned himself. A man gets himself loaded and he becomes careless. He owlishly studied the other occupants of the car for some small indication of menace. Then he sighed with relief and a sense of well-being. Nothing had changed. The cardplayers were unsmilingly intent upon their games. The scene was warm, pleasantly lighted, comfortable, and as secure as a homeside hearth. Here he was safe.

2

🌿 HEAD propped against a pillow, long legs stretched the length of the divan, Sol Madrid watched the smoke from his cigarette rise and disappear with the invisible current of the air-conditioning system. His dark, lean face was in repose but there was an odd, speculative luster in his eyes as though something secretly amused him. He had been in this position from the time the Super-Chief had pulled out of Chicago. When he was thinking, he liked to lie down and he was thinking now, seriously and with a curious sense of baffled curiosity. Nothing dropped into form as it should. There were intriguing bits of a puzzle in his mind but they refused to fall into place. The whole thing just didn't make any sense.

He drew heavily upon the cigarette stub and lit another from its coal. A small tray on the floor beside him was all but overflowing with twisted butts. Intuition, experience, told him this was no fantastic coincidence and yet it had to be. Why should Dano Villanova's accountant, Harvey Mitchell, be on the same train with Villanova's girl friend, Stacey Woodward? Further complicating this inexplicable situation there was the twinkling-eyed, rosy-cheeked Roy Gaines. It was Madrid's business to know but not be known and he was leafing through a mental dossier on Gaines, who had the appearance of someone's benevolent uncle, a department store Santa Claus, a kindly old gentleman who would sit in the park on a warm spring day and feed the pigeons. Instead, Roy Gaines was a "button man," a killer of icy, impersonal ferocity for the Detroit *borgata*. Why? Sol rubbed the knuckles of a heavy hand against his nose as though this rough massage would draw out the answer. What Mecca brought these three pilgrims together?

His mind retraced the known habits and associations of the trio. It was highly improbable they knew each other. Villanova kept his life with the Woodward girl a thing apart. She lived alone in all the luxury Dano generously provided. When they traveled together they occupied separate suites in the same hotel or ship. It was unlikely she had ever met a single member of the "family." Certainly it was beyond imagining she was aware of the existence of Harvey Mitchell, who burrowed like some quiet mole among the complicated ledgers, accounts and manifold financial dealings of the Chicago branch of *Cosa Nostra*. Logic told Sol this. Intuition denied it. Roy Gaines. Where did he fit here?

Madrid swung up from his lounging place, poured himself a drink of fine bourbon and stood by the window, sipping the liquor appreciatively. A witches' brew was being stirred. For whom and to what purpose?

He had been mildly interested when he had first seen the Woodward girl at the station. She was a thing of beauty although, he grinned, perhaps not a joy forever. She had background, breeding, education. Fifteen, twenty years ago she might have been called a moll, a fluff, a twist. Those terms were as old-fashioned as the word gangster.These days society had to deal with a new breed, a second generation from the mob rulers who once held Chicago, Detroit, Los Angeles, New York, Cleveland, Miami and other cities as their private fiefs and shooting preserves. The Capones, Schultzes, O'Bannions, Lepkes, Colls and Lucianos were men of musty fiction. In their places were shrewd businessmen, many of them graduates of Eastern universities. They lived quietly, circumspectly and in an aura of respectability. Yet their well-manicured fingers still held the same old threads. Dope. Gambling. Prostitution. The manifold rackets from the numbers with their five-and-ten-cent bets to silent partnerships in hotels and casinos from Nevada to Puerto Rico, Las

Vegas to Acapulco. Nothing had really changed. The operation now was suave, polished and sophisticated. Murder was done and often but it no longer roared around a corner in a black sedan. It came quietly and with finesse.

The Woodward girl, he mused, was part of the new look. He had watched her from a point outside her vision. For all her appearance of casualness her attention never strayed for long from the train gates. So, he had told himself, she is waiting for someone to show but it wasn't Villanova. If she and Dano were taking a trip together she would have gone directly to her bedroom suite as Villanova would have gone to his. The small traveling case at her feet could only mean she was taking the Super-Chief. If so why the hell didn't she go to her car instead of standing there pretending to read a magazine?

Madrid decided to wait. There was time. His curiosity was piqued. Then, in the file of passengers he caught sight of the rolling-gaited figure of Gaines as he checked through at the conductor's stand. Madrid had whistled softly for he was familiar with the habits of Roy Gaines. He was a slipper-and-armchair man who was devoted to his extensive library of classical music, a small flower garden with a hothouse, a pair of Siamese cats and his neat home in suburban Detroit which he rarely left except on business; a contract which meant the quietly efficient extermination of someone who had offended against the notions of *Cosa Nostra*. So, he wondered, what was putting Mr. Gaines aboard the Super-Chief? A few minutes later he saw Mitchell, cautious as a wounded ferret, accompanied by a porter, trying to shrink himself into invisibility among the others. Then, and only then, had the Woodward girl moved. Without haste she picked up her case and joined the line. So she had been waiting for Mitchell. Why? He shook his head. The idea of Stacey Woodward running away with Harvey Mitchell was so fantastically ludicrous that Sol dismissed it immediately. Just the same there was a connection between their movements.

Madrid had dropped his cigarette, mashing it out with the toe of a shoe. Tiny crinkles of perplexity drew themselves about his eyes. He was positive Mitchell did not know the girl by sight. But then, and the question came to him automatically, how did Stacey Woodward recognize Harvey Mitchell? Taking his leisure he had followed the strangely assorted three to the train. Now Woodward, Mitchell and Gaines were in cars 103 and 104. Sol's bedroom was in 102.

Balancing himself against the rhythmic swaying, Madrid poured himself another small drink and laughed abruptly because this was one hell of a funny situation and he was going to have some thirty-six hours or so to watch it develop.

A week ago he had been in the State of Sonora, in Mexico. There, in the countryside, the garnet poppies grew. Acres upon acres; hectare bounding hectare of satin beauty. They shone in the sunlight like exquisitely fashioned bulbs of sheerest crimson leaf but they brought no esthetic pleasure to the women and girls who worked among the rows after the petals had fallen and covered the ground with soft radiance. With sharp blades they expertly incised a spiral cut about the downy pods. It was delicate work. The knife must not cut too deeply, for the sticky secretion would then not bleed to the surface. From the gum collected, carefully scraped away and wrapped in leaves, came the opium. A fairly simple laboratory process transformed this into a morphine base, slightly brownish in color. From this, by a more complicated method, came the white powder of heroin, the enslaver.

Listening to the song of wheels on rails Sol thought of a couple of lines from a poem written many years ago, in World War I. He transposed them:

> *In Sonora's fields the poppies grow,*
> *Beside the crosses, row on row.*

Only, he mused, the crosses were not in Sonora but stretched around the world. They marked uncounted graves, were the signposts of murder and every violent crime of which man was capable. They threw their shadows on the mean walls of filthy pads, prison cells, hospital wards, expensive apartments and single rooms for the junkie was confined to no class. He could live on Park Avenue, in New York, or the shabby slum district of Los Angeles. The crosses were the invisible racks upon which the addicts writhed, clutched at their bowels, doubled themselves up in agony and screamed in helpless torment. They were the guideposts for the kids who first experimented with marijuana and, when the kicks from the weed were no longer enough, graduated to the H. To get the money they stole, first from their parents, and then in desperation mugged an innocent pedestrian in a side street, held up a liquor store, hot-wired a car and sold it to a shady dealer for one or two hundred dollars. High school girls first gave themselves to a pusher for a paper of the stuff and when he tired of them turned prostitute. Always the monkey on the back demanded more to keep him quiet. Five, ten, twenty and fifty dollars a day. There was only one way for most of them to get that kind of money. Murder and robbery. Men and women clawed at each other, crawled and abased themselves for a fix when the torment was upon them. Heroin produces no dreamy euphoria. The addict lives in no world of pleasant, softly hued dreams. Once hooked he screamed for the drug only to ease the incredible pain which took possession of his body as the effects of the narcotic wore off. No one who had ever watched a "cold turkey" withdrawal where the addict screamed, rolled upon the floor, beat his head against a wall, scratched at his body until the skin shredded, scuttled as some broken crab beneath the bed, begged, pleaded, howled in a nightmare of convulsions, could feel anything but horrified pity and a loathing for those who fattened themselves upon such human misery.

No one knew how many addicts there were in the United States. A half million? A million. More? No accurate count was possible. During his ten years with the Federal Bureau of Narcotics, Madrid had watched the traffic grow. The sources were, seemingly, unlimited and they fed a vast syndicate from the Mafia, in Sicily, to *Cosa Nostra,* in the United States. Every agent knew where the drug came from. A map could be drawn from the poppy fields in Turkey with the raw opium moving into Syria. From Syria it went to Beirut, in Lebanon, and from Beirut to Naples or Marseilles. In Southern France there were scattered, illicit laboratories which turned the opium into heroin. It found its way in cargo, passenger baggage, diplomatic pouch and the hand satchel of an airline stewardess to American ports and landing fields. It came from China, Cuba and now, in increasing quantities, from Mexico. Such men as Dano Villanova were the financiers of the operation. They were arrogant, contemptuous of the law and its underpaid officers and tremendously powerful in the nether world in which they lived. The flow of money was endless and the smuggling of heroin preyed upon every human weakness—fear, greed and the appetites of the flesh. Nothing was overlooked and the drug moved through strictly prescribed channels. There was first the smuggler who brought it into the United States. The powder then came into the hands of the "wholesaler" and this dealer sold to the "ounce man," the small peddler. From a kilo of heroin, a little over two pounds, the "wholesaler" realized a profit of close to fifty thousand dollars. The "ounce man" sold his packets to the addicts for from two to five dollars, depending upon how it was cut with milk-sugar powder. It had been estimated that between five and six million dollars changed hands on a single street corner in Harlem in a single year.

The men who directed and financed this network of evil kept themselves beyond reach. The couriers, the wholesalers, the ounce men, had no idea of their identity. The agents of the Federal Bureau of Narcotics knew who they were but they couldn't prove it. The vast, shadowy empire was cynically referred to as "our thing" and it was just that. Each major city had its "family" and every family its *Capo,* boss, top man. Beneath him ranged the *Sotto Capo,* the second in command, and below this rank were the *Caporegima,* lieutenants; the *Regime,* made up of privates in the army; and finally, the *Consiglieri,* usually a corps of lawyers who acted as advisers, steering the activities between the legal shoals, setting up outwardly respectable and legitimate business enterprises which served as a front. Beyond this hard core, the cadre, was the invisible system which fed the octopus: hole-in-the-wall bookies; elaborate betting parlors which were furnished with the quiet elegance of a private club; newsstand vendors who served as outlets for the numbers racket into which were fed the nickel and dime bets for an annual take of millions. Then came the whores, organized and moved from town to town, brothel to brothel; sometimes operating from trailers at construction sites or from single rooms in nearby towns. This was the lowest stratum of regulated prostitution. On a slightly higher scale were the call girls, euphemistically referred to as "models" or "TV actresses." Once, in the Hollywood glamour days, they were known as "starlets." Their fees ranged from twenty to one hundred dollars, depending upon the time spent with a client. There was no crime, save the wildcat, unpredictable holdups, the murders of sudden passion, in which *Cosa Nostra* did not have a hand. But the great fountain of evil from which gushed untold millions, keeping green the lush pasture of organized lawlessness, was the H, the Horse, the heroin.

From Matamoros, across the Rio Grande from Brownsville, Texas, Neuvo Laredo at Laredo, Juarez at El Paso, Tijuana, with its crossing into San Diego, the deadly fruit of the poppy found hundreds of openings. It was impossible to police this extensive border. What Washington tried to do was close the big gaps. With the help of Mexican authorities, undercover agents, informers, the Federal Bureau of Narcotics fought an endless war. Mexico did its best to shut off the source. Sometimes, Sol thought wearily, the whole thing was like a worn tire. You patched it up here and it blew out there. In Mexico City he had talked long and earnestly with Mexican officials, government agents, local police. They had flown over the State of Sonora and looked down upon the hidden poppy fields. It seemed incredible that such malignance, terror, agony and torture could stem from the small plots of shimmering beauty. The existence of the fields here and in other states was no secret. Mexican *Federales* made constant raids. Helicopters flew over them and dropped napalm bombs but this was dangerous, causing disastrous forest fires, destroying timber, spreading to innocent farms and villages.

In Washington, Sol had carefully prepared his report. It contained little of which the Bureau was not aware and served only to keep some sort of a check on the current activities. The Mexican Government supplied him with the names of suspected dealers, wholesalers who might give information for a price. They were indifferent to the fact that this would result in the detection and arrest of a client at the border. Another buyer would take his place, for the gains outweighed the risk. The wholesaler would already have collected his price for the sale. So he had nothing to lose and was, actually, paid twice. The present value of heroin on the Mexican market was around $350 an ounce and it was cut many, many times by the time it reached the addict.

Madrid's transfer to Los Angeles was not unexpected. He had worked there before. In his mind there was a file of the names of the "ounce men," the pushers, the hangouts of the desperate addicts.

Ordinarily he would have flown but he had a few days' vacation coming to him and he took the Super-Chief because he had an almost childish delight in trains. He loved the sound of wheels, the chatter as they spun across a switch, a sense of boring into the night; the keening wail of the diesel engine's horn; the sheen of stainless-steel cars; the gentle movement as of a cradle when he slept at night; breakfast at a window with the countryside flashing past; the effortless service aboard such a luxury train. Now—and he smiled at his reflection in the glass—he had this interest-provoking situation to watch. Woodward, Mitchell and Gaines. This was no chance meeting but the answer eluded him. The odds against it being without plan or purpose were so impossible they had to be dismissed. He crushed the paper cup in his hand. Whatever this ill-assorted trio was up to was really none of his business. So, he chuckled, he'd simply take his seat in the orchestra and watch the show. Whatever was of interest to Dano Villanova always occupied a small part of Sol Madrid's mind and Dano's girl, along with a "button man" and the Chicago family's accountant, would certainly interest Villanova if he was aware of their movements.

Shirt open at the throat, suspenders drooping limply about his hips, Roy Gaines was bent over the gleaming washbasin in his compartment. He heard the door open and close with the faintest click. For a moment he held soapy palms to his face. Then, slowly, he began to rotate them over the pink cheeks. Carefully, deliberately, he rinsed and reached for a towel. He didn't turn. There was no need for it. In the cabinet mirror he could see the reflection of the girl with the honey-colored hair. Her face, unsmiling, reposed, was framed in the glass. Their eyes met without recognition. Mr. Gaines turned heavily.

She was leaning, almost negligently, against the door. In the fingers of her left hand she held a cigarette and a small gold lighter. She lifted the cigarette to parted lips and flicked the lighter until a flame leaped from its wick. During all of this she didn't shift her eyes or her stance of graceful indolence. The right hand held a .32-caliber automatic which was pointed at Mr. Gaines' paunch.

"Stay right where you are." She whispered the order in a cloudy, unhurried voice. Then there was the trace of a smile as she added, *"Mr. Williamson."*

For just a fraction of a second the eyes of Roy Gaines narrowed and then quickly reassumed their innocent wonder over the strange behavior.

"My goodness," he was helplessly flustered, "a pretty girl like you shouldn't enter a man's compartment, especially without knocking, and"—his bewilderment increased—"carrying a gun, too."

The automatic flicked with an impatient motion. "My mother always told me to carry a gun when I went to a man's room. Turn around now," the order was crisp, "and put your hands on the wall above your head."

Gaines' expression obviously deplored the state of things but he did as he was told. He felt the muzzle of the .32 jab into his back. The pressure was hard, viciously determined. Rapidly, expertly, one of the girl's hands went over him, slapping down his shirt from both armpits, running down the outside of his trousers, touching deftly at his bulging hips, moving quickly across his thighs.

"Move." The girl prodded him again with the gun, forcing him toward the door. "Nice and easy."

Roy Gaines wheezed softly. "I wouldn't be surprised"—he spoke with unhappy solicitude—"if you didn't end up as a very bad girl. I certainly never thought things like this went on in such a nice train."

"You never really know, do you, Mr. Williamson?" She was indifferently matter of fact. She opened the cabinet door and felt in behind the Thermos carafe and beneath the stacked towels. Next she picked up Roy Gaines' coat. Holding the collar between her small, white teeth she patted the pockets and then the lining. Satisfied, she let the garment drop in a shapeless pile to the floor.

Not by gesture or inflection did Roy Gaines drop the pose that he was a bewildered old gentleman inexplicably wedged most uncomfortably into a corner.

"Could I move a little, miss? It is very close here."

"Turn around."

Gaines edged about until he was facing the divan. The girl sidled behind him and thrust inquisitive fingers into the pockets of a gabardine raincoat on a hanger. Gaines' hand strayed cautiously toward the small plate on which the button for the porter's bell was set.

The girl didn't hurry. With cold precision she stabbed the red-hot coal of her cigarette into the knuckles of Roy Gaines' hand and the sparks showered down.

Gaines made no sound but a tremor ran over his body as he stared at the seared flesh. He raised his hand away from the bell.

"Get out your suitcase." She nudged him and waited.

As he stooped to drag the case from beneath the seat Gaines was aware of her perfume—a fresh, brook-moss scent. He placed the bag on the green cushion.

Stacey Woodward flipped open the lid and began tossing out shirts, pajamas, socks and a couple of magazines.

"It was so nicely packed," the man murmured regretfully. "I like things neat and tidy."

A pair of black, high shoes was at the bottom of the case. The girl looked at them for a moment. She picked one up, weighed it in her hand and then tossed it aside. She reached down for the other, hefted it, and the tiniest of smiles crept to her mouth. With a snap of the wrist she turned the shoe upside down and a Police Positive .38 thudded heavily into the suitcase lid. Roy Gaines didn't display the slightest interest or surprise.

With the pleased expression of an inquisitive child who has solved a perplexing riddle the girl picked up the revolver. Flipping out the cylinder she shook the wicked-looking shells into her hand and transferred them to her handbag. Then she tossed the firearm on the couch, hesitated and searched in her bag until she found a small tube of cold cream. This she handed to Gaines.

"Smear some of that on the burn." She was pleasant, almost sympathetic. "Sorry." She dropped down at the far end of the seat and seemed to release a load of weariness. "You had me wondering there for a minute," she confessed wryly. "I think I'd like a drink." Gaines rubbed the cold cream over his scorched knuckles. "I wouldn't be at all surprised," he spoke gently, "if I didn't become awfully angry about this after awhile."

"I don't blame you." She was in quick agreement. "By the way, you can drop the Foxy Grandpa act. I know who you are and the name isn't Williamson." She was amiably at ease. "You are out of a job, Roy. At least," she added, "until I have what I want. Then I don't give a damn. Ring for the porter and order us a drink."

There was nothing in Roy Gaines' attitude to reveal he was disturbed or surprised. He touched the bell button and then stood, staring pensively out of the window. Stacey Woodward sat, handbag in her lap, the .32 automatic concealed beneath it. Her fingers drummed softly on the leather. The only sounds were the soft whirring of the fan, the subdued nicking of wheels on rail joints. After a few moments, almost as an afterthought, she reached out, retrieved the gun she had taken from Gaines and stuffed it in her purse. Then they waited until the door buzzer sounded. Gaines went to the door, the porter was framed in the opening.

"Order a double Scotch on the rocks for me." She continued to look out of the window.

"Double Scotch on the rocks and a bourbon and straight water for me."

The porter nodded and withdrew. Whatever opinions he had about a young and beautiful girl in an old gentleman's compartment were not reflected on his face. He closed the door.

Stacey Woodward lit a fresh cigarette, drew the smoke heavily into her lungs and exhaled softly. She studied Gaines and then grinned with a curious, impish expression.

"How were you going to handle it?"

"Handle what?" Gaines was all perplexed innocence.

"The hit." She was impatient and then relaxed. "You don't look like someone who could do the big one." She thought this over. "I suppose that's why you are so good at it. Dano always said you were the best."

Gaines maintained the pose. "I find your slang all but incomprehensible." He was interestedly pedantic. "But, it seems to imply some sort of violence to someone."

"No one is going to be violent with Mitchell; not right away, anyhow."

"Mitchell?" Gaines tested the name.

"Oh, stop it!" She was impatient. "You know damn well that little ghost who calls himself Cameron is Harvey Mitchell and I want hands off him until we do some business together."

Gaines thought this over, chewing at his lower lip. "Your interference," he spoke sadly, "is going to make some people in Chicago exceedingly annoyed." He clucked unhappily. "Haven't you thought of that?"

"I've thought of everything." She smiled.

"You could save yourself a lot of trouble." The eyes of Roy Gaines were suddenly frosty. "You could save everyone trouble by giving me back my revolver."

The door buzzer sounded again and a waiter from the club car came with their drinks. After he left, the girl sipped meditatively, the tip of her tongue caressing the ice cubes. Roy Gaines swallowed half of his almost angrily. It was the first real emotion he had shown.

"Mr. Mitchell," she spoke dreamily, "has a quarter of a million dollars with him. I want it all or half." Her eyes crinkled. "I can't see how giving you back your gun will help."

Roy Gaines slipped back effortlessly into his role. "I'm afraid Mr. Mitchell is a completely irresponsible and, perhaps, reprehensible character. I am not sure we should even be seen at dinner with him. My employer is quite determined he be taught a lesson. And," he was momentarily saddened, "I am afraid your intrusion into the situation will eventually place you in the same untenable position."

"Perhaps," she agreed. "Just the same, I'll finish my business with Mr. Mitchell and get off at K.C. or Albuquerque, depending on how long it takes. Then I'll give you back your gun and what you do after that is none of my affair."

Gaines gave the impression of a man distressed. "Don't you see that any business you may do with Mr. Mitchell at this time will, sooner or later, make you very much my business? The gentleman in Chicago would not be satisfied with anything less. And, as you yourself said: I am very good at it."

"Tell them a girl took your gun away." She grinned.

Mr. Gaines twinkled. "My goodness, I'm not worried about that. You'll give it back to me."

She stood up, glanced into the mirror and touched at her hair. "I'll give it back when we make a deal. You let everything ride nice and easy here on the Super-Chief until we get to Kansas City. By that time I'll have what I want."

Gaines was miserable, reluctant to refuse the request of such a lovely young woman.

"I just couldn't enter into such an agreement without the consent of the principals in Chicago and I am quite certain this would not be forthcoming."

"Right now you and I are the principals." She nodded brightly. "I'll see you at eight o'clock for dinner."

The door closed softly behind her. Mr. Gaines sat down, crossed his hands meditatively over his paunch and stared out of the window. He did hope that Mrs. Longworthy, his housekeeper, was taking good care of the cats. They always missed him whenever he had to be away on business and this trip, with the interference, might take him all the way to California. He sighed.

Sitting across the table in the dining car from the girl with the honey-colored hair and Mr. Williamson, Harvey Mitchell was disturbed, aware of a small undercurrent. The awareness of danger had sharpened his senses, honed them to a fine edge. There was, or so it seemed, an indefinable intimacy between this Judith Royal, as she had introduced herself, and Mr. Williamson. It was something new and hadn't been apparent at their first meeting in the lounge. Mitchell tried to analyze and isolate this intuitive warning that everything was not as it seemed but the solution eluded him. He ate mechanically, every instinct alert, yet nothing was said over the table to confirm what he felt. Mr. Williamson was eagerly chatty, his pink face creased with a happy smile. The novelty of eating on a train, the impeccable service, crisp linen, polished silver, made the meal an adventure and he said as much several times. The girl was poised, softly charming. She divided her attention between the two men, but now and then glancing at Mitchell with what, he was certain, was a veiled expression of invitation. She suggested they shared an amused tolerance for Mr. Williamson's naïveté.

I could be, Mitchell warned himself, a little drunk and imagining things. He had taken three drinks of Scotch in his compartment. It gave him a comfortable feeling of boldness. It could be that this Miss Royal was only being friendly. She was certainly a well-bred young lady. Anyone could see that. Just the same, and the notion excited him, you could never be sure.

The light drizzle that had accompanied them from Chicago's outskirts had changed into a steady, drumming rain. Water beat against the broad, plate-glass windows as the train slashed its way through the night. The downpour made the dining car's interior seem warmly secure.

Mr. Williamson finished his apple custard dessert and drank the last of his coffee with a sigh of satisfaction. He folded his napkin in a neat oblong and placed it beside his plate as though from long habit.

"That's what I call a real good meal." He beamed. "Or maybe it's like they say. Good company is the sauce for food."

"I'm sleepy." The girl made the simple statement seem a shy confession.

Mitchell could have sworn she looked directly at him and one of her eyelids drooped in an unmistakable wink. He felt his heart pound with excitement. Maybe—his imagination took off in a soaring flight—this was one of those things you heard about which were always happening to other people on trains or ships. Experimentally, he inched his foot forward beneath the table until he felt it touch hers. The contact could have been accidental. He waited expectantly, pretending a great interest in the rain outside. Instead of pulling away the girl actually slid her foot until her ankle rested against his. Mitchell felt his mouth go dry. He didn't dare look at her and kept his face turned. In the dark mirror of the window he could see her face as it lifted slightly. There was a faint smile of invitation on her lips. He was sure now and pressed boldly against her leg and she didn't shift away. He marveled breathlessly that this could be happening. Never in his life had a girl as beautiful as this one ever so much as glanced at him with interest. He preened himself and thought that maybe when a man had money, a quarter of a million dollars, it gave him a confidence, a luster, to which women responded. He felt himself towering above everyone on the train.

"I wonder if it would be worth while staying up to see Kansas City?" Roy Gaines, still in the role of Mr. Williamson, glanced brightly at the girl.

"The people of Kansas City don't think so." Mitchell whinnied loudly, pleased by his wit.

"I'd hate to miss something in Kansas City." Mr. Williamson seemed to be weighing the inconvenience of staying awake against the purely speculative attraction of Kansas City's Union Station.

"I'd sure hate to wake up tomorrow morning and find out I had missed something."

The girl's tongue touched lightly at her lower lip and there was a shrouded amusement in her eyes. She lit a cigarette, leaned back in her chair and studied Mr. Williamson.

"Maybe you ought to stay awake then."

"I'm a light sleeper. I suppose if anything really happened . . ." He left the conclusion to the sentence unfinished.

Mitchell darted a quick glance at the girl and then at the old man. Something in Williamson's words, the tone, suddenly made him wary. It was as though this Miss Royal and Williamson were sharing a secret. That was ridiculous, he told himself. How could they? He'd had too much to drink. That and the excitement of the girl's touch were making him imagine things.

From a table at the opposite end of the car Sol Madrid had watched the trio. The backs of the Woodward girl and Mitchell were toward him. He faced Roy Gaines and once, for just a second, their glances had met and a faintly puzzled expression had crossed Gaines' features. It lasted but a second but in that brief interval it seemed as though Gaines was trying to remember something. The three rose now, Mitchell and the girl in the lead, Gaines almost waddling behind. As the car's steward held the door open Roy Gaines turned and looked back the length of the car. Again his eyes held on Madrid but there was no recognition in them. What did show was a speculative curiosity. Then he passed through the door with his companions.

In the dimly lighted vestibule Mitchell and the girl paused. Gaines wheezed lightly. The girl's hand rested lightly just within the crook of Mitchell's arm with a confiding pressure. Harvey wondered how they were going to get rid of this pest. After that he'd suggest casually he and the girl go to his compartment for a nightcap.

"I think I'll just go back to the club car and sit up for awhile." Williamson solved the problem.

"Well. Fine." Mitchell was hearty. "We'll see you in the morning." The use of the plural was pleasantly titillating.

Williamson left them. Mitchell waited until he had disappeared. A plan was incubating in his mind. The comment about Kansas

City gave it substance. Why not? He'd slip off the train, leave his bag after he had taken out the envelope. He'd just step off, pretending to stroll the platform, and lose himself. The city would swallow him.

"It's chilly out here." The girl pressed closer to him.

"Well . . ." The accumulation of the drinks gave Mitchell courage. "How about coming to my compartment?" He actually giggled, although to him it sounded like a worldly laugh. "I'll show you my etchings."

Her expression didn't change. "Why not?" There was a sultry, smoky quality about the reply. "That's what a rainy night is for."

They walked to the car and Mitchell's hand was actually trembling as he opened the door to his compartment. The lights were on, the berth made up. For a second he was actually shocked by the sight of the turned-down covers. Well, he thought, if she comes in now she will certainly know what she's doing. He stood aside to let her pass and then turned his back while he slid the lock into place.

"We'll have a little drink. I have some Scotch. How about it?" He turned expectantly and then his mouth slacked open.

She stood, regarding him with a contemptuous loathing. Never in his life had he seen such scorn on anyone's face. A short, nervous and uncertain laugh cracked in his throat. He didn't know what had happened but he took a step and laid a reassuring hand on her arm.

"Take your fingers off of me, you little creep." She slapped him across the mouth.

"What's the matter?" He backed away, unable to comprehend what was happening and stunned by her fury. "You wanted to come, didn't you?"

"That's right, Mitchell. I wanted to come."

It took a couple of seconds before he realized what she had said. She had called him Mitchell and not Cameron, as he had introduced himself. Fear glazed his eyes. He ran a dry tongue over drier lips.

"How?" He could barely utter the word and his legs almost collapsed. Tears were in his eyes, scalding and salty. "How did you . . ." He could get no further with the question. Then a hysteria possessed him. "Get out of here." His scream was shrill. "Get out of here before I call the conductor."

She laughed at him. "You're dead, Mitchell. You've been dead since yesterday evening when the bagmen came in with the collections. You know," she seemed to commiserate with him, "all of these years with Villanova and then you settle for a lousy quarter of a million; commit suicide for it." She shook her head slowly as though unable to comprehend the timid stupidity.

"I don't know what you're talking about." The words squeaked like the small cries of terrified mice. "My name is Cameron. I'm going to call the conductor. You'll see. They'll throw you off the train."

Her hand was in the large pouch bag hanging from her shoulder by a strap. It came out unhurriedly and with it the revolver taken earlier from Roy Gaines.

"There are six bullets in this which say you won't call the conductor."

"You can't do this." Mitchell was crying without shame. "I never thought they'd send a girl. Look," he pleaded. "Whatever they offered I'll pay more. What do you want?"

"That's better." She was easy, relaxed. "Counting my time and trouble it comes to exactly two hundred thousand dollars with no discount for cash." Her eyes lighted with humor. "That will leave you fifty thousand which is more than you'll have time to spend."

Mitchell breathed easier. She wasn't a gun after all. Just a chiseler. They hadn't sent her. She had come on her own and for the money. This he could understand and deal with. He felt his confidence return. With a bravado he didn't quite feel he straightened his thin shoulders.

"I'm going to have a drink." He made a swagger of the sentence.

"Pour two." She motioned toward the wall cabinet.

"I'm going to have a drink." There was more assurance now. "Then I'm going to call the porter. You wouldn't dare use that gun. Someone would hear it. That ass Williamson knows you left the dining car with me. Now, get out!"

What she did then really surprised him. With an indifferent gesture she replaced the gun in her bag.

"I didn't intend to shoot you, Harvey." She made the use of his first name sound warmly intimate. "Ring the bell. Call the porter, the conductor, the brakeman. Anyone you can think of."

He studied her, bewildered by the assurance. "This is some sort of a trick." He made the statement uncertainly. "What?"

She nodded agreeably. "You're right, Harvey. It will be quite a trick to keep you alive and I'm the only one who can do it."

"You're lying." Fear and doubt tugged at him. She was too sure of herself. There was something he didn't yet understand. "You're trying to bluff, to scare me." His lips attempted a curl of scorn but they trembled.

"Maybe." She lit a cigarette. "Maybe you're right, Harvey. But you can't be sure, can you? That's why your hands are shaking; why your mouth quivers. I know something you need to know—where and how the hit is to be made; who has the contract. I have a silly, girlish idea you ought to be willing to pay for that information."

Mitchell thrust his hands into his pockets to hide the palsy. "How do I know you are telling me the truth?"

"You don't." She nodded understandingly. "I could be lying. But then, you could begin asking yourself how I knew who you were or that you were taking this train. Try starting with those things."

"No one could have known I was taking this train." He was fighting for time, trying to account for her presence.

"They all knew it."

"Then why did they . . ." He was afraid to finish the question.

"It might have been a little messy the other way, I imagine. Villanova's accountant with his throat cut, a slug in his belly, found somewhere in or just outside Chicago. So, they set you up in someone else's backyard."

"Please. Could I have a drink?"

"I told you to pour us both one."

The whisky slopped as he half filled the paper cups. He handed her one and then gulped his with greedy haste. After a moment some of his courage returned.

"Suppose I say to hell with you? What's to stop me from walking off the train at Kansas City?" He studied her, hoping to find a trace of hesitation in her manner.

"Nothing." She lit a cigarette.

"Or Albuquerque?" He probed again.

She laughed with an honest amusement. "Nothing. But," she was deliberate, "you won't get off before I tell you to because you can't be sure someone isn't waiting in Kansas City or Albuquerque. Now maybe, just maybe, you can get off and walk through the Union Station at K.C. and nothing will happen. But, maybe again, that is just what they expect you to do and someone will be waiting. You won't take that chance, Harvey. I'll bet you two hundred thousand dollars you haven't the nerve."

Mitchell sank down weakly at the opposite end of the divan and stared bleakly at her.

"Who are you? How do you know what you do?"

"I was Dano's girl." She said it without inflection.

He looked up, incredulous. "Then why, if you're Villanova's girl, do you want to take what I have; what I risked my life to get? You don't need it."

"You don't understand very well, Harvey. I said I *was* Dano's girl."

"What's your name?" He still didn't quite believe her.

"Stacey Woodward."

He nodded dumbly. He had made out too many checks to furriers, jewelers, exclusive dress shops, restaurants, automobile dealers, for things purchased and charged to the account of Dano Villanova by Miss Stacey Woodward. She had to be who she said she was.

"How did you know me?" The question was a whisper.

"I have a good memory for faces. Three years ago you flew down to Nassau and brought Dano's tax returns. The two of you sat by the pool of the Royal Victoria Hotel. Remember? He went over the forms with you and signed them. I was in a deck chair on the other side of the pool and I thought how funny it was. Dano in bathing trunks signing a check for, maybe, a million dollars. I watched your face. It twitched with envy and greed. I thought then you were a thief and wondered why Dano didn't know it. As I say. I have a good memory."

"But you don't need money," he pleaded.

Her short laugh was harsh. "*Il Capo* holds a tight leash where money is concerned. I have clothes, a new car every year, an apartment with an Italian maid who is Dano's spy, furs and jewels but"—she twisted the soggy paper cup—"the real stones are in Mr. Villanova's safe deposit box. He has phony copies made for me to wear. Don't ask me why. It is the devious Florentine mind. As for money,

I have less than a thousand dollars in the bank. Dano says: 'Why do you need money? Charge what you want.' So, Harvey," she smiled at him, "when I heard about you making off with two hundred and fifty thousand of Dano's I decided to cut myself in. They had an *arguiamenda* about you this morning in my apartment. You know what that is?"

Mitchell's inclination of the head was one of frightened misery. An *arguiamenda* in *Cosa Nostra* was a meeting, held to decide a matter of policy or action. It usually resulted in something extremely unpleasant happening to someone. He, Harvey Mitchell, was the someone.

"You know," she was conversationally pleasant, "Dano wasn't really angry. He laughed. He was in fine humor as though he had been told a funny story. He said: 'Imagine that little son of a bitch stealing from me, and a lousy two hundred and fifty grand at that.' Just the same they let the contract on you. After all, when you put your hand in the candy jar without permission it has to be slapped otherwise someone else will try it."

Mitchell stared blankly out of the window. The rain was an almost solid sheet now and the silvered cars tore through it, boring a tunnel of flying spume.

"Suppose I just sit here. Maybe they count on my getting off at Kansas City. I stay in the compartment all the way to Los Angeles and then ask the conductor for police protection?" He voiced this with small hope.

"You'll be all right then, won't you?" She made it sound as though he had struck upon a particularly ingenious solution.

Mitchell pressed his forehead against the cold window glass. It was no good and he knew it. Wherever the Super-Chief stopped, someone would be waiting. He could no more lose himself in Los Angeles than he could in this compartment.

The door buzzer made a soft, rasping sound. It was so lightly done that at first they paid no attention to it. Then there came a gently persuasive knock. The girl stiffened alertly and Mitchell's breath came with an audible gasp. The tap was repeated and there was something almost sinister in the gentle request that the door be opened. Stacey Woodward looked at Mitchell and was fascinated by the terror she could see. The buzzer sounded again, a split second of whirring. It almost seemed to say there was no real hurry; no immediate need to open the door. Whoever stood outside made his presence felt and with it a patient assurance. He was telling Harvey Mitchell: I can wait but you know I am here, on this train. Then he was gone. They could feel the vacuum the departure left.

Mitchell had shrunk within himself. He stared at the girl and his head began nodding. It moved faster, in small, spasmodic jerks until an uncontrollable twitching took possession of his entire body.

"All right. All right. All right." The repeated statement kept time with the spasm. "But you'll have to stay here in the compartment. Stay until you can get me off. Tell me where. I—I trust you. See? I trust you."

"The money." The reminder was toneless.

Awkwardly, Mitchell fell to his knees and pulled frantically at the suitcase. He took out the thick envelope. The collections of the bagmen came in small bills and even silver, but before turning it in to the accounting department it was changed into fifties, hundreds, five hundreds and thousands. The bank deposits were made with this in half a dozen accounts throughout the city. Dano considered it less likely to incite a teller's curiosity than would sacks of small currency. Besides, it was easier to handle. Grasping the envelope in both hands Mitchell pressed it to his chest and his eyes beseeched her.

"Half?" He whispered the offer.

She shook her head and reached toward him. "Two hundred thousand for me. The rest for you." She waited.

While she watched he counted out fifty thousand dollars. His fingers fluttered among the bills, selecting, discarding aimlessly. They were tiny rodents racing through a mound of paper, reluctant to leave the pleasant warmth of their den. Finally, he finished his count, stuffed the notes haphazardly in his pockets. The balance he miserably returned to the envelop and handed it to Stacey Woodward.

"You'll keep your bargain?" He stared at her. "You'll tell me where it is safe for me to get off? How I can do it? Don't forget now." There was a momentary brightness of foxy cunning in his eyes. "You're in it with me. You've taken the money, too. If they want me they'll want you. That's the way it is, isn't it?"

"Pardner, ol' hoss," she burlesqued the drawl, "that's the way it is."

Despite the fact it had cost him two hundred thousand, Mitchell actually seemed relieved to have someone sharing the guilt and its danger. His lips contorted themselves into a smile.

"Maybe, we ought to have a drink on it. I—I'm really not used to liquor." Again there was that curious, nervous giggle. "But then, I'm not accustomed to any of what is going on."

"I'll have a drink." She agreed without enthusiasm. "But don't get drunk on me, Harvey. Things are complicated enough as they are."

They had the whisky straight in the paper cups, she sipping at hers, he gulping as though it were distasteful but necessary and then staring down into the empty container.

"Two hundred thousand dollars is a lot of money. A real lot of money." The complaint was there but mild.

"I'm an expensive sitter."

"You're not very good company for what you charge." He was being roguish.

"That isn't what you paid for."

"Are we going to sit up all night?"

"We're certainly not going to bed together if that's what you're suggesting." She stuffed one of the pillows into a corner and turned on the dim, bluish night-light. "Anyhow," a smile curved about her mouth, "not side by side. You take that corner." She tossed him the other pillow.

Rain hit the window with the sound of scattered pebbles. The storm which had swept in from the Pacific was lashing at the broad plains and slightly rolling country. Trickling streams had been turned into boiling water. Rivers were swollen, roads were flooded, and in some places small communities were battered and drowning. From the Rockies eastward it had been raining for days, grounding airline traffic, stalling trucks and private cars on the highways. In some sections only the trains were running. Of these things Mitchell and the girl were not aware. Although the lightning outside flashed and writhed with the frenzy of crazed serpents they were securely locked within the compartment.

Stacey Woodward's eyes closed. Mitchell watched her. Maybe, when she went to sleep . . . The idea only half formed itself before it was dismissed. Suppose she did sleep and he could get the gun out of her purse? What would he do with it? He was trapped and she held the key to the only safe door. She knew what he didn't and for that he had to pay. It was, the liquor gave him a hazy philosophy, better, maybe, to live with fifty thousand than to die with two hundred and fifty thousand. Just the same he would wait and be very, very careful. The chance to get his money back and still be safe might come. If it did he'd take it.

3

THE Super-Chief bored through the storm, straining to be turned loose. The engineer, his eyes aching from trying to fathom the night, held the train at three-quarters speed. He had the weather reports over the radio in the diesel's cab. There was nothing but rain ahead all the way to the Coast.

Sol Madrid awoke suddenly and without reason. This often happened to him when he was attempting to work out a problem or was troubled by something he didn't understand. He would come awake completely, all of his senses keyed and with a tightness in his belly. Then the tension would drain and he would relax again. He snapped on the reading light and looked at his watch. It was 1:40. At two o'clock they were due in Kansas City. He lit a cigarette, turned off the light and lay smoking in the darkness. Suburban communities were blurred smears of scattered streetlights through the rain. He could feel the reduced speed of the crack train and knew, in a few more minutes, it would begin to creep upon the vast complex of the Kansas City yards. Kicking off the covers he moved down to the window end of the berth and sat there, his feet propped into a corner, smoking meditatively and wondering a little at his preoccupation with something which was of no concern at all to him. Yet, he mused, whoever and whatever touched Dano Villanova sooner or later moved into his sphere. The Woodward girl and Mitchell, mistress and accountant to the *Capo*. They orbited slowly in his mind and beyond them, like some solitary and badly defined figure, was Roy Gaines.

He was wide-awake now and restless. He stripped off the pajamas, pulled on slacks, ducked into a golf shirt, put sockless feet into a pair of loafers, shrugged into a jacket and took a gabardine raincoat from a hanger. Then, he left the compartment and walked down the narrow aisle to the vestibule. The porter was there, four pieces of luggage beside him. At the sound of the door's opening he turned and recognized Madrid as one of his temporary charges who was booked through to Los Angeles.

"You're not gettin' off here, sir?" There was a faint surprise in the question.

"No. I couldn't sleep. Thought I'd walk up and down, stretch my legs while we're in the station."

"Not much of a night for walking, that's for sure."

They said nothing more until the train was switched into the tracks of its platform. Two heavy-eyed passengers joined them. The porter swung down, reached back for the bags and set his alighting stool in place. Sol stood aside until the pair left the car's end and then he followed. Vague shadows moved along the Super-Chief's shining length. A baggage truck trundled past, transfer vans were at the express cars, sacks of mail were being tossed into a high-sided cab. Few passengers left the train here but there was a shadowy, nocturnal activity concerned with the movement of this train.

Standing back, just outside the circle of an overhead light, Sol listened to the steady pounding of the rain. Now and then a gust of wind whipped a heavy spray over the length of the platform and the moving figures ducked beneath its force. Somehow, he wasn't the slightest bit surprised to see Roy Gaines.

The man stood where he could watch the steps leading to cars 103 and 104. He made no effort to pretend an occupation beyond just what he was doing—waiting to see if anyone left either of the cars. His hands were thrust into the slit pockets of the light topcoat he wore and his face, shining with moisture, bore a bland expression of mild curiosity when a truck or baggage handler passed him. Sol lit a cigarette with difficulty and cupped it within his hand to keep it dry. Then he strolled toward the dumpy man.

"Nasty night." He spoke casually.

Gaines displayed no surprise at being spoken to by a stranger at 2:15 in the morning of a wet and miserable day. There was just a flicker of doubt in his eyes, as though he were trying to remember something which, perhaps, never really existed. Then the expression was gone.

"Indeed it is. The porter tells me it's raining all the way between here and California. I suppose, though," the smile was warm, friendly and interested, "it stops at the California state line. The Chambers of Commerce would never permit it to enter. At least, that's what I hear; sunshine three hundred and sixty-five days out of the year." He beamed up inquiringly at Madrid.

"They have a man with an atomizer who goes around, now and then, spraying everything lightly." Sol made the statement gravely.

Gaines cocked his head slightly with a curious, birdlike alertness. There was, in his manner, something which said: There is something about you I should know; a thing I ought to remember. What is it?

Madrid dropped the cigarette to the concrete and it died with a sharp hiss in a puddle of water. He was sensitive to Gaines' intuition, the odd wariness, although he knew the man had no possible way of knowing who he was.

"Well"—he spoke with a casual friendliness to Gaines—"I think I'll turn in again."

"Good night." Gaines nodded. His eyes followed Madrid as he went to his car.

Within the dark compartment Stacey Woodward and Harvey Mitchell watched through the window.

"What do you suppose that fool Williamson is doing out there in the rain?" Mitchell spoke crossly.

"Maybe he just likes the wind and the rain in his hair." The girl had taken sharp note of the exchange between Roy Gaines and the tall, lean man with the predatory features of a hawk. "You're too jumpy, Buster." She lit a cigarette and wondered if there was a connection between Gaines and the stranger.

"You have your money," Mitchell persisted. "Suppose I left the train here, in Kansas City. Would it be all right?"

"No." She wondered why she didn't let him go. It would be simpler that way. She was dryly amused by the plucking of her conscience. Why not tell him to leave the train and be done with him? Let Roy Gaines pick it up from here as best he could. "No," she repeated. "I think you're better off here."

"Who did they send?" He snapped the question at her.

"No one you would know. But when the time comes I'll point him out."

The time the train spent in the terminal seemed endless. She was weary, wanting her own compartment and bed. Irritably she punched the pillow into a small mound and tried to make herself comfortable. With eyes closed she wondered what Dano Villanova must be thinking. Had he missed her? possibly not. There were days at a time when he didn't even call, let alone see her. But she was always expected to be there or her telephone service be able to locate her within minutes. Even if she went to a movie, a fashion showing, or simply a drive she had to check regularly to find out if he had called and to leave word where she was. It was part of the arrangement, the *deal,* as Dano called it. Yet, and this amused her slightly, he had an unadmitted respect for her. First of all she was beautiful; someone, something, to be shown off as one might be vain over the possession of a fine, blooded animal. It pleased him to be seen with her in a restaurant, a night club, the theatre. I am, she mused, a status symbol; a really elegant broad, a beautiful bitch kept in a plush-lined kennel, perfectly groomed, bathed, brushed, powdered and scented. I am, also, a fine lay. Tired as she was, this idea stirred her. There was no doubt but that Dano was a great stud. They coupled in a perfect, fierce and primitive union. At such times he was crude, brutal, inexplicably vulgar, and the words he used as he spent himself in her had a strangely erotic effect. She found herself, at times, cursing back at him and softly whispering every obscenity she had ever heard. Why had she left him? The question was not easy to answer. Dano was a handsome and consummately dangerous man. The latter, she admitted, was an attraction; undisguised evil, she thought, always was. The Medusa's head was irresistible. One must look at it with ambivalence. She stirred and kicked off her shoes. She had been Dano Villanova's girl for three years now. Her mouth twitched in a little smile. Girl was the word. Mistress had some small connotation of dignity. Girl, dame, broad. These were better suited although, and this also amused her, Dano would never have referred to her as such even in his own mind. She was unidentifiable in ordinary terms.

She felt the train begin to move. It was eased from a standstill with a barely perceptible motion which would awaken none of the sleeping passengers. She heard Harvey Mitchell as he went to the door again and tried it to be sure it was locked. They would find Harvey even though, for the moment, she could protect him from Gaines. But there was no hurry. The *borgata* was thorough. Roy Gaines or someone else would eventually make the hit and everyone in the "family" would know why. Her thoughts returned to Villanova. Her leaving him would strike at his pride. Girls just didn't walk out on Dano Villanova. They were thrown out, locked out, scared away, but they didn't leave of their own volition. What happened to her now depended on how angry he was or would become. He could say: To hell with Stacey Woodward and install someone new—a model, show girl or whatever captured his fancy—in the apartment she had so abruptly vacated. Or if his vanity was sufficiently wounded he would set the delicately geared machinery into operation and have her found and brought back. Or again, she could be beaten, hounded and driven from place to place and there would be no sanctuary. This would happen if the *Capo* felt he had been mocked and made to look ridiculous. She experienced a small shiver of apprehension. Her leaving had not been the result of a spur-of-the-moment decision. She had been thinking about it for weeks, months. She had grown increasingly restless under the restrictions Dano imposed. Every minute of her days and nights must be accounted for. To be kept was one thing but the realization that she was not only a kept girl but a prisoner to her keeper began to rankle. Until she learned of Harvey Mitchell's theft, his flight and destination, there had seemed no sensible way of escape. Sensible? No. That wasn't the word. Practical, perhaps. She had no intention of leaving with only a few hundred dollars in her purse. She had credit cards for airlines, hotels, restaurants; charge accounts everywhere but no cash. Then Harvey Mitchell provided the solution and without too much regard for the consequences, or thought as to where she would go once she had blackmailed the little man out of the money he had stolen, she left. She had heard Dano on the telephone giving the contract to Roy

Gaines. It was only by the merest chance that she knew what Gaines looked like. Dano had pointed him out one night in a Detroit restaurant. "That's Santa Claus with a gun." She could remember his words. "You want to know what a rod looks like, baby? There it is." She had been incredulous—this benevolent-appearing, mild-mannered elderly gentleman. "He's the best in the business," Dano had continued, enjoying her astonishment, "Roy Gaines, because he doesn't look as though he would say scat to a cat."

She was suspended somewhere halfway between sleep and a drowsy wakefulness and, in the darkness, had the feeling Harvey Mitchell was watching her with quiet malevolence. He was. Tears salted in his eyes and he writhed in his humiliation and the sense of injustice. To be cheated this way after he had planned everything so carefully. To have the money, or most of it, snatched from his hands after everything had gone so well. And, how did he know she wasn't lying? Maybe she was the only one who had suspected he would risk the train. Her whole story could be a lie. But, and his misery increased, he couldn't be certain and was trapped. Doubt, suspicion and fear nagged at him with the throbbing of an ulcerated tooth. He tried to compose himself, courting sleep as an antidote.

Steadily the train drove westward; into the vast plains now with the incredible downpour of rain obscuring the countryside. Down the length of the shining cars only an occasional light showed in the vestibules. Stacey had no idea how long she had slept or that she had slept at all. The rasp of hastily applied brakes, the abrupt deceleration, threw her forward and her head banged against the window. Mitchell also was jerked upright and brought fully awake from his uneasy dreams.

"What's happened? What's happened?" He repeated the question.

"How do I know?" She put a hand to her temple and then switched on the light.

Mitchell went to the door, put his fingers on the bolt and then hesitated. There were sounds outside, muted voices of other passengers who had been awakened. Mitchell looked back at the girl.

"Go ahead and open it." She massaged her brow.

Cautiously, turtle-like, Mitchell put his head outside. The porter was moving down the aisle, reassuring passengers who stood in their doorways.

"There's a washout ahead," he soothed everyone. "Crew already at work on it. Nothing to worry about. Hold us up some. The conductor'll be along in a minute." He repeated the words as he passed.

Mitchell shut the door again and locked it. Without looking at Stacey he went to the washbasin, drew it down, filled the bowl with cold water and splashed the sleep from his face. He ran a tongue about the foul cavity of his mouth. There was nothing worse than the dead taste of old whisky. He wiped his eyes and cheeks, ignoring Stacey. Hatred for the girl seethed within him. He went to the window and, shading out the compartment lights with both hands, tried to fathom the night. In the darkness he thought he caught a glimpse of distant lights and pressed closer to the pane. For a second the wind tore away the curtain of rain. There were lights out there but it was impossible to judge their distance. Slowly, fearfully, he began to grope toward an idea. Here on the plains, the prairie, the train was halted. It was an unscheduled stop. No one could possibly have anticipated it. He could take the few necessary steps down the corridor and into the vestibule. He could drop from the train into the rain and darkness and walk in safety toward those lights. No one would follow. Harvey Mitchell could simply disappear. He began to smile. It was an unpleasant expression, baring his teeth into an animal's snarl. First, though, he wanted his money from this girl. He was afraid to look at her for fear his expression of slowly dawning triumph would betray him. Besides, he was arguing with himself, he was certain she had lied. How could Dano have guessed he would be on the Super-Chief? How could a hit have been set up in so short a time? She was a thief and a liar and he would rid himself of her for good. How? He turned and glanced at the wall cabinet. In it was a heavy, nickeled Thermos carafe. He could reach in and take it by the neck, pretending a need for a drink of water. One fast turn and he could crash the bottle on her head.

Casually, trying to whistle a note of indifference, he opened the cabinet door. He must be careful not to alarm or warn her until he could bring the weapon down in a single, terrible blow. His fingers closed about the neck.

"I'm way ahead of you, Harvey." Her words were spoken with an amused contempt. "Put back the jug."

He spun about. The revolver was half lifted, the muzzle, ugly and sinister as a snake's head, pointed at his quaking belly. The strength went out of his hand and the Thermos dropped to the floor.

"I started getting ahead of you," she continued disinterestedly, "from the time you looked out of the window. I could see the little wheels beginning to turn."

"I—I don't know what you're talking about," he protested weakly.

She stood up, the gun level and unwavering. "Go ahead." She was encouraging. "You can get off here. No one is waiting out there for you. Even Dano isn't that smart. He would never have figured the Super-Chief would be stalled somewhere out in the prairie. But," she indicated the bag, "what I have I keep."

"I think you've been lying to me all the time." He almost screamed the words. "I don't believe they sent anyone."

"Maybe not," she agreed without interest. "You will probably never really know, and if you're lucky enough to stay alive it will bug you for the rest of your life. Did Villanova's broad con me out of two hundred thousand just because she was smarter than I am? you'll keep asking yourself." She half smiled and moved between him and the berth.

The whirring rasp of the buzzer startled them both. Stacey looked quickly at the door.

"Just a minute." There was a note of something close to elation in Mitchell's voice. "Who is it?"

"The conductor, Mr. Mitchell."

For the first time Stacey Woodward displayed an uncertainty. She hesitated, half turned, and then quickly replaced the gun in her bag. Mitchell, directly behind her, leaned forward and slid back the door's latch. She tried to push away but he blocked her. The door opened and the conductor stood there. There was a brief second of surprise on his face at seeing Mitchell and the girl, fully clothed at this hour; surprise and doubt, even, at seeing a girl in the compartment. But he masked it.

"Everything is all right. There is a bad washout of some track. A crew is on it now. It may hold us up for a few hours." He nodded pleasantly and turned away, closing the door.

She tried to whirl away but it was too late. From behind her Mitchell's arm had come up simultaneously with the closing of the door. The bony forearm bit into her throat, choking off any outcry. Desperation, avarice and fury combined to give him an unsuspected strength. He locked the free hand about his wrist and pulled, feeling an almost insane pleasure in what he was doing. She writhed and twisted in a silent battle. Her body jumped, the hands flying up helplessly to claw at his arms and fingers. Mitchell's breath came in a sharp, whistling sound. Sweat poured from his face and his teeth bit into his lower lip until the blood came. He wanted to kill her. His arms ached with the relentless pressure.

He felt her sag but still did not release his hold. She was deadweight now and he held her upright with straining effort, afraid to let go. Then he knew she was unconscious. There seemed to be no life and he wondered if he had really killed her. When he released the armlock she crumpled to the floor. He watched, his teeth pulled back in a vindictive snarl. He wanted to kick her, stamp his heel into the back of her neck.

Pulling the handbag from beneath her body he took the thick sheaf of bills and paused at the sight of the revolver. He had never fired a gun in his life. This would be no good to him. If it came to the point of shooting he was dead anyhow because whomever Villanova had sent would be fast, deadly and come in secret. He left it there. Methodically he put the two hundred thousand back in the envelope with his fifty thousand. He then thrust the bulky package into the waistband of his trousers. Facing the mirror he straightened his tie, smoothed his hair. He started for the door, stepping around Stacey Woodward's body. He wondered if he had really killed her. With his hand on the latch he remembered to snap off the lights. Then calmly, unhurriedly, he stepped out.

Mr. Williamson was bent over at a window in the narrow corridor. At the sight of him Mitchell jerked to a halt. Didn't the damned old fool ever go to sleep? Williamson's arms were folded on the small handrail. He was peering into the night but at the sound of the door he turned to face Mitchell.

"Well, now!" Mr. Williamson seemed pleased to be able to share the adventure with someone. "You got dressed in a hurry, Mr. Cameron. Lucky thing for me I hadn't really gone to bed yet. I wouldn't have missed this for anything. Just wait until I tell my daughter I was in a train wreck." His bulky form blocked the narrow corridor.

"There isn't any wreck. Just a washout. Didn't the conductor tell you that?" Mitchell made no effort to hide his impatience. "Will you please move so I can get past." Roughly, he tried to shove through. Williamson didn't move. A sudden panic welled unreasonably within Mitchell. It just couldn't be. "Let me through!" he screamed.

Williamson's expression was one of pained surprise but he didn't shift away. Feeling trapped and hunted, Mitchell twirled about and away, in the opposite direction. He almost ran.

"Mr. Cameron." Williamson sounded hurt and bewildered.

Mitchell ignored the call. Panic nipped at his heels. He raced for the vestibule.

Effortlessly the mask of a kindly, innocent old gentleman slipped from the face of Roy Gaines. He was no longer Williamson. He jerked open the door of Mitchell's compartment and showed no surprise at the prone figure of Stacey Woodward. Callously he snatched at the large over-the-shoulder bag. His hand dug into it and came out with the revolver she had taken from him earlier. When he left he didn't even bother to close the door. Instead of following Mitchell he made for the closer vestibule at his end of the car. For a heavy man he moved with incredible speed. He threw open the door and dropped into the rain and night.

Sol Madrid, still unable to sleep, had stood in the vestibule of his car smoking. He saw Mitchell as the man all but dove from the door of the car, pulled frantically at the vestibule closing and, when it was finally open, jumped the distance to the ground. This had taken only seconds. Madrid went to the opening but already Mitchell was lost in the steaming curtain of rain. Then, as he glanced down the length of the train he saw Roy Gaines for just a moment before the downpour obscured him.

"Mitchell." The voice of Roy Gaines rose on a high, insistent note. He no longer maintained the pretense of believing Harvey Mitchell was Horace Cameron. "Mitchell. I want to talk with you."

The rain then hid both pursuer and pursued. So, Madrid thought, it was Mitchell Roy Gaines was after. What, then, about the girl? Where did she fit? On an impulse he pushed open the door of the adjoining car and strode down the silent corridor. The porter, standing transfixed at the entrance to Harvey Mitchell's compartment, looked up with the incredulous dismay of a man whose brain refuses to believe what the eyes see.

"She lyin' there." He made the statement numbly.

Sol moved quickly past the attendant and knelt beside Stacey Woodward. Bruises were beginning to discolor the smooth skin of her neck. Her lids were down, the face peculiarly mottled. She seemed not to be breathing but there was the tiniest flutter of a pulse at her throat.

"Get the conductor and see if there's a doctor on the train." He snapped the order without looking up. "She's still alive."

Madrid studied the lovely features. He had no idea what to do with a case of strangulation. Maybe, he thought, the treatment was the same as in a case of near drowning. Air must reach the lungs. He straddled the prostrate body and with his hands began a gentle, pumping motion. He was almost guiltily aware of his thumbs as they inadvertently pressed against the hard contours of her breasts. They ought to have a pulmotor, he thought angrily and then, despite the situation, he grinned. Passengers weren't usually strangled on the Super-Chief. It was a contingency the Santa Fe would hardly prepare for. Amazingly now he felt a small shudder run through the girl and a moment later he was aware of figures behind him. He looked up as the conductor, disbelief and, under the circumstances, a strange disapproval in his expression, moved into the compartment, accompanied by a youngish man with the unmistakable black bag of a doctor.

"I didn't know what to do," Madrid half apologized, for his position astride the unconscious girl now seemed outrageously lewd. He stood up. "I don't think she's dead."

The doctor made a quick examination and nodded in silent agreement. His fingers traced delicately over the throat. "Can't tell yet"— he seemed to be talking to himself—"how badly the cartilage is damaged. Help me put her on the bed."

They lifted her gently, the worried porter clucking and fussing, arranging a light blanket and the pillows. Stacey Woodward murmured unintelligibly and seemed to choke. The doctor took a syringe and a sealed phial of adrenalin. He glanced at Madrid, the conductor and porter, dismissing them without words.

"Mr. ——?" The conductor looked at Madrid.

"Madrid. Sol Madrid. I'm in Car 102."

The conductor consulted a list. "Yes. Mr. Madrid. I'll have to make a report. Would you mind?"

Sol followed the man to a vacant compartment. The conductor was nervous, worried and uncertain. Sol took a seat and lit a cigarette.

"I . . . how did you happen . . . ? I mean . . ." The man was so obviously unhappy with the situation he found it difficult to form a coherent sentence. "Did you know her?"

Sol thought for a moment. It would serve no purpose to say he knew who the girl was. He took out his wallet, flipped over the cards and showed the conductor his identification.

This unmistakable testification of authority and identity bolstered by the vague power of the Government and the Bureau obviously relieved the trainman. He sighed audibly.

Sol told him only what he thought necessary. He had been unable to sleep. Came out of his compartment when the train stopped. Walked from his car and into the next one. There was a small light of curiosity in the conductor's eyes at this. He seemed to be wondering to himself why a passenger would go from his own car into another. But he said nothing. Madrid continued in an even tone. He saw the porter standing at the open door. The girl was lying on the floor. That was all.

"I suppose there will be some identification in her bag?"

"The doctor says she will be all right. You can ask her who she is and what happened." Madrid was logically soothing.

"Yes. Yes, of course." The man grasped eagerly at this comfort. "After all we don't—we don't have a—a murder on our hands, do we?" He anxiously included Madrid in the troublesome affair.

"No." Sol uncrossed his long legs, stood up and smiled. "No. We don't have a corpse."

The conductor flinched at the word. "Even so," he was unhappy, "it is going to look very strange on my report. I don't think anything like this has ever happened on the Santa Fe before."

"I'm certain it hasn't." He hesitated. "I'll be at the Ambassador Hotel, in Los Angeles, for a few days if you want me. I'll repeat what I have told you, if necessary."

"Thank you, Mr. Madrid. Thank you very much." The conductor impulsively grasped Sol's hand.

"I think I'll go back and see how the girl is." Madrid made it a statement and not a request for permission.

"Yes. Yes. Of course."

The rain's sound on the steel cars was a snarling rattle and it came in heavy, windswept gusts. Somewhere beyond the warm, secure comfort of the train Roy Gaines and Harvey Mitchell were engaged in this strange and silent contest. Leaving the conductor Madrid wondered why. What had brought them to this moment? He halted at a window and his eyes tried to pierce the night. Water washed in streams across the pane. He could see nothing.

Struggling through the dank undergrowth, fighting like a terrified animal, Harvey Mitchell struggled for breath. This Williamson, the pleasant old gentleman, was the rod. He had to be. Otherwise how would he know Harvey Mitchell was not Horace Cameron? He ran now, bent into the wind; stumbling, half falling, plunging through the thickets which tore at his face and clothing. The elements whipped and lashed him and the soggy weeds and dank brush were waist-high at times. He felt as though he were being tossed upon some dark and terrible sea. He tried to draw upon a confidence he really did not feel. He could outrun a fat old man. He had to outrace him. Somewhere beyond this terrifying stretch of desolation he could be safe.

The rain sang a constant, whispering lament as it whipped and hissed. A gumbo mud sometimes held his feet and ankles captive and he knew the frantic terror of helplessness. After awhile he had to stop while his lungs fought for air. He looked back over the way he had come and could see nothing; not even the lights of the train. Some assurance had begun to reassert itself. He had lost Williamson, if that was his name. The old fool was probably as spent as he was. Maybe he had even given up.

Mitchell bumped into a tree, looming suddenly out of the murky shadows in which everything assumed twisted and grotesque shapes. He leaned against it, resisting an all but overpowering desire to slide down and lie upon the ground. The night cloaked him in invisibility. It was his friend, his companion. With it he was safe, but when it left him in the morning he would be naked upon this scraggly plain. He forced himself to move, plodding like some heavily burdened beast.

As he drove himself to the exertion he tried to remember how far away had been the distant lights he had glimpsed so briefly from the train. There was no way of telling. In the lightning's flash he had seen this barren; beyond it a heavy line of trees and the faintly, yellow gleam in windows or on streets. He thrust weak and trembling legs forward. This was an agony of effort. The thick envelope holding the bills kept slipping down from his waistband. He tried to hold it, doubled over as a man who had been kicked in the groin. Tripped by a tangle of roots he could not see, he lay face down in the cold muck. He raised his head, wiped mud and water from mouth and eyes. It was then he was certain Williamson was following him. He heard no sound, but with a hunted thing's instinct he could sense the relentless pursuit. Only the wind and the rain surrounded him but he could feel the presence of something sinister, heavy-footed and determined.

"Mitchell!" The call came with nerve-shattering abruptness. It was plaintive, fluted, coaxingly deadly. "Mitchell, you're not going to make it."

Headlong, consumed by complete panic, Harvey Mitchell tore through the brush. It had been impossible to locate the voice. All he knew was he must put it behind him.

"Mitchell." The cry was the mewling pipe of a seabird. "Mitchell, I won't let you get away."

Clawing for every foot of ground, slipping, rising, staggering drunkenly, Mitchell ran and dodged in senseless desperation. His shoes were sodden, coated heavily with mud, and the effort of lifting his feet was intolerable. The pain in his chest was excruciating. He felt as though he were being repeatedly stabbed by a knife. He was closer to the fringe of trees now. It should be higher there, the footing easier. He tripped again and fell. He lay there sobbing without control.

"You'd better wait, Mitchell. We ought to have a little talk." Again the voice, nearer now, with its terrifying cooing sound. "I'll find you, Mitchell."

He ran again, through the narrow line of trees. Lightning forked in the sky and he could see a ditch and beyond it the shapes of darkened houses. He drew upon the last remaining resources of mind and body. Down the ditch where the water churned and boiled; clawing with his fingers he kicked and scrambled up the other side. A black ribbon of road lay ahead and beyond it a lantern or oil lamp glowed in a single window. Slobbering, weeping, running, falling, Mitchell literally screamed his way toward the light.

Roy Gaines wheezed and panted. His heavy body rolled forward with the uneasy, swaying motion of an elephant. He was angry with Mitchell, himself, the night and the way things had gone. Gaines was a neat man in his work, a perfectionist. Now, what should have been clean and simple had unaccountably become sloppy and complicated. Who, though, could have anticipated the Super-Chief would stop where it had never halted before, and with its stopping, allow this situation to develop? Years of pleasant, easy living had made him soft. He was not accustomed to slogging through the dark in rain, wind and mud. The contract had been an impersonal one. He had felt nothing for Harvey Mitchell. Now he hated the man. It would give him a great deal of satisfaction to kill Harvey Mitchell. He pushed through the thin line of trees which served as only a windbreak. This way Mitchell had gone. He would follow. In the impenetrable gloom he could not see but simply feel his way. The lightning flash which had guided Mitchell did not now show the way. Gaines could not anticipate the ditch and on its muddy lip his footing gave way. He fell back, trying to check the abrupt descent, but it was too late. He slid as a cumbersome toboggan, accelerated by the ooze, and hit the roiling water with a mighty splash. For a moment he went completely under and felt himself being swept away. He flailed with his arms, churning the current and finally regaining his feet. About him the water swirled. Ahead loomed the opposite bank. He thrust himself forward, hands groping for the slope. Beyond this, he told himself, there must be solid ground, for he could dimly see the skeletal metal towers which carried the rural electricity. The sides of the ditch offered no hold. His fingers dug into the yielding earth. He tried to crawl upward like some great, wounded saurian. He lay, winded, upon the slanting earth and cursed with slow, methodical fury. He was trapped here in this goddamned sinkhole.

Lightning, white-hot and almost blinding, ripped open the darkness and Roy Gaines saw the dangling black thickness of the wire. In his anger he did not stop to think as the wind whipped the wire in a half circle toward him. He reached out with both hands and grasped it and the world about him exploded. Death came quickly to Roy Gaines. He was electrocuted instantly in this contact with the high-tension wire and the wind sang a weird and mournful threnody as the rain lashed at the night and steamed within the ditch.

Sol Madrid sat in the compartment's single chair. He was bent slightly forward, big hands dangling loosely between his knees. The smoke from a cigarette between his fingers twined upward in a wavering vine. Stacey Woodward, in the berth and covered lightly with a blanket, stared at him with a puzzled, all but frightened fascination. There was a compelling, saturnine quality about the man. He seemed gentle and yet, somehow, quietly deadly. It was an unusual combination.

"Why did Harvey Mitchell try to kill you?" The question was repeated softly.

Her eyes were wide. Mutely she expressed her astonishment. Her throat was still hurting although the doctor had given her a light opiate to ease the pain. It was an effort to speak above a whisper.

"How did you know?" The words were barely audible.

"It's my business to know." Madrid was not abrupt. The reply was almost quizzically amused.

"Who are you?"

For a moment it seemed as though Madrid had not heard. He drew upon the cigarette and then leaned to press it out in a tray. Finally he reached for his wallet, opened it and held the card for her to read.

"Oh!" She was relieved.

"I got curious." He spoke with an abstracted detachment. "You, Stacey Woodward. Roy Gaines. Harvey Mitchell. It only needed Villanova and some of the boys." He tilted his head back and stared at the ceiling. "You don't have to answer, of course, but I'd still like to know why or what drove someone like Harvey Mitchell to try murder. What made him so desperate?"

She shook her head, refusing to answer. Her eyes searched his face with undisguised curiosity.

"Roy Gaines has a contract on Mitchell." This was a statement and not a question.

"Little Harvey is a thief." Her voice was husky. She watched him.

Sol tapped the knuckle of a forefinger against his teeth, his gaze never leaving hers. Suddenly a slow, amused smile of comprehension touched his features. He whistled, a low note.

"Mitchell steals from the *Capo*. Gaines gets a contract. You try and shake Harvey down." He closed his hand about his throat with an expressive gesture. "You almost got away with it, too." He laughed shortly. "Mitchell dove off the train like a seal into a tank. Gaines went after him. Where does that leave you?"

"With a bruised throat." There was an odd, impish grin about her lovely mouth. "Thanks for your help. The doctor told me."

Madrid stood up. "Ordinarily, in my work, I don't come across many beautiful broads on the floor. In bed, sometimes, but very, very rarely on the floor. Like mystery story stuff, huh?"

"Yes." She was demure. "Like mystery story stuff."

He paused at the door, turned to look at her. "I'm going to be at the Ambassador Hotel for a few days. When your throat gets so you can swallow a drink I'd like to buy you one. Unless, of course, you're meeting Villanova. If so, give Dano my regards. Tell him Sol Madrid still wants him."

At the mention of Villanova her eyes clouded and something close to fear was a quick shadow across her face. She did not answer but her head turned to watch him as he passed through the door and closed it behind him. For several seconds she stared at the blank panel and then dropped back to rest against the pillows.

In the diner, lit by a single, battery-powered hand light on a shelf, the counterman leaned against the warm urn and studied the hunched figure on the stool. The little man had come stumbling in out of the night, panting; hardly able to walk. He was covered with mud, his eyes were glazed and he could barely speak to ask for coffee. His eyes kept darting toward the door and he drank two cups of scalding coffee, gulping them without sugar or cream.

"There's someone—someone I don't want to see." The words came in a torrent. "He—it's possible—he may be along any minute." Hands fumbled for a wallet. "I'll give you fifty dollars if you'll close up for the night. Lock the door. Pull the shade. Don't answer if anyone knocks." Two twenties and a ten were laid on the varnished boards.

"Mister, I wouldn't take in two dollars on a night like this. No one is likely to come along. I'm wonderin' how you got here."

"Never mind." Mitchell pushed the bills forward. "Take the fifty. Close up. Don't let anyone in, not anyone. I trust you."

The counterman shrugged and folded the money, putting it in his pocket. Then he went to the door, bolted it and drew the blinds over two windows. He paused then and turned.

"The law ain't after you, is it?"

"Oh no! Nothing like that. I give you my word."

"All right. I don't want no trouble with the law."

"No. I'd—I'd be glad to see the law. If—if a trooper should come along and you're sure who it is, let him in."

"Hell"—the counterman's suspicions were quieted—"if you're in that kind of trouble there's a phone there. Call in an' ask for help. No," he corrected himself, "the line's dead. Power lines down. Everything out." He came back to stand again beside the urn. "For fifty dollars you can have some ham an' eggs if you like."

Mitchell shook his head. "Where am I? What is this place?"

"This here is just a place by the road. Nearest town is Perry."

"Is there a bus or something?"

"There sure as hell ain't no buses runnin' this night. Tomorrow, maybe, one might come through goin' to Topeka."

"Could I sleep here? Just rest, maybe?" Harvey looked around the single room.

"Mister," the counterman chuckled, "for another fifty dollars you can own the damned place." He motioned toward one of the side booths lining one wall. The seats were padded with imitation leather. "Why don't you kind of stretch out in one of them? I'll bring you some more coffee if you want."

"Yes. Thank you. Maybe I will." Gratitude flowed with the words. "You're sure that door is locked?"

"I'm sure. But like I said, no one is likely to be comin' along save maybe a line crew from the power company. You're all right. I got your fifty. You got my word."

"Thank you. I guess I will rest a little."

The counterman watched speculatively as Mitchell went to one of the booths and hunched himself into a corner. He was sure one scared little man. He wondered what he had done. He drew a fresh cup of coffee and carried it to the table.

"Thank you." Mitchell glanced up.

"When you're feelin' better you ought to wash up some. You're about the muddiest man I ever seen. There's a basin in the toilet."

"Yes. Thank you. Later. Right now I'm tired."

The man nodded and left. There was no sound within the small lunchroom save the incessant pounding of the rain and the faint, steaming sound of the nickeled coffee urn. The counterman reached for a toothpick and began to probe thoughtfully at a decaying molar.

4

ON weekends the traffic at the border gates between Tijuana, in Mexico, and San Ysidro, on the American side, moves in a heavy, sluggish stream of cars bumper to bumper. During the morning hours the tide flows into Mexico with the tourists bent upon the bullring, the track at Caliente, the beaches or simply to wander up and down Tijuana's main street with its garish bars, strip joints and souvenir shops. Late in the afternoon the current reverses itself. The visitors, heavy-eyed from too much good Mexican beer, tacos, enchiladas, frijoles, mole, tequila and whisky, push against each other, anxious to pass through United States Customs and Immigration and streak along the freeway leading to San Diego and Los Angeles.

Just to the right of the crossing into Mexico is a small, single-story building and before it a sign which carries a warning to all drug addicts to register before entering Tijuana. They come, the old and the young. They are neither ashamed nor belligerent, frightened nor swaggering. They are given a form to be filled out. It requires their name, address and addiction; the date of departure from the United States and the expected time of return. On the reverse side the addict must list his convictions, the type of drug used and the sentences imposed. The document is then countersigned by the officer in charge and given to the user, who must carry it with him and turn it in to the authorities when he reenters.

To the casual observer the regulation seems pointless. The addict, with the "tracks" of the needle plainly on his arms, comes to Tijuana with only one purpose in mind—to get a "fix." The men of the Bureau know this. The "junkie" knows they know it. To make them register when both or all parties are aware of the situation serves little purpose beyond making it possible for the Bureau of Narcotics to keep some sort of a count on the increase or decrease of the users.

Madrid sat at one side of the room, his chair canted against the wall, eyes brooding on the Sunday traffic outside. Heat ran in shimmering waves. The cars moved slowly. Here no search was made by either American or Mexican authorities. But police with typewritten lists in their hands stand and check the license plates for a "hot" car, a wanted man. There is little sanctuary in Baja California for the automobile thief, the runaway juvenile, the man or woman fleeing from the law. Actually it is a trap, for there is no way out save at Mexicali or Tijuana unless transportation can be arranged across the Gulf of California to land the pursued in Sonora, Sinaloa and from there into Chihuahua. Once on the Mexican mainland, those who run from prosecution find themselves in a precarious situation unless they are well supplied with funds. They cannot find work and a gringo beggar is quickly picked up by the police. It is when the visiting cars turn back that the dull, fatiguing routine of checking and questioning begins. Car after car. The same questions endlessly repeated. Where were you born? Are you bringing back any purchases made in Mexico? The officials have ears sharply attuned to the trace of an accent in the replies for there are always those who attempt to enter the United States illegally here. Also, their senses of observation have been sharpened and they have developed an almost extrasensory perception. Time after time they will hold up a car for thorough search for no other reason than "there seemed something wrong about the way the driver acted." Sol knew and understood this feeling. Many times he had experienced it and most of the time the hunch had paid off. Now, though, listening to the soft hum of the air-conditioning unit, watching the scurrying of the tourists who parked their cars on the California side and walked into Mexico, he was only idly interested in the routine he had observed many times. He had come down to escape a dull weekend in Los Angeles. Suddenly he laughed softly to himself. What in hell could be duller than sitting in this office talking shop with a couple of Bureau men who would have given anything to be able to spend the same weekend in Madrid's room at the Ambassador or around the hotel's pool?

"I thought you were going to the races," Blakely, one of the men in charge of the office, said to Madrid. "If you do, make a bet for me. Fifth horse in the fifth race."

"That's a system?" Sol smiled. "Scientific?"

"It's as good as any until the horses learn to read the *Racing Form.*"

"I don't know." Madrid lit a cigarette. "Maybe I'll take a room, have a cold shower and lie under a fan until bullfight time."

"Take a room, a shower, a broad and a fan. Let the bulls fight it out among themselves." Blakely grinned and nodded toward the outside. "Like that guy. Look at the action on her. Wow! You could chin yourself on those knockers."

Madrid's eyes followed the young couple as they sauntered toward the gate. The girl wore what had become a standard costume for a certain type which seemed to flourish in the West Hollywood section of Los Angeles and spent the weekends in Tijuana. First there was the imitation felt hat, black and low of crown with a knotted cord beneath the chin. Then there followed a cheap copy of a matador's shirt, ruffled and pleated, drawn tightly over jutting breasts and tucked into stretch pants which were so form-fitting as to reveal each crease of their bodies. On their feet they wore high-heeled boots of simulated leather, cheaply stamped in scrolled designs to give the appearance of being hand-tooled. The wearers of this outlandish garb seemed totally oblivious of its ludicrous effect. Their male companions also ran to a pattern. The butch or crew cut, khaki shorts, T-shirt, feet in heavy wool tennis socks and sneakers. Over their shoulders was slung an imitation goatskin bottle which would later be filled with a cheap red wine and boisterously drunk at the bullfight or thrown into the arena as a tribute to the matador. So uniform was their dress, their habits, gestures and speech that they all seemed to have been cast from a single mold. This strict conformity, Sol thought wryly, was their idea of nonconformity. In his mind he could follow their progress through this border town. They'd scramble aboard one of the rickety buses or share a taxi with another couple and head for La Sierra Nevada, a block-square motel filled with their counterparts, all intent upon getting drunk as quickly as possible. They would argue without any real heat, fight without anger, fall into the swimming pool and come out to sit and drip-dry at one of the tables. The place would be crowded with the worst possible type of Americans. Hard-eyed Lesbians and their *femmes*. Fairies and their sullen, contemptuous boyfriends. Men and their girls. Men and their wives. Men and other men's wives. Until 3:30 or so the place would be a shrieking bedlam and then begin to empty as the noisy mob straggled toward the bullring a couple of blocks away. There they would crowd into the sunny section of the arena's seats, yelling, shouting, tossing their phony wineskins back and forth. They would get drunker and louder and the fights would break out, vicious now; and the Mexican police would eventually step in and club the worst offenders into insensibility and drag them off to Tijuana's filthy jail. Those who remained had no real knowledge of bullfighting. They howled their *Olè!* at the clumsiest of *faenas*. Watching and listening to them, Sol had often thought they would shout *Olè!* if the bull halted to take a leak. The Mexicans tolerated this weekly incursion with silent contempt. Tijuana lived upon its tourist trade but there was no mistaking the scorn in the eyes of the waiters and taxi drivers. These Americans, Madrid thought, were the shabbiest of ambassadors for the United States.

His brooding was interrupted by the entrance of a couple, a man and a woman in their late twenties. They came without self-consciousness, displaying no more emotion than they would in signing a hotel register. He watched as they filled out the required forms. They did this with brow-creased concentration as though they were intent upon an examination for a driver's license. When the blanks were completed, signed and countersigned, they folded them carefully and put the papers in pocket or purse.

"Keep out of trouble now." The official spoke with a resigned weariness.

They nodded indifferently, familiar with the routine. If they came back "high" they would be turned over to the San Diego police. Both knew this. Now they were intent only upon getting out of here and to "the man" for the fix which would stay the growing torment for awhile. They would behave themselves and be quiet, seeking out their own kind. They found no pleasure in drink and little in food. There was no excitement in the bullring or race track. The day would pass and evening fall and they would begin to wonder desperately whether they would be able to make a buy when they got back to Los Angeles.

Sol's eyes followed the pair as they left and entered a parked, yellow Ford convertible with its top down. Watching them, seeing the tight hunger on their faces, Madrid wondered, as he always did, how so many of them managed to support the habit, for as it grew it could cost as much as fifty to one hundred dollars a day. To get it they would sacrifice everything—honor, pride, their bodies and minds.

He dropped the front legs of his chair to the floor and nodded to Blakely.

"I'm going up to the Caesar Hotel, get that shower and a drink. If I go to the track I'll play that fifth horse in the fifth race for you. Two on the nose. So long."

Blakely raised a hand in a half salute and watched Madrid with small envy as he slid in behind the wheel of the rented car and jockeyed it into the traffic lane.

Harvey Mitchell sat within the shaded *portal* of a hotel in Chihuahua. In the patio's center a fountain bubbled slowly. There were only a few guests at the scattered tables. White-jacketed waiters moved among them bringing coffee, beer, or frosted drinks of rum and lime. It was too early for the daytime meal which was served around two o'clock in the afternoon. Harvey could not accustom himself to eating this heavy variety of food in the daytime. It always left him torpid and sleepy but it was the custom of the country and, he thought, probably accounted for the siesta. He refilled his glass with the ice-cold beer. He was waiting for a man as he had been for the past three days. During his years as Villanova's accountant he had stored away a great amount of information on the dark workings of *Cosa Nostra*—names, contacts, sources from which the drugs were funneled into the United States. He had made a contact in Juarez and the word had been passed along to Chihuahua. He had done this openly and without fear, for those he spoke with were not aligned with the Chicago *borgata* but simply served its needs. They could have no knowledge of Harvey Mitchell's defection or that a contract was out on him. This man for whom he waited would come. Of this Mitchell was certain. He would come because he smelled money but he would come with caution and in his own time.

Mitchell's gaze roved over the occupied tables. Tourists with their cameras, souvenir sombreros on their heads, machine-woven serapes over their shoulders. All the cheap gimcracks which they bought with such avid excitement and suspicious haggling, certain they were being cheated—as they were. Harvey felt an arrogant scorn for them all. They chattered and laughed with the shrill insistence of parrots. They were simpletons and he was superior and aloof from their kind.

He sipped the chilled beer and marveled a little over what had happened to him within the short space of a week. He had stolen a quarter of a million dollars from an organization which did not take such derelictions lightly. He had killed a girl. He wasn't really certain about this but if he had, he felt no remorse. He had outwitted the *borgata's* hired killer and left him floundering about somewhere in the darkness. He had plotted his moves carefully after that night in the roadside diner somewhere in Kansas. When the weather cleared the following day he had taken a bus to Peoria; then a flight to Topeka and from there to El Paso. A tourist card had been picked up at the Mexican Consulate in the Texas town. He had driven across the river, found the man he sought, given him a message for the one in Chihuahua. Then, back to El Paso and the plane to Chihuahua. Here he had deposited the money in the Banco Nacional. Its translation into pesos at the exchange rate of something over twelve to a dollar had mounted to an astounding sum in Mexican currency. He was a millionaire. The realization of this gave him confidence and a tremendous satisfaction. He glanced at the tourists patronizingly. If they only knew what manner of man sat at a table across the patio from them. His smile was tightly smug. He traced a line down the frosted glass with one finger. When the man came they would talk, cautiously. Then eventually, when each was satisfied, a deal would be made; a small apparatus, at first, set up. Harvey would supply the money. The man would lead him to the supply of heroin. Then they would arrange with those who were willing to take the chance of smuggling it across the border and into the hands of those who would cut it and sell it to the ounce men. All of this must be done with care and in another's name. Harvey Mitchell would cease to exist. There was, of course, the risk. This he was prepared to take, not because he was a brave man but because he was a greedy one. In a few years he could be wealthy beyond imagining. It would take time but Harvey was no longer in a hurry. Against every move he made he must constantly weigh the possibility that the long arm of *Cosa Nostra* would reach out and find him. Even now it was like the tentacle of an octopus, weaving, searching blindly, constantly seeking to fasten upon him. He must avoid it.

With a finger he picked at the colorful label on the beer bottle, chipping it off in small fragments and then putting them together again on the table like a jigsaw puzzle.

"Señor?" The word came softly.

Harvey looked up quickly, his heart pounding. When, he thought, will I get over this feeling of panic whenever a stranger speaks to me? The man wore a suit of dusty, blue serge although the season's heat demanded lighter clothing. His face was round, innocent, smooth, and lightly colored to the shade of creamed coffee.

"I am Aguiella." The accent was barely noticeable. "It has been said you wished to see me."

"Yes." Harvey nodded. "Sit down." As an afterthought he added, "Please."

The man took a chair and lit a cigarette. His eyes did not meet Mitchell's but flicked around and over the tables and the tourists.

"Will you have a drink? Beer? Tequila? Coffee?"

"Nada, gracias." He corrected himself. "Nothing, thank you." He gazed at the cigarette's tip and blew gently upon it. "How is it you know of me?" His gaze was direct, a little cold, but the question was asked tonelessly.

"I have friends in Chicago."

"Many people have friends in Chicago." The tiniest of smiles touched the lips and was gone.

"I have been associated with those who have done some business in Sonora; business in flowers, the poppy."

"Ahhh!" The sound was a slow, indrawn breath.

This was a form of oral fencing with which Mitchell, in his present frame of mind, had little patience. To have it out in the open where they both could look at it was the only way.

"I have the money." He spoke determinedly. "You have the knowledge. We could put them together."

"But," Aguiella did not lift his glance, "let us suppose you are not exactly what you say you are. It has happened before. An agent from the Treasury Bureau working with the Mexican police. From such a thing we could have a difficult situation. Is it not so?"

Mitchell recognized the man's need for caution. He wondered how it could be overcome. There were names, the names of men in Los Angeles, Chicago, Detroit, New York, Brownsville, Matamoros who were engaged in the traffic, but he doubted they would mean anything to Aguiella.

"I have no way to prove I am what I say." He shrugged with a small admission of defeat.

The Mexican nodded understandingly. "No," he agreed. "There is no sure way." He paused. "I am," each word was being weighed, "only a very small man in this flower business but I have friends in the mountains where the little, hidden fields grow the blossoms. I would like to be a big man. It is a dream of mine to have a great house, servants, cars, lots of women. I will not get them without some risk. *Verdad?*" He was silent for a moment. "Let me think on this for a little while, a day or so. If I decide you are telling the truth and you are what you say you are, then perhaps we can negotiate some business." For the first time his eyes searched those of Harvey Mitchell. They were sharp and penetrating. "It comes to me you are frightened of something. I am not sure why. If you were an agent or working with the *Federales* this would not be so. It is this which makes me believe you are telling the truth." He stood up. "I will come back in a couple of days. You are comfortable here?"

"Yes." Mitchell experienced a sudden confidence. The man would come back. "Yes. I am quite comfortable."

"*Adiós* then. I will let you know." He nodded and left.

Mitchell watched him go and fell into a pleasant daydream of things to come. They would set up the machinery. The fortune he knew to be waiting was no longer so far out of reach. He knew how the illegal growing of the opium poppy in Mexico persisted despite the Government's persistent efforts to stamp it out. High in the mountains of Sonora and Sinaloa, hidden in the valleys, visible only from the air, hundreds of families and, sometimes, entire villages cultivated the deadly bloom in small bowls of land. Heavy fences of thorn branches surrounded them, for the grazing cattle had an insatiable appetite for the pods and their narcotic effect. The peasant farmer sold the gum to Mexican peddlers for one or two pesos a gram. These men, traveling the remote regions with their burro-loads of tinware and small household articles—cloth, needles, thread—brought the opium to the cities where they sold it for one hundred and twenty-five to one hundred and fifty pesos a gram to the laboratories, which refined it into heroin. From this point on the powder commanded incredible prices when smuggled across the border. What Mitchell must have, with Aguiella's help, was the chain of peddlers, the sources of constant supply, a chemist and a small laboratory. The process of transforming the opium into heroin was not a complicated one. They would move cautiously, starting on a small scale and expanding as the apparatus began to function. They had no need to concern themselves with the market. It was there, ready made, and always seeking more and more of the product. The demand always seemed to outrun the supply.

From one small field, opium to the value of $10,000 could be extracted and there were uncounted numbers of them tucked away in hidden recesses. Within Mexico itself all the risk would be taken by the *campesenos* who furtively cultivated the poppy. It had been said, and not without reason, that for every grower arrested two soldiers died in their never-ending effort to destroy the secret fields. They were ambushed, fallen upon and cut down with machetes or fired upon from places of concealment. When the *Federales* arrived unexpectedly, every man in a village or a farm would mysteriously disappear. When questioned, the women and children would shrug and protest their innocence. They knew nothing of the poppies which bloomed so abundantly. They had no knowledge of who had sown the seed. It was God's will, perhaps, that flowers should show themselves in a region where there was little beauty. Their men? Again the shrug. Who knew where men and boys went? It was not the business of a woman to question their goings and comings.

As he sat in the pleasant light of early afternoon, thinking of the fortune lying so close to his hand, only one thing disturbed Harvey Mitchell. Sooner or later he would have to go to California and make contact there with the wholesalers who bought in the quantities of kilos. In this there was danger for he must expose himself to questions and suspicion. He knew those he should see only by name. He was well aware they worked on the fringe of *Cosa Nostra,* not being a part of it but only a necessary adjunct to its operation. There lay the real danger, for the Chicago *borgata*—and Dano Villanova in particular—were not likely to forget what Harvey Mitchell had done. He would have to move with great care and secrecy; change his name, shave the mustache, alter his appearance as best he could. He counted, though, on the insatiable avarice of those who trafficked in the drug. If he could supply them, they would find it profitable to protect their source. All this now, however, seemed happily remote. Here he felt security and a sly sense of triumph. He had done what no one should have dared to do. All would go well if he was careful. He signaled a waiter for another beer and relaxed in his chair, turning his face to the warming sun.

In a small apartment hotel off Wilshire Boulevard in Los Angeles, near Westwood Village, Stacey Woodward stood at the window, listening to the traffic headed for a Sunday's outing on the beach at Santa Monica or the stretches of sand along the highway which skirted the coast all the way to San Francisco. She could hear the rushing sound of motors and tires but was not really aware of it. She was deep in troubled thought. A light breeze plucked at the sheer negligee and she was totally oblivious of the lovely picture she made. Hers was a cool, poised beauty. Yet she was far from poised in her mind. There was the very real problem of what she was to do from here on and it could not be dismissed. In a case of soft Italian leather were the credit cards which would have enabled her to stay at any of the luxury hotels in Beverly Hills, eat in the city's finest restaurants, charge what she wanted at the most exclusive shops.

She could not use them. Eventually the bills would reach Dano's office and her whereabouts immediately known. In her purse there was something over three hundred dollars and when that was gone she had no idea where she would get more.

She lit a cigarette and thought a little grimly she could go on call. This body, and she unconsciously ran a hand down a slender hip, had served her well. Upon it had been lavished much expensive care —exercises, massages, soft oils, perfumes and clothing. Villanova had found a wild, animal pleasure in it. She had sold it to him, after a fashion, although this had not really occurred to her before. Now, what she had done with one man she might have to do with many. The idea repelled her but she was not really outraged by the notion. She was actually quietly amused, for Los Angeles, or that part of it called Hollywood, was not the most ideal place for a girl to start in "business." The field was overcrowded. Even though motion pictures had long ago shed their luster to television the young, pretty and eager still crowded in, pitifully hopeful of being discovered somehow, somewhere by someone. Some eventually went back home but most stayed, unwilling to admit their disillusionment. Eventually they realized they had nothing to trade with but their bodies. There was, she knew from the things she had heard, a district in West Hollywood between La Cienega Boulevard and Fairfax Avenue, bounded on the north by Sunset and the south by Santa Monica Boulevards, where the apartments were filled with call girls. The going price was twenty dollars. She did some mental arithmetic. Five men at twenty dollars. One hundred. Five or six days or nights a week. Five or six hundred dollars. She had spent that much on a dress. There were alternatives: a job modeling clothes, posing for nude art calendars, a salesgirl, a receptionist. To hell with it!

Crossing the room she took her purse from the bureau and counted her money. Three hundred and sixty-eight dollars and twenty-seven cents. It was far too nice a day to stand brooding at a window. She'd get dressed, rent a U-Drive-It and join the beach traffic, finding some place along the way to have a couple of cold martinis and lunch and watch the sun go down over the Pacific.

As she showered and then dried herself she thought of Harvey Mitchell. In this she hadn't been very smart. She had wanted it all, or most of it, and this had driven the timid little man to unexpected heights of desperation. She should have offered him a deal which he would have accepted; even gone along with him for the ride for as long as the money lasted. She wondered what had happened to him. Had Roy Gaines caught him, scurrying like a terrified rabbit on the wind- and rain-swept prairie? Was he dead? The little bastard had tried to strangle her. Her fingers touched her throat. It was something to remember. Never drive a man, particularly a frightened one, too far.

She dressed, tailored slacks, sandals, a plain shirt open at the throat. Ruefully she realized things hadn't been planned at all well. The wardrobe she had packed was scanty. For a moment she looked at the telephone and was tempted to put in a call to Dano. He was probably furious but he would take her back. No. She shook her head. That was harlotry on schedule, a timetable; punching a clock. "Be here. Be there. Where the hell did you go? Why didn't you leave word?" There must be something better. It came to her as a small shock that she was lonely. There were people she could call but they were all friends or acquaintances of Dano. She didn't know one damn soul. Madrid. She halted in the act of binding her hair with a bright kerchief. What was his first name? Sam? Sul? No, Sol. Sol Madrid. That was an odd one. She had never heard of anyone named Madrid. Impulsively she picked up the bulky telephone book, found the number of the Ambassador and waited while the operator rang Madrid's room. When there was no answer she had him paged in lobby, restaurants, bar and poolside. There was really no reasonable excuse for her calling him. They were strangers even though he had accidentally come to her assistance and had seemed honestly concerned. Still, there had been something about him; a genuine warmth, a curious strength of purpose which was, at the same time, oddly gentle. Disappointed, for it was too nice a day to spend alone and she would have liked to share it with someone, she left her name and number. Then, taking her bag she closed the door behind her, walked down the two flights of stairs and out into the bright, warm sunshine.

With a cold viciousness which would have startled even those who knew him well and were aware of a vindictive anger, Dano Villanova systematically ripped and tore every dress, suit, robe and gown filling the closets and chests in the apartment on Lake Shore Drive, near Oak Street. He hurled bottles of perfume, toilet water, creams and lotions against the bathroom's tiled walls. In the living room he jerked pictures from their hangings, stamping heels through glass and frames. With a leg broken from a chair, he wrecked the well-stocked bar, tore drapes from the windows and smashed album after album of records for the hi-fidelity installation. He roamed like some enraged ape from room to room, bent only upon destruction. His eyes were black coals of fury and the normally handsome face a contorted mask. He behaved as though everything he touched and ruined was the soft, yielding body of Stacey Woodward. There was murder in him and he cursed with appalling obscenity, low in tone, terrible in meaning.

The unbelievable had happened. A girl had walked out on Dano Villanova. His vanity screamed at the incredible outrage. The bitch. Always she had made him feel just a little uncomfortable, as though the clothes he wore were somehow just not right, his speech coarse, his manners clumsy. She had made him unsure of himself although this was something he never admitted. And he, the sucker, had let her get away with it. He had been too good to her. From the very beginning he should have slapped her around until she knew fear and had come to heel like a well-trained dog. Some of the cool independence should have been knocked out of her from the start. It had worked with other girls and they had become tearful, supplicating, eager to please, abasing themselves. Deep in his heart, even though it was filled at the moment with hatred, he knew this would not have touched her spirit. Dano Villanova was a man who lived on the fears of others. He had grown wealthy and powerful on their weaknesses, their vices, their helplessness. He displayed the arrogance of a man whose authority was unquestioned and certainly never disputed. He had ordered the execution of a dozen men and had a feral instinct for treachery. He was the undisputed *Capo* of the Chicago *borgata* and when the "family" gathered in a *commissione* he was listened to with quiet respect. Now this had happened to him and it was not something which could be swept away and hidden. Sooner or later it would be whispered and there would be secret smiles, a sly word dropped out of his hearing. The *Capo's* muff had walked out on him. The humiliation gnawed and he felt his fingers tighten as though her slim throat cracked in their pressure.

Why? He paused and stared around the wrecked apartment. Why would any girl leave this? Cars, clothes, furs; everything she had wanted had been hers. Travel? They had gone to California, Hawaii, Miami, Nassau, Europe. The best, always the best. He had treated her like a lady. There had even been times when he thought about marrying her.

For two days, while his innate violence boiled under control, he refused to believe she had actually left him. No girl in her right mind would walk out and leave all or most of her clothes and furs behind. He had waited, telling himself he would knock out a few of those beautiful teeth when she came back. He called her telephone exchange for a message, left one for her. Nothing. It was then he began to admit the impossible had really happened. There had been no trouble, no row, no shouting or recriminations. Staccy never permitted herself to be drawn into a quarrel. When something annoyed her she merely picked up a book and read, or pretended to, ignoring him; refusing his suggestion they go out to a night club, theatre or restaurant. Her controlled behavior always put him on the defensive. She remained aloof and in complete possession of herself. Her voice was never raised. She allowed him to do the talking, spend his momentary annoyance and anger until he felt cheap and futile. No dame should be able to do that to a man. Her manner and acceptance of things as they were never admitted she was being kept. She accepted everything as her proper share in an arrangement to which she contributed as much, if not more, than he.

He searched the bar for an unbroken bottle. The floor was littered with glass. Finally he found some cognac in a cabinet. Without seeming to do so she had taught him many things; an appreciation of good brandy, wines and food. The admission of this now only served to goad him further. A bitch with her nose in the air even when her ass was on a bed. He opened the brandy and drank from the bottle, carrying it with him to a chair by the window where he could look out upon the lake. The drapes of soft blue with gold threads running through them lay in an untidy heap. He kicked them aside.

Where the hell had she gone and why? Florida? Not in the summertime. Besides, he permitted himself a small smile, he knew damn well she didn't have much money. He had kept things that way deliberately. She had airline credit cards as well as those for hotels, restaurants, rented cars. He'd have the accounts checked and see if they had been used and where. Deep within the anger was a small kernel of baffled resentment. It was childish but there. Why had she left him?

He took another drink. All of a sudden things started going to hell. That little rabbit of a man, Harvey Mitchell; a keeper of books, a worm with his "Yes, Mr. Villanova. Certainly, Mr. Villanova." He had seemed so harmless Dano had trusted him far beyond what his cold judgment might have dictated. So the sneaking son of a bitch had made off with a quarter of a million dollars. Well, in time he'd find him. Then there was Roy Gaines, who had never defaulted on a contract. Gaines had been found dead in a Kansas ditch. The stupid bastard had electrocuted himself. But, and this had puzzled Dano when he read the small item in the *Tribune,* what in hell was Gaines doing off the Super-Chief? The only answer was he had been chasing Mitchell; Mitchell who had known or recognized the Detroit gun. He had inquired of the Santa Fe and found out the Super-Chief had been briefly halted while a washout was being repaired. So Mitchell had jumped the train and Gaines followed.

To the goddamned hell with Roy Gaines and Mitchell. He threw the bottle against the opposite wall. He wanted Stacey Woodward and he would find her. A hundred tracers, small veins through which flowed the intelligence, the commands and intrigue of the *borgata,* would be put to work. Sooner or later they would find her. Then he would see to it that she knew such agony and debasement as she could not believe possible. She would crawl and he would see her ruin. She would scream for the mercy of dying; plead for relief, search a faltering and panic-stricken mind for escape. First would go all honor and pride; the fastidious care with which she had always maintained herself. Dignity would yield to a beggarly supplication and when this failed she would begin to sell Stacey Woodward piece by piece, soul and body, until there was nothing left anyone wanted. He had seen it happen too many times not to know the deadly process of attrition.

He felt better now and the thin lips almost smiled. Reaching back to where the telephone lay upon the floor near an overturned table he picked it up, listened for a moment to the humming tone and then dialed slowly. He needed to make but one call. From this the order would be transmitted, fanning out through a vast and invisible web. The *Capo* wanted something done. Find a girl by the name of Stacey Woodward. Find her and take care of her but good.

5

MADRID swung off the freeway at the downtown ramp, wound through the all but deserted maze of lower Los Angeles and then picked up Wilshire Boulevard, which stretched like an almost empty cavern. The freeway would have been faster but on a Sunday every bastard with wheels was crowding it at seventy miles an hour or more. Sweaty, hot, tired, irritable and unreasonably aggressive, the drivers dove at each other, courting sudden death at every mile. He didn't feel like coping with them. On Wilshire he loafed along, clocking his speed to the staggered traffic lights so he moved with only an occasional stop.

The *corrida* had been dull; a *fracaso* as the Mexicans called it, with undersized, cowardly bulls who refused to charge. The matadors were indifferent. Actually, he admitted, you couldn't expect much at Tijuana. The best bulls went to Mexico City for the big winter season. The men who fought made this summer tour of the border circuit because it was part of their contract. They were well aware that most of those who filled the arena's seats hadn't the slightest appreciation for what was happening on the yellow sand below. So, for the most part, they took the easy way with flashy but relatively safe passes and made their kills without going in over the horns. It was a day's work and nothing more. Sol had left early, avoiding the traffic rush at the border gates.

He glanced up at the cloudless sky. It was almost six o'clock but with daylight saving, darkness wouldn't fall until around eight. For a change the air was fresh and clean without the smog which had steadily crept upon the city for years. Now it had become a creeping, yellow horror, filtering up into Beverly Hills, Westwood and even into parts of Santa Monica. The residents had learned to live with it but the stuff was a festering blight and the price Los Angeles had paid for its sprawling growth. Idly he wondered why everything had to be BIG. All over the country, in towns and cities, the Chambers of Commerce and civic organizations were constantly pressing for more industry, greater population. Even San Diego, which once had charm and character, was desperately contesting for additional plants, extended naval facilities, taller buildings, expanded aircraft production; all of the things which would make it just one more faceless city. A bridge was being built across the harbor to the quietly rural town of Coronado and one more retreat would vanish. Suppose, he mused, everyone just said to hell with it? We like things as they are. Build your factories, your plants, your oil refineries someplace else. Let us be SMALL, contented. He smiled. This was heresy. They could string you up for such thoughts. They were un-American and an affront to man's soaring spirit. To be big was to be wonderful.

At the Ambassador he turned the car over to a parking attendant and went directly to his room. Below was the landscaped patio with its palms and colorful flower beds. The sunshades were huge blossoms and a few bathers were still stretched out on pads, feeling the last of the day's warmth on their half-naked bodies.

A tiny red bulb glowed on his telephone, indicating a message. He called the operator and was told that a Miss Woodward had left her number. Nothing more. There was a small frown about his eyes. Then it cleared. After all, he had told her where he would be. It had been an invitation to call. She had, but, and this annoyed him because he realized it was becoming a habit, he wondered why. Not to thank him. This she had done on the train.

He stripped off his clothes. In the shower he let the water run lukewarm and then full cold. Wrapping himself in one of the oversized towels he poured a drink from half a bottle of bourbon, stretched out on the bed and lit a cigarette. The telephone rang softly. For a moment he did nothing. When it sounded again he reached and cradled the receiver against his ear.

"Madrid." He spoke without emphasis.

"Sol. This is Eddie Collins."

"Go away."

"You go. Mexico."

"I just came back from there. Tijuana."

"That's not Mexico. That's L.A. with an accent."

Wearily Sol swung up and sat on the bed's edge. Collins was an old friend out of the Bureau's District Office. They had worked together often.

"I have two more days of vacation coming before I'm suppose to report to you, Mr. Collins." He tried to make it sound firm.

"I teenk you make beeg mistake, frien'." Collins was softly insistent. "I teenk you work a'ready."

"An' I tink," Sol put the cigarette out, "you make a lousy dialect comedian. What kind of an accent is that supposed to be?"

"I'm Pancho. You Cisco Kid. You go to Chihuahua. Big Chief say so. I only work here, too."

"For Christ's sake." Sol was honestly angry. "I just got back. He knows that. Why can't someone else make the trip?"

"When you got a guy with the name of Madrid on the payroll you just naturally got to send him to a Spanish-speaking country."

"Well, I'm only half Spanish so I'll go halfway."

"There's something moving, Sol." Collins was abruptly crisp, businesslike. "We had a call from Colonel Ortega, in Chihuahua. There's some action going on. He isn't sure what but wanted to let us know and offered all the cooperation if we wanted to send an agent, an observer. You know how Ortega is. He doesn't worry about protocol or that the Bureau intrudes in his territory, as long as a job gets done. There was a small squeal but it has to do, maybe, with a big rat. No one is certain. It's just a whisper. Right now there is a little mouse nibbling around. Dano Villanova's accountant. Harvey Mitchell. You know him?"

"Sure I know him." Madrid was suddenly alert. Mitchell in Chihuahua. "He was on the Super-Chief with me on the way out but he ducked off. Remember Roy Gaines, out of Detroit?"

There was a curious silence for a moment. When Collins spoke again all trace of banter was gone.

"We got a routine memo from the FBI. Mr. Gaines was found in a ditch, west of K.C. He had grabbed a hot wire. What goes on?"

"Gaines was after Mitchell. A contract, I'd guess."

Collins whistled a long, low note. "Who in hell would have the nerve to put a contract out on Villanova's accountant?"

"Villanova, maybe." Madrid dropped the suggestion casually.

"You're kidding."

"I'm guessing. Also, my zealous friend who can't wait until Monday to start lousing up my vacation in the sun, the *Capo's* girl friend, by the name of Stacey Woodward, was on the train. Someone tried to kill her."

"Why?"

"If I knew all the answers, Mr. Collins," Madrid spoke wearily, "I'd be Chief of the Bureau or, at least, a District Administrator instead of a lousy peon who gets chased across the border every time someone brings in a half-smoked cigarette of marijuana."

"I think I'll call the boss. He may want to talk with you tonight."

"Listen, pal. Whatever is going on can sure as hell wait until tomorrow. Do me a favor. Stay away from the telephone. I'll be in the office first thing in the morning, around daybreak if you say so. We'll lay everything out then."

"You got a dame in your room?" Collins was suspicious.

"I wish I did have. You got a number?"

"Now," Collins was pious, "you know nothing like that goes on in Los Angeles. The Chief of Police says so. The only tail around is on the horses at Hollywood Park."

"I never tried a horse." Madrid was gravely reflective.

"They're undependable, friend. All right," Collins was easy, agreeable, "I haven't talked with you. Come in tomorrow. Have fun."

"I'll try but you've sure spoiled it for me."

"You really want a number?"

"I have one. Now get the hell off the line while I call it."

"Good luck."

"In this town you don't need luck, only twenty bucks."

Sol dropped the receiver back into place and lay against the pillows for a moment. Then he got up, made himself another drink and dialed the number Stacey Woodward had left.

Well north of the Malibu colony, on the broad highway skirting the Pacific, there is an exceptionally fine restaurant, the Trancas Inn. The service is deft, unobtrusive, and the food excellent. In a corner booth, looking out upon a terrace and rock garden with a miniature waterfall, Madrid sat across the table from Stacey Woodward. He turned the stem of the glass, holding a sour Daiquiri, between his fingers and regarded her with unconcealed admiration. There was an unflawed, crystal beauty here and yet, he thought, there was mobility of feature which gave it light and shadow. This was no cold ornament of a girl but one which held the fire and color of a fine diamond.

He had called. She answered. The exchange had been brief, impersonal almost to the point of indifference, but he had felt a warmth, something close to a pleased gratitude, as her voice came across the wire. It was as though she had been expecting and dreading another call and was happy his wasn't it.

"This is Madrid. Sol Madrid. Will you have dinner with me tonight?"

"I'd like that very much."

"What time and where do I pick you up?"

"Seven thirty or so." She gave him the Westwood address. "And—and thank you for calling."

From her small hotel they had driven out Wilshire Boulevard, through Santa Monica, down the big, sweeping ramp and onto the highway. They had not talked but it was a silence without constraint or the awkwardness of strangers.

"Any place in particular you'd like to go?"

"I always leave that to the man." A surprising smile touched her lips. "Do you know, for years I have wondered about the notion that wherever you see trucks parked at a restaurant you can be sure the food is good. Why are truck drivers supposed to be gourmets?"

"I don't think they mean good. They mean plenty. You know. Big slabs of overdone Yankee pot roast, mounds of mashed potatoes with synthetic gravy, heavy slabs of pie. Most of the time the food is lousy but the myth persists. It belongs with the idea that a cold shower first thing in the morning is good for you."

They had said little more—a word, an observation, trivialities—until he had swung into the Trancas parking lot and a few moments later were seated and the iced drinks before them.

Now she met his gaze without embarrassment. There was even a small, quizzical light of amusement in her eyes.

"Was this invitation tonight social or are you being snoopy—a detective?"

"I'm not a detective. You know that. I'm a Treasury Agent assigned to the Bureau of Narcotics. Also," his grin was disarming, "I try, whenever possible, to be honest. So maybe it is a little of both —snoopy and social."

She nodded, satisfied. "May I have another Daiquiri?"

He ordered again for them both and they said nothing until the waiter brought the drinks.

"You're wondering a little, aren't you, what I'm doing in California without Dano?"

"Wondering possibly, but I'm not too upset about it."

"On the train you seemed to know so much. Who I was. Who Gaines and Mitchell were."

"I collect odd bits of information; lint on a blue serge suit. By the way," his eyes lighted, "do they make blue serge anymore? You never hear the word."

She shrugged. "I think Du Pont did blue serge in." The small smile vanished. "Was your being on the Super-Chief just a coincidence?"

He nodded. "I like trains and had some extra time coming. It was only another trip until I saw you waiting near the gate. Then along came Mitchell and Gaines. When you followed Mitchell I began to get interested even though it was none of my business. I couldn't make myself believe the three of you on the same train was a thing of chance. Someone was after someone or something. I began to wonder who and what." He studied her. "Why did you try and lean on Harvey Mitchell?"

She hesitated over the answer as though trying to make up her mind whether to answer. Then her eyes met his with candor.

"I've left Dano. I heard him on the telephone and knew Mitchell had taken a quarter of a million dollars. Then he talked with Gaines in Detroit. I needed money. Mitchell seemed to be the answer. I almost got away with it."

"You damn near got yourself killed. And," he measured the words, "what you tried to do makes both you and Mitchell thieves." He said it unemotionally, reciting a fact.

She lifted one shoulder with a gesture of indifference. "I suppose so." There was a small defiance in her gaze and then it dropped. "The word has a harsh sound. Somehow, though, stealing from a thief doesn't seem as bad as just stealing."

"Semantics." He paused and then opened a menu for her. "Let's order."

"You do it. Anything will be fine."

He beckoned a waiter and ordered lightly; a salad and then Lobster Thermidor and with it a bottle of the fine, California Pinot Chardonnay. When they were alone again he finished the Daiquiri.

"Mitchell is in Mexico. Chihuahua. We, the Bureau, think he is setting himself up in the flower business with Villanova's money. Poppies."

There was an almost imperceptible start of surprise. Then, again she was completely poised.

"Dano will get him. He dislikes initiative on the part of the hired help."

"What about you?" The question was unnecessarily crude and he wondered why he had voiced it. "I'm sorry."

Unhappiness was a brief shadow. "No, I don't think you are. You're reaching for something. Oh!" The tone changed. It carried, now, the open simplicity of a child. "He'll get me, also. That is, if he is angry enough or really wants me back."

"You're frightened." It was a statement and not a question.

"Of course."

"Why did you leave him?" He pursued her.

"I'm not sure. I think, maybe, I just got tired of being what I was. I don't think you'd understand."

"You've been Villanova's girl for three or four years now. Wasn't it something you could have talked over with him?"

"You don't talk things over with Dano. You listen." Her expression was one of admiring curiosity touched with a certain mockery. "Is it possible your Bureau is this thorough; to know how long I have been Dano Villanova's mistress? Or is the information from your own private file?"

"More lint on a blue serge suit." He smiled and then sobered. "I know everything about Villanova but nothing I can prove. I've wanted him for a long time. The Bureau wants him. One of these days he'll make a mistake."

"Did you think I'd help you help him make one? Is that why we're here tonight, together?"

"No." He drew the word out slowly. "But," the explanation came with a certain difficulty, "there was a fringe area I wanted to explore."

She wasn't annoyed. "In the first place I wouldn't help. In the second place I don't really know anything. Oh! I know his friends, his associates, some of the people who work for him, but he is not a man who exchanges confidences. I was only a small, diverting part of his life. I served a certain necessary function; let's say a hostess with bedroom obligations. I know he is a big man in a big and frightening organization. But," again the smile came slowly with a soft radiance, "those are things you know."

"The money that has kept you these years. You knew where it came from?"

A small, perplexed frown darkened her eyes. "I can't understand why you're not making me angry. Your manner and questions are insolent. You're presumptuous and trying very hard to push me. But," the frown disappeared, "for some reason I don't mind. It seems you have a certain ugly charm, and perhaps at the moment I'm susceptible."

"Have you any plans?" He changed the subject effortlessly.

"No." It was a flat confession of uncertainty. "What plans, ideas I had, went with Harvey Mitchell. But I've always made my own way in one fashion or another."

"I'll be in town for a couple of days at least. I'd like to see you again."

"No more questions? No more talk of Dano?" She was quietly emphatic.

"I'll just be my charming, ugly self and you may grow a little more susceptible."

"I hardly think so in two days."

"It has happened."

She slanted her eyes up at him. "Yes." She paused. "Yes, I can believe that although I'm not sure why."

They left the inn and he drove northward through Oxnard, Ventura and finally into Santa Barbara. The night air was warm and fragrant and a moon gave the rolling Pacific a silver wash. She didn't ask where they were going and seemed happy simply to relax, leaning back against the seat, her shoulder occasionally brushing his with unaffected intimacy.

"Is Madrid really your name? Sol Madrid." She seemed to test it on her tongue like some unfamiliar flavor. "I never knew anyone with the name of Madrid. Is Sol short for Solomon?"

"No. It's just Sol. For that matter, I never knew a girl named Stacey."

He made a left turn off the highway on a street leading to the harbor. At the end of a long, wooden pier there was a frame building with its windows softly lighted.

"We'll have a drink, if you like. Some brandy and coffee and then I'll take you home."

She rested her cheek against the upholstery and glanced at him with a sidelong speculation.

"I've never been here before. It's all new. I thought maybe you were motel minded and this was it."

"Suppose it had been?" The car was barely moving over the loose boarding.

"I don't know." She answered without hesitation. "I really don't know. And," the admission came thoughtfully, "I'm not sure why."

"This is one of the really fine restaurants in the country and I practically never get motel minded. It is something I am particular about."

She straightened up and with a quick, impulsive gesture brushed his cheek with the barest touch of a kiss.

"Thank you, Sol Madrid."

He made no move to touch her; to press for an advantage in a sentimental moment. What he felt was a tenderness. He crossed his arms upon the wheel, resting upon them, eyes fixed upon the bay's colored lights. Then, he seemed to give a brief nod as though answering a question asked of himself.

"When I leave here I'm going to Mexico. You may need help. I'll give you a number, a close friend at the Bureau. Use it. He'll know about you and he's a good man when things get tight. Now," he took her hand for a moment, "let's have that drink."

This was a small cantina and restaurant in Chihuahua. Dusty, faded streamers of colored crepe paper ran from the corners of the ceiling and were fastened in a drooping bow to a center cluster of dim, low-watt bulbs.

The man Aguiella sat across the scarred table from Harvey Mitchell. There was a glass of tequila, a saucer of quartered limes and a shaker of salt before him. The room was all but empty and quiet save for the sharp click of the dominoes as the players at the game slapped down their pieces. Mitchell poured the remaining beer in the bottle into a glass. He was tense and his hand, in motion, was a mechanical thing.

"I have given much thought to what we talked about." Aguiella spoke without raising his eyes. "I do not think we can do the business."

Mitchell took a swallow of the beer. There was something in the tone of the refusal that disturbed and frightened him. In this place, the city, this dim and somehow sinister cantina, he felt alien, vulnerable. There was a strange, indefinable menace in the air. He pressed back against the chair and felt the pressure of the small Italian automatic he had purchased in El Paso. It fitted neatly into the palm of a hand. He had no real idea, at the time, why he had bought it. Fear and the instinct for self-preservation. He had never carried a gun before, never even fired one; but its possession had given him a small confidence as he walked with it from the run-down pawnshop in the Texas city. Now he slept with it beneath his pillow and its size made but the slightest and almost unobtrusive bulge as he carried it with him. He wasn't really certain he could use it if and when the time came. Now he watched the man Aguiella.

"Why?" He tried to keep the impatience from his question. It had been ten days since he had seen or talked with the Mexican in the hotel's patio. "What has happened?"

Aguiella turned up the palms of his hands. He was indifferent to Mitchell's querulous annoyance. He took a small swallow of the colorless liquor after a touch of salt and then sucked pensively upon a piece of lime.

"Do you know how it is, *señor?*" He lifted his head to gaze at Mitchell. "Sometimes, when you take a handful of sand? No matter how tightly you hold it a few grains sift through the clenched fingers."

"What are you talking about?" Mitchell's anger showed itself.

"It is only that a few grains from someone's hand have dropped to the ground. They were brought to my attention." He paused. "I think it is, *señor,* you ride the white horse."

Mitchell stared uncomprehendingly at him, trying to make some sense out of the words.

"It is an expression of my country," Aguiella explained gently. "A man who rides a white horse." He slowly drew a fingertip across his throat in an unmistakable slash.

The shock of the pantomime so jolted Mitchell that he jerked upright in the chair. It was a convulsive movement and one over which he had no control. He felt the damp chill of a sweating fear on his body. So soon, he thought; already, down here, it was known to the *borgata* where he was?

As though he understood what was passing through the American's mind Aguiella shook his head with a small sign of understanding sympathy.

"No." The Mexican shook his head. "It is not known exactly where you are or even you are in Mexico. But the word is whispered in many places that it would be of an advantage to someone if he found of your presence and let certain people in the Estados Unidos know. So," he smiled briefly, "you see how it is. You make a dangerous partner."

"But the money," Mitchell spoke with a desperate urgency, "think of that. Together we could become wealthy beyond your imagining. We could be careful. I would not appear in the business. There are small villages where I could settle and supply the funds to you. No one need know."

Aguiella's smile was regretful. "Your partner would also ride the white horse and such a rider has no need for money. I prefer to be the poor man I am, doing small dishonesties with little risk." He finished his tequila.

Mitchell experienced a weakness. All confidence drained from him. There was another chance at the fortune for which he lusted. In Hermosillo, a man by the name of— He searched his memory frantically. Batuc! That was it. Juan Batuc. He could recall now how, and under what circumstances, he had first heard of the man. There had been a meeting, an *arguiamenda* of the *borgata,* and because he was familiar with all of the financial transactions Villanova had sent for him to sit in on the session. There had been a long discussion and it was finally decided to use this Batuc as a supplier from Sonora. Later, there had been a dispute over the wholesale price of the heroin and Batuc had been dropped in favor of another who offered a better deal. So, he reasoned to himself now, this Batuc could well be a man of resentment and still angry over the *borgata's* action. Together they might do business. But, and again the cold fingers of apprehension ran down his spine, could he trust Batuc when he found him? Could he trust this Aguiella with the information he now possessed? Could he trust anyone? Even as they sat here, with the Mexican pretending regret, he may already have betrayed him and passed on the word of his presence in Chihuahua. Villanova would pay well for the information. If this had not crossed Aguiella's mind it would certainly occur to him that Harvey Mitchell was a valuable piece of property. There was in him, at the moment, the wild desire to leap up and run out into the covering darkness of the night. Aguiella was and would continue to be a constant threat. Harvey Mitchell was nothing to him; no ties of friendship bound them. Why not turn his knowledge into a profit? Somehow, and again he fought to control an unreasoning panic, this Aguiella's mouth must be made silent. It was with an effort he nodded a quiet understanding of what the Mexican had said.

"I will find someone." He spoke with an exertion, trying to make it sound casual.

"Of course, *señor.*" Aguiella was agreeable. "It is possible that I, for a fee, could put you in touch with someone who has not my caution and a willingness to live humbly."

Mitchell could feel the sly hypocrisy in the suggestion. He fancied he could divine the methodical working of Aguiella's mind. To pass the word and keep him here in Chihuahua until Villanova had been informed. Then, someone would come or a killer hired in Mexico and that would be the end of Harvey Mitchell. He held his features stonily composed.

"I have other connections." He rejected the Mexican's offer with an elaborate indifference. "I will stay here in Chihuahua until they are made." He wanted Aguiella to believe there was no haste, that he had no suspicion of the man's treachery.

"So." Aguiella rose. "That is good. If you will accept I will now drive you back in my small car to your hotel and we will say *adiós* with no bad feeling. You understand how it is, *verdad?*"

You're damn right I understand how it is, Mitchell snarled to himself, but he smiled an acceptance of the offer and they walked from the cantina. The domino players did not look up from their game. The man who served the bar and tables was reading a lurid comic book in Spanish.

They drove through Chihuahua's badly lit and roughly cobbled side streets. In his hand now Mitchell held the small automatic. It was no larger than a cigarette case. He cautiously moved a thumb to release the safety catch, wondering fearfully if it would make a tell-tale sound. It didn't.

Two blocks from the hotel, in the dark shadows between the widely spaced streetlights and beneath the overhang of a jacaranda tree, Aguiella drew the rickety car to a shuddering halt. He spoke with an almost embarrassed note of apology.

"It is only two *caudras,* two blocks," he amended, "to your hotel. If you would not mind walking them? It is not too safe, I do not think, to be seen now openly in your company. And who knows what eyes are watching? You understand how it is?"

"Yes. It is not important."

Mitchell half turned in his seat as though to offer his hand in a good-bye and then he shot Aguiella three times through the neck and throat, pressing the stubbed barrel into the flesh and pulling the trigger as fast as he could. The sound was muted, no louder than the snap of a lash at the end of a whip.

Mitchell jerked away, fearful of the blood which might stain his clothing. Then he stepped from the car, peered cautiously up and down the street and found it deserted. As an afterthought he went around the car, reached in and turned off the ignition. The engine died wheezingly. Now the car would attract little attention. He walked, without haste, in the direction of his hotel.

He experienced a most curious feeling of exultation. It was almost as though he were a little drunk. His body was weightless, his step airy, and his feet seemed not to touch the uneven pavement. Never before had he felt like this. It was power. He had killed a man. He, Harvey Mitchell, the timid keeper of books and accounts had, by his own hand, eliminated a menace to his safety. The knowledge of what he had done was intoxicating. He wanted to sing, whistle. Never again, he told himself, would he be fearful of anyone. A man died so easily, without a struggle, and all things were possible for someone with determination. He was momentarily contemptuous of Villanova and the *borgata's* hired guns.

Approaching the hotel, caution slowed his steps. Small errors must be avoided and it was better no one see him coming in. Instead of going through the main entrance and lobby, past the room clerk's desk, he went down the side of the building, an inconspicuous shadow within the heavily treed and shrubbed gardens. A wooden door opened on the patio. He tried it and the latch raised without pressure. The patio was empty, an occasional light bulb glowing weakly before the guest rooms on the ground floor. From the hotel's bar came the wailing music of the *mariachi* band. Here the tourist guests lingered over their drinks. Unhurriedly he walked along the *portal* until he came to his room; unlocked it, entered and closed the door behind him.

In the mirror he surveyed his clothing. Then he removed the suit and went over every inch of it for the smallest stain. There was nothing. Aguiella had fallen forward, over the wheel, and the blood had gushed upon his own knees and the floorboard.

The little automatic? Mitchell wondered about this. Should he rid himself of it? Would the police, when Aguiella was found, take the slugs from the body and test them for barrel markings? Probably. Would anyone connect him with the dead man? The waiter who had served the two of them in the patio ten days or so ago? Maybe. Someone at the cantina? He didn't think so. No one there had spoken to the Mexican and it was logical that he had selected an out-of-the-way place where he was unknown and his association with the gringo tourist would be a matter of indifference. Just the same it would be better to get rid of the pistol. Tomorrow would be time enough. He broke the gun down into three pieces, magazine, barrel and stock. In the morning he would join the inevitable sightseers on one of the guided tours and at each stopping place would inconspicuously rid himself of one piece at a time in widely separated places.

Again he knew the heady wine of power and decision. With neat precision he hung up his clothing and put on pajamas and slippers. Then he called room service on the telephone and ordered a whole bottle of Scotch. This was something he had never in his life done before. Within the space of a few minutes he had been transformed. It would be soothingly pleasant to get a little drunk here in the safety of his room and, maybe, even have a girl. He wondered about this also with amazement. What was happening to Harvey Mitchell? Where had he gone? Who was this stranger who towered and felt the need for a drink and a woman? He lay back on the bed, reveling in the sensation and waited impatiently for the whisky and the boy who would bring it. He would tip him well and ask about a girl who might be slipped into his room.

6

⚘ IN the spare office of Colonel Ignacio Ortega, *Comandante* of the *Federales* for the State of Chihuahua, Sol Madrid sat in one of the heavy, uncomfortable chairs and smoked thoughtfully as the officer talked.

Ortega, called Nacho by his intimates, was a handsome man in his early forties. His jet hair had silvered lightly and his features were clear and sharply intelligent. Unlike most Mexican officials Ortega had no small jealousies, no petty desire to hold and exercise all authority. He never felt that, in accepting the assistance, knowledge and experience of someone else he was admitting to subordination. Really qualified men, he knew, were rare and there were many problems which required the combined efforts of many persons. He and Madrid had known each other for several years and were on a first-name basis. Each respected the other.

Briefly Madrid had related what he knew of Harvey Mitchell's defection, his embezzlement of a quarter of a million dollars from the Chicago *borgata's* treasury, and his flight from the stalled Super-Chief. Now he listened with mild astonishment to what Ortega had to say.

"This Aguiella," the Colonel lit a second cigarette from the stub of the first, "was a small criminal of no consequence. He was unimportant save in the general picture of narcotics in my country. His value to those who deal with the stuff was the fact he had the confidence of the country people, the peon who has a secret poppy field tucked away in a valley. He could make the connections. To our knowledge he never attempted to take any heroin across the border. Save for his tenuous association with the narcotic trade from the poppy to the concealed laboratory I would not have interested myself in his death but left it to the local police."

"Harvey Mitchell killed him?" Sol was incredulous.

"Oh! Of this I am certain," Ortega assented. "But it is not something I can prove. We questioned him. He admitted freely he had known Aguiella but insisted the acquaintance and relationship was only that of a tourist and a guide. He had engaged Aguiella to show him around. He made no attempt to deny what we already knew, that he had been with Aguiella on the night of the murder. They were planning a tour for the following day. Aguiella had driven him from a small cantina to the hotel and left him there. On the following morning, after waiting for his guide to appear, Mr. Mitchell grew impatient and joined a guided limousine tour. Nothing would move him from this story."

"The gun?" Sol asked.

"We searched thoroughly. *Nada.* But it was of a very small caliber and could easily have been disposed of between the time Aguiella was found and Mr. Mitchell interrogated. It could well be buried somewhere about the hotel grounds."

"Where is Mitchell now?"

"Here, in the city. Since I had no idea what was on your mind, since your telegram said only you were coming, I suggested to Mr. Mitchell he remain in Chihuahua until our investigation was completed. He was extremely indignant and talked of going to the American Consul, writing his Congressman. However, he remained. I only advised your Bureau of his presence here because we were aware of his meeting with Aguiella."

"I wonder why?" Sol stared at his locked fingers. "I wonder why Mitchell would kill his contact? It just doesn't make sense."

Ortega shook his head. "It puzzled me. It was a curious riddle.

But now, since you have told me of the Chicago affair, some small light begins to show itself. Suppose Aguiella had learned the Chicago *sindacato* wanted Mitchell? He was *hot*—a smile flashed—"as the idiom of your country has it. Assume Aguiella found Mr. Mitchell too dangerous to associate with? Let us imagine he told our friend this and politely withdrew from their projected venture? Mr. Mitchell becomes alarmed and suspicious. Aguiella, knowing where he was, might well turn this information over to those who would pay him well. Mitchell couldn't take the risk. This, I think, would lead even such a little man to murder."

Thinking of the incident on the Super-Chief, Sol was inclined to agree. Mitchell was a desperate man, and as such, was capable of desperate measures.

"As you know," Colonel Ortega continued, "we have a convenient statute here in my country. The 'Thirty-Three.' It covers a multitude of things and under it we deport anyone as an 'undesirable alien.' Would you like to have Mr. Mitchell back across the border?"

Sol didn't reply immediately. On the flight down from Los Angeles he had carefully examined the problem of Harvey Mitchell. There had been no instructions from the Bureau's District Administrator. There was no plan, no set of rules to be followed. First. What was Mitchell up to? Find that out and then meet the situation as it developed. He knew Ortega would deport the man back across the border if the Bureau requested the action. But Harvey Mitchell was too valuable to lose and that was what would happen if he returned to the United States without protective custody. To hustle him over the Rio Grande would only expedite Dano Villanova's lethal plans. But Mitchell alive in Mexico, using Villanova's money to cut into *Cosa Nostra's* monopoly of the drug, was setting up a situation.

"No." He shook his head now and answered. "Let's leave him alone for awhile and see what he is up to. Let's see if he can set up an operation and with whom. If he gets deeply involved we may have something. First, he will be way out of his depth. He may have been a good accountant for Villanova but he won't know how to handle the men here. They will use him. When he really begins to flounder he'll get scared. If he is frightened enough he may be willing to trade information for protection. I want Harvey Mitchell singing. I want the whole story of *Cosa Nostra* told to a federal grand jury. Harvey

Mitchell knows it all, from the *Capo* and the top men in the *Commissione* to the mules and ounce men."

"As you wish," Colonel Ortega agreed. "He will be told he is free to travel about as he wishes. His activities may clear up some things for us. One thing. Does he know you by sight?"

"No." Sol was positive.

"That is good." Ortega nodded. "I have a feeling, a hunch as you say, he will not stay long in Chihuahua. Now." He sat back and stared at the ceiling. "Where would I go," he ruminated aloud, "if I wanted to make a connection and had a quarter of a million dollars to finance it? And, this must be considered, remain inconspicuous?"

"Sonora?" Madrid answered the question with one of his own.

Ortega smiled with pleasure. "Yes, my friend, I think I would go to Sonora; to Hermosillo, possibly. So. If we are guessing correctly would it not be a good thing for you to be already in Hermosillo if and when Mr. Mitchell arrives?"

"It would be a very good thing, *compadre.*" Sol grinned. "Can you arrange for my introduction to and acceptance by some of the more disreputable citizens there?"

"I think so. I will have you picked up immediately by the police. Your arrest and detention will be heard of in the proper places. We have men working undercover in this traffic who will later vouch for you and see to it you are certified. By the time Mr. Mitchell arrives you will be established on at least a tentative basis. I need not warn you, however, that you may get yourself killed in this sort of a venture. Our little stool pigeons, our informers and even our own secret agents sometimes disappear in a most disagreeable fashion. All criminals are suspicious by nature; the Mexican more so. Their weakness is greed and a conviction they are smarter than the police."

"I am a careful man by nature."

"Keep it that way." Ortega regarded him with a friendly twinkle. "I will hold Mr. Mitchell in a state of detention for a week or so more despite his protests. That will give you a little time in which to adjust yourself to Sonora's climate."

"Is there a flight into Hermosillo today?"

"Passage will be arranged and you will be arrested the moment the wheels touch down at Hermosillo and held only long enough to make contact with one of our men we will have planted there." A dry smile lit his face. "Forgive us, if you will, the facilities of our jail there. It is not in our philosophy to make the lawless comfortable. We do not believe in cell radios, motion pictures, baseball games in the yard, individual toilets and showers as you do in the United States. Our prisons are dirty, the food awful. Those who are jailed in Mexico may not come out better men but they are most certainly chastened, temporarily, and have no desire to return."

"And if we are wrong? Mitchell does not go to Sonora?"

"His movements will be tracked. You will be kept advised."

Sol rose and Ortega followed. Their hands met in a firm clasp, for there was real friendship between them. The officer was a dedicated man. He led the way to the door.

"Our man will approach you in jail." Ortega halted with his hand on the knob. "Would you like some dramatic word of recognition or something simple?"

"Simple. It will get complicated enough as we go along."

"*Bueno.*" Ortega thought for a moment. "He will say his name and that he is from Juarez. By this you will know him."

"That's good enough." Madrid removed the small, leather-covered identification card from his wallet and handed it to the officer. Also a check drawn upon the Bureau's contingency fund. "I don't think anyone ought to find this card on me. Will you have the check deposited? I may draw on it to make a buy just to get things started. Thanks for everything. Keep Mitchell on ice for a week or so."

"I will but I promise you it will not keep him cool. He continues to talk about his rights. So. *Adiós.* Go with God. We will be in touch."

Although he knew it was dangerous, Harvey Mitchell could not rid himself of a feeling of smug complacency. He had discovered unsuspected facets about himself. He had eluded the *borgata's* hired gun. He had recovered two hundred thousand dollars from the little tramp who had tried to shake him down on the train. He still wondered, now and then, whether he had killed her. It no longer made any difference. Without the slightest tremor he had killed a man here in Chihuahua who might have betrayed him. With these things a timidity of years left him. He had proved himself smarter than any of them. He walked now with a cocky assurance. He had made fools of the authorities who had questioned him regarding the murder of Aguiella. Not once had they been able to shake him from the story he told. His detention here was temporary. They would have to release him and from then on he would move with assurance. He continued, though, to exercise one caution. He did not leave the hotel. In the evenings he sat in the bar, surrounded by the tourists, steeling his nerves against the interminable din of the *mariachis* who wailed and lamented in songs of love about their *alma* and their *corazón*. He thought it was probable there would be no music in Mexico if soul and heart were removed from the vocabulary. But the musicians and the tourists were a protection of sorts and he merged himself with them, even striking up a few acquaintanceships with the transients; standing his share of the drinks but limiting himself to an occasional beer. He discovered that whisky in quantity gave him a sense of invulnerability and this could be fatal. Never for a moment could he dismiss the fact that he walked the high wire of danger. So, as much as possible, he kept himself surrounded by others; taking the dreary sightseeing excursions; listening to the endless complaints about indifferent waiters and how hot water always came out of the C tap because Mexican plumbers thought C was for *caliente*.

Now and then he thought of Villanova and laughed secretly, knowing the *Capo's* fury at being made to appear foolish and this was exactly what had happened. The sheep had taken a nip out of the wolf. Compounding Villanova's anger was the disturbing knowledge that his meek, self-effacing accountant's head was crammed with damning information. If pressed too hard, hounded without being disposed of, Harvey Mitchell might be forced to go to the FBI, the Internal Revenue Service and the Federal Bureau of Narcotics. This would worry Villanova and everyone in *Cosa Nostra*. So, if he wanted to live, he must constantly be wary and alert. He could never take anything for granted; trust no associate, no hireling. For, whatever Harvey Mitchell could pay for his own protection the *borgata* could and would pay more to have him removed for good.

He did not like to think about this. His future and security lay in building for himself a tight and efficient organization and operation. He knew well what the profits could be and with enough money he could buy a loyalty of sorts and bodyguards. Men who were making money were less inclined to treachery. *Cosa Nostra,* wide flung though it might be in the States and through its connection with the Mafia in Sicily and eastern Europe, did not exercise quite the same power and terror in Mexico. The Mexican had a highly individualistic character. He would have to depend, somewhat, upon this trait. In the meanwhile, here in Chihuahua he would blend himself, chameleon-like, with the tourists and surroundings. He would remain quietly patient until the authorities finished their ridiculous inquiry and gave him his freedom to move about. Then he would go to Hermosillo and find this man Batuc. Maybe they could do business together.

There were many times when Stacey Woodward regarded herself in the mirror with a sardonic ruefulness. It needed a sense of humor and a highly developed feeling for the ridiculous to survive this strange interlude in her life. Once, not so long ago, there had been closets filled with clothes and furs; a maid to draw her bath and attend her every need; a chauffeur, if she wished, to drive her to a luncheon engagement with Dano. Now she had this single cubicle with its bathroom in which she could barely turn around. Her wardrobe was limited to half a dozen or so acceptable dresses. This she had brought upon herself and she was frequently at a loss to understand fully just why. Something defying all logic had made her rebel. Of course, and this she had admitted readily enough many times, she had counted on getting most of little Harvey Mitchell's stolen money. That would have made the big difference. When this failed she should have called Villanova, been properly humble and returned to Chicago to face and soothe his anger if possible. He would have taken her back. Yet, even now, she found this alternative distasteful. It had nothing to do with morality. The association with Dano had gradually eaten away at character and individuality; she moved and behaved like a beautifully groomed, animated doll until she felt her mind becoming as vapid as a doll's face. She couldn't recall exactly when she recognized the emptiness of her life; there was no stimulation of mind or thought. To Dano, music was something you heard in a night club. Books filled empty spaces on shelves. Pictures were things shown on a screen and made in Hollywood. The distaste for the life must have been latent for a long time and came, quite unexpectedly, to the surface. But she couldn't help but wonder at times whether the rebellion had been worth the price.

It had been necessary to find a job. She had thought first of applying at a modeling agency. She photographed beautifully and wore clothes with an undeniable flair. This was the work she had been doing when Villanova first saw her and sometime later made his proposition. After considerable thought she rejected the idea of becoming a model again. It was too conspicuous. Maybe Dano was satisfied to let her go. Possibly he hadn't or wouldn't make an effort to find her. But she couldn't be sure. He was a terrible man in anger. Her leaving him would scar his vanity. As a photographer's model her picture would appear in national advertising and from it she could be traced if that was what Dano wanted. Modeling in any of the exclusive Beverly Hills shops, she would always risk being seen by someone, the wives or the girls of Villanova's associates in California, and the word would eventually get back to him. He was capable of any vengeance; to scar her for life, to have her killed. It all depended on how much his pride had been hurt. She couldn't risk it.

She had finally found work as a hostess in one of the many restaurants in Westwood which, although a part of Los Angeles geographically, was more or less an extension of the UCLA campus which sprawled over acres and acres. It wasn't really unpleasant work—taking customers to a table, laying the menus before them, supervising the service. She was an unobtrusive part of the scene. The clientele was mostly students from the University and they treated her with a breezy, friendly familiarity. Now and then one of the older boys asked her, with an uncertain casualness, for a date and once, in a moment of loneliness, she accepted. It turned out to be a wrestling match from a parking spot on the beach at Zuma back to Westwood. After that she decided college men were a little out of her league.

She faced the truth candidly. She was desperately lonely. This was a life to which she was totally unaccustomed. Now and then, on her day off, she would go to a movie or recklessly spend part of her small salary on a rented car just for the pleasure of driving along the beach highway or up through the Malibu hills and down into the Valley. Most of the evenings, though, she spent at home reading or listening to music on the small radio, since she could not afford television. Once, she bought a bottle of good French cognac and deliberately got herself royally potted. With a hangover the next morning she decided this was a bad solution and the way men and women became solitary drinkers and subjects for A.A.

The restaurant was near the intersection of Wilshire and Westwood boulevards and within easy walking distance of her small hotel. When the place closed at ten o'clock she liked to stroll through the pleasant quiet of the village which, miraculously, retained an oddly rural atmosphere even though it was part of a big city. She would stop at a corner and buy an early edition of the Los Angeles *Times*, chat for awhile with the news vendor and then save the paper to read with her coffee in the morning. The management permitted a percolator but refused her request for a cat or a dog. She wanted some small companionship; something to which she could come home to. Even a mongrel from the pound or a stray kitten would have made the room less cold and barren.

She caught herself thinking frequently of Sol Madrid and wondering if he was still in Mexico. And Harvey Mitchell—what was little Harvey doing with his two hundred and fifty thousand dollars? Was he hiding in fear in some out-of-the-way village or living it up with some girl or girls in Mexico City? His every waking hour must be filled with apprehension. Villanova and the "family" would not forget him. He was an unsettled account on the ledger. Maybe, she had said to herself once with dry humor, I should have teamed up with Harvey. We would make a good pair. Both of us a target for the *Capo's* vengeance. We could have gone on just one hell of a bust and spent the quarter of a million, letting tomorrow take care of itself. It was, she knew, an outrageous idea. Never for a moment could she have endured the greedy pawing of this frightened, ineffectual man.

She remembered what Madrid had told her. Mitchell in Mexico, going into "the flower business." If this was true then Harvey must be truly insane, for they wouldn't give him a chance. If *Cosa Nostra* didn't get him then Madrid and the Federal Bureau would. But then, maybe this timid man had steeled himself to an unsuspected recklessness. It had taken nerve and planning to steal from Villanova; sharp decision to do what he had done to her on the train and then elude Roy Gaines. It was barely possible he might get away with an operation in Mexico. She wondered, for it was a fantastic notion—Harvey bucking a syndicate.

Once, she was tempted to call the number Madrid had given her and ask if he was in town. There was an attraction about him, a curious, dark and predatory nature. In him she sensed the hunter, the relentless stalker. Yet, with her he had displayed a contradictory gentleness. She could remember him with something close to a wistful tenderness. If he was in Los Angeles and wanted to see her again he would have made the effort.

Alone, as she was much of the time, her mind frequently strayed into capricious channels. Maybe it might have been better if she had gone in for a little discreet whoring. On call, at least, she wouldn't be so damnably lonely. She tried to imagine how it must be to share a bed with a succession of men who were strangers. How did one behave? Could the mind be disciplined to accept this intimacy as business and nothing more; a transaction without affection or respect; simulated passion for a fee? Was it, for a man, little more than going to a toilet; a form of release and satisfaction? She had no idea, but the speculation intrigued her even though she knew she would never be able to bring herself to work as so many girls did. Morality did not enter into her musings. She had been bought before but in a different way. She could be no comfort station for the passing male. I'll take this now for what it is, a period of stagnation. Something has to happen. It was incredible that her life would become nothing more than standing by the cashier's desk near the door, a sheaf of menus in her hand and a welcoming smile on her face.

The room was richly paneled in dark walnut and the lights were subdued. Down the center there ran a long table. In the chairs flanking it sat a dozen men. They were, for the most part, indistinguishable from hundreds of successful Chicago men who sat at board meetings and discussed, with the aid of graphs and charts, the course of their enterprises.

The air was heavily scented with the perfume of fine cigars. A cabinet, its doors open, offered a selection of good whisky, wine, brandy and rum. Ice frosted a silver bucket. Glasses were of finest crystal. All were untouched. Later, perhaps, some would take a small drink.

Here were gathered the *Commissione* of the *borgata*. They were elderly men, in their late sixties; squat, impassive and inclined to fat although they belonged to their country clubs and determinedly played bad golf for exercise and high stakes. They rode the fairways in their electric carts and went home to eat enormous meals of *pasta*, meats with their rich sauces, heavy desserts and wines. Their features, some of them scarred by old knife slashes, carried the unmistakable cast of their ancestry: Italian. Sicilian. Levantine. Their names: Petrucci. Barbetta. Ricco. Bataliano. Guiliana. Their speech was still crude and illiterate for they had come from the slum gutters of New York, Philadelphia, Boston, Detroit and Chicago's South Side. All had known the gang wars of forty or more years ago. They had been young then and had killed ruthlessly and without conscience. They were products of the great racket days and the era of prohibition with extortion and murder as the by-products. Now they were old but time had not erased their accents nor softened their will and rapacity. They were still capable of violence but they directed it now instead of executing the crime. All the years had taught them was a certain animal caution. To this end they cloaked themselves in anonymity wherever possible. They patronized the best tailors. Their shoes and shirts were custom-made. Their homes were spacious and in the most exclusive residential districts. Their sons and daughters were reared with only a slight suspicion of their fathers' backgrounds and they attended the colleges and schools in the East. The old men accepted age and semi-respectability with a certain amount of resignation but their instinct for power and their methods were as keen and ruthless as ever.

The things of which they had talked today were not of Chicago alone. The interests of all of them had many spreading and interlaced roots, from gambling to narcotics, controlled prostitution, a tight grip on innumerable unions, "the fix" in a hundred or more cities and towns. Always they sought to broaden their profitable fields, for the only excitement left to them was the accumulation of power. Of money they had plenty. Rarely within these walls was there an argument. Those who were privileged to sit here were the elder statesmen and they treated each other with respect. They even had a word for it, *cortesia*. It was a manner of behavior and none violated it. There might be differences of opinion but they were quietly voiced. It was said only: "I think this is a good thing." Or "I do not believe it should be done. It is bad for us." Shielding the real operations of the *borgata* were innumerable legitimate enterprises —laundry chains, trucking lines, restaurants, night clubs, motels, taxi fleets, a small steamship line, car rental services. These things were the front, the shield. The profits were meticulously filed with the Bureau of Internal Revenue for they had learned from the example of others how disastrous it could be to play carelessly with the Government. But, the big money from the illicit operations could be concealed. For these no books were kept, no accounting made beyond the "family."

At the head of the table, immaculately groomed, darkly handsome, Dano Villanova presided. He stood out from the others like a polished rapier among heavy clubs. He was the youngest but had been chosen because the older men instinctively recognized his capacity for sharp decision, an inexorability and a cruelty which displayed itself in the agate darkness of his eyes. To him was accorded the deference due the *Capo* and when, sometimes, a matter could not be resolved his was the final word settling the problem. He was of the new generation; limited in education and taste, bearing a surface sheen and arrogance which passed among his associates as a true polish of sophistication and knowledge. His judgments were keen and his methods without compassion. He was well suited to occupy the chair of the *Capo*.

The meeting was nearing its close. A variety of things had been discussed; small questions disposed of, minor weaknesses in the chain of command strengthened and one or two petty offenders with ambitions of their own marked for discipline or erasure. There had been a lengthy discussion over a surprising offer which had come to the "family" by way of an intermediary from Cuba. Castro's government, desperately in need of exchange, had suggested that perhaps one or two of the lavish casinos and hotels which had been exappropriated could be reopened and operated as before with a percentage of the profits going to the Cuban Revolutionary Treasury. Under certain conditions it was a tempting offer. Gambling, upperbracket prostitution and the luxury hotels had once been a source of tremendous income.

Villanova had listened and then shook his head. "It is a crazy man's idea," he said flatly. "Who the hell in Cuba has the money to gamble with? Tourists? They're scared to death of the place. Throw Castro out and we have something but who is going to do that? The Cubans who might have done it, the real resistance, sit on their asses in Miami and argue. There is no one left in Havana to argue with Castro. We'd be suckered into something that doesn't have a chance." He rose to indicate the matter was closed and the meeting over. "If we could get into the Bahamas, Puerto Rico, Jamaica. That is worth thinking about." He went to the cabinet and poured himself a small glass of brandy. "One thing," he resumed speaking without turning, "none of you has talked about here is Mitchell. This is good respect as it should be. Mitchell is my affair. The amount he stole is nothing but that he did steal it is important. He was my man. I trusted him. So, I will take care of him in my own way."

"They laugh a little about this in New York, Cleveland, San Francisco and other places." The one who spoke was of the name Barbetta. His skin was as dark and wrinkled as a walnut and he walked with a small limp. There was no malice in the words, no suggestion of criticism. "They think it is funny a bookkeeper would have the nerve to do such a thing."

"Sometimes, when I do not imagine a knife in his guts, I think it is funny, too." Villanova turned, glass in hand. "Who would imagine the mouse had such big teeth and appetite? Anyhow, I give you my promise he will be taken care of and in such a way no one will laugh or ever do such a thing again. The word has been given on him. Sooner or later he will be found. I think he is in Mexico but where I don't know just yet. The money he took I have replaced from my own account. For that two hundred and fifty thousand I purchased Mr. Mitchell. He is my private and exclusive property."

So well disciplined was Villanova in the presence of the *Commissione* that no trace of the hot anger he felt showed itself. He might have been talking about some unprofitable but unimportant investment made.

Two or three of the members drifted to the bar and suited their various tastes with the liquors there. Others stood looking out of the window, down at the street fifteen stories below. In their minds they were remembering Chicago as it had been in the wild and reckless days of their vanished youth. Then the mobs had divided up the city, as some great, private estate, into territories. There was no central authority. Each gang fought to hold its own or to take over from another. Not a glass of beer, a shot of whisky, was sold without permission. No weary young whore walked the streets or worked in a house until she had made the proper arrangements. Murder was so commonplace that, unless it was a particularly dull day, the newspapers' city desks put it under a one-column head and not always on the front page. They elected the mayors, bought judges, police commissioners, captains and lieutenants. No one but the unimportant punks ever went to jail. Nothing, from the smallest delicatessen to the largest department stores, escaped the extortion of "protection." All this while the good people of Chicago pretended it wasn't happening. There had never been a time like it before or since. Now it was all organized, centrally directed and as well run as any large corporation. It was safer, more profitable, but the strong, heady wine of rivalry had been diluted. They were old and with no real stomach for the contest now but they had known the power of feudal lords and the memory of it would not leave them.

They left the room, singly and in pairs. Below, their cars and chauffeurs waited. They would go, now, to the dull domesticity of their homes to lounge in deck chairs beside their pools or play a few hands of gin rummy with a companion. Others, as to a ritual, went to the steam baths to sweat in uncomfortable silence under the impression it was good for them. One or two might have themselves driven to a country club, where they lunged and hacked at golf balls. But nothing they did carried with it any real excitement and in their hearts they knew it.

Villanova was the last to leave. He shook hands with grave politeness; inquiring after families, expressing an interest in the forthcoming marriage of a daughter or the plans for a son in college. These were the good manners expected of the *Capo* and he went through the formalities with dignity, but the smile accompanying the words never passed beyond his lips to reach his eyes with genuine warmth. Now, alone, he drank a second brandy in moody contemplation and found it without bouquet or stimulation.

Dano Villanova had no small diversions as did the others. He belonged to a country club as a matter of status but rarely entered it. There was a luxurious cabin cruiser moored at a yacht club on the lake but it was infrequently taken from its berth. He disliked golf and cards, rarely went to a ball game and never to the theatre unless it was a musical or the opening had social overtones. He had gone through three years of high school and then dropped out to take a job, first as a messenger, then a collector, under one of the men who was now a member of the *Commissione*. He was tough and unswerving in purpose. Under his patron's direction he brought the brothels of the district into line; beat up stray prostitutes who dared attempt to operate on their own. Then he was promoted to the post of organizer, forcing small businesses to subscribe to an "association" for their protection. He had applied himself with nerve and pitiless energy and his ascent in the *borgata* had been rapid. There was in him no capacity for conviviality, no patience for inconsequential talk. He read nothing save the gossip columns and his only interests lay in beautiful girls and the accumulation of influence and authority.

In the apartment once occupied by Stacey Woodward he had installed a tall, willowy and magnificently breasted creature who still could not believe the incredibly miraculous thing which had happened to her. Out of the anger seething within him he had thrown furs, jewelry, clothing, servants and a car at the breathlessly bewildered girl, who only a couple of weeks ago had been appearing as a half-naked, statuesque beauty in a night club. Now she was Dano Villanova's, surrounded by everything of which she had ever dreamed. It all seemed too wonderful to be true.

Villanova treated her with an indifference close to contempt. In her presence he was constantly aware of the contrast, remembering the cool poise of Stacey Woodward; the grace and manner of her breeding; the almost regal detachment with which she sometimes regarded his fits of temper, his sulking moods and his eventual awkward attempts to apologize without actually doing so. There was no substitute for class, which was the word he unconsciously applied to her. This other one, sometimes he couldn't even remember her name, was pathetically eager to please. She abased herself in many ways, submitting to every physical indignity. She was fawning, anxious, fearful that this incredible dream might end. Mentally he spat in her beautiful face even as he sated himself with the pliant fervor of her body. He showed her no courtesy, no affection and this she accepted with tremulous gratitude. The comparison between her and Stacey Woodward only stimulated his black fury for the girl who had dared to walk away without reason or explanation. He had been good to the bitch, treating her like a lady. His hatred, now, was an evil cancer, flourishing unseen but eating away at him constantly. Never would he forget or forgive the insolence of Stacey Woodward. Her punishment had become an obsession. It kept him sleepless at night and walked a mocking shadow beside him during the day.

He was furiously impatient with those he had put upon the search. Stupid bastards who couldn't run an errand. One small bit of information only had they brought him. A girl answering her description had been aboard the Super-Chief on the same run that carried Roy Gaines and Harvey Mitchell. This had to be an accident if it was true. But then Gaines gets himself killed on the goddamned prairie. Harvey Mitchell disappears. So, what had happened? Had she teamed up with a louse like Mitchell for the sake of a couple of hundred grand or so? That was too fantastic. The three had no connection. So, Stacey Woodward had gone on to California. This had been checked out through the porter and conductor. More than that, someone had tried to choke her to death. Why? Who? The mystery chewed at him. He followed one line. She had gone on to Los Angeles but L.A. was a big city, California a big state. There was no sure way of knowing whether she had stayed there. Las Vegas? He dismissed this. Too small, too many persons knew her for they had gone there together often. Beverly Hills? The same answer. If she was hiding it had to be somewhere he would never think of looking. That she was hiding he was certain. She knew him well enough to realize he would take her desertion as the greatest of all insults. She would not risk his anger, knowing his temper, his capacity for revenge for the offense. So, somewhere, she was tucked away without money or working at a job. She would be frightened, looking back over her shoulder every time she stepped out the door, her nerves screaming at an unexpected knock or a telephone call. Well, he would have every foot, yard, mile, acre west of the Rocky Mountains from Seattle to Baja California, combed until she was found. Once this was done she would really learn about Dano Villanova and what it meant to walk out on him.

This he promised himself. But, and it was a thing not yet fully admitted, he was superstitiously disturbed by the things which had happened. Mitchell, a nothing, had dared to steal from the "family" treasury; risking what he knew would be certain death, for such a thing could not go unpunished. Then, Roy Gaines—a good workman who had never left a contract unfilled—misses on one set up for him so simply any punk could have done it. Finally, Stacey disappears without reason. Christ! If they had had a fight. If he had knocked her around as she sometimes deserved. This he could have understood. Put together they all formed an ominous pattern, filling him with an uneasiness he had never felt before. It was like, he thought, a man scratches at a flea bite and dies of blood poisoning. Deep within him there was a peasant's mystical conviction of unseen, unknown evil surrounding a man. It was a thing to be exorcised but the only incantation Dano Villanova knew was force and he could not put his hands on anything solid. He reached and his fingers closed upon the air.

7

❦ THE police, who had picked up Madrid only moments after the airliner had touched down at the Hermosillo airport, had been impassively and impersonally efficient. From their manner it was obvious they were only carrying out orders and knew nothing beyond the fact an American on this flight was to be arrested.

There had been no hearing, no formal booking, no charge. Sol protested loudly for everyone's benefit and to make it look good. He was taken to the jail and roughly pushed into a cell occupied by four Mexicans who eyed him with hooded curiosity. They were in varying degrees of dishevelment, unshaven, unwashed, bleary-eyed. They said nothing, not even among themselves. Each, by common consent, occupied a section on the dirty floor with his back against the wall. Sol neither spoke nor nodded but found a place of his own. He lit a cigarette but made no offer of sharing what he had. Hunched together, knees drawn up, he smoked with a sullen concentration. He was a man who had suffered an unwarranted arrest and humiliation. A half hour, at least, passed before a word was uttered. Then one of the prisoners, with an unemotional matter-of-factness, said to his cell-mates, "He sleeps with his mother."

The obscenity, in Spanish, is shorter and uglier and Sol well un-

116

derstood the reason for it. By no movement or flicker of the eyes did he betray his knowledge of the language. His head remained half bent over the cigarette but he could feel the derisive glances upon him. They were all waiting to see if he knew what had been said. After a moment there was soft laughter. Then they began to talk among themselves, ignoring him. It was the senseless chatter of lazy, idle monkeys—women, money, things remembered. They scratched at their crotches, slapped at the flies and spat at the cockroaches as they scurried over the stone. From the things they said Sol gathered they were minor offenders, thrown into jail because of drunkenness, fights, the beating of a woman. The cell had the acrid odor of urine, the moldy smell of a place long unaired. Wryly, Sol thought Colonel Ortega had not made an understatement when he described the condition of the Mexican jails.

"You got more cigarette?"

The question was asked abruptly and in heavily accented English. Madrid lifted his head and stared unwaveringly at the speaker. Finally, he nodded and drew the pack from his shirt pocket. He took out four and tossed one to each of the men. For the first time he could sense a cautious warming.

"*Gracias.*" The word came in a muted chorus. Save for the one, the others apparently spoke no English. "*Mil gracias.*"

Madrid shrugged indifferently and, as an afterthought, handed over the packet of matches. They lit one and frugally used it for all four cigarettes. Then it was passed back to him and for a few moments they smoked in a wary, companionable silence.

"For what reason they put you here?"

"Who knows?" he replied to the English-speaking one. "Maybe they don't like my face."

A rapid translation was made for the benefit of the others and there was an understanding murmur. The bastard *policía* were always throwing a man into jail for no excuse. Was a little too much tequila, a fight, the beating of one's woman a reason? They were all normal, natural things for a man to do if you looked at it in the right way.

Sol made no effort to maintain a conversation. He wondered if one of the four could be the contact arranged for him by Colonel

Ortega. Somehow, he didn't think so. He smoked his cigarette down to the final, pinching end, as a man who had no idea when he would get more might reasonably do. He leaned against the wall, watching the roaches, wondering on what mysterious insect errands they were engaged as they raced.

Around two o'clock in the afternoon the guard came with food. It was a single *casuela* of frijoles with a stack of cold, tough tortillas. There were five spoons and they ate from the communal pot, spreading the beans on the tortillas and then rolling this into a cylinder. Later, an earthenware pitcher and mugs were delivered and they drank the strong, black coffee with satisfaction. Madrid again distributed his cigarettes. The Mexicans were all easier now. They addressed their remarks to Madrid, including him in the talk even though they were aware he didn't understand. Sol dozed a little. It was goddamned uncomfortable here and he thought he and Colonel Ortega might have arranged something a little less devious.

Half-awake, he heard a drunken shouting in the dark corridor. It was the indifferent, ribald cursing of an amiable drunk. The door was unlocked and the guard, with a head-shaking tolerance and a half-grin, pushed the new prisoner in.

He stood in the center of the cell, weaving and peering owlishly at the occupants. He wore a suit of dark blue. It was wrinkled and soiled. His necktie was askew and there were small splatterings of blood on a once white shirt.

"Jalisco." The prisoners greeted the new arrival with familiarity and delighted surprise in which there was a certain admiration and respect. *"Que pasa?"* They stood up to surround him.

The man called Jalisco pushed them away irritably and glared belligerently.

"What happened is that I'm in this bastard of a jail." He glanced at Madrid and jerked his head toward him. "Who's the Yankee?" All that had been said was spoken in Spanish.

"Who knows? A tourist, maybe. He doesn't speak the language."

"The sons of bitches never bother to learn." Jalisco was contemptuous. "They think everyone should speak nothing but English. I spit on them all."

"What did you do to get arrested?"

Jalisco rocked back and forth, spread his feet to steady himself before answering.

"A tourist comes to the hotel." He spoke with the weary resignation of a man who should have known better. "He wants a guide. He wants girls. They always want girls. Maybe they can't get it from their own women. So, we drink together and I take him to La Ranchita. He gets drunk. I get a little drunk and one of the *putas,* she takes some money from his wallet. When he wakes up he's mad. He wants to fight me. I haven't done anything and don't want to fight but he keeps at it and finally we do, not really hurting each other but making a lot of noise and *la patrona* calls the police. This tourist says I stole his money. So, here I am." He grunted his disgust and stared malevolently at Madrid. "All Yankees are bastards and so are you. How do you call yourself?" This he said in English.

"Chingas tu madre." For the first time Madrid spoke a word in Spanish. It was a deliberate insult and one of great filth.

There was a quick indrawing of breath from the original four and they backed away, watching Jalisco expectantly for it was not possible he would allow the curse to pass.

Jalisco hunched his shoulders and peered at Madrid. He scowled at Madrid's indifferent, lounging posture. Then a grin crinkled his features and he began to laugh uproariously.

"So, you do learn some Spanish, Yankee, even if it is dirt. That is better than nothing. I do not feel like fighting right now but if you knew who I was you would not say such a thing to me. They call me Jalisco, because I sing the song so good, but I come from Juarez."

"I still say go do it to your mother or yourself." Sol was truculent for a reason. He did not want to reveal an interest beyond this.

Jalisco sank wearily to the floor, regarding Madrid with a curious, amused, roguish air.

"My mother would beat me and to do it to myself gives me a headache. It always gave me a headache, even when I was a *chamaco.* So, I don't think I will." He refused to take offense. *"Cristo* but I was drunk last night. I'm going to sleep now. Maybe, later I will stick a knife in you for what you said. We will see. Maybe we get along fine, Yankee. Who knows?" He pillowed his head upon an arm and curled himself into a fetus-like position. His eyes closed.

The prisoner who spoke English looked from the drowsing Jalisco to Madrid. He seemed to be a little puzzled by the exchange of words between them and the Mexican's refusal to resent the insult.

"You speak the Spanish?" His curiosity was evident in the question.

"A few words. *Pochismo*. Border talk. *Nada mas*." Madrid was casual, unconcerned.

"That Jalisco. He's a very bad man, sometimes."

"So am I."

The English-speaking one translated for the others. They regarded Madrid with a speculative respect. Jalisco snored and the sound, somehow, seemed to relieve the small tension within the cell. Madrid was aware of the relaxing. He wasn't quite sure why or how it had come about. Perhaps it was Jalisco's indifference to the affront, his acceptance of the Yankee as a man of quick temper which he had provoked. Sol couldn't be certain but he was willing to let things ride as they were.

The hours were interminable and there was nothing to relieve the monotony. They simply sat and the stone floor grew rougher and colder. Jalisco slept and Sol wondered if he had really come to the jail drunk. If not he was one hell of a fine actor. He wished now Colonel Ortega had told him a little more about the man. Was he of the police, an undercover agent, or simply a stool pigeon? As a matter of policy, Madrid mistrusted all informers. What they sold to one man they would sell to another.

It was late, five thirty or so, before Jalisco awoke. He sat up, stared about him as though to identify the place in which he found himself. Then he chuckled.

"I had a dream I was in jail. Now, I'm awake and I am in jail. I sure don't think I'll dream that dream anymore." He addressed Madrid.

The listening Mexicans turned questioning glances upon each other, wondering what had been said. Jalisco repeated his words in Spanish and they laughed understandingly at the joke.

Sol's stomach rumbled, flatulent with the beans and cold tortillas.

"Can you get food sent in here from a restaurant outside?"

"If you have the money. Food and even a woman, if they keep you for a long time. She should be your wife but it isn't always so. For this the jailer takes a small bite. The *mordida*. Like you say, a bribe."

"I have money. Call the guard and tell him what we want."

"For everyone?" Jalisco cocked his head to one side with an odd gesture of questioning.

"Como no?"

Jalisco again translated and the Mexicans became interestedly alert. Then he went to the cell door and bellowed a summons down the corridor. After this he turned to Madrid.

"What do you want?"

"Well," Sol grinned, "I sure don't want a woman with all this company. Some decent food; a steak or chicken, maybe. A drink. Scotch for me. Tequila for the others if that's what they prefer."

Jalisco loosed another shout and finally the jailer came, muttering angrily. Jalisco spoke rapidly, explaining the Yankee's wishes. Sol listened.

"So," the guard replied sourly, "he must be a wealthy tourist to buy for everyone."

"All Yankee tourists are wealthy. Only we Mexicans are poor. Haven't you learned that?" He gave the order and the man began counting on his fingers. Then he stared at the ceiling, doing some mental calculating. "How do you figure?" Jalisco was impatient.

"Tres cientos pesos."

"He says three hundred pesos. That's some thirty dollars *más o menos.* Like you say. More or less. It includes a small bite for a hungry man of a guard."

Sol nodded and counted out the money from his wallet. The Mexicans watched the action with sharp and greedy eyes.

"Tell him to bring the Scotch and tequila first with some fresh water. We'll eat later."

"Bueno." Jalisco spoke with satisfaction and delivered the instructions.

When the guard had pocketed the money and shuffled off, Jalisco spoke to the others. They bobbed their heads with eager approval and spoke together.

"They say for a Yankee tourist you have a good heart."

"Screw." Madrid was unimpressed. He wanted to maintain the role of a scornful, angry man in front of the others. "If I tried to eat and drink alone they would probably kick my head in during the night."

"A tontas y a locas? Or like you say. Without reason?" He studied Sol for a moment. "You'll do, *compañero*." The words were quietly spoken but carried an honest tribute with them.

The Scotch was good and from the noisy exclamations of approval from the Mexican quartet the Cuervo tequila equally satisfactory. The guard, figuring his *mordida* was a little more than generous, had voluntarily added three packages of cigarettes to the list. One was the expensive product from the United States which had a heavy duty. The others were of local manufacture and had the acrid taste of cheap cigar scrappings which bit at the throat, but neither Jalisco nor the others seemed to object. They were, Sol decided, a cultivated taste like mescal.

Madrid drank sparingly, savoring the fine, smoky taste of the good Scotch. He noticed, also, Jalisco was careful with the tequila. Now and then their eyes met but without recognition beyond this brief encounter. Whatever the method of operation was to be, the Mexican would have to point the way.

By the time the evening meal was delivered they were all suffused in a mild glow of goodwill. Madrid went over to a corner and inspected the stack of filthy pallets. He could see the bedbugs and lice crawling within the seams. He turned to Jalisco.

"What's the bite for a poor man of a guard for some clean pads?"

"A little." Jalisco smiled. "A couple of dollars in your money. Like the Yankees say," he added without rancor, "in real money."

Madrid nodded. Many times he had heard a tourist ask: "How much is fifteen pesos in *real* money?" They seemed completely insensible to the gross discourtesy the question implied.

"Let's have them, then."

"You'll ruin these *hombres*." Jalisco turned a thumb toward the original four. "From now on whenever they go to jail they'll want you along." He lit a cigarette. "Tomorrow, maybe, we get out of here and then we make some talk together, eh?"

Madrid spent a restless and uncomfortable night. His mind refused to compose itself but persisted in ranging over the many-faceted problem, for there was no clearly defined starting point. It was like trying to determine the beginning of a circle. He caught himself thinking of Stacey Woodward and realized with a small jolt of surprise that she crept, unbidden, many times into his musings. Also, the pallet on which he lay was stuffed with corn shuckings. They rustled and crackled with every turn. There was no pillow and the canvas sacking was abrasive to his cheek. The Mexicans snored blissfully. The tequila and a large meal had left them happy and satisfied. Jalisco, also, seemed to have the facility of adapting himself to his surroundings. He went to sleep immediately. Madrid wondered about him, for he seemed to be treated with a half-humorous tolerance, if not respect, by both the guard and the prisoners. He was, evidently, a local character of some reputation.

In the morning the guard brought coffee and the hard rolls. Later he came back, opened the gate and called the names of Jalisco and Madrid. Their four cell companions crowded about Sol, slapping him on the back with good-natured envy.

"Bien suerte, compañero. Hasta otro día."

They were led down a long corridor, up a flight of stairs and into a small courtroom within the jail itself. Sol thought he looked properly disreputable. His clothing was wrinkled, his shirt soiled. The stubble of a beard was heavy on his face.

An uneasy group of minor offenders against the peace and tranquillity of Hermosillo sat on the bare benches awaiting their turn before the *juzgado,* the magistrate. Studying the man on the bench, Sol thought how curious it was that the border Texan had turned the word *juzgado* into *hoosegow,* for a jail.

One by one the prisoners were led forward. Below the magistrate two clerks shuffled papers endlessly. Everything in the nature of an official transcript in Mexico is done in at least quadruplicate. As the names were called, one clerk would stamp all four forms. Then he passed these to his co-worker, who solemnly imprinted them with his own cabalistic notation. Listening to the cases Madrid understood this was a court for petty offenses. Most of the men wore the peon dress, the *calzónes,* a white, pajama-like suit of cotton. They were quickly disposed of. Few had the money with which to pay a fine and they were given varying terms in jail.

Jalisco was fined one hundred pesos for being drunk and disorderly, for the breaking of furniture in La Ranchita and creating a general disturbance. The tourist had withdrawn the charge of robbery. The judge wearily passed the sentence and it was obvious, from his manner, that Jalisco was an old offender who was always in some minor trouble.

The *juzgado* studied the complaint against Madrid with obvious uncertainty. He leaned down and whispered something to one of the clerks, who shrugged an indication of his ignorance. Then the magistrate addressed Madrid.

"Do you speak Spanish?" The question was asked in the language.

"Yes, your Honor," Madrid replied in kind.

This seemed to relieve the magistrate. He poked an accusing finger at the complaint and spoke sternly.

"It tells me here you were drunk and noisy on a plane from Chihuahua. This caused great inconvenience and distress to the other passengers and danger to their lives and the machine. The pilot radioed the Hermosillo police who arrested you upon arrival. Is there truth in this?"

Sol had no idea who knew what. He could only assume the *juzgado* was ignorant of his identity. Colonel Ortega had simply arranged this charge with a high-ranking officer who would keep the information to himself. He was detained and jailed without the local police being aware of anything beyond the order. It was important that as few persons as possible knew who he was.

"If the paper," Madrid pointed to the document in the magistrate's hand, "says it is so then it must be the truth. I don't remember too well."

"It is a serious danger to have a drunken man in an airplane. You are a guest in our country." The magistrate was indignant. "It is advisable you remember this and conduct yourself with respect and courtesy for our laws. Do you wish a lawyer?"

"No, thank you. I am sorry for what happened."

"I do not like to place a tourist in jail. I will fine you one thousand pesos. Are you prepared to pay it?"

"Yes, your Honor."

The entire exchange had been carried out in Spanish and there was a murmur of pleased interest from the others in the small courtroom. It was good to see a Yankee tourist made to pay for such disgraceful behavior. Always they acted without courtesy. To them every girl was a whore and every man a thief. They should stay in their own country with their Yankee dollars and bad manners.

The clerks and Madrid whispered in quiet argument over the rate of exchange and what a thousand pesos came to in United States dollars. When they reached an agreement Sol counted out the fine and then slid an extra twenty-peso note beneath the hand of each. They gave no evidence of being aware of what he had done but their hands remained flat on the table with the bills covered.

Madrid bowed shortly in the *juzgado's* direction and then walked from the courtroom, aware that all eyes were following him with envy and dislike. Here was a Yankee tourist who could pay a thousand-peso fine and walk away as though nothing had happened.

Outside, in the bright, warm sunshine, Jalisco leaned against the wall. He fell in beside Madrid.

"What," he asked with innocence, "would be expected of a man who has just been released from jail?"

"That he would go, first, for a drink and some decent food."

"It was in my mind, *amigo*."

They walked a block or two in silence and then, with a touch on the elbow, the man guided Sol down what was little more than an alley and into a cantina. It was dim in there, the only light and air coming through the open door. Two men sat at a table playing dominoes and drinking coffee. They looked up and spoke Jalisco's name in greeting and stared curiously at Madrid.

Seating themselves at the rear they ordered beer and then fried eggs with ham and fresh rolls. The beer was cold and they finished two bottles apiece before either spoke.

"You will call me Jalisco, as does everyone." The man spoke softly and in English. "I am, for your information, Lieutenant Carlos Mendoza. But," he spread his hands in a humorous gesture of resignation, "I have been underground, as you say, in this business for so long I sometimes forget who and what I really am. It is no more a part I play. I am Jalisco. We have things to do together?"

"That, I think, was what Colonel Ortega had in mind." Madrid smiled. "He said only that a man would contact me. I wasn't sure how the meet could be carried off. Too many people had to get into it."

"The jail seemed to be as good a place as any. Already you have made friends. Not of the first class, maybe, but they will remember and speak well of you."

Briefly, Madrid outlined his interest in Mitchell and the hope the man might eventually help him to uncover the trails leading back to Villanova and the Chicago *borgata.* The officer listened intently, his intelligent face responsive to Sol's words.

"So. You think your man comes here now?"

"It makes sense. In Mexico City his presence would be too quickly known and the word passed on."

"It is your idea to wait and watch while he tries to put an apparatus together?"

"With your government's permission."

"We are much ashamed of what happens here. Many good officers, the police and *Federales,* have been killed trying to stamp out the traffic. I also will be interested in this Mitchell's activities. How do we give you a cover?"

"Get the word around that I am in the market. I'll make a buy and take it over at Juarez. It will be set up at the border for me to pass. The news of this will get around. I will do it a couple of times. After awhile I will become known as a man with good connections. When Mitchell starts operating he will have heard of me. Mitchell is a little fish but if he annoys the big fish they may come out and snap at him. We can't be sure. If I force him into trouble he may talk to make a deal. It is the only thing I have to go on. Of course, there is always the chance they will kill him first. Part of my job will be to keep him alive and, maybe, take him back to the States."

Lieutenant Mendoza lit a cigarette. "In all of Mexico there are not more than four men who know who I really am. You make the fifth. Colonel Ortega must have great confidence in you to permit this information to rest in your hands."

"I will be careful with it."

Mendoza assented with a brief lowering of his eyelids. "I despise the people who traffic in this stuff. It is a hatred that consumes me. Because of it I have sacrificed an open career, marriage, home, children. For ten years I have played the good-natured clown. Jalisco. He sings at the top of his lungs when he gets drunk. He is generous when he has a few pesos and there is enough larceny in his heart to satisfy everyone. He is a guide for the tourist. He knows where girls are to be had. He can arrange a fix for an addict. He can, after all credentials have been examined, arrange for the wholesale purchase of heroin. He hears things but pretends he doesn't and so a secret poppy field is located and destroyed or a hidden laboratory raided and the chemists arrested. No one ever connects these things with Jalisco. He gets into small trouble with the police and sometimes spends a month or so in jail. Everyone knows him. The authorities do not take him seriously for he is only a minor nuisance and sometimes he makes the stool pigeon for them. So, he is tolerated on one side; laughed at with some affection by others. He is a character, the Mexican who sleeps in the sun with his hat over his eyes. Believe me, my companion, it is not what I would have as a good life."

"We also have such men in the service." Madrid could understand.

"Someone must do it. Only," there was sincere regret in the admission, "I often wonder why it must be I or why I chose it. It was, after all, my own doing. Now," he blew smoke in a thin, tight jet, "we must think a little about you. How and where you should live. I would suggest a small, rented house instead of the hotel. It would be better if you give your business here some frame of permanence. With a house you would have freedom of movement and privacy. I know of such a place. By the way, would this Mitchell recognize you on sight?"

"No."

"That is good." Mendoza paused. "He cannot be coming here without some idea of a connection. We will have to watch and see what he does; who he seeks out and how. He, also, must move with caution. As to your own operation, I don't imagine it will be much different from what you would do in the United States. Make yourself a familiar figure in certain places. I will give you their names. I will see to it that word is passed from reliable sources you are here to make a buy. Sooner or later you will be approached. Somewhere, in the background, you will find me. Don't pretend we are unacquainted. After all, we were cell-mates. This also will be known." He smiled with an engaging humor. "You are not entirely without credentials."

All of what the officer had said made sense and it would take time. Any suggestion of haste would only arouse suspicion. One didn't buy half a kilo of heroin as one would a pound of coffee. Also, it was important that Harvey Mitchell establish himself. There were, though, certain things to be set up between Madrid and Los Angeles, El Paso and the bridge at the crossing to and from Juarez, the gate at Tijuana and San Ysidro. None of these things did he like to intrust to the mails, telephone or telegraph services. This he explained to Mendoza.

"My government's courier service is at your disposal. Colonel Ortega will arrange it. There is no possibility of a leak there. You are right not to take anything for granted. Now," he stood up, "I am Jalisco and your guide for awhile. You will spend a few days at the hotel until the house is arranged for. Tonight we will behave as any tourist and guide. We will drink and eat, be seen in the hotel bar and a few cantinas. I will take you to Hermosillo's very best whorehouse. These are the normal pursuits of a *tourista*. Everything we do will have a purpose. I think we make a good pair. There is about you something which gives me confidence."

Harvey Mitchell leaned back against the worn upholstery of the old DC-3's seat and peered down at the rugged countryside. The plane bounced and shuddered from the updrafts and the motors pounded. It had long ago outlived its time and was held together now by faith, constant patching and repair. It was the only service into the State of Sonora and he had taken it in his eagerness to get out of Chihuahua. His apprehension over the flight was tempered a little by the memory of the profuse apologies tendered him by the authorities for his detention. It had been a regrettable but, they hoped, understandable error. The murder of the man Aguiella was now officially entered as being a thing of vengeance by an unknown enemy. The Señor Mitchell, it was hoped, would be in sympathy with the police, who must explore all avenues. The questioning of him had been routine. It was hoped he would enjoy his visit to Mexico and accept the sincere regret of the Government for the inconvenience suffered.

Harvey had listened to the excuses and the polite phrasings with the slightly impatient air of a man who had been subjected to a stupid indignity. In the end he relented sufficiently to express his understanding of the situation. He left the police station with the brisk, half-angry stride of a man who had been long delayed and now must be about his personal and important affairs.

The plane was dropping now, coming down into Hermosillo. As he fastened the seat belt he considered, briefly, registering at the best hotel or *pension* under an assumed name. This notion he almost immediately discarded. His six months' tourist card listed him as Harvey Mitchell. Some minor accident or incident might make it necessary for him to produce it. Then there would be the problem of trying to make a satisfactory explanation for giving a false name. The disadvantages outweighed the small security such a move would give him. No, he would conduct himself quietly, unobtrusively, toward the locating of the man Batuc who had once supplied the Chicago *borgata*.

At the small airport he claimed his luggage and was almost immediately accosted by a smiling, deferential man in a shiny blue suit who respectfully removed his hat and asked if the gentleman would like a guide who was familiar with everything and whose name, jestingly spoken, was Jalisco.

"What is there to see?" Mitchell allowed the volunteer to take his bag.

"It depends upon what the gentleman looks for." The reply was given with a small laugh and a knowing wink. Good places to eat, a few interesting things to see, such entertainment after dark as Hermosillo offered. "Whatever it is you desire I, Jalisco, can find it for you."

"For a few days perhaps," Mitchell agreed. "Until I know my way around."

"I am to be trusted." Jalisco darted to open the sagging door of a rickety cab. "Everyone knows me and I know everyone. The management of the hotel will assure you I am a person of honesty." He followed Mitchell into the taxi and gave instructions to the driver.

"How is it you speak English so well?" Mitchell was mildly curious.

"It was taught to me in the school in Juarez when I was a boy there. In my business as a guide it comes in handy and always I listen to the tourists, picking up new words."

Mitchell stared without curiosity out of the window and then, suddenly and without warning, he became the tormented victim of suspicion. Fear raced through him. Was it really by chance this man was at the airport or had he been waiting there for Harvey Mitchell?

Was this bland, friendly innocence a pose behind which was a deadly purpose? The thing had him by the throat again, shutting off his breath. He darted a quick glance at the guide who called himself Jalisco and saw only an artless smile, an eagerness to be of service for a small fee. Mitchell shook off his apprehension. No one could possibly have known he would fly from Chihuahua to Hermosillo. No one, he soothed himself, really knew he was in Mexico. Just the same he must be careful. No one was to be trusted completely. He would not be too often alone with this man or any other until he knew him better.

"Do you meet all the planes coming into Hermosillo?" He thought his voice had the tiny squeak of fright in it.

"There are not many, sir. Two a day. These I meet in the hope of a client. The touring buses also, but there is little business for me with them because they usually carry a guide. Has the gentleman been in Hermosillo before?"

"No." Mitchell felt the strain lessen. "This is my first visit."

"In the winter," Jalisco was anxious to be informative, "there is fine dove shooting for those who like the sport. Sonora is a flyway for the birds going farther south. In the summer, as now," a humorous shrug accompanied the words, "there is rain and the tourists, although most visitors prefer Mexico City, Cuernavaca and other better known places."

"All I want to do is rest and be quiet."

"Then you will find no better place to rest. It is what we do best. You will be comfortable in the hotel. When we get there you will, perhaps, wish to have some lunch and a siesta. I will remain about the lobby and at your service."

Mitchell was silent for a moment. He chewed at his lower lip and then impulsively spoke of what was uppermost in his mind. It was bold and, maybe, indiscreet but he could not stifle his impatience.

"I have friends who had a friend here." He tried to make it sound indifferently casual. "His name, I think," he frowned as though trying to remember, "was Burdick. No." He snapped his fingers. "Batuc. That's it. Juan Batuc." He drew a short breath and waited.

"Batuc?" The name was repeated with a half-mystified air. "There is a village in Sonora, not too far from Hermosillo, called Batuc."

"This is a man's name." Mitchell was annoyed by the obvious stupidity. "But," he tossed it away, "it is of no real importance."

"Batuc?" Jalisco contorted his features in an effort to be helpful. "It seems to me I have heard of such a one. I will make inquiries. Yes," this emphatically, "I will ask about and see if such a one still lives here."

"I said it wasn't important." Mitchell had the queasy sensation of having spoken rashly. If this fellow knew of Batuc then he would know of what he did. "As I said, he is only a friend of a friend."

"It is always pleasant, in a strange place, to know the friend of a friend." The guide was not to be deterred from being helpful.

"Well," Mitchell agreed unenthusiastically, "you might ask around."

Harvey registered at the hotel, asking for a room overlooking the patio. Jalisco stood nearby and when the formalities were concluded, snapped his fingers sharply at the porter, pointing to the bag. Then he turned to Harvey.

"I will be here when you want me. I am completely at your service. As it is said in Spanish," he smiled, *"a sus órdenes, señor."*

8

❧ THE word was spread quietly and it rippled out as does a lake's surface when lightly brushed by the wind, leaving no trace of its source.

Juan Batuc heard it as he was meant to and pondered over its meaning. Batuc was grossly fleshed and a man of cunning evil. His skin always glistened as though freshly oiled, and he panted wheezingly at the slightest effort. His belly was that of a woman in her ninth month of pregnancy and it swayed and quivered when he moved or walked. He sat, now, in the *sala* of his home and a thick lower lip jutted forward in a pouting expression of thought. Nearby a slender Indian girl of surprising beauty, with the complexion of a dusty red rose, was perched on the arm of an ugly overstuffed chair. She waited with the patience of her people for the mood of the man to show itself.

"*Más cerveza.*" Batuc grunted the order.

She arose with a lithe grace, went to the kitchen, took a cold bottle of beer from the electric refrigerator, uncapped it and brought it to him. There was a servant girl who could have been called but Batuc liked her to wait on him. This she knew.

He drank from the bottle, belched and blew out his cheeks.

"This man Mitchell, who asks about me," he spoke in Spanish for the girl understood no English, "I do not know him. What is it he wants?"

"Why do you not ask the question of him?"

Batuc looked up, surprised, for he had been talking more to himself and expected no reply from her. She met his stare, kicked a loose sandal from her foot and scratched lazily at the instep.

"Come here."

She moved obediently to stand beside him. His hand moved up over her leg and thigh, then tugged her to his lap and his fingers squeezed and fondled the hard young breast. She was unresponsive but as docile as a tame fawn.

"Wherever I go," he continued crossly, "someone comes up to whisper this Mitchell's name to me. He lives at the Hotel Monique and wants to see me. What about? I do not like to talk with strangers. I particularly do not like to talk with gringo strangers. They are all bastards; worse than Mexican bastards. Is it not so?"

Her shoulders lifted. "How should I know?"

"Because I tell you." He was suddenly angry. "Look what they did to me. There was a time, once, when I could have been one of the wealthiest men in all Mexico. Then the gringo bastards tipped me over to make a better thing for themselves. After that I could sell nothing. Every kilo of the stuff I got together was destroyed or stolen from my men, who were beaten and killed. Those who still bought a little from me were always caught at the border because the officials were told in advance who they were, when and where they would try and cross. The peon in the valleys was threatened or chased away. If he did not go or do business with them, his poppy fields were burned with a fire oil dropped from a low-flying airplane. Finally, everyone is frightened off. No one will do business with Juan Batuc because it is too dangerous. Now I sit and the fine ideas I had are nothing. How do I know who this Mitchell is?" He repeated himself with the petulance of a spoiled child.

"Could it harm you to see him and find out?"

"It could harm me if he stuck a gun in my guts and pulled the trigger."

"Why would he want to do that?"

The simplicity of the question seemed to infuriate him and he pushed her away roughly. She stumbled and almost fell. For a moment she looked at him and then dropped the other sandal and walked to the other side of the room. From there she called the maid to bring coffee and a slice of fresh pineapple. He glared at her, grunted and heaved himself up.

"You are the head of a burro," he shouted.

She smiled a little. "You do not mean that, Juanito."

After a moment: "No, I do not mean that. You are good to have. It is only when I don't understand something I become cautious and suspicious. It is of my nature."

She drank the strong coffee into which hot milk had been poured and nibbled at the dripping slice of pineapple, wiping her mouth with the back of a small hand.

"I will not go to see him," Batuc made the decision, "but I will permit him to come here and see me. That way, if there is something about him I do not like it can be handled easier." He raised his voice, calling the maid.

The girl came quickly, silently, on her bare feet, and stood obediently before him.

"You will tell your brother," he spoke slowly, "he is to go to the Hotel Monique. There he will find a man who calls himself Mitchell." He took a ruled pad and a pencil from a table and printed the name. "Here." He gave it to her. "Your brother will say to this man that Juan Batuc will see him here at the hour of seven this evening. If he does not speak the language your brother will ask the hotel clerk to translate for him."

"*Si, señor. Ahorita.*" She left as quietly as she had appeared.

"Now," Batuc appeared relieved, "we have a finish to this nonsense of a game and find out what is to be."

Lieutenant Mendoza stood in the lobby of the Hotel Monique near the desk. When the boy from Batuc came, holding the scrap of paper as though it were explosive, the officer listened as the youngster spoke haltingly to the clerk and then pushed the paper at the man. Mendoza reached and took it.

"As you know," he told the clerk with a lofty air, "I am in the employ of the Señor Mitchell as a guide. I will take the boy to him."

The clerk nodded indifferently and went back to reading his paper.

Outside Mitchell's door Mendoza knocked on the panel.

"Who is it?" Mitchell's query came sharply.

"Jalisco, *señor*. I have a messenger for you."

The lock turned, the door opened on a chain and Mitchell peered through the slit. Then he closed the door, took the links off and opened it fully.

"I have had great success." Mendoza was modestly elated and beamed upon his employer. "This friend of friends of yours, the man called Batuc, has been located. He sends this messenger," he indicated the boy, "to say he will be happy to see you at the hour of seven." He addressed the youth in rapid, questioning Spanish and then turned again to Mitchell. "He has given me the Señor Batuc's address. I will guide you there myself. It is an easy distance."

Mitchell successfully concealed his relief. He had fretted and worried these past three days. Without the contact of Batuc he had nothing. The guide Jalisco, he thought, was one to be trusted. He would use him now with more confidence. The important thing at the moment, though, was that a meeting had been arranged. It was a start.

"Give the boy a peso, Jalisco," he instructed, "and add it to the expense account you keep."

"It is done, *señor,* and I will be waiting for you in the lobby at fifteen minutes to the hour of seven. Until then."

Juan Batuc's jowls were folded and sunk upon his chest but he managed to peer up with hard, agate eyes at Harvey Mitchell.

"All of this could be some sort of a trick." His English was heavily accented.

"Why should I want to trick you?" Mitchell was sweating. He was confronted by a stubborn suspicion. Nothing he had said during the past half hour had made a favorable impression and he must have this man's confidence. "I have said everything."

"You could still be one of them. God knows for what reason. The bastards left me nothing. You could be of the police, also, or working for them. How do I know? Prove something to me."

"I was not one of them." Mitchell leaned forward earnestly. "As I told you, I was employed to keep the books, the accounts, to write checks and draw the cash for them. Because of these things I knew your name and where you lived and that you were the supplier for them until the arrangement was broken off. What reason would I have to lie?"

The nervous, almost pleading attitude of the little man reassured Batuc somewhat. He was a mouse wanting to be the cat. He had done something and because of this he was afraid.

"To do what you suggest will cost money, for we must buy into a laboratory with chemists and assistants, equipment. I do not know about these things too well, only the finished product. What these men do with the poppy gum is illegal, they take great risk."

"I have plenty of money. You have the knowledge of who and what must be bought. We need each other."

"It is also dangerous. There will be killing. We will have to tip them over as they tipped me. Their supply will have to be shut off. For the killing, when necessary, I can hire the *pistoleros* to be trusted. They are expensive also. You must know what you risk." The statements were emphasized to make them almost questions.

"I have thought of all these things." Mitchell was desperately anxious to convince this man. "There is no question of money; only that we make more. A fortune for us both. We are partners. I know the names of men in Los Angeles, El Paso, Brownsville, Tijuana who will buy. As I told you. I kept the records. We give them a better price and force the others out. In time we will control it all save what comes into Vera Cruz, Tampico and other places by ship and airplane from the Far East and the Mediterranean."

Batuc's chins sank another fold as his head fell lower. There is something about this one, he thought. He is a frightened man. In everything he says there is desperation. I wonder why?

Batuc's head lifted. "What is it you have done? You are running too fast."

Mitchell snapped upright, eyes wide. "What makes you think I have done anything?" His mouth dried suddenly and he could not swallow.

"I have seen fear before. You shake inside. You sweat and are reckless. I need to know why before we go any further in this."

Mitchell understood they had come to the place of decision. Upon what he said now depended the success or failure of the venture. Reluctantly but because he knew there was no alternative he told Batuc what he had done, how he had done it, and of the money on deposit in Chihuahua.

For the first time the scowl left Batuc's face. His belly heaved silently. Then he began to laugh until his whole body was in motion. This insignificant one. To take a quarter of a million dollars from them and get away. Who would have believed it? He shouted his delight and tears came to his eyes. He clutched at the mound of his abdomen and shook his head incredulously. To use the Chicago *sindacato's* own money to ruin its operation here was the greatest joke of it all. Even as he laughed his mind was working on another idea. This was a chicken to be plucked and left to run squawking in the yard without a feather. The opportunity, even with all the dangers from outside, was too great a one to be missed. The operation would be set up with the money and then, when all was working well, the Señor Mitchell could be disposed of. There would be the double joke in this.

The laughter subsided slowly. "I believe you," Batuc said. "It is too *fantastico* not to be true. We will do business together, *compañero.* I give you my hand on it." He lumbered up and thrust out his hand. "We have a drink on it. A *copita,* eh? Like good brothers we will be from this moment."

"I do not drink much." Mitchell released the damp fingers and unconsciously wiped his own along a trouser leg.

"But a very small one," Batuc urged. He turned and called, *"Joventina. Aqui. Venga."*

The Indian girl came. She wore a bright skirt of banded colors and a white blouse. Her feet were in sandals, her hair worn in long braids. She regarded Batuc questioningly.

"This is one I will do much fine business with." He spoke to her in Spanish. "The Señor Mitchell."

"Con mucho gusto, señor." She studied him somberly and with some pity. Batuc would swallow him, she thought to herself. Swallow and vomit him up.

"We will have a drink," Batuc ordered and turned to Mitchell. "A little tequila, some Scotch?"

"Perhaps a small Scotch and water."

Batuc translated for the girl and she left them for the kitchen. The man laid a heavy arm across Mitchell's shoulder.

"We will do important things together, for now I know I can trust you."

Mitchell squirmed uneasily. He did not like to be touched with such familiarity. Instinctively, he disliked this man and mistrusted him but he had no choice. The money, after all, was his. He would hold the purse and use it to take command. This he told himself but he could not quite shake off the feeling of being on the end of a pin.

In the hired car outside, Lieutenant Mendoza smoked a fourth cigarette. His eyes roamed over the high wall with its deadly shards of glass implanted in the mortar at the top. It enclosed the house and garden. He would have given much to be invisibly present at the conversation taking place behind it. The knowledge of what was being said would save many hours of work. They would be careful with each other, this Batuc and Mitchell. But in the end, they would reach a cautious agreement. It had to be this way. From what Madrid had told him, he knew Mitchell must have Batuc. The Mexican police would also like to have Batuc. They had wanted him for years but he was as cautious as a weasel. This time they would get him, for he must take open risks to make the operation successful. There would be murder done now in the mountains, on the roads, in the town. Mendoza was a practical officer. No matter what his superiors might say he was quite willing to let them kill each other off. It would narrow the field and save the Government the trouble of catching, arresting and trying them all. He was not at all certain the trouble and what would happen here would move those in Chicago to overt and violent action. They were too accustomed to having the killing done by contract. However, that was Madrid's concern. He was satisfied to allow a situation to develop.

As the heavy wooden gate opened and Mitchell, followed by Batuc, appeared he leaped from the car to stand with a smiling display of obsequiousness by its door. The two walked toward him. Batuc squinted suspiciously.

"*Muy buenas noches,* Señor Batuc." Jalisco removed his hat respectfully and half bowed.

Batuc's expression cleared. "Jalisco," he replied indifferently. This one was a clown who did small errands, hung about in cheap cafés, stole a few dollars from a drunken tourist. He had seen him often around the town. From him there was nothing to fear. *"Que tal?"*

"Nada, señor. It is only," he added in English for Mitchell's benefit, "that I have great pleasure in uniting friends of friends."

Batuc grunted and placed a hand on Mitchell's shoulder.

"I will call for you tomorrow, my friend, in my own car and we will take a drive into the country. I will show you what there is to see."

Almost hurriedly Mitchell entered the car and stared straight ahead. There was something sinister in the very appearance of this Batuc, who stood with his hands upon his belly as they drove off.

"And now, *señor,*" Jalisco was anxiously polite, "where is it you would like to go? Some music? A girl, maybe?"

"Back to the hotel, Jalisco. Tomorrow I will not need you, but keep in touch with me. It is possible I will have steady employment for you."

"As you wish, *señor.*" There was disappointment in the reply. "I am always at your service."

Lieutenant Mendoza left Mitchell at the hotel and watched as he scuttled out of the street and night into the lobby. Then he drove to a comfortably unpretentious house in the better section of Hermosillo's residential district. A maid answered his ringing at the gate, left him standing there for a couple of minutes as she went to give his name to the *patrón* and then came back to show him into the *sala.*

Madrid was stretched out on a couch. He started to rise but was pinned back by an all-but-imperceptible shake of the officer's head.

"I am here with the car as you requested, Señor Madrid."

"Oh! All right." Madrid stood up. "What the hell is your name? I keep forgetting."

"Jalisco, *señor.*" It was spoken humbly.

"Let's go then, Jalisco." Madrid slipped on a jacket. "Some music, dancing, a few drinks and a girl."

"They are all waiting, *señor.*" Mendoza stood aside respectfully, allowing the American to precede him. "I have arranged it."

They did not speak again until they were away from the house.

"The servants," Lieutenant Mendoza said, "they are all good, simple people but like servants everywhere they talk. Don't trust anyone. It is better I remain Jalisco, a guide and sometimes petty thief as they may have heard of me. Tonight," he lit a cigarette and inhaled with deep satisfaction, "I put our friends together. Mitchell is frightened but they will do business. I could tell by Batuc's manner. Now we will begin to do things about you."

Sol regarded him with an honest admiration. "I'm beginning to suspect," he said quietly, "you are one hell of an officer, Lieutenant."

"In my own way I get things done. It is not always pleasant. I did not want to communicate with you before Batuc and Mitchell had their meeting. How have you passed the time?"

"Reading the newspapers and improving my Spanish. The courier from Colonel Ortega came to see me. I sent certain information to Juarez and El Paso, Nuevo Laredo and Laredo, Matamoros and Brownsville. I'll make my first crossing at one of those places."

"That's good." Mendoza chuckled his approval. "You are going to be a tremendous success as a narcotics smuggler. You make a buy here, carry it across safely and return. You will be watched. The word will get about. In a short while you will be in great demand. Batuc and Mitchell will hear of you." He drew on the last of the cigarette and threw it out.

Madrid leaned back against the seat and whistled a melody of his own fashioning. He was thinking how preposterously easy it was to smuggle narcotics from Mexico into the United States. The Bureau couldn't stop and search every car. The agents could only make spot checks or rely upon the information of paid informers who, as often as not, dealt themselves a double hand. Anyone with some money, a car and a willingness to take the risk could become a smuggler. A buy could be made in practically every border town in the country. Most of the small ones got through. Now and then they caught a big one. The last two had been a South American diplomat, attached to his country's embassy in Mexico City, and an airline stewardess. The diplomat had used his immunity to carry large quantities of the stuff into the United States. The airline stewardess, he grinned in the half-light thinking about her outraged protestations of innocence, wore a special girdle. The garment was made in double folds and in the space between the layers of elastic cloth she could carry a kilo or more of the white powder. The ingenuity sometimes discouraged him.

"You know," he spoke abruptly, "what we said back there in the house about a few drinks, some music and a girl begins to sound real good after three evenings of reading newspapers."

Immediately Lieutenant Mendoza became Jalisco, the guide and panderer, sly and infinitely wise.

"*Señor,*" he whispered, "I know exactly the place you have in mind. Good whisky. Fine, young, clean girls. All virgins." Honesty overcame him. "Well," he admitted, "almost virgins. I, Jalisco, will take you to this place."

"You do that, Jalisco," Madrid approved. "I just don't think I ever heard of an almost virgin before."

Stacey Woodward walked homeward in the soft night. Overhead there was a powdering of stars in the sky. Along Wilshire Boulevard the traffic had thinned but it was still sufficiently heavy to make the constant *shushing* sound of a light sea. She had stopped, as was her habit, to buy the early edition of the Los Angeles *Times* from the old man on the corner at Westwood Boulevard. She encountered no one. Few persons walked in Los Angeles, and in Beverly Hills a late stroller was usually halted and questioned by the police. She liked this walk home after the confinement of the restaurant. It was quiet and a pleasant feeling of solitude enveloped her. With the passing of time, the daily routine of her job, the same young faces at the same tables every evening, much of the early uncertainty and apprehension had left her. She was strangely contented even though a little lonely at times. She had no friends, only the most casual contact with the other employees. Now and then she thought of Chicago and Dano Villanova, but it was with a curious detachment as though they were part of a movie once seen or a book read; without reality or lasting substance. She also meditated at times upon her future. What really lay ahead of Stacey Woodward? It had to be more than this. Sometimes her musings turned upon the strange man with the odd name. Sol Madrid. What had become of him?

A light wind riffled through the trees and set the leaves trembling. She was conscious of the sound of her footsteps on the pavement, crisp and assured. It was good to walk, breathing deeply, lifting her face to the sky. She felt curiously young and lighthearted. She turned a corner off the boulevard. Halfway down the block was the small hotel and her room. She had bought herself a secondhand television set. It was her companion at night. After a warm bath she would usually mix herself a drink and sit, watching an old movie and savoring the fine Scotch which was one of the luxuries in which she indulged. Sometimes she laughed to herself at this routine. *All I need is a parrot or a cat to become a young old maid.*

The car was drawn into the shadows and she could see the figures of a man and a girl. The rear door was open and the girl leaned upon it in a posture of misery. As Stacey approached she fell to her knees, sobbing uncontrollably. The man stooped and was patting her shoulder with clumsy reassurance. Stacey started to pass. This was none of her business. A quarrel, probably, or a girl in the sort of trouble girls sometimes found themselves. Yet the kneeling figure was so forlorn, so abjectly wretched, that she couldn't bring herself to ignore her.

"What's wrong? May I help?"

The weeping girl looked up, staring miserably. "Please." This was her only word.

Instinctively, automatically, Stacey stepped to the aisle of grass separating sidewalk from curbing. The weeping stopped. The girl's arms closed about her ankles in a football tackle. The man fastened upon her, one hand clamped over Stacey's mouth to shut off the scream already welling in her throat. She was literally thrown headlong into the car with her assailant on top of her. She struggled, fighting with a desperate terror to free herself. Nothing she did could unlock the imprisoning arms and hands. It had all been accomplished so silently. The door slammed shut, striking cruelly at her feet, thrusting her legs and knees up in an agonizing fold. She was sprawled grotesquely in an awkward bundle on the floor mat. The man's weight pressed upon her. She heard the motor start, felt the car roll forward and knew there would be no one on the dimly lit street to see what had happened. She made a savage attempt to bite at the hand across her mouth but the pressure was so relentless her jaws could not move. She felt herself suffocating. Then the man, straddling her almost in a position of copulation, twisted her head around. She screamed silently within her throat at the sharp pain. For a moment she stared up at an unfamiliar face. It yielded nothing but indifference; no anger, no compassion. The eyes were blank.

Then the man hit her, using the boned edge of his open hand like a cleaver to strike just off the point of her chin with expert precision. The world became a dark, whirling void in which she was lost.

It had all taken no more than a minute.

Some time later, she had no way of knowing how long it was, she clawed her way back to a dim consciousness. The first sensation was one of horror. Something had happened to her mouth and lips. They would not open. Then she realized heavy strips of some material, tape probably, bound them. She tried to move her feet but the ankles were also secured. Her wrists were similarly fastened. She was on the car's floor. The vibration of the vehicle's progress was carried to her ears and body. A blanket or overcoat covered her. There was nothing but complete darkness. She could feel the man's feet resting heavily in the small of her back. She made an attempt to move and the pressure of the feet increased in a warning. As from a distance she heard the words.

"If you want it again I'll give it to you. If not, keep quiet and we don't have trouble."

Her jaw was filled with an almost intolerable pain and she wondered if it was broken. Then it occurred to her that at no time had she asked herself why this was happening. She knew. Dano. Dano hadn't forgotten or forgiven. All these weeks and months they had been quietly, relentlessly, looking for her. In how many places? Who, by the merest chance, had either come into the restaurant or seen her on the streets of Westwood? She was appalled by the ferocity of Villanova and the pressure of the search he had ordered; the net, cast here and there by tireless fishermen. How long had her movements been followed from where she worked to where she lived? The unvarying schedule had been clocked until this man and woman had known to the minute when she would reach that particular section of the street. The rest had been simple. Now what? If Dano had come himself she would have understood better. To slap her around. To vent his anger personally. This she might have expected and even understood, for he had been injured beyond his capacity to endure. His vanity had been flayed. Another man might have dismissed her leaving with an indifferent shrug. Not Dano Villanova. She had committed the unforgivable error of making him small in his own eyes. No matter what he told others, he would know the truth and it would tear constantly at him. No girl kissed off Dano Villanova.

The texture of the road changed. The car had swung from a paved highway to what must be a secondary road. She was bounced and rolled slightly as the wheels traveled over a rutted surface. Where were they taking her and for what purpose? Her initial terror had subsided but the fear lingered. Certainly, she thought, they wouldn't go so far as to kill her. Murder is not so easily come to. Maybe Dano was waiting. He was quite capable of beating her terribly.

They drove for what she thought might be fifteen or twenty minutes more and then the car turned and traveled for a few hundred feet before coming to a smooth halt. The man's feet raised themselves from her side and a hand reached down to pull away the blanket. Her eyes stared upward and out of the window into the semiblackness of the night. From far away came the barking of a dog. The motor died and there was no sound. Hands now reached down and stripped the tape from her mouth with a searing pain. Tears scalded her eyes but she uttered no cry. The same hands ripped the tight binding from wrists and ankles. Even in her misery she could think ruefully of the nylon stockings as they shredded off with the tape.

The car's door was opened by the girl who had caused her to halt on the Westwood street. The man slid across the seat, stepping down and out over her body.

"You get out now," he commanded. "Yell if you want to. No one can hear but I'll clip you just the same for the fun of it."

Stacey got to her hands and knees on the constricted space of the floor. Her body was so cramped she could not make it function.

"Will you help me, please?"

Hands reached in, hooking themselves beneath her armpits, pinching her breasts with complete impersonality. She was dragged forward, the man holding until her feet came out in a nerveless tangle. She leaned against him and he forced her upright. Her knees buckled and she would have fallen if he hadn't propped her with his body. She swayed with the uncertainty of a drunk while every muscle and nerve screamed in their pain.

She stared questioningly at the girl who stood a little apart; a vague, amorphous form whose features were indistinguishable. Then her gaze attempted to bring substance out of the landscape. There was a large house with lights of butter yellow behind drawn shades. The car was halted at the mouth of what might have been a barn or a garage for several cars. There was a faint perfume of orange in the air and she could make out the orderly mass of what seemed to be a grove. There was nothing to tell her where she was, but as the strength of her body reasserted itself, her mind began to work. They were probably somewhere in the San Fernando Valley. That would account for the oranges and the scent of earth which had not yet cooled from the hot day's sun. Wearily she thought it didn't really make any difference.

"Can you walk?" the man asked impatiently.

"I think so."

The girl came forward and took her arm. There was no real sympathy or concern in the gesture. It was simply a measure to save them the trouble of picking her up if she fell.

Stacey took a tentative step, flanked by the pair. The second was easier but she moved with the doubtful certainty of a convalescent.

As they drew closer to the rear of the house a back door opened and an oblong of light fell upon the ground and cast a small illumination. Stacey looked at the girl, really seeing her for the first time. She was young, twenty or thereabouts, and there was nothing to distinguish her from a million others to be found in towns and cities all over the country. She appeared to be completely without emotion. She neither smiled nor frowned. Her face was just a pretty mask.

They mounted the steps, crossed a narrow porch. A second man held the door open for them. He regarded Stacey without any real curiosity. After they were inside he closed and locked the door.

They passed through the kitchen, which was large and orderly, into a dining room and from there into the living room, brightly lighted and furnished with the unimaginative pieces to be picked up in sets at almost any store.

Seated in a chair was the largest woman Stacey had ever seen. She had the build of a wrestler and was dressed in the white uniform of a nurse, even to the shoes and stockings. For one, wild moment Stacey thought she was going to laugh. The woman, she told herself hysterically, looks like Casey Stengel.

"Hello, dearie." The words and tone carried the artificial concern of a professional nurse or, Stacey thought, the madam of a whore-house. "You look just fine." She rose and took Stacey's arm. "I'll take care of you now."

Stacey pulled away. Anger flooded her. This whole thing was some outrageous joke or, hope came quickly, a mistake. She looked from the woman to the others.

"I don't know any of you. Why am I here?"

"We'll get acquainted, dearie." This time the woman's fingers bit into her arm. "We're going to know each other just fine."

Stacey tried to spin away but there was a sudden and tremendous strength in the hand holding her. The sudden jerk didn't unbalance the woman for a second. The nurse, if that was what she was, smiled and her false teeth shone brilliantly.

"I want to know why you brought me here."

"Now sit down, dearie." The woman gave her a shove which all but threw her into a chair. "It's not going to do any good for you to get upset. You have a friend in Chicago who was worried. He didn't like to have you living alone and working in a restaurant so he asked me to take care of you."

It had to be Dano, Stacey thought. There was no other answer to this senseless kidnapping. She glared at the woman, who seemed to be in complete charge. The others just stood around, listening and watching with the intent preoccupation they would have given to a television program.

"Is Dano here? I want to see him."

"Your friend is a very busy man," the woman confided intimately. "He just might want to see you later when he comes out this way. I think that's what he has in mind."

"What am I supposed to do in the meantime? Get clubby with you and the goons?"

"Now, that's not a nice way to talk. You'll hurt someone's feel-ings."

Stacey slumped in the chair, defeated. There was no point in try-ing to fight the situation. She was more angry than frightened now.

"Could I have a drink and a cigarette? Mine are in my purse wher-ever it is."

"Of course, dearie." The woman turned to the man who had opened the door for them. "Get the lady a drink, Jensen." She dug in her uniform pocket and pulled out a pack of cigarettes and a book of matches. "Keep them, dearie. I've got plenty more."

Stacey forced herself to hold her hands steady as she lit the cigarette and inhaled deeply. She couldn't keep her gaze from the woman's face. Never before had she seen such bland malevolence. After a moment the man called Jensen returned with a water glass in which there was an inch or so of whisky.

"You want something with it?"

She shook her head and took the drink in one swallow, gagging a little on the heavy bourbon but managing to keep it down. She smoked and the tobacco's bite was good in her throat. No one said anything. After a couple of minutes the whisky began to assert itself. She felt warmth and the pleasant sensation of relaxation.

"What do you intend to do with me?" She was easier now.

"Why, you're going to like it here just fine, dearie. Your friend wanted you to have the best of everything. From now on you'll get your regular medication. Just as much as you want. As often as you want it." The smile broadened with happy approval. "We're going to make a junkie out of you, dearie."

9

☙ JALISCO had done the groundwork well. From the mouth of one to the ears of another the information was passed along an invisible chain until it reached those for whom it was intended. Then there was a period of waiting while someone put together such information on the Yankee as was available. It wasn't much but those who came to Mexico to make a buy rarely offered credentials.

At around five o'clock of an afternoon, some three weeks after Madrid had arrived and settled in Hermosillo, the maid came to him saying a man was at the gate, asking for the señor. He did not give his name, saying it would mean nothing. Would the señor see him?

At the rear of the house there was a garden-patio with a *jacalita*, a small, thatched shelter with a table and chairs, where Sol frequently had a drink in the early evening. There the man waited. He did not rise with the usual courtesy of the Mexican when Sol approached. Their eyes met, each making a quick estimate of the other. Madrid kicked out a chair, sat down and lit a cigarette. He pushed the pack over toward the Mexican's hand.

The man ignored the gesture. He balanced a narrow-brimmed felt hat on his knees with his fingertips resting lightly on its crown.

"Do you speak Spanish?" His eyes never left Madrid's.

148

"Yes."

"How does that happen?"

"Do you speak English?"

"Yes."

"How does that happen?"

The faintest light of amusement kindled itself behind the visitor's eyes at this exchange. He reached forward now and shook a cigarette out of Madrid's pack.

"Gracias."

"De nada."

"I think, perhaps," the man said, "we will speak in the language of the country. Your Spanish is better than my English. It has come to me you wish to purchase some souvenir of Mexico to take back to the United States."

"It was in my mind."

"How heavy would this thing be?"

"A kilo more or less, at first."

"Ah!" There was a moment of thought. "This would not be too heavy for you to carry?"

"I can carry it if the price is right."

"It is possible an agreement can be reached."

"This," Sol proceeded slowly, "is for a friend in the United States. So, I would want it to be of the first class."

"That is the way it would be."

"When?" Sol was abrupt.

"A certain amount of care must be taken in these matters." Again the tiniest flicker of humor touched the eyes. "I do not have a license to deal in souvenirs. You have a boy who works here about the garden." It was a statement and not a question.

Sol nodded.

"It so happens I, also, employ a boy for little errands. It could be arranged between us that your boy, with the money, could meet my boy with the souvenir. These things could then be exchanged without our bothering ourselves with the details."

"That would be satisfactory. I can trust my boy. Can I trust yours?"

"In this souvenir business it is necessary we trust each other some.

It would be foolish of my boy to be dishonest with you. Is it not so?"

Madrid leaned back in the chair. "A dishonest man who deals in souvenirs does not stay in business long. I give you my word on this." Sol's voice carried an unmistakable edge. "We must settle on the price."

"In your money it would be ten thousand dollars."

Madrid laughed softly. "I have bought souvenirs before in Mexico. In Laguna Salada, near Mexicali, one of the same size can be purchased for five thousand."

The man thought this over and then nodded. "It seems a reasonable number."

"Do you want it in pesos or dollars?"

"Dollars. You have it ready?"

"No. I will have to fly to Chihuahua and take it from the bank. This is Tuesday. Let us say Saturday?"

Suspicion clouded the Mexican's face. "It is strange that a tourist looking for a souvenir would not have the money with him."

"It would be stranger still if I kept that amount in the house or in my pocket."

The man considered this and then inclined his head in agreement. "Then, on Saturday night at the rear of the cathedral, on the hour of seven, your boy will meet my boy." He stood up.

Madrid remained where he was. "You will remember what I said about it being of the first quality?"

"It is eighty percent. There is no better."

Sol merely nodded in agreement and watched the man as he crossed the garden and let himself out the gate. Eighty percent pure. It would be cut to ten percent by the time the pushers, the ounce men, got it. The profit on a kilo was fantastic.

The following morning he flew to Chihuahua, drew the money from the bank and returned. His garden boy met the carrier at the appointed time and returned with a package wrapped in newspaper. Sol touched a minute amount of the white powder to his tongue. It was as the dealer said; of the first quality, only slightly cut with milk sugar.

From now on, he knew, his every move would be watched. Invisible eyes would follow him with great interest and each step would be reported back. How and where the Yankee went. Whom he talked with. In what manner the heroin was taken across the border. Was this a real buy or a trick? Sol packed a bag and took the flight from Hermosillo to Chihuahua. From there he took a connecting plane to Juarez and went directly to a restaurant called La Casita.

The girl was waiting, seated at a table in a corner. She looked up as Madrid entered and their eyes met. She tapped out her cigarette for a signal as arranged and immediately lit another. Madrid crossed the room and took a chair at her table. His bag was beside him. When the waiter came he ordered a beer. His back was to the entrance.

"You had a tail from the airport." The girl spoke in a conversational tone.

"I know."

"He just came in."

"It's all right. I expected it." He drank half the beer. "They have tracked me all the way over to see how I was going to handle it. You have a car?"

"Sure." Her easy smile was one of amused conspiracy. "I'm an American floozie who comes across the border for her kicks. I've been doing this every day for a couple of weeks, ever since your information was delivered. Now I'm part of the scene, a character."

"It's all set up? I want it to look good."

"It will move. The Mexicans will check your baggage only. The American Customs will inspect the baggage and the car but not your person. It will all look legitimate to your friend at the bar; thorough but no more than that."

"Let's don't keep him waiting." Madrid finished the beer, dropped change for the check and a tip on the table and followed the girl out.

"A real tart's car, huh?" She thumbed in the direction of a flashy yellow convertible. "Throw your bag in the back." She slid behind the wheel, took out a compact and carefully studied herself. "Your friend is coming out."

"Give him all the time he needs. It has to look right."

"It will. By the way, what did you do with the stuff?"

"Wrapped around my waist."

She nodded and set the automatic transmission button, her eyes on the rearview mirror. In it she could see the man who had been following Madrid get into a nondescript black sedan. She waited until he was settled before pulling away and watched as the sedan followed.

"My name's Karen. Karen Phillips. I'm new with the Bureau down here."

"I thought you must be. Otherwise I would have remembered you."

"That's a compliment?"

He smiled for the first time. "That's a compliment."

"We're going to a motel in El Paso. Mr. and Mrs. Sol Madrid. One of our men will come this evening to pick up the stuff. It will look like a regular contact to your friend. Is this a big operation?"

"It could be if it develops right." He glanced at her profile, watched a smile play about her lips. She was new enough at this to be excited by what was happening. "I think I like the motel part."

She laughed without turning. "It's all in the line of duty. For God and Country."

At the Mexican Customs and Immigration Sol turned in his tourist card and opened his bag for inspection. They usually looked for silver which did not bear the guild mark or a pre-Columbian figure, an object of art or antiquity which Mexico would not permit to be taken out of the country. There was no indication from anyone that the inspection was other than routine.

"These are special men," Karen said after the officers had passed them, "put on for the day. We requested it. The Bureau didn't want to trust anyone else with the information. They know who you are, of course."

On the American side the search was more thorough, as a spot check might be. The car was gone over carefully and Madrid's bag minutely inspected. There wasn't the slightest recognition of Sol's or Karen's identity. Madrid answered the usual questions. Place of birth. No, he had made no purchases in Mexico and was bringing nothing back with him. The bag was closed, the Customs sticker placed on it. They were waved through. In the mirror Sol could see the black sedan move into its place.

As they entered the traffic of downtown El Paso, Karen divided her attention between the other cars and the rearview glass.

"We've picked up another tail. Light me a cigarette, will you, please?"

"You talk like a gangster's broad." He lit the cigarette and passed it to her. "Picked up a tail."

"I'm saturated with television. Private eye stuff." She glanced at him quickly. "Are you really as tough as they say you are?"

"I once hit a little old lady from Pasadena. That's how the whole thing started. It just grew into a legend."

"I'll bet."

The motel room was large, bright and airy with sliding glass doors opening on a garden. Karen sat on the edge of a twin bed and watched with interest as Madrid removed his coat, stripped off his shirt and unwound the flat waistband of elastic. Flap pockets were sewn into it and in each one was a glassine packet of heroin. He dropped the belt casually over the back of a chair and stood, rubbing at his stomach muscles.

"Do you want a drink?" She leaned on one elbow and reached for the telephone.

"Order a bottle of bourbon for me. Whatever you want for yourself."

"Bourbon with a Coke is all right with me." She asked the operator to send a bellboy over and then looked up at Madrid. "You may not believe it but I've never been in a motel with a man before. It's sort of gee-whizz like."

Sol couldn't hold back the smile. "How old are you, Karen?"

She hesitated and then answered almost defiantly. "I'm twenty-two and still intact." There was a pause. "Although that no longer seems as important as it once did."

"You're pretty young for this sort of work."

"I don't think so; neither does the Bureau. Anyhow, I've been assigned to you. I'm your girl. They thought it would look better to have the same broad meet you whenever you came in."

"You're about as un-broad a broad as I have ever known."

"I thought I was doing pretty well."

"You'll do. I don't often have this kind of a contact. The next time I come in will be at Laredo."

"I'll be there. You don't mind if I'm a little excited over what is going on? I've done my best to act bored and worldly but it is all so new."

"You'll get worldly fast enough. I'm going to take a shower. When the boy comes have him bring some newspapers and plenty of ice." He picked up his bag and started for the bathroom.

She called after him, "Will you take me out to dinner tonight like maybe I was your girl?"

He turned and looked back over his shoulder, nodding. "Like maybe you were my girl." He shut the door.

She listened for a moment until the rushing sound of the shower filled the room. Then she leaned back with an ecstatic sigh. One after another she kicked her slippers off, throwing them high until they hit the ceiling and fell to the carpet.

Stacey Woodward stared blankly at herself in the mirror. What in the beginning had been an incredibly fantastic nightmare of horror was now a reality. She pushed with her fingers at her hair, thrusting it up. It was without luster, as dry and lifeless as her skin. Her eyes were without light. Unconsciously she scratched at her arm. Sometimes her body felt as though it were being crawled over by thousands of invisible ants. What she refused to believe could happen had happened. The monkey was there and its appetite grew. No longer was it possible to deny this.

At first they had forced her down on the bed. Her arms and legs were pinioned by the two men and the girl while the nurse, calmly and without haste, had given her the injection. She had screamed and fought in mounting terror. They ignored her pleas.

"Dearie," the woman had held the hypodermic up, pushing out the air. "You just don't know how lucky you are. There are a million junkies who would give anything for this kind of service. Clean needles, good stuff, someone to do the shooting." She had felt expertly for a vein, talking all the while. "You ought to see what some of them use. An eyedropper with the point filed down until it is sharp enough to pierce the skin. It leaves a nasty track and sometimes they get blood poisoning. When we put you out you'll get down on your hands and knees, begging to get back. You'll remember how good it was here. You got on the mainline right away. Wait until you try and do it for yourself with a dirty spoon and a candle or match to dissolve the fix in water. You'll scream for me then, dearie. Yes, indeed you will."

She could no longer recall the sensation of that first injection. The time and the effect were clouded in her mind. She had refused to accept the possibility one could become an addict against one's will. Addicts were mentally disturbed persons who went on narcotics as a defense against a world in which they had no place. A healthy, normal person would have no need of drugs. They cannot, she assured herself, trap me into this. She knew, now, how specious this argument was. Heroin fed upon itself, creating its own hunger. During that first week she found herself resisting less and less and was not humiliated by the nurse's sardonic chuckle as she became submissive. They gave her the freedom of the house with limitations. The shades were always drawn so she had no idea of the landscape. A heavy, wire screen covered her bedroom windows and at night there was always someone in the room. The injections were given on schedule and she could remember the growing terror which took possession of her the first time the nurse deliberately allowed hours to pass before coming with the hypodermic. She had bit upon her lips to keep from screaming, pleading mutely with her eyes. Finally, when she could endure it no longer, she had shrieked, her nerves unable to suffer the torment.

"For God's sake, don't you know what you're doing to me? Help me, please. I'm going out of my mind."

"Of course, dearie." Unhurriedly the woman had put away a magazine. "I just wanted to see how long you could take it. You're coming along just fine." She went to the kitchen and prepared the syringe.

The nurse watched her disintegration with a clinical interest. The others regarded her with an openly amused contempt. She was no longer ashamed. Food, cigarettes, liquor, had no appeal. She picked over her plate, turning away from the meals with loathing.

"You really ought to eat something, dearie." There was mockery in the solicitude. "It will build your strength."

She had run to her room, throwing herself on the bed in a numb fear.

Now the irregularity of the injections was more calculated and deliberate. They let her go until she writhed in an unbearable torment; scratching at herself, clawing the bedsheets, unable to control the spasmodic jerking of her body. She moaned and keened and finally came to dropping to her knees beside the nurse in her chair, begging without dignity.

"In a little while, dearie." The woman would rock back and forth, thumbing through greasy magazines and not even looking at her. "In a little while. You've got to know how it is because when we let you go it won't be easy. Oh, we'll give you a contact all right. Your friend in Chicago wants it that way. But it's going to cost a lot of money, dearie. You'll have a big habit by then; maybe a hundred dollars a day. Somehow, you'll have to get it. You ought to take better care of yourself. The only way you're going to get enough money to feed the monkey is from men. The way you look now you'll be lucky to get ten dollars for it. A ten-dollar whore, dearie, is going to have trouble coming up with a hundred dollars a day."

There were intervals, after she had been given a fix, when she was temporarily filled with the sensation of unassailable strength and power of will. I'll kick it, she would assure herself. Right now. This minute. Cold turkey. When the time comes I won't ask for it. The resolution dissolved with the hours as the effect of the narcotic wore off. Little by little she could feel the gnawing, the pain, the nausea, the cramps and incredible itching. Then came the fear. Suppose it was now they cut her off completely. Just one more time, she prayed. A relief from this moment. The next time I'll be stronger. The next time. I really mean it, God. Just this once and then I'll show them they can't do this to me. All courage and pride, though, was ultimately consumed by the voracious monster which would not leave her. She no longer believed the things she told herself.

Once, they had let her go for a full twenty-four hours, watching as predatory animals might look upon a disabled thing they would eventually devour. She crawled, tore at her skin, ripped her clothing, beat her head against the wall, rolled over the floor, doubled up with the knotting pain. She cried and screamed in complete abasement. The nurse had finally given her the fix, not out of pity but because she could no longer bear the noise which was interfering with a television program she was watching.

"You just ought to get a better hold on yourself, dearie." She clucked her annoyance. "How is it going to be when you're out on your own and it's twelve o'clock at night and you can't make a connection or haven't any money? You ought to think about that, dearie, and discipline yourself a little."

She lived now in continual dread of the time when they would turn her out on some side street in Los Angeles or Hollywood, alone, broke and friendless. Each morning she awoke with the shaking fear. It could be today. No, she would feel a small relief, they wouldn't take a chance during the daytime. But, she would start an uncontrollable trembling, it could be tonight. Then she would go to the front room with the question in her eyes, the dumb, stricken look of uncertainty drawn upon her features. If the woman was in a good humor she would get her fix after only a little delay, and the hours would be tolerable for awhile.

It was in this hell she existed.

The Bureau's district man sat in a chair facing Madrid and Karen. Over his lap was the waist belt. He hefted it once.

"You made a big buy, a kilo I'd guess." He reached for his drink.

Sol nodded. "I wanted it to look like a big operation. Take it in kilo lots and you get quick attention."

"What now?" The El Paso Bureau's man was named Thomson. He was tall, loosely jointed and had a slow, engaging smile. "How do you move?"

"The next buy I make will be from the competition. That will start them snarling at each other."

"You know what could happen?" Thomson mused.

Sol nodded. "One side or the other will tip you off that I've made a buy and am coming over. I'm counting on that." He glanced with quiet amusement at Karen. "When that happens, you or Laredo will let me know. I'll have a meet here with the broad." His grin widened. "That's what she calls herself. She'll take it over. Then they'll be sure I have the connections and the juice is in where it counts. It's going to make the Customs Service look like a pretty crummy lot."

"I suppose that's the way it has to be." Thomson finished his drink and stood up. He fastened the belt around his waist and closed his coat over it. "Someone will pick this up in the morning. I don't go near the office. No one knows me around town or across the bridge." He shook hands and eyed Karen with speculative interest, nodded and left.

Madrid put out his cigarette. "Where do you want to go for dinner?"

"It's fine right here. The dining room is good and they have a small combination for dancing. You know," she was sparklingly demure, "this thing has all sorts of possibilities."

"Well, we'll have a couple of drinks, dinner, and then you can get in your floozie's car and go home."

"Uh-uh." She shook her head. "My instructions were to stay with you."

"The Bureau didn't mean *stay* the way you say it."

"I'm not supposed to wonder what the Bureau meant. I was told to meet you in Juarez and stay with you as long as you wanted me. You can put your own interpretation on the verb *to stay*. Anyhow," she was wide-eyed, "suppose the tail who followed us here is still watching? Don't you imagine he might think something funny is going on if I leave? That isn't natural. Thomson comes and goes. I go. He'll begin to wonder why so much activity when it isn't necessary and maybe suspect the whole thing is a plant, a real phony. You wouldn't want that to happen, would you?"

"No, I wouldn't want that to happen." He was grave. "You put up a good argument." He took a tie from his bag and knotted it in the collar.

"I know," she conceded dubiously. "And I always thought I'd be arguing from the other side when the time came. And," she slid from the bed and went to the dressing table, "I have an idea the time has come. Good-bye *intacto*." She glanced in the mirror, moistened her lips with the tip of her tongue, and with as lewd an expression as she could contrive, winked at him.

10

JUAN BATUC folded his hands across his paunch and rotated his thumbs slowly over each other. He was digesting the intelligence which had come to him and wondering about this gringo who had gone so boldly over the border with a kilo of the white stuff concealed on his person.

The news of what Sol Madrid had done spread swiftly through the sections of Hermosillo where such a crossing was noted with more than casual interest. Was it a trick or were this Yankee's connections so good he could do this thing successfully and without concern of detection? Batuc had great respect for the integrity of the United States Customs Service. The defection of an official in his own country would not have surprised him. They were badly paid and the *mordida* was accepted as a necessary fact of life. But the American officers at the border were of a different breed. Always, though, he admitted there was the chance of a bad one or two. This Madrid must have found the rotten fruit. Batuc whistled softly in admiration. He would have a talk with the gringo. Much business could be done between them if the fix was really in.

Things were going well for Juan Batuc. Already he had gathered together some of the peddlers who made their slow rounds of the mountain villages. The opium was beginning, once more, to reach him in the leaf-wrapped packets. He had sent men he could trust into the hidden valleys and they dealt directly with the peons who grew the poppy. This was a hard and tiresome job and he delegated it to others who had worked with him before. After all he was the *jefe,* the chief, and could not be expected to do this himself. More to his satisfaction, though, was the discovery that Harvey Mitchell was a greedy fool and he had found small ways in which to milk him. The man was in terror of his life and lived in a constant state of frightened agitation. As an experiment Batuc had whispered to him that a stranger, a Yankee, was being seen in the cantinas and he asked, always, the same question. Is there one in Hermosillo by the name of Harvey Mitchell? The response had been gratifying. The sweat of panic had broken out on the little man's brow, his hands trembled and there was stark fear in his eyes. Slavishly he appealed to Batuc for protection. *Pistoleros* to be hired to guard him. He left the hotel immediately and found refuge in Batuc's home. After two days of this Batuc shrewdly gauged the time. The stranger could be taken care of. There was no need to worry. A small matter of five thousand dollars, then—he popped his thick lips and pulled an imaginary trigger—it was done. When Mitchell protested the cost Batuc merely shrugged.

"You must," he acknowledged sadly, "know the value of your life, *señor.* Poor man that I am, I would think mine worth five thousand dollars."

Mitchell had drawn the money, a staggering amount in pesos, and meekly handed it over to Batuc. Juan had happily pocketed the sum, for no one had inquired about Harvey Mitchell. He wondered how often the same trick would work. Not often, he admitted regretfully; twice, maybe, but no more. Mitchell was a scared rabbit but he was no fool.

In everything he did Juan Batuc managed to pad the amounts to be spent, draining off the surplus for himself. He went to Mexico City and on the outskirts, beyond the stretch of the *pedregal,* that expanse of ancient, volcanic rock which scars the landscape, he had found a concealed laboratory where a team of chemists worked to transform the opium into morphine and heroin. They arrived at an arrangement. After some calculation Batuc gave Mitchell a figure which was twice the amount per kilo the laboratory was actually charging. He waited for a protest and when none came he marveled at Mitchell's ignorance. How would a man go into this business without having some real knowledge of it? Now he continually searched his mind for new ways to feed upon Mitchell, the timid man who had so much money and so little courage. Perhaps this gringo Madrid might supply part of the answer. The market in Medico's border towns was open. Here there were always buyers for the heroin. But, and this nagged at Batuc, the real money lay in the stuff when it was in the United States. This was the big operation; to deal directly with the wholesalers there. He forced himself out of his chair, took his hat and went out to his car. It was shabby now. The fenders were dented and loose, the body scarred and the motor noisy. Next year he would have a new one; a big, shiny Cadillac with bullet-proof glass. He was warmed by the notion that Harvey Mitchell would pay for it. The idea gave him a good feeling in his belly.

From a window in his room Harvey Mitchell watched Batuc leave. He had come to hate this man but was helpless without him. He was certain Batuc was cheating him outrageously but he had no way of proving it. Fear was his constant companion and he would awake in the middle of the night with a nameless dread and the chill of death upon him. Long ago he had abandoned his original plan of eventually going to Los Angeles and making contact with those persons whose supply of heroin came through the Chicago *borgata*. This, he realized, would be suicide. The news of his presence would get back to Dano Villanova. No. He must rely upon Batuc and the knowledge of his dependency revolted him. He was being cruelly manipulated and was powerless to escape. Almost daily the pig found something new which called for additional money. He went to the bureau and poured himself a small glass of tequila. This was a thing he had rarely done before—take a drink in the daytime. Now he was coming to depend upon it to quiet his ragged nerves. He had the frantic desire to gather his money and flee. Where? To what place would he go? The dream of power, a fortune, beautiful women, a small palace somewhere overlooking the sea, servants to cater to his slightest whim, had vanished. He was but a small piece on the board to be moved about at will because he could not command the situation. He should never have allowed Batuc this hold. Now, he thought miserably, he was doomed to exile in this dismal place while what he had risked so much for was frittered away. With the empty glass in his hand he sat upon the bed and cried. Tears of mortification, anger and frustration smeared his cheeks. What good would a fortune do him here even if Batuc didn't find a way to bilk him out of it? His thin shoulders sagged despondently and he wiped at his eyes with the back of a hand. It would almost be better to go back to Chicago. Give Villanova what was left of the money and take his chances. But he knew there were no chances. Villanova would not forgive what had been done. Where, he wondered morosely, had Batuc gone now? What scheme fermented in his head? He was told nothing, only when more money was needed. When, he had asked plaintively, would the money start returning? Batuc had merely raised his shoulders and answered *"ahorita."* With these Mexicans it was always "ahorita," in a little while. Batuc, though, had unbent enough to tell him what was common gossip in the cantinas. The gringo with the odd name of Madrid had good contacts at the border. This was certain. He was a man with whom an association could be a very profitable thing. No middleman to squeeze the profits. The stuff could move directly to the United States with maybe, in time, their own pushers. There was where the fortune lay. Harvey thought about this now. He was suspicious of all Americans but Madrid might offer a way out. He was Batuc's prisoner. There was no other word for it. Suppose he could talk with Madrid and, if things went well, offer to finance him? He would be dealing with an unknown but almost anything would be better than Batuc. Hatred seethed within him as the tequila gave him courage. He would send the gardener's boy to find Jalisco and bring the man to see him. Jalisco knew everything and could be depended upon. That was the thing to do.

He went to the kitchen and out into the patio where the boy worked. With the few words of Spanish he had picked up he told the boy to bring Jalisco. Then he went back, ignoring the veiled stare of the maid, and had another drink. To hell with Batuc.

While Juan Batuc talked in slow, persuasive tones Madrid half listened. In his mind he was running over the file which Lieutenant Mendoza had given him on the man. He had been in and out of the traffic for years. He was without principle and would cut his mother's throat for a profit.

Batuc was speaking. "You do not know me, Señor Madrid, but I have heard of you. There was a time when I was big here in Sonora. Then the bastards tipped me over. Now I am going to be big again. We could do business together. I have the supply. You, it seems, have good connections at the border." He waited.

Madrid appeared to be thinking. "I like to do things quietly and without trouble. I made a buy. It was satisfactory. Why should I change?"

"That Vargas who sold to you is a yellow dog." Batuc spat the words out. "He was one, with those in Chicago, who helped tip me. Vargas was a big fool in making a sale to you. This will get back to the ones in Chicago and they will not like it. Also, I will give you a better price; say forty-five hundred a kilo in your money." There was an unmistakable eagerness in Batuc's manner.

"How good is it?"

"It can be ninety percent."

"I need to be sure of the quality. Where does it come from?"

Batuc allowed himself a smile. "You do not expect me to tell you that? Maybe, later, we make the operation. It will not just be a seller and a buyer but partners. Then you will know what is needed to be known."

"It was told to me you have a partner."

Batuc shrugged. "He will not last in this business. His guts are water but he has money I need."

"A partnership with you doesn't sound very attractive."

"With you it would be different. We would understand each other."

"*Cajo!*" Madrid made the word sound as offensive as it was. "I wouldn't trust you around the corner."

Batuc was not disturbed. "That is a good way for it to be with partners. Neither trusts the other too much. Everything, then, has to come out in the open where both can examine it." He waited expectantly.

Madrid let the offer lie where Batuc had dropped it. He stood up, walked to the window and stood looking out. Finally he turned.

"I'll take a kilo now at your price. We'll see how things go. Later, maybe, we can talk something else. When can I have it?"

"At the end of the week. Come to my house at six o'clock on Saturday. It is Calle Moreno. 17." He laughed suddenly and with unexpected good humor. *"Compadre.* You tell me how you have the grease in at the border and I will tell you where my supply comes from. How does it sound?"

It was Madrid's turn to smile. "I'll see you Saturday. Until then."

Sol waited until Batuc had left. Then he strolled down to the central plaza. He bought a newspaper, had his shoes shined, paused in idle curiosity to watch the public letter writers. They worked in the shade of the park on ancient Oliver-typewriters. Their clients, mostly illiterate peons, sat stiffly on a chair and haltingly told them what to write. Then he walked over to the hotel and took a table on the sidewalk and in the shade. Over a beer he read his paper, waving off the beggars, the boys with Chiclets, the women peddling *rebozos* and the men offering machine-made *serapes.* After a moment a shadow fell across his paper. He looked up. Lieutenant Mendoza, in his shiny blue suit, a broad, obsequious smile lighting his face.

"It is a good day, *señor.* Can I be of service?"

Madrid wondered at the man's patience with this perpetual disguise and the effort of maintaining the character he had created for himself.

"It is a good day, Jalisco. So good I will buy you a drink."

The officer wiped the perspiration from his face, took a chair and signaled a waiter. Madrid ordered the beer. When it came, Sol pushed his pack of cigarettes toward Mendoza.

"I had a visitor."

"I know."

They talked in ordinary, conversational tones. There was nothing unusual in Jalisco's sitting with a tourist. He was always hustling a peso from the Americans where he could. Sol smiled to himself, wondering how the man gathered his information. Nothing seemed to surprise him.

"I am making a buy Saturday. A kilo."

The officer sighed. "I would very much like to know where it comes from. When he went to Mexico City we had a man on him from the time he landed at the airport. But he's tricky, suspicious and fast. Our man lost him in the market."

"He will have a kilo at his house on Saturday. You could pull him in on that."

"No. Someone else would take his place. I want the works—the laboratory, the chemists, the peddlers who bring the opium, the fields and the peons who are growing the poppy. Make your buy and take it across. I'll see to it that Vargas hears you are dealing with Batuc. It will build a fire under him."

"Batuc is ready to dump Mitchell but not until he has sucked him dry."

Jalisco pretended an absorption in the gaudy label on his beer bottle. "There is a man," he spoke without looking up, "at the far table near the hotel door. He arrived this morning. When you get a chance take a look. Maybe his face means something to you. I think he comes for Mr. Mitchell. He asked for him when he registered." He arose and half bowed politely for the benefit of the others at the tables. *"Gracias, señor."* The words were clearly spoken. *"Hasta la vista. A sus órdenes."* He left with an assumed briskness, moving in an odd, half-trotting step.

After a few moments Madrid moved his chair about, as though to get a better light for his reading. He had only scant seconds to study the occupant at the table but it was long enough for Sol to know he had never seen the man before. This in itself meant nothing. There were triggers all over the country ready to take a contract. The stranger was having coffee and rolls and was inspecting a lottery ticket purchased from a plaza vendor. If he had come for Mitchell he would probably get him, for those Villanova hired were good at their job. Sol wondered how much time Harvey had. The little man's head was filled with information Sol wanted. Wearily he thought he would have to try and keep Mitchell alive, get him back to the States and let him sing. First, though, he would have to be doubly frightened, eager for help and grateful when it came.

A heavy fog swept in from the Pacific through the funnels of the canyons leading back through Santa Monica. It draped itself over the trees and houses, brought traffic on Highway 101 to a creeping snarl and smeared the windows of the liquor stores, restaurants, hole-in-the-wall hamburger and hot dog stands. It was clammy and unpleasant, seeping in beneath doors and through cracks until rooms and clothing became damp and musty.

In the dimly lit booth of a small bar on Channel Road, Stacey Woodward linked the fingers of her hands with a tight, twisting motion and fought against screaming. A half-filled shot glass of bourbon was before her. She had ordered it out of desperation, knowing as she did so it would do no good. She was clutching at anything to stave off the inevitable for just a little while.

Six nights ago they had dumped her out of a car near the tangled clutter of small cottages and sleazy motels on the fringe of the Malibu colony. In her purse they had put one hundred dollars and a card on which was scrawled an unintelligible symbol.

The nurse had patted her shoulder with hypocritical concern as they prepared to leave the house. "You see, dearie, it's like I told you it would be. We just wouldn't turn you out of here without a penny to your name. You're hooked real heavy and will need a contact. Now, you go down by the Santa Monica pier and wait. Every night at seven o'clock a man will come. He'll wear a soft brown hat with a little red feather in it. His name is Paul. You show him this card and he'll sell you a paper of H. Now, you be real careful, dearie. The hundred won't last long because you've got a big habit. Maybe you can hustle some, although all that amateur stuff around the beach makes it hard for a professional girl to pick up even a ten. The vice squad keeps things nailed down. You'll just have to do the best you can."

It had been late at night when they told her to get dressed. The nurse had given her a last fix. She had put on her clothing with a slow indifference. Her skin was pale, almost without life. It had the quality of translucent porcelain. She had been blindfolded and forced to lie on the bottom of the car. She had no idea where she had been held these past two months. It was somewhere in the Valley. Of this she was certain. It really didn't make any difference.

When she was ready to leave, the nurse had surveyed her critically.

"You don't look too bad for a junkie; a little drawn, maybe, and you've lost some weight. Of course, right now you're high and that helps. Your clothes are nice and clean, new stockings and everything. You've got to keep your looks if you can, dearie. They are all you have to trade with."

Even through the temporary tranquillity of the narcotic Stacey was aware of a creeping fear. What would she do in the morning when the demon began to rip at her nerves? She had pleaded and crawled without shame and in complete degradation, crying to be allowed to stay. She shrank in horror from the world beyond this house. It was hostile, cruel and filled with unknown terrors. The police would pick her up. The pusher would not be where they said he would wait. She would lose the money they had given her and be helpless. Indescribable fears grew and were magnified. She had no illusions about the monster's appetite or her puny resolutions to defy it.

"Please let me stay. I won't make any trouble. I'll do anything you say. Anything."

"Now, dearie," the woman had been impatiently patient, "what could you do any of us would want? Here now," she added with hearty generosity, "I'm going to make you a present." She put a hypodermic and needle into a small case, dropping it into Stacey's bag. "There aren't many junkies with an outfit like this. Why, you'll be a queen of the pads where they shoot with anything they can stick into a vein."

When they dropped her off it was past midnight. Only an occasional car spun past. Here and there a light showed in a window. Farther down the highway there was a bright cluster marking an all-night restaurant. She shrank against the dark wall of an unoccupied cottage and watched the car that had brought her make a sharp U turn and vanish. For several minutes she stayed where she was, merging herself with the shadows. Desperation was her companion. She was alone in a terrible and alien world. She began to walk toward the illuminated section. Crouching away whenever headlights appeared. She had to avoid being spotted by one of the squad cars regularly patrolling the area. If she was seen here the police would wonder what she was doing alone, on foot and at this hour. They might even take her in for questioning and find the syringe in her purse. There were the telltale tracks on her arms. It wouldn't take them long to discover what she was. She must get off the road.

Fighting to control her panic she pushed through the restaurant door. A couple and two or three men sat at the bar. One of them turned and eyed her with calculating appraisal. There were a few single bills and some change in her bag; the money she had when they had snatched her off the street in Westwood. That, she thought numbly, was years and years ago. At the pay telephone she called a Santa Monica cab and then stood in the doorway until it came. First she must have a room, a hole into which she could crawl. She fought to keep her voice steady.

"Do you know of an inexpensive motel that's clean and quiet?"

The driver was an elderly man. He sensed something was wrong but was indifferent. He had troubles of his own. Sixty-five and pushing a cab on the graveyard shift. He hated the world and everyone in it.

"You ain't goin' to get into any good place without baggage." He snarled the reply. Goddamned tarts. Lousy bitches. "Where do you want to go?"

"I don't know." She was helpless. "Won't you please help me?"

"There's a place on Entrada, run by a man an' his wife. It ain't a joint. Maybe she'll take you." He was uncompromisingly sullen.

The motel, in the shape of an L, stood on a slight rise a block or so up from the beach. Stacey put her finger to the bell at an entrance marked OFFICE. From inside she could hear the sound of a television set as a late movie was unrolled. After a few moments a woman came to the door. She wore a loose flannel nightgown, buttoned to the throat.

"Do you have a vacancy? I-I'd like a place for a week, at least." She added the last in the hope it would lend some respectability to her request, appearing as she did at this hour without luggage. "I'll get my bags tomorrow."

"We don't allow girls to have no visitors." There was sharp suspicion in the reply.

"I won't have any."

"It's seven dollars a day, five by the week."

With shaking hands Stacey counted out thirty-five dollars and gave them to the woman. In return she was handed a key.

"Number four. Remember now, no visitors. I got good eyes an' I keep them peeled. This is a respectable place." She pointed. "It's right over there."

Alone in the dingy little room with its cheap furniture Stacey sat on the edge of the hard bed and smoked one cigarette after another until her throat was parched. Then she simply stared bleakly at the curtained window. For the moment she was all right but by morning the teeth of the thing would be sharp and gnawing. Morning? God in heaven. It would be seven o'clock tomorrow evening before the pusher would show. She couldn't even be sure of this. By that time she would be climbing the walls, every nerve rasped and bleeding. She began to shake with an uncontrollable chill of apprehension. What would she do with the hours? How to pass them without going insane? Her teeth bit into a lip and she tasted blood but felt no pain. Fumblingly, she put a quarter in the pay television set. It would run for an hour. She turned it down, muting the sound, and was indifferent to the program. Digging her face into a pillow she choked upon her sobs.

That first day had been a time of incredible agony. She went to a liquor store on the corner and bought a pint of the cheapest bourbon they had. It gagged her and solved nothing, for the greedy incubus would not be tamed by such pallid stuff. She drank half of it without any effect. By seven o'clock she was stretched upon the rack in torment. She waited on the beach near the pier, her eyes frantically searching for the pusher, knowing she teetered on the high cliff of madness. She locked the welling screams within her throat; felt the itching, the worms on her body, the first twinges of the cramps which would convulse her. Then she saw him. He stood near the pier, leaning against a wall, smoking a cigarette and staring at her indifferently.

She wanted to run toward him but caution slowed her footsteps. Wordlessly she handed him the card. He looked at it and nodded without interest. Brown eyes, in which there seemed to be no pupils, studied her with a contemptuous flicker. He half smiled.

"You're in bad shape, doll."

"Please give it to me." Fingers dug at the bills in her purse. "For God's sake." The first note of hysteria edged her voice.

"Not here, doll. We don't pass it here." He turned and his gaze swept the beach, the pier, the highway and the palisades beyond. Then he reached out and deliberately moved his palm over one breast and then the other. "You're not too bad, doll, nice hard knockers. I got nothin' to do right now. We'll go to my place."

He had taken her to a parked car. She followed with dumb obedience. They drove four or five blocks to a section of ranch-style, single-story apartments.

She remained with him for two days, submitting with dull-eyed patience while he spent himself upon her. In return he fixed her twice a day. It wasn't enough. The heroin was heavily cut but it kept her from insanity. On the morning of the third day he turned her out. She gave him all the money save for a few singles and in return he handed her five papers of the stuff.

"Don't look for me, doll," he warned, "unless you've got some bills. You don't have anything I need. I can get all the gash I want; young, high school stuff, for a couple of papers."

"What am I going to do?" The familiar terror clutched at her.

"How the hell should I know? You junkie broads are all the same, thinking you can trade a little cold ass for the stuff. Come back with the bills and we'll do business. Now, blow. I got things to do."

Now, in this musty bar with the patrons bent over their glasses in the silent concentration of lonely drinkers, she stared fixedly at the remaining whisky as though it were a crystal ball in which she could read the future. What she saw only sharpened the cold edge of fear. This was the dark, blind alley filled with unimaginable horrors. There was no one to hear her cry, no one to whom she could turn; no understanding, no relief from this hungry thing upon her back. The rent at the motel was paid for one more day and night. After that she would be on the pavement. Where would she go, where hide? The question terrified her. There was in her no strength, no will to resist. In her purse there were two or three dollar bills and some change. The pitiful amount might just as well have been pebbles. It had no value, for there was not enough of it to buy what she so desperately needed. She had searched out the pusher's apartment. He had laughed in her face and shut the door. She had stood there unashamed, and cried, begging for help. Later she had walked the side streets of Santa Monica, loitering near the bars, hoping a man would speak to her. She was pathetically eager to sell the only thing she had for enough to make a small buy from Paul. No one, not even the drunks, gave her more than a passing glance although there was an open invitation in her effort at a smile. Catching her reflection in a window she could understand why. She was drawn, haggard, afflicted with the nervous uncertainty of the habit. Her hair was without sheen. Her complexion had the waxy pallor of the addict. There was nothing about her to attract a man. A spasm of trembling took possession of her body. She fought it, bowing her head, crying silently.

The bartender, taking glasses from a table in an adjoining booth, stopped to examine her. Women drunks were always a problem.

"You all right?" There was no sympathy in the question. His only concern was that she might be on a crying jag and disturb his patrons.

She nodded without raising her eyes.

"Well, you sure as hell don't look it. Why don't you go on home?" He was anxious to be rid of her.

"When I finish my drink," she flared, struggling for control.

He hesitated for a moment, then shrugged and went back to his place behind the bar.

With a fumbling hand she searched through her bag for cigarettes. They satisfied nothing. It was the same with liquor and food. She couldn't remember when she had eaten last. There was only hunger for the drug and the release it could bring.

Over and over the same question pounded at her. What am I going to do? How is it I stand upon this barren plain without a friend, someone to take my hand? After tomorrow she could only walk the streets, find a park bench or a place on the beach for a few minutes' rest. The police would surely pick her up in time. Long before tomorrow, though, she would be a screaming maniac in a hostile and scornful world. In it there was no place for the afflicted. The healthy shunned them as lepers, afraid of contamination.

Her hand came out of the bag, spilling coins, bills and cigarettes over the table. With them was a card given her long ago by Sol Madrid. On it he had penciled a name and telephone number. She stared at it for a long time and his words came back to her. "I'll give you a number, a close friend at the Bureau. He'll know about you and he's a good man when things get tight."

What could she say to this unknown man? She didn't know. It was a small thin hope; a friendly, understanding voice, someone to lead her out of this labyrinth. It was this or the police or suicide off the pier into a dark ocean.

For a moment she fought for mastery over her sweating and trembling body. Then she went to the public telephone, shut the door and dialed the number. It was late. The Bureau must be closed. Madrid had neglected or forgotten to tell this man about her. The apprehensions crowded into the booth with her.

"Treasury Department. Bureau of Narcotics." The voice came over the wire.

"I know it's late"—she kept her voice steady, apologizing—"but I must get in touch with Mr. Collins."

"This is the night operator. There is no one here at this time. Can I help you?" It was impersonal but assured.

"No. Only Mr. Collins. My name is Woodward. Please."

Some of her panic and urgency communicated itself. There was a moment's silence.

"Hold the line, Miss Woodward. I'll try a couple of places and see if I can reach him. If I do I can hook you up through the switchboard."

The line was open but silent. She sat upon the small seat which folded into a corner of the booth. Her legs were without the strength to support her. Icy perspiration gathered on her face.

"Collins speaking." The connection came alive suddenly.

"You don't know me, Mr. Collins." The words tumbled over each other. "My name is Stacey Woodward. Sol Madrid gave me your number. I'm in trouble. For God's sake help me."

"I remember, Miss Woodward." There was something reassuring in the voice. "What can I do?" He was soothing. Her desperation had transmitted itself.

"I don't know. Please. I know it's late. I have no right." She was becoming incoherent. "If I knew anyone else I wouldn't have bothered you. It's hard to talk."

"All right. Take it easy. Hold on to yourself." He recognized the hysteria. "Where are you?"

"In a bar. A place called Mike's. On Channel Road in Santa Monica."

"You're not drunk, are you, Miss Woodward?" There was a weary suspicion in the question.

"No. Please believe me. I wouldn't have called you for that."

"All right." He didn't sound annoyed at the intrusion. "It will take me about half an hour to get there. Can you sit it out?"

"I'll try but please, please hurry."

"Stay where you are. I'll be there." He hung up.

It seemed hours. She crowded herself into a corner of the booth and held tightly to the table's edge. Behind the bar was an electric clock advertising a beer. The large second hand swept around in a relentless circle. It had a hypnotic effect. Once or twice the bartender glanced her way with scowling indecision.

Collins came in, fog drifting behind him. He looked around and came directly to her table. Her eyes met his and then fell away. He was too familiar with the signs to have to ask a question.

"We'd better get out of here, Miss Woodward."

She nodded and slid across the seat. He took her arm.

"Do you owe anything?"

She shook her head.

The bartender watched them leave. A slopped-up dame. Maybe her husband came for her. He didn't give a damn just as long as she got out. Broads alone in a bar always caused trouble sooner or later.

In the car she sat with head bowed, struggling to control the agony which was taking possession of mind and body. Small, strangled cries escaped her and the cramps were dull knives twisting in her stomach.

He started the motor. "How long have you been without it?"

"Twelve hours, longer maybe. I've lost track." She looked up with a pleading hopefulness.

"You know I can't help you with what you want." He covered one of her hands with his own.

"Oh, my God!" Somehow, against all reason, she had expected a miracle.

"The best I can do is have a doctor, a friend, have you admitted to a hospital for the night. They don't like a case of withdrawal but they'll take you if he asks it as a favor. It's going to be rough but a lot better than jail. That's where you were headed."

"Just one, a small fix. Just this once. Then I'll kick it. I promise. I know a pusher. He'll give it to me but I don't have any money left. Won't you help me, please? I'll do anything you say after that." She leaned forward and beat her fists on the padded dashboard.

"There isn't any such thing as just one more time. You know that. I want to help you but you'll have to help yourself."

She locked her arms about her abdomen and rocked back and forth, fighting the torture. Watching her as he drove, Collins wondered if he could get her to a hospital before she lost all control and became unmanageable. He wished all the young kids who thought it was smart to play around with goofballs and marijuana could see this girl. She still wore a beauty but it was succumbing to the ravages of the drug. The years of experience told him what she was suffering and, in a sense, he shared her misery.

"I don't think I can take it." She moaned. "Will they give me anything?"

"A heavy sedation maybe, but it won't do you much good. You have to know that. There's only one way and that's cold turkey. You'll never have it any rougher." He pulled in at a darkened filling station where there was a telephone booth.

While she waited Stacey was tempted to wrench open the door and run out into the night. She had an idea what would happen at the hospital. No one would really give a damn. Addicts were a nuisance and private institutions couldn't be bothered with them. They'd close her in a room with maybe a nurse to watch over her and she could scream, beg, crawl and pound herself against the walls until they put her in a restraining jacket. But if she ran now, where would she go? It would only be exchanging the known for the unknown. The impulse had arisen out of sheer panic.

Collins came back. He lit a cigarette and offered it to her.

She shook her head, twisting about to wrap her hands about the back of her neck; moving with the convulsive jerks of a spastic. She was barely aware of his words.

"The doctor will meet us at the hospital." He was talking in the faint hope of diverting her momentarily. "The important thing is how you feel about it. You have to want to kick the habit. All the doctors in the world won't do any good unless you help."

"Please, for God's sake get me somewhere before I start to scream. You can't know what this is like. If there is a hell I'm in it. I'm going mad. Just one fix. I'll be able to handle it the next time."

With one arm holding her tightly as she twisted and writhed, clawing at herself, Collins drove as fast as he dared through the silent streets.

11

✿ ALONG the footpaths and the straggling roads leading down from the hills and the valleys to the highway into Hermosillo an unmistakable pattern of violence began to display itself.

No one could say who the men were or where they came from. Sometimes they wore the white *calzónes* of the peon, traveling afoot or on burros. Again they were dressed in the clothing of city dwellers and waited where the trails from the mountains merged into the single artery of travel. Always, though, they carried guns and their methods were the same. They paid scant attention to the women carrying their chickens, eggs, a duck, baskets or ornamental gourds to market. The men and boys, though, were searched and sometimes stripped and the leaf-wrapped packets of opium taken from them. Then they were beaten. The punishment was not senselessly brutal but was administered with a calculated thoroughness; almost as if it was ordered by authority as a corrective measure. It was the same with the peddlers who traveled on regular circuits, their pack animals loaded with cheap household items and patent medicines to be sold in remote communities. For years they had brought down the drug from hidden poppy fields, delivering it to their contacts in Hermosillo. Their packs were ripped open, the contents strewn over the ground. Those who had secreted the lumps of opium in their merchandise or on their person were methodically whipped and the deadly fruit of the scarlet flower carried off. Such raids from the soldiers of the *Rurales,* the *Federales,* were accepted as reasonable hazards of the rich traffic. But, these *bandidos,* the *ladrones,* these *hijos de putas,* did not behave themselves like men in government service. The opium did not turn up in the usual channels and no one could say where the thieves came from, in whose pay they were or what they did with the stuff.

So thoroughly were these raids conducted that there was fear now in the countryside. Those who grew the poppies still had their women collect the gum from the pods but they were afraid to take it into the city. The peddler no longer made his deals with the mountain peon and the once flourishing trade in the narcotic dwindled to the merest trickle.

In Hermosillo there was angry confusion and meetings filled with loud words of fury, recriminations and suspicion. No one trusted anyone. Juan Batuc raged with heavy trampings about his house. He was just getting started again and now this thing happened. He was forced to listen to the whining complaints of Harvey Mitchell, who plagued him with questions. What had happened to the money he advanced? When would it begin to return? How was it, if Batuc had such good connections, he could no longer supply the raw opium to the laboratory in Mexico? In a rage Batuc had hit him, sending the little man sprawling in a corner.

It was the same with Felipe Vargas, who had taken over as the principal supplier for the wholesalers in Los Angeles who operated under the direction of the Chicago *borgata.* Two men from the "family" flew in from California and held a long meeting with Vargas. They were cold-eyed and skeptical. How was it this thing had been allowed to happen? Who was responsible? Where was the stuff going? Was he, Vargas, making a better deal for himself with someone else? Fearfully Vargas protested his innocence for he did not underestimate the purpose of these men nor their ruthlessness in handling a defector. The profits of the Mexican operation were too rich.

"It is that whore's son Juan Batuc." He sought desperately for a satisfactory explanation. "Of this I am sure. He has hired these thieves in Mexico City, maybe, to ruin me. I, personally, will open his guts and feed them to the buzzards."

The two men from Los Angeles said nothing. They simply stared at him with icy calculation. Vargas understood they believed nothing he told them. Then a most curious thing happened. An officer from the Gobernación Nacional, in Mexico City, arrived in Hermosillo and called upon the two visitors. Politely he told them that the Government considered them undesirable. Their tourist cards were requested and they were put on an outgoing plane with a guard of two soldiers who would see to it they were landed back in the United States.

On this Felipe Vargas pondered as did Juan Batuc when he heard of it. How was it the Government knew of these men? Who had seen to it the authorities were notified? It was a thing over which to ponder. It made a man uneasy.

To Juan Batuc the man Jalisco carried the word that the Yankee, Madrid, was ready to make another crossing; this time at Nogales. He would buy a kilo. When could Batuc have it ready?

This goaded Batuc into an outraged bellow. "Where do I get it? That *cajo* Vargas is behind all this trouble. He and those from Chicago again who are out to tip me over just as I am getting well started. I will cut out his nuts and stuff them in his mouth. You will see."

Then Jalisco, who seemed to circulate aimlessly and somehow find a receptive ear into which to drop small bits of information, carried the same word to Felipe Vargas. The gringo Madrid was ready to make another crossing. He would buy a kilo or more. Then Vargas screamed.

"It is that bastard Batuc. Of this I am certain. Because I ran him out of business once he is out to ruin me. I, personally, will open his guts and feed them to the buzzards. You tell the Yankee I will get it for him somehow, only the price may be higher. It is not so easy to come by. I may have to go to Mexico City for it."

All of this Jalisco relayed to Madrid when, as frequently happened, they encountered each other in the plaza and the Mexican gratefully accepted Sol's invitation to have a beer at his table.

"They are beginning to reach for each other's throats. Soon they will start telling everything they know; where the other's laboratory is and who are the border contacts. Then," he finished his beer, turned the glass upside down to imprison two flies upon the table, "I shall have them like this!"

"Who is causing all the trouble?" Madrid offered his cigarettes and lit one for himself. "Who is doing the hijacking all of a sudden?"

Jalisco pinched his nose between two fingers and his eyes brightened with suppressed laughter.

"It is a nice frame, is it not? Naturally, my Government knows nothing of it officially. Its participation would be most emphatically denied. If the truth ever comes into the open it is only Lieutenant Mendoza who is responsible. It will be said he exceeded his authority and he will undoubtedly be dismissed from the service in disgrace."

"Colonel Ortega . . ." Sol left the question unfinished.

"Colonel Ortega would have to be the first to denounce me, strip me of my rank and turn me out with indignant protestations that I am acting on my own and the Mexican Government was innocently involved." He shrugged. "That is how it would have to be."

Sol glanced around at the adjacent tables. "The man," he spoke with no more emphasis than if he were discussing the weather, "you pointed out to me. The one who sat here last week and lives quietly at the hotel. You were right about his coming for Harvey Mitchell. His name is Scarpi. Carlo Scarpi. He leaves his fingerprints on glasses or the tableware at a meal. I sent them to Washington. He is a gun from Detroit."

"We could save trouble by having Mr. Mitchell 'Thirty-Three'd.'"

Sol shook his head. "No. When he goes back to the States I want him to go willingly, eagerly, with me. I want him to be so grateful he will talk."

"I don't think you will get him." The officer was thoughtful. "The finest intelligence service in all Mexico comes through the servants. They know everything and one talks to the other. Your Mr. Mitchell is a prisoner through his own fear. He never leaves Batuc's house and Batuc will take good care of him as long as Mitchell has money. I don't believe either you or this Scarpi can get to him."

Sol considered this. "You may be right but Batuc needs action. He has to begin to show a profit. Harvey may be scared but not out of his wits. He can still add and subtract. Sooner or later he will figure

Batuc is taking him for a long sleigh ride. Then he'll look around for a better connection; Vargas, maybe, or make a contact with you. I think I'll have a talk with this Scarpi first. I don't want my canary shot up before he gets a chance to sing."

"There are easier ways of getting rid of Señor Scarpi. He gets put on a plane for the States as an undesirable."

"And next week they'd send someone else down." Madrid rejected the suggestion.

The lieutenant nodded and arose. *"Bien suerte.* Don't underestimate either Batuc or Vargas. They are getting desperate. Their buyers in the border towns are hurting. The stuff is harder and harder to get. There is pressure on them. The junkies are screaming. The peddlers are begging for merchandise."

"I'll be careful. *Hasta la vista."*

Carlo Scarpi was bored to hell-and-gone with Mexico and Mexicans. He had a job to do and couldn't find the opportunity to do it. He knew where his man was but was unable to get near him. He sat in the hotel by day and brooded over this. At night he found nothing to amuse him. The hotel bar was noisy and filled with the persistent wailing of the *mariachis.* The cantinas were dingy. The whorehouses depressed him. How the hell could a man enjoy himself in a place where the girls sat around breast-feeding their bastards between customers. Scarpi's instincts were not finely attuned but this sort of thing—a girl handing her baby over to another girl to be cared for while she went into a scabby room for a quick trick—unnerved him, as did the religious pictures on the walls, the crucifix and Christ's agony above a tin prophylactic washbasin, the Virgin's figure on a chest of drawers. He stopped looking for diversion in these places. Scarpi had never been a drinking man and he found small pleasure in the stuff now. It made him torpid and bad-tempered, quick to anger and impatient with minor annoyances—all dangerous emotions in his business. He would have given the whole thing up and gone back to Detroit save for the fact it would reflect upon his competence. A good craftsman would not leave a piece of work unfinished simply because it was difficult.

He ate the usual heavy lunch, drank two cups of strong coffee, stared indifferently about the patio and decided to go to his room for a nap. Somehow there must be a way of getting to this bastard Mitchell. The men in Chicago were becoming impatient. They refused to accept the explanation that the hit could not be made because the target refused to show itself. Already he had received two telephone calls and his weary answers only brought angry demands for action.

At the door of his second-story, balcony room he fitted the heavy iron key and found it unlocked. Innate caution made him hesitate. He kicked the door open and stood to one side.

Madrid sat in a chair facing him. Their eyes met without recognition or surprise. After a moment Scarpi stepped inside but left the door open.

"How did you get in here?"

"With a hairpin." Madrid put out his cigarette.

"So? What do you want?"

"A little talk."

"A cop?"

"No."

"Then out. I don't feel like talking to strangers."

"We'll know each other better in a few minutes. I want you to lay off Mitchell."

"Who the hell is Mitchell?"

"All right." Madrid ignored the question. "Let's put it this way. I have a nice thing going for me here. I don't want it fouled up. Mitchell is part of the nice thing. If he gets hurt I get hurt. My nice thing isn't so nice anymore."

Scarpi's expression lighted with understanding. His manner became easier.

"You act like a cop. You sound like a cop on the take. All cops are bad but one with his hand out for the ice is worse. Now, get the hell out of here before we have trouble."

Madrid leaned forward in the chair. "I don't seem to be getting through to you. If anything happens to Harvey Mitchell I'll be looking for you. So, whatever you're getting for this job won't be worth it."

"Screw you."

"That's been tried. No one liked it." His glance sought a suitcase in a corner of the room and he nodded toward it. "There's a gun in your bag. The Mexican police don't like Americans bringing guns into the country. They're afraid someone might start a revolution. If I make a call they'll come and search. Your ass will be in a can with the lid soldered down."

Scarpi crossed the room quickly. He bent and tried the lock. It was still fastened. The bag had not been opened. He looked up. Madrid was smiling.

"It had to be there." Sol was satisfied. "I looked everyplace else. I didn't figure you'd be fool enough to carry it around with you. The Mexicans are funny about tourists with guns."

The change in Carlo Scarpi's manner was all but imperceptible. Some of the tightness was gone. He studied Madrid, then took a cigarette from a pack, lit it and inhaled deeply.

"At first I figured you for a Mex who talked good English. You're an American."

"Yes."

"What the hell are you doing in this crappy place?"

"I told you I had a thing going."

"It's too bad"—Scarpi was relaxed, he sat on the bed's edge—"it's too bad you got a thing goin' I got to interrupt. You're like, maybe, a guy I could get along an' talk with; some company in this ass-hole town. Jesus. I been in some places but nothin' like this. All I want is to get a job done and blow. You know what I dream about? A white girl on a brown sheet."

"You'll never see it if you lean on Mitchell." Sol got up slowly. "Stay away from him because if you don't I'll get to you fast."

"I believe you." Scarpi was amiable. "But in a trade like mine you gotta take some chances. You know, like guys who jump in parachutes for kicks because they know there's maybe a time when they don't open or a joker packed them with sawdust. We got no hard feelings?"

"No hard feelings. I'm only trying to save everyone trouble."

"About the iron in the suitcase?"

Madrid shook his head. "I don't blow a whistle for something I can handle myself."

"Then it's like just between you an' I?"

"It doesn't have to be anything if you don't keep pushing. If you do, then it's just like between you and me." He paused. "When you took the contract did they tell you about a gun named Roy Gaines?"

Scarpi's eyes narrowed. He peered at Madrid with an unasked question in his expression.

"You're a spook." There was a small admiration in the statement. "An honest-to-God spook. Nobody knows about Roy."

"You do. I do. Villanova does."

"Get out, will you?" The order was without anger. "You're beginning to give me the creeps."

"Try a plane trip for them. Back to Detroit." Sol nodded briefly and walked from the room.

Carlo Scarpi stared at the empty doorway. He attempted a short laugh but the sound wouldn't come.

The boy who worked in Juan Batuc's garden, and did the small odd jobs about the house, stood back and admired the waxed polish on the old Cadillac's hood. This was one of the things he liked best about what he was told to do. He had the Mexican's almost childish delight and wonder in and for all mechanical contrivances. He never ceased to marvel they could be made to run and sound; the noisier the better. To blow the horn, race the motor, created an inexpressible ecstasy. Above all, though, when he had finished with the waxing and polishing Señor Batuc permitted him to back the car out of the garage and drive it to the front gate. In time he hoped to be the *señor's* chauffeur and sit proudly behind the wheel, wearing, maybe, a uniform cap. He put away the rags, the tin of paste and scrambled behind the wheel. The key was turned in the ignition lock, the starter pedal pushed.

The blast tore the garage walls apart, broke all the windows in one side of the house, sent masonry, plaster, shards of glass and pieces of the boy catapulting through the morning air. It reduced the cook and maid to screaming objects who ran hysterically about the garden without purpose, covering their heads with their aprons as though this could ward off further destruction. It temporarily stunned Juan Batuc and then sent him stumbling in a quivering mass of fear to the patio. He looked upon the destruction, watched the dust swirl and settle in a hazy cloud. Then he vomited at the spectacle of the blood-splashed pieces of flesh plastered against the adobe wall. The Indian girl Joventina, who had been washing her hair, stood transfixed with water streaming upon the tiled floor. Harvey Mitchell, pitched from a chair, cowered on hands and knees screaming in high terror. He had no idea what had happened but was certain its intent was to kill him.

Then, from the houses nearby, people came running, followed by yelping, frenzied dogs. They crowded and milled about the gaping hole, peering with awestruck fascination at pieces of Señor Batuc's Cadillac. There was a fender here, a door there, the mangled torso of the *joven,* a crimson, shapeless thing in the dusty road. After awhile the *policía* came and later, with sirens and bells clearing a way, the fire department, although there was no real fire to be put out. The police took notes from the dazed Batuc, the servants. A multitude of copies would later be made of their questions and the answers and filed away for what purpose no one was really sure. The firemen poured water upon the smoldering wreck and then regretfully went away, because there had been nothing spectacular for them to do. The crowd drifted off, talking with excited gestures, arguing and explaining the thing to each other.

Batuc sat in a chair in the *sala,* shaking with an uncontrollable chill. His lips moved with soundless gasps as does a fish when taken from the water. The Indian girl, her hair still wet but brushed into a heavy cascade, brought him a bottle of tequila, the salt and limes. He drank from the bottle and seemed unaware of what he was doing. His eyes stared and saw nothing.

In all of his time Juan Batuc had never known such a thing as this to happen. Men had been shot or knifed. This he had done. But what had just occurred was something one saw only in the Yankee gangster pictures. It was not the Mexican way of assassination. So, it must be those bastards in Chicago again who were jealous because Juan Batuc was back in business and would tip him over for good. But, and he considered this carefully, there were no strangers in Hermosillo. A few tourists came and went, spending only a day. The gringo, the one named Madrid, was no longer an unknown. He was in business also and had no reason to hate Juan Batuc. There was another who called himself Scarpi. Juan fingered his lip. This Scarpi was of a mystery. He sat out the days at the hotel. For awhile he had spent his nights in the *casa de putas,* La Ranchita. Of those who came and went Juan Batuc kept himself well informed. As yet this Scarpi had given no indication of what his business was. So. Could he have been the one who did this upon orders from those in Chicago? Batuc mulled upon the question. No, he decided. To do such a thing one must have several sticks of dynamite, the caps to set it off, a knowledge of the car and how it was possible to enter the garage through a small side door. A Yankee did not come into Mexico carrying explosives in his suitcase. The stuff would be discovered at once by the Customs officers. So who, then, had committed this offense? Vargas, the whore's son? It would have to be Felipe Vargas, who was already responsible for the searches and the beatings, the waylaying of those who brought the poppy gum down from the mountains.

The layers of fat shook, trembling like a weak custard with Batuc's fear and anger. His mind darted and twisted in an effort to escape the inescapable. They were out to kill him. It was not enough that his supply of the raw drug was being shut off. Juan Batuc was to be taken out of business altogether; erased in a bloody smear somewhere as was the gardener's boy this morning. He took another drink and for the first time was aware of Mitchell's presence. The man babbled incoherently, his voice rising and falling in a frenzy. It came slowly to Juan he was being blamed for the explosion.

"Shut up, little man." He spat at Mitchell.

"You will have us both killed." Mitchell's words spilled from him and the sentences were disconnected and made no sense. "And all of the money you have taken from me? What has it been spent for? You have lied and cheated. Of all the money you asked for only a miserable amount has come back. What of your fine connections, the protection you promised; how we would have a good operation going and with nothing to fear from anyone. *Mas dinero.* More money. It is all I have heard. Now this. You are a thief." Mitchell was panting.

"Shut up. I say it again, little man." Juan swallowed again from the tequila bottle. "Or I will kill you myself." He eyed Mitchell with icy hatred and an abrupt suspicion entered his mind. "It was maybe you only they wanted to kill. Those you stole from in Chicago. It did not matter if I and the others were killed. It was because of you this thing happened." He was shouting hoarsely, almost believing what he said. "No more will I give you my protection. My house is no longer yours. You will get out now, today. Go where you will and take your chances. I have no need of you. I would rather be alive and poor. To be with you is to walk with disaster. From the beginning I felt it. I do not even know your name from now on."

Mitchell was barely aware of the angry words. He stumbled blindly from the room, his breath coming in short gasps. He would get out of this house. But, the question posed itself with startling clarity, where would he go? Until he could leave Hermosillo he must again stand naked in the street, alone and friendless. He felt the danger closing in again from all sides. The money. He would draw it all from the bank and take a plane for Mexico City. From there he could choose. Guatemala, Brazil, Argentina, Chile. He would be content with what he had. He was no criminal hunted by the law and could travel openly. The only thing he had to fear was Villanova. Because of this, then, he must always keep on the run but he would be alive. He began to throw his scanty possessions into the suitcase.

Batuc, the tequila soothing his insides, was already regretting what he had said to Mitchell. It was not the little man's fault and in his anger he had tossed away a very good thing. He had turned out the one man who had the money he needed. The bomb had been meant for Juan Batuc alone. He was the one who could be expected to sit behind the wheel and tramp upon the starter. There was only one man who could have planned it and that was Felipe Vargas. He half rose with the intention of going to Mitchell's room and placating the frightened and angry man. Then he sank back wearily. Instinct told him nothing he could say would change Mitchell's mind now. So, he told himself, I must repair the damage as best I can and look for another contact. Slowly the image of the Yankee, Madrid, took shape in his mind. It was possible. They could work together. It would not be as with Mitchell, of course. This gringo Madrid was tough. He was not running. If they did business together it would not be Juan Batuc who gave the orders and made the decisions. He sighed. A small piece of cheese, to a hungry man, was better than no cheese at all. Also, he felt certain if Felipe Vargas pressed Madrid, the Yankee would take care of him. He glanced up to see the Indian girl watching.

"Send Chela to me." He reached again for the tequila.

The girl left silently and returned with the little maid, who was still so frightened she could barely control her movements.

"You will go to the plaza, Chela," Batuc rumbled, "where, at this hour the American, Señor Madrid, usually takes his coffee and reads the paper. You remember him? He came once to the house before."

The girl nodded.

"The American speaks the language so you will ask him if he will be good enough to come to our house at his convenience. If this is not possible I will come to him. You understand?"

Again she nodded but could not speak. After a moment of indecision she went away.

Batuc sat with his hands folded in his lap. Perhaps it was not too bad a thing Mitchell was leaving. With Madrid he would not be the *jefe*. There would be no easy access to money. Just the same, it was good to have a strong man at one's side. He would make the best of it.

In the plaza the report of what had happened at Juan Batuc's house was being told and retold with many elaborate variations. The old women in the market, before their heaps of peppers, melons, tomatoes and cloth-covered mounds of tortillas, clattered to each other. They repeated what they had heard and colored this with their imagination. The men in the cantinas put aside their dominoes and discussed the matter, offering grave opinions. The few police, on their rounds, maintained a lordly silence, implying they knew more than was being told. Little concern was expressed by anyone for the dead boy.

At the sidewalk tables Jalisco threaded his way between the seated tourists. Today he was peddling a spurious, pre-Columbian figure. As always he approached Sol Madrid with a fine display of humility. This, for some reason, seemed to delight him and he made a great show of his obsequiousness, bowing and holding his hat at his chest.

Now he unwrapped the statuette and offered it for Madrid's inspection, lowering his voice in a conspiratorial whisper.

"It is an object of rare antiquity, *señor,* and I am offering it at a great sacrifice. It is undoubtedly true Aztec, or perhaps even Mayan."

Sol took the figure for inspection and inclined his head in solemn agreement.

"New Jersey Aztecs, I would say."

"Perhaps so." The faintest of smiles came with the words. "Although it is told to me there are some noble Aztecs working in a Mexico City factory. You have, of course," he continued in the same tone, "heard what happened this morning?"

"In all its variations. Do you know another?"

"No, but I could make a good guess. I would say it was a business dispute. You know how those things are. Anyhow, there will be alibis for all. Of more interest, though, is the sudden departure of your Mr. Mitchell from the *casa* of Señor Batuc. He arrived at the Hotel Monique in a state of agitation and is now, I believe, locked in his room."

"I can't say I blame him." Sol frowned. "I can't afford to lose him, though. If he leaves here I have to start all over and I'm getting tired."

With a shrug of regret, Jalisco took back his figurine, unhappy he had been unable to make a sale. He wrapped it in old newspaper.

"I talked with Colonel Ortega." They were at an isolated table beyond which their words did not carry. "My instructions are the same; to be of all assistance to you. If Mitchell tries to leave Hermosillo he will be detained. It will be explained the authorities are investigating the bombing and his testimony is needed. This he may not like but will have to accept."

"Thank you."

A small shadow moved up near the table and a tiny voice whispered, *"Permiso, señor?"*

Batuc's maid stood in timid hesitation. She looked questioningly at Jalisco and then at Madrid. Carefully, then, reciting from memory, she gave Madrid Batuc's message. Then, almost fearfully, she hurried away. The gaze of both men followed her.

"This I like very much, my friend." The lieutenant spoke with satisfaction. "You and Batuc will make fine partners, if that is what is on his mind and I suspect it is. He needs a strong friend with good connections."

Sol nodded and a sudden grin flashed over his face. He waved away a waiter who approached with the coffeepot.

"I would like to see or hear Scarpi when he finds out Mitchell is in the open and he still can't get near him."

"Mitchell is safe as long as he doesn't leave the hotel or walk in the garden at night. Even then I don't think he would dare make a move. Anyhow, we shall see."

"Do you have time to sit down?"

"But of course." The lieutenant unwrapped his figure and again placed it on the table. "It will be assumed we are only discussing this rare object of art." He accepted one of Madrid's cigarettes.

"I have an idea Mitchell is ready to hit the panic button. It only needs a little push to send him screaming. Maybe this Scarpi will give him the nudge. He must realize Villanova will never give up. Harvey is only incidental to the *Capo* but he is there, unfinished business which has to be taken care of. He has to understand his only chance is to go back with me."

"Then you do not intend to talk with Juan Batuc?" The officer could not keep the note of disappointment from his voice.

Madrid was quietly thoughtful. He looked up to meet the lieutenant's gaze.

"My Government wants the lid on this operation here nailed down as much as you do. It's only one source, but if we can shut off Sonora then we can move on to something else."

"But Mitchell comes first?"

"That's the way it has to be. I want him ready and eager to talk; to spill his guts to a federal grand jury. He is familiar with every phase of the Chicago operation; its connections, its channels, its payoffs, the sources of income, the division of profits. He can tear this thing wide open for us."

"My Government," the officer reflected, "has been working on this for a long time. Many times we could have arrested Batuc or Vargas but that would have accomplished nothing. Others would have stepped into their places. The apparatus is complex. Until now we have never been able to get an operative as close to Batuc as you are right now. He wants, needs, a deal with you. Your trips over the border have been impressive. They were not wasted. He would like to use your knowledge, your connections."

"You didn't really think I was going to walk out on you?"

"I hoped not." The officer's expression brightened.

Madrid shook his head. "Just let me arrange this in my own way. A deal and the information we want from Batuc is not something I will get in one meeting. I'll see him this evening and set things up for further talks. I will be making a trip to the States. This I will tell Batuc. What he won't know is that Mitchell goes with me. Then I will come back to Hermosillo as I have done before. There will be nothing in my movements to make Batuc or anyone else suspicious. You get Mitchell to Tijuana and I'll pick him up there."

"It could work that way," the officer agreed. "It could very well work as you have laid it out. There is nothing in it to raise a question in Juan Batuc's mind. I am happy with it."

"Just be sure Mitchell stays alive. I don't want this Scarpi picking him off while I'm on another errand."

"There is a man flying in from Mexico City today. He will be assigned to watch Scarpi. It would still be easier to deport him."

"Then I am empty-handed," Madrid objected with a quiet intensity. "I need Scarpi to put the final scare into Mitchell."

"Very well, we will try things your way, *compadre*. Things work slowly but they work. There will be difficulty with Mitchell. Right now he is a turtle who does not want to stick his head from the shell for fear someone will snap it off. I think I should see him first. After all, I am only Jalisco who was his guide and friend when he first arrived. He has no reason to mistrust me. He may even listen but I will really tell him nothing. That I leave to you."

Madrid watched the young Mexican as he moved away between the tables, clutching the worthless stone figure. Never did his instincts fail him; never did he drop, for a moment, the character; always he walked the high wire of danger with cocky assurance. Sol was proud to call him friend and the word, *compadre,* he had used was not given lightly.

12

GREED and suspicion moved in alternating shadows across Juan Batuc's face as he talked and studied the indifferent pose of the man who was sprawled negligently in the chair opposite him.

Sol Madrid had listened with an air of polite detachment as Batuc laboriously skirted what was uppermost in his mind. He was, by nature, devious and could not bring himself to stating frankly what must, sooner or later, be discussed between them. On a tray were bottles of Scotch, tequila, ice in a bowl, limes, salt and water. Neither had finished his first drink. Madrid reached over and added two ice cubes to his glass. His eyes never left Batuc. They glinted with a hard light of amusement as the Mexican tried desperately to pass him the conversational ball. Sol ignored the effort and glanced at his watch.

"Why don't you get to it, Batuc?" The question was sharply impatient. "What's on your mind? You sent word you wanted to see me. I'm here."

Batuc wiped at his face with a slightly soiled handkerchief. Nervous perspiration glistened on his jowls and ran in small beads down his neck.

"Between strangers," he muttered unhappily, "it is not always so easy to be frank. One is never sure how far the other can be trusted." He paused hopefully. Madrid said nothing. "As you have heard, I had some trouble this morning. My car . . ." He left the sentence unfinished.

"Tell it to the police." Madrid was bored.

"The police do not give a damn." A small touch of humor came to his tone. "Batuc and the police are not exactly *simpatico*. They would probably think it a very good thing if I had been blown up along with the gardener's boy."

"What do you want from me?"

"It was in my mind we could do business together. For this reason I wanted to see you."

Madrid's short laugh had an unpleasant sound and Batuc flinched beneath the derisive accusation.

"The way I look at it," Sol spoke slowly, "any guy who is in the trouble you are would make a lousy partner. Who tried to kill you?"

"I will be sure first and then he will be taken care of." For a moment Batuc showed an angry resolution. "You must know I was once a very big man here. I will be again. There are jealousies." He spread his hands to encompass the world and its cupidity.

"You had a partner. Mitchell. I know all about it. What happened?"

Batuc made a sound of spitting. "Mitchell! He is a *gusano*—a worm. A little trouble and he runs screaming like a woman. With such a one I cannot do business. But I *can* use a man like yourself. *Muy valiente!*" He beamed at Madrid as though he had paid him a rare compliment.

Sol shook his head. "I'm not sure I want to do business with you. After what happened today, I think possibly you're poison. Anyhow, just in case, we ought to get things straight. Maybe we can put something together. I don't really need you. But remember this—you don't *use* me."

"Forgive me." Batuc was eagerly apologetic. "It is my bad English. The word was not meant as you make it sound."

Madrid could detect the urgency in the man's voice. He was badly shaken by what had happened but still unwilling to commit himself completely. He could be led now if it was done carefully.

"I already have a proposition." Sol lied deliberately. "Felipe Vargas."

Batuc's face swelled in speechless fury until it resembled a child's purple balloon. He tried to speak and strangled on his words.

"I turned it down," Madrid continued blandly, "because I don't like his connections. The slice is too big. I can do better on my own."

Batuc's inarticulate anger subsided. "I will cut Felipe's feet off at the ankles. I will leave him nothing to stand on."

"You're in trouble up to your ass." Madrid ignored the boast. "I know it. You know it. So, what you will or will not do to Vargas doesn't mean a damn thing. If they want to, the friends of Vargas will run the wheels right over you. Now"—he finished his drink—"I will give it to you straight down the line." He leaned forward in an attitude of earnestness. "I am no Mitchell. There will be no money handed over to you. The soft touch is finished. If there are payoffs to be made I'll make them, and I want to see the man whose hand is out. I want to know where the stuff comes from; the laboratory in Mexico City. I want to know the police who are taking a bite to pretend it isn't there. I want to know who your contacts are in Tijuana, Juarez, Nogales and Mexicali and how much they can handle. In other words, I want the whole operation spread out for me so I know to the ounce what is going on."

A wary doubt expressed itself in Batuc's eyes. He shifted unhappily as a man might who finds himself in an uncomfortable position.

"What you ask for, *señor,* is a lot. What do you propose to contribute in return?"

"The thing the machinery needs most—connections at the border. You know I have them."

"I have wondered about that." Batuc was suspicious again. "To have what you call the fix-in at so many places. A man who can take a kilo across without concern." He shook his head wonderingly.

"You're not the only one who likes money." Sol was contemptuous.

"The connections in the border towns," Batuc mused. "They are mostly men of the *sindicato* with whom, now, Vargas does the business. What good will it do you to know who they are?"

"Because before I am finished I will have Vargas and the *sindicato* out of business. We will get rid of the old and set up new connections at the border. This time, though, they work for us. We wholesale directly. No man in the middle to squeeze the profits. We'll cut it to strength ourselves and run it across with our own mules. It goes straight into the hands of our ounce men and from there to the pushers. We don't need to go outside California for a market. The whole operation belongs to us. You said you wanted to be big again. You'll never have a better chance."

"You can do this?" Batuc marveled. "The men of the *sindicato* do not worry you?"

"I can do it. So, you can come in or stay out."

Sol could sense Batuc's reluctant wavering. He was dazzled by the profit to be made when the whole thing, from source to sale, could be held between the two of them. He held back now because he disliked the idea of trusting anyone so completely. To share his knowledge, all of it—from the flower to the powder, the location of the laboratory, the identity of the police and the *mordida* paid them—was to reduce himself in stature. In this partnership he would not be the key man, the *jefe*. This struck at his pride. Yet right now he had need of this Yankee. Studying him, Madrid could almost predict his decision but he realized he had applied enough pressure for this first meeting. Let Batuc turn it over in his mind. The appeal would grow with time. He stood up.

"You wanted to see me. I made the proposition. Take your time and think it over. But it has to be as I say. You hold nothing back. In a day or so I go to Los Angeles to set up a couple of things. When I return we can talk again but not for long. It will have to be yes or no. In the meantime," he laughed softly, "stay out of automobiles."

Harvey Mitchell stood at one side of the window and stared unseeingly down at the flower-decked patio. It had been a day of unnerving developments. He had left Juan Batuc's house in an unreasoning panic, convinced the bomb had been meant for him. Without any real idea of what he would do next he had checked back in at the Hotel Monique, locking himself within the room. He wondered miserably, now, why nothing had gone as planned. From the time he had stepped aboard the Super-Chief until this morning everything which, in his avarice, should have been simple had become increasingly complex. He had been forced to murder; to lay himself open to the plundering of Juan Batuc; to seek protection and sanctuary when, with two hundred and fifty thousand dollars of Dano Villanova's money, he should have been able to walk boldly. The truth was, he told himself miserably, he did not have the stomach for any of this. For the hundredth time he wished he was back in Chicago, surrounded by the familiar things of his office, secure with his weekly salary, his comfortable apartment. No longer did he indulge himself in the luxurious dreams of unlimited money and power; the seaside villa somewhere and the fawning of beautiful women. All he wanted was a place where he could hide in anonymous safety. He could think of no land where he would ever feel completely secure again.

Earlier he had overcome enough of his fear to go to the bank. He had drawn some money and closed out the account with a cashier's check. Batuc had bilked him out of close to twenty-five thousand dollars with his lies and imaginary expenditures. The knowledge of this filled him with anger and mortification. With his business at the bank completed, he had returned to the hotel and asked the clerk to get him a reservation on the first flight out of Hermosillo to Mexico City or a connecting point. Then he went back to his room, sat behind its locked door and tried desperately to see beyond it and into the future.

Scarcely fifteen minutes had passed before the clerk called to say an officer of the police wished to see him. With the caution which had become his constant companion, Mitchell asked the hotel's employee to accompany the policeman upstairs and to his room. He wanted the presence of a third person in the event the policeman was an impostor. He would take nothing for granted.

The police officer, a sergeant, had been polite and his words were filled with regret. It would be necessary for the Señor Mitchell to postpone his departure from Hermosillo. The bombing of the morning at Señor Batuc's was being most thoroughly investigated. The testimony of Señor Mitchell would be required.

Harvey protested vehemently. He knew nothing, had seen no one, had been in his room at the time of the explosion. All of this he had previously explained. His objections only increased the officer's carefully rehearsed apologies. It was an inconvenience, to be sure, but the *señor* must understand there were inescapable formalities to be gone through. All members of the household would be required to give their version of the unfortunate affair. This could not be done on a moment's notice. Harvey had encountered this polite stubbornness of the Mexican official mind before. Finally, after considerable argument, he had nodded a weary assent. He would remain for the inquiry and only hoped it would be completed in the shortest possible time.

A knock on the door now spun him around from the window. Even the simplest thing set his nerves to screaming. He was hemmed in by invisible dangers. When the knock was repeated he drew upon his small courage and asked who was there.

"It is Jalisco, *señor*. Would you permit me to enter?"

Recognizing the voice but puzzled by the visit, Mitchell cautiously opened the door.

"What is it? What do you want, Jalisco?"

"With your permission, *señor,* only a few minutes of your time."

Almost irritably Mitchell stood aside and then carefully relocked the door. Jalisco stood, hat in hand. He nodded approval as the key was turned in the lock.

"It is good, at this time, to take all precautions, *señor.*"

There was something different here. Mitchell could give it no name but he was aware of an oddly changed attitude on the part of this man who had acted as his guide. The distinction was subtle. Jalisco, as always, was deferential but he now bore himself with a strange confidence, almost authority, which was puzzling but also in a measure reassuring. Harvey wasn't quite certain why.

"What is it you want, Jalisco? I am leaving Hermosillo. I have no need of a guide or help."

"Believe me, *señor,* you do have need of assistance. Because you keep your door locked I know you are aware of this. Is it permitted to sit down for a few minutes?"

Here was a friendly, familiar figure, and because of this Mitchell began to feel easier. He nodded an assent. Jalisco carefully placed his hat on the floor beside a chair and sat down. After a moment, Harvey also took a chair.

"Señor Mitchell." Jalisco spoke slowly. "You are in danger." He shook his head quickly as Harvey started to speak. "I am not talking of the bomb which exploded this morning at the home of Juan Batuc. It was not meant for you."

"How do you know?"

"I hear things." Jalisco rested back in the chair. "I have come to help if you will accept what I can do. A man can only run for so long and then the road ends."

Harvey started to protest, to deny, to assert his confidence. But there was something in Jalisco's manner which stayed him. He opened and then closed his mouth soundlessly.

"You come very close to the end of the road now, *señor*. Believe me, I do not say this to frighten you." He was unsmiling and held Mitchell's eyes with his own. "That has already been done."

"What is it you want from me? Money?" There was a rising note of anger in the questions.

To himself Lieutenant Mendoza sighed. How simple it would be to identify himself; to impress upon this small, frightened man that his only chance for survival was to trust him and, later, Sol Madrid. He discarded the idea. His cover had been too painstakingly built over the years. He was Jalisco, the man of small dishonesties. Everyone knew him. He must keep it this way until the job was finished. He lifted his shoulders with a characteristic gesture of wry amusement.

"Money? It is always welcome. If what I have to say is of value, then your generosity will tell you." He managed a crafty expression.

"Why should I believe you?" Suspicion was in the question.

"You make it difficult, *señor*. But, suppose I say a name to you." He paused. "Carlo Scarpi."

All color drained from Harvey Mitchell's face. He stared and could not utter a word. Villanova and the Chicago *borgata* had used Carlo Scarpi many times. In Mitchell's presence the name had been spoken often, the charge for his services discussed. Mitchell himself had drawn cash for payments on contracts. Scarpi was relentless, as coldly venomous as a cobra. But, and his mind whirled in spinning confusion, how could this Mexican, this guide and peddler of cheap souvenirs, a runner of errands, possibly know who and what Carlo Scarpi was? Fearfully he slid from the chair and in the same bent position backed away until he was wedged in a corner. His hypnotized gaze never left Jalisco's face.

"No, *señor*." Jalisco was soothing. "I did not come in his place. I have nothing to do with this man Scarpi. I gave you his name only to make you listen to what I have to say."

"Then how . . ." Mitchell could find no words beyond the unfinished question. "How could you . . ."

"How could I know?" There was almost a faint sadness in the reply. "I am a small man who finds a peso here and there. I listen and I hear things. That is why I said you are coming to the road's end unless you trust me a little."

Mitchell remained where he was, as though the triangle of wall was a sanctuary. His eyes searched the Mexican's face. In it he could find nothing but an odd expression of sympathy.

"Why should you care what happens to me?"

"It is possible I don't care at all. A tourist who lives or dies, to me it is nothing. A man wants to talk with you. He believed you might trust me a little. He paid me to come and deliver his message. So, I am here."

"Who paid you? Scarpi? Whatever he gave I will give more. See." Mitchell dug at his coat, pulled out a wallet. One hundred *peso* notes fluttered out as his fingers scattered them in their nervousness. "Whatever you want. I have more. You will help me get away tonight. It would be easy for you. There are ways. You must know them."

"Out of here? This hotel? That is simple. Then where do you go? I have known such men as this Scarpi. They do not give up, because killing is their business. Time is on their side. Scarpi has paid me nothing; neither has the other one. I owe him a favor. This is it. Will you talk with him?"

"Why should I?" Mitchell began to believe Jalisco offered no threat. Some of his bantam arrogance again displayed itself. "What is this man to me? He must want something."

"This one has the strange name of Madrid. He wants to help you."

"You're crazy." Mitchell all but shouted an angry protest. "He is with Batuc. They did some business together. It is only a trick. I don't want anything to do with him. It will only be money, money, money."

"The other one—Scarpi—is after your life. Which would you rather keep?"

In Mitchell's mind now the turmoil and fear began to be sorted into order. Panic gave way to reason. It was simple enough. This Madrid wanted to sell him protection against Villanova's hired killer. The whole thing could be a lie. Batuc, Jalisco and Madrid had planned it between them to get this money. But, and again doubt crept back, how would Jalisco know of Carlo Scarpi? He hesitated.

There was a sharp, unexpected knock on the door.

"Don't answer it." Mitchell cringed as though he would make himself invisible. "Let him knock. No one is here." He whispered the last.

Briefly Jalisco studied the cowering, abject figure. Then he went to the door and opened it. Madrid stood within the frame.

"I have done what I could, *señor*." Jalisco nodded toward Mitchell and made a resigned gesture with his hands. "Now it is up to you." He slid past Madrid, who took a step inside the room and shut the door.

Mitchell started to protest but the only sound which came from his throat was a terrified squeak. His eyes were bulbous. Madrid reached behind him, turning the key in its lock.

"Sit down." Sol's words were those of a tired man. "I'm not going to hurt you. That isn't what I came for."

There was something in the tone. Mitchell could not identify it. But of this he was certain, it held no menace. If, as he suspected, this man had come with a demand for money, an offer of protection, he would handle it. Payoffs were something he understood. Moving from the corner he sat tentatively on the edge of the bed, his gaze fixed upon the visitor.

"I'm going to tell you certain things." Madrid spoke as a teacher to a student. "When I have finished you can make up your mind how it is going to be. I know everything about you. You were the accountant for Dano Villanova and the Chicago family. You stole two hundred and fifty thousand dollars and got out on the Super-Chief. There was a girl named Stacey Woodward who tried to shake you down, and a gun from Detroit by the name of Roy Gaines who had a contract on you. Somehow you got away from Gaines and came to Mexico, to Chihuahua. There you killed a man by the name of Aguiella."

Mitchell licked at dry lips and stared with complete fascination at Madrid. Finally he found his voice and whispered, "How do you know this? Who are you?"

Sol ignored the questions. "I'm going to give you a choice. You can come back to Los Angeles with me or the Mexican Government will deport you as an undesirable alien and you can leave with Carlo Scarpi on your back. If he doesn't get you, someone else will."

"How do I know . . ." The words trailed off.

"Who I am?" Sol finished the question for him. "My name is Madrid. I am an agent of the Federal Bureau of Narcotics. I couldn't take the chance of having identification found on me on this job. Colonel Ortega, in Chihuahua, will vouch for me. You've talked with him on the Aguiella killing. Anyhow, I think you know I am telling the truth."

Mitchell did not question the statement. It had the undeniable quality of authority. This man was what he had said. Suddenly he was tired, exhausted from the running, the constant feeling of hands reaching for his throat, of danger hiding within every shadow. Exhaustion and a strange, almost blissful lassitude took possession. He was almost grateful that it was over. Oddly enough his first thought was of sleep; to go to bed and not start at every small sound in the night.

"What do you want of me?"

"First your safety; to get you out of Mexico before you do something foolish and someone gets to you. Then I want your testimony before a federal grand jury. I want the whole story of the Chicago *borgata*. How and where the records are kept; the lines of communication; the whole, interlocking complex documented with names and dates. Who is being paid off. No one knows these things better than you."

"They'll kill me." The words were barely audible.

"They'll kill you anyhow, Harvey. The minute you leave this hotel without me you're a walking corpse. Back in the States the Government will give you all possible protection. With it you have a chance to live. Without it you have none."

Mitchell had no illusions about the protection the Government would provide. FBI men would be assigned around the clock. But sooner or later, he would have to be on his own. They couldn't take care of him for the rest of his life. Would it be better to take his chances now? There must be some remote spot where no one would ever think to look for him.

"If I say no?" There was a small defiance in the question.

"If you say no I'll have a deportation order here by this afternoon. You'll be put on Aeronaves de Mexico and flown to Juarez, taken across the river and turned loose in El Paso. And," his voice grated, "right behind you will be a man by the name of Carlo Scarpi. I'll see to that also."

Harvey Mitchell began to cry. It was no wild, hysterical outburst. He wept as a child might over some disappointment. Elbows resting on knees, hands covering face, he sobbed his frustrations and humiliations of a lifetime. He was unashamed, weeping openly, and the cry went back to childhood. He was the timid boy bullied at school, ignored by the cliques, scorned by girls. He had dreamed of being big physically, dominating the schoolyard, the leader. Instead, he had been pushed, shoved, mocked for his frailty. His adult life had been the same. Harvey the bookkeeper, the mole who meekly took orders and abuse. Then, back in Chicago, had come a chance and he had taken it. Now it had come to nothing.

Madrid watched him and listened with an understanding compassion. From the beginning of this adventure Harvey Mitchell never had a chance. He had been out of his league from the start. He lit a cigarette and waited while Mitchell's agony of soul ran its course.

Mitchell rubbed at his face with a handkerchief. Then he went to a bureau drawer and took out a bottle of Scotch. He poured some in a glass, drank it and took a deep, shuddering breath.

"All right." He looked over at Madrid. "I'll go back with you." His pale eyes glistened. "I don't seem to have much choice, do I?"

"A couple of things." Sol was crisp. "I still have a job to do here; something I will have to come back and finish. My cover is complete. Batuc and the others take me for what I am supposed to be. I can't endanger it by taking you out of Mexico myself. You'll be flown to Tijuana in a Mexican Government plane. An American officer will meet you there and take you to Los Angeles. There will be protection for you every mile of the way. I'll follow by regular airline. No one in Hermosillo must even suspect there is a connection between your movements and mine. A Bureau man by the name of Collins, in Los Angeles, will arrange your hotel accommodations and you will be given a twenty-four-hour-a-day guard. As for Scarpi, he will be arrested here within an hour on a charge of bringing a gun into Mexico without a permit. He will not know you have left. No one in Chicago will hear of it. You'll be all right. This much I promise."

Mitchell nodded a dull assent. Nothing seemed important any longer. What was to have been the great adventure with glamour and excitement had ended in the failure which had been the pattern of his life.

"One more thing," Madrid continued. "I can't risk coming back here again today. At three o'clock Jalisco will be hanging around the lobby. You will go down and hire a car as you have done before, engaging Jalisco. The car's driver will be an officer of the Mexican police. He will take you to the airport and to Tijuana. Our men will be waiting at the International border. It will be simple, fast and safe."

Harvey sat down again. He had listened without interest. The moves were being made for him. He studied the carpet at his feet and then glanced up at Madrid.

"The money? I have some cash and the rest in a check on the bank."

"The Bureau has no interest in the money. As far as the United States Government is concerned, it doesn't exist. As far as I know, Villanova never reported an embezzlement to the police. You are not wanted by the law and the money is yours. Keep it for what it is worth. You may still get a chance to have some fun out of it."

Surprisingly, Harvey Mitchell began to laugh. Fun? He had never really known what the word meant. A quarter of a million dollars and all it had done was to weigh him down as he tried to run.

13

 IN one of the palm-shaded bungalows on the grounds of
the Beverly Hills Hotel Dano Villanova awoke, as he had for the past
three mornings, to a seething anger. He glanced across at the twin of
his bed and studied the girl lying there. She slept in a curled position.
Blond hair fell over one cheek and her mouth, in sleep, had a soft
petulance. He thrust a leg out from beneath the covers, stretched
and kicked her. She stirred and finally awoke with a drowsy reluctance but no resentment.

"Call room service and order some breakfast." He reached for his
cigarettes on the night table.

"All right, honey." She was submissive; yawned and then, as a
delicate afterthought, covered her lips with a hand, patting at them
with fingertips. "What do you want?"

"For Christ's sake," he snapped, "do you have to be so dumb?
You ought to know what I eat by now. Juice. Coffee. Danish."

It never occurred to the girl to protest his surly mood. She had ad-
justed herself to him and it. He was always bad-tempered these days.
She never even wondered why. Gentleness, consideration, a small
respect, just weren't part of the bargain. She had clothes, furs, jewels,
charge accounts, an apartment and car back in Chicago. A girl

would have to be out of her mind to expect more. Knowing this, she was careful not to irritate him or she might lose what she had. Sometimes, after he had gone to sleep, she would think a little wistfully how wonderful California could be if Dano were different. She gave the breakfast order now and then propped herself on one elbow, looking over at him. He lay on his back scowling and smoking. Idly she wondered what he was thinking about in this black humor. She was also curious as to why they had come to California. He never wanted to do anything like dance, go to a night club, have people in for a party. During the day he sat by the pool, wearing dark glasses, drinking orange juice and reading the papers. At night they had food sent to the bungalow. Now and then someone called George came to the hotel. He seemed to be some sort of a press agent or something. He and Dano played gin rummy and never talked; at least, not when she was around. Once he had told her to take her clothes off in front of George so he could see a "stacked broad." No one was embarrassed.

Waiting for room service, she thought Dano had never really been what she would have called nice. Secretly, she wondered why he kept her. Sometimes he made love to her but not often. He was real good in bed when he wanted to be; rough, mean and growling. For kicks she used to imagine she was being raped by a gorilla. For the past couple of days he had become increasingly irritable and his explosive anger was frightening. Like last night. A fellow by the name of Johnson or Jensen, something like that, had come to the bungalow. Dano sent her into the bedroom. She could hear them talking and Dano's voice rising. Now and then the man would mumble something. He was scared and apologizing, making excuses.

Dano had yelled, "You stupid bastard, I told you to keep track of her! That's what I wanted. To see her hooked and crawling. So, she's lost. Well, you'd damned better find her and quick."

Jensen, if that was his name, tried to explain. She could hear the whining note in his voice. Then Dano was hitting him. The sound of fist on flesh and bone came clearly. Jensen was whimpering, pleading. She could almost see him backing away, trying to cover himself. Finally there was the slam of a door and then quiet. After awhile she went back into the living room. On the floor was a bloodstained handkerchief on which Dano had wiped his raw knuckles. At her entrance he whirled about.

"Shut your goddamned mouth," he snapped.

"But, honey," she protested wonderingly, "I didn't say anything."

He had slapped her across the face then. It was a vicious, senseless blow which made her cry because it was the way a brutal man might kick an inoffensive dog.

He drank a lot of brandy that night and then had the operator place a call for Mexico. Whomever he talked with there had only made him angrier and he finally slammed the receiver down and then spat on the instrument. It had made her a little sick.

Now he was sitting up in bed with the telephone on his lap and telling the operator to get him Mexico again. It was some place called Hermosillo. He wanted a man named Carlo Scarpi at the Hotel Monique.

The waiter came with the breakfast table and she cautioned him to silence with finger at mouth. He tiptoed out after a wary glance at Villanova. Dano was yelling at the hotel operator.

"Get me someone down there who speaks English, real English so I can understand what he's saying."

She poured coffee. He reached over for the orange juice, drank it and took a swallow of coffee. She lit a fresh cigarette for him and he took it without acknowledgment. The call was completed and he asked for Mr. Scarpi. Whatever it was the operator said in Mexico only made him angrier. He demanded the manager and repeated his request for Scarpi. He listened and then shouted.

"What the hell do you mean he's in jail? What for? He's an American citizen. What did he do? Well, how do I find out? All right. All right. Let it go." He hung up. "How do you figure a dumb-head like that?" He wasn't speaking to her. "Getting himself picked up like any cheap punk. Jesus! Isn't there anyone around who can do a decent job anymore?"

"Are we going to Mexico, honey?" she asked hopefully.

"Shut up and eat your breakfast. Go take a bath. Do anything."

"I always take a shower in the morning." She was offended.

"Then go stick your head in the toilet." He finished his coffee.

In the paneled room high above Chicago's dirty streets the *Commissione* was gathered at the long table. There was only one empty chair, the one at the head reserved for the *Capo*. That it was vacant was a matter of the traditional *cortesia,* the respect accorded the *Capo* even when he was not present. No one would have thought to occupy it even though the elders of the *borgata* were gathered for the sole purpose of discussing the future of Dano Villanova.

For what seemed to be a long time no one said anything. The ones who smoked drew reflectively upon their cigars and stared past those sitting opposite them. The others made small, meaningless marks on little pads of paper or sat with their hands clasped, waiting patiently for the senior member to speak. This, also, was the *cortesia.* No one was restless or in a hurry, for this thing was of somber importance and must be approached with thought and dignity.

Alberto Petrucci was as dry, weathered and gnarled as a Monterey cypress. He still had the hawk's eye and his mind, despite seventy-five years, was sharply honed. When he spoke, his words came with a harsh, grating sound. He talked and his hands, twisted with arthritis though they were, made flowing and decisive gestures.

"So we make a mistake and don't cry over it like old women. Just the same we got a problem." The statement came abruptly and when he talked, the sentences were a blend of Italian and accented English. They had all acquired this habit. "Maybe he was too young to take what we give him but it didn't seem so at the time. He had the fire and was full of moxie. Something we all lost. Now we gotta decide what to do."

There was a soft murmur of assent but no one ventured an opinion.

"What," Petrucci continued evenly, "we gotta look at today is the danger. A thing should have been done quickly but it wasn't. Dano's mind's been on something else. A muff! At the bottom of all trouble with a stud like Dano you find a muff. His brains go to his balls. He don't think of nothin' else." He allowed himself a thin smile. "Even I was once like that. So, maybe we all remember how it was to be young but it don't settle nothin' for us. What this Mitchell took don't mean nothin'. Dano made it good with his own money. But we got this Mitchell alive. He runs because he knows someone runs behind him. Maybe he gets real scared. He goes to the Federals and makes a deal. They give him protection. He talks. Then we got real trouble. It ain't like one of them Congress investigations with only a lot of talk. This is, maybe, a federal grand jury with indictments, like they call them."

No one interrupted. This had all been discussed in pairs or threes.

"So," Petrucci did not pause, "we gotta first get this Mitchell hit. He can't be that smart. First he gets away from Gaines and now this Scarpi says he can't get near him. All right. We give out a dozen contracts on him no matter what it cost. One of them gets him and the mouth is shut. So, now, we come to Dano. We don't take the *Capo* outa the chair like he was a Chairman of the Board an' ask him to resign. In all my life I don't remember no more than maybe, a couple of times when the 'family' let a contract on the *Capo*. It ain't an easy thing to do. It shakes everything from top to bottom. Like they say, it rocks the boat. Just the same this is, maybe, what we gotta do." He paused and looked about the table. "And we're all, maybe, a little tired. Who takes Dano's place? You, Barbetta? You, Valetti? You, Mario? Someone must sit there. Dano forgets his duty."

"We vote the same as always." This was Barbetta, almost as old as Petrucci.

None of them really wanted the honor, the responsibility. Yet, the position had its roots deep in time. The head of the "family" went back to the earliest days of the Sicilian Mafia, where the life of a man could be completely dominated by the organization, and the patriarch carried with him an almost mystical aura and undisputed power. It was inconceivable to these men, reared in such a tradition, that the chair at the head of the table should be even temporarily unoccupied.

One by one they wrote a name on the pads before them; tore off the sheet, folded it and pushed it with the others to the table's center.

"You, Mario," Petrucci directed, "make the count."

"Petrucci," Mario read from the first slip. "Petrucci. Petrucci. Petrucci." There was no break. No other name intruded.

Petrucci stood up. There was no gratification in his expression. His eyes roved from one member of the *Commissione* to the other and he nodded his acceptance.

"I am too old for the honor, but I guess maybe we all are except Mario here." He moved slowly from his place to the table's head and, after a moment's hesitation, seated himself in Dano Villanova's chair. His hands rested on the arms, his head was bent in thought. Then he straightened. "Always the family sticks together. You, Mario, I make *Sotto Capo* and put weight on your shoulders. Find out what's with this Mitchell business and why Scarpi does not fill out the contract. I want it done if it takes a dozen men. We get rid of him before he makes trouble."

Mario made no reply. None was expected of him. The order had been given.

"Now," Petrucci's tone carried with it a note of regret, "we gotta come to Dano. It's too bad but we got no choice. I myself will take care of this. A man goes to Los Angeles. The hit is made. It is finished." He leaned forward on his arms. "The business of the family goes good. We got a fine organization with everything under control. So, before I sit too long in this chair I'm gonna take a little vacation. I think, maybe, I ask my daughter, son-in-law and two grandchildren with me to Hot Springs. I lie in the baths for awhile. They don't do my arthritis no good but the kids like the Springs so I pretend Grandpa enjoys it too. We talk together again after Dano and Mitchell are taken care of."

He arose and the others followed. His gaze rested on them individually for a second or two. Then he nodded.

"Such a long time together, all of us. You do me a great honor. I would like to be forty years younger. That is the age to be the *Capo*. Not now." He took his hat and walked with painful slowness from the room.

Corona is indistinguishable from a thousand other Southern California towns of similar size. Somehow, they all look alike. It lies southeast of Los Angeles in the citrus and farming belt and only one thing sets it apart from the surrounding communities. In 1961 the California legislature enacted into law a Civil Addict Program, and Corona was selected as the site for this experiment. The buildings are loosely known as the Corona Rehabilitation Center.

Here a drug addict may voluntarily commit himself for treatment. Or, as often happens, he or she may be sent there at the request of a relative, through the district attorney's office or at the order of a judge. It is, for many, the last, desperate effort to save themselves from the torture and misery of lives which have become unbearable. These were the voluntary patients and their period of commitment is two and one-half years. For those who are sent by court order, the time is seven years. In special cases the volunteers, upon recommendation of the staff, may leave after six months. But he or she is subjected to the strictest outside supervision. Five times a month the addict must report and take the Nalline test, which shows immediately if the use of drugs has been resumed. When the test is "positive" the user is returned for further treatment.

Stacey Woodward was at a desk near a window cataloguing some books which had been donated to the Center's small library. She worked with unhurried efficiency, sometimes smiling a little as she glanced through one of the volumes or noted an absurd title. The sunlight caught the new sheen of her honey-colored hair and tinted a fresh glow upon her skin. There was health here now and a vitality. The horror had not left an indelible stigmata. This was a hospital, a sanitarium, but strict security measures were enforced. She had not chafed under them. There was no rebellion. In her there was only gratitude for the miracle which had brought her back to life.

She had not been unhappy here. Her commitment had been voluntary after that first, terrible night when a stranger, Eddie Collins, had answered her lonely cry for help and come to take her from the bar in Santa Monica. It was difficult now to recall the incredible agony of withdrawal. It had been a time when she thought she must go completely insane. She knew now she would have committed any crime, including murder, for a fix. Then, slowly, time began to work for her. The craving and appetite lost its consuming fury. She awoke to no uncertain day of terror. A measure of confidence returned. She could talk calmly, in the therapy sessions, of the addiction. Unlike many of the others she never spoke of the manner in which she had become an addict. Most of the patients had gone the same route. First had come the Benzedrine, the "goof pills," to give them a lift. Then followed the marijuana to relieve a fit of depression, a disappointment, an unhappy love affair, a feeling of inadequacy. Then a sniff of cocaine, an injection of morphine. Finally, the H from which there was no escape. Always there was a pusher lurking nearby.

There was a sharp but unadmitted distinction between those who had come voluntarily for treatment and those who had been committed to the Center by despairing relatives or the courts. The latter arrived with sullen anger, filled with resentment and hatred. They schemed endlessly to have a fix smuggled to them or to escape and lose themselves in the murky world of the addict. They were the disturbed and adolescent, or delinquent, mentalities who had sought in the drug a bulwark against a society with which they were unable to cope. Most of them would return to the habit. Upon release they would gravitate to familiar haunts, seeking old companions. The addict found he had nothing in common with those who were not also users and so they tended to move in tight, clannish circles. They would seek them out with a sure instinct and set their feet once more upon the thorn-strewn path.

No one was really sure how successful the program of the Center was. The volunteers had the best chance. They, at least, had recognized themselves and their lives for what they were and wanted help. It had never occurred to Stacey, once she had passed the initial stages of treatment, she would want to return to the drug. She was free. Of this she was certain.

Eddie Collins had been a frequent visitor; coming, perhaps, more often than the regulations permitted. Stacey thought he probably used his position with the Bureau of Narcotics to have the rules bent a little. But he had been there when her need to reach out and touch someone had been the greatest, and all the professional therapy in the world would not have satisfied the desperate longing for companionship. She wanted to be reassured she still belonged in a world of normal people. Collins, with compassion and a rare understanding, provided the mental bridge over which she could cross from the dark horror into the light. In him she had discovered warmth and humor and she thought this a startling contradiction. The very nature of his work should have made him callous and impatient with an addict. Instead, he seemed to share their misery. In her life there had been no other man who would have taken the trouble to help lift a stranger from the pit. In her heart there was affection and gratitude.

Once, when they were permitted to walk about the grounds in the approaching dusk, she had asked him about this.

"Does this happen to you often? I mean, the contact with an addict?"

"No." He had smiled at her. "You're my first case. In my job we deal with the source, trying to shut it off. The users fall to the police. But then," he had reached to take her hand, "you were not an addict as we usually define one."

At first she knew he did not believe her story. It was a crutch, an excuse, an outrageous fabrication. No one ever had addiction forced upon him by physical restraint. When he finally realized she was telling the truth, she could feel his tightly controlled fury. His expression had hardened, his voice became charged with bitter anger. Thereafter when he came he questioned her in minute detail, going over her recitation many times, trying to catch something he might have missed. What about this farmhouse which she thought was somewhere in the San Fernando Valley? Wasn't there anything she could remember which might provide a clue? The sound of a train at a certain time of day or night? An airplane or airplanes passing at approximately the same hour each day? The sound of trucks on a nearby highway? When someone left to replenish the food stock how long did it usually take to get to the village, market or town and back? Could she recall the last names of any of those who held her prisoner? She could only tell him one. It was Jensen and was, probably, a surname. The house and barn or garage? It seemed as though the buildings were within or on the edge of an orange grove. She had never been outside in the daytime; had no idea of the shape of the house or on what sort of a tributary road it stood. As to the other queries, she was unable even to answer partially. After the first couple of days her life, her world, were fixed upon one thing alone. The time when the woman would come with the syringe and needle. She lived, existed, for this. Nothing else was real.

"You're not much help." He was disappointed. "I'd like to nail the bastards. I've been around a long time but this is something new. What sort of a mind would conceive of putting a girl on the junk because she hurt his self-esteem, his ego?"

"Dano," she replied simply. "Dano Villanova. If you knew him, you would understand. Even I underestimated him."

One thing she did remember—the name of the contact, the pusher, in Santa Monica. Paul. She described him the best she could, the apartment house in which he lived, the neighborhood. These things she told to Collins.

"It's a start." He was pleased. "We'll pick him up and maybe if I can get a little time alone with him, he'll talk. In time," he was encouraging, "something will come to you. It may give us a lead."

Once she asked him about Sol Madrid, for the memory of the man remained with her. What had he said that brought Collins to answer her call from Santa Monica and lift her from the gutter?

"Sol?" He lingered over the name with a quiet smile. "He didn't say much and that made me think it was important to him. It certainly wasn't enough to send me out on what I was pretty certain must be the wild ramblings of a lushed-up dame. I guess maybe it was the way he sort of dropped you in my lap. We've been friends for a long time and there is an obligation between us. All he said was: 'There's a girl by the name of Stacey Woodward. I have a feeling she may need help. I gave her the Bureau number. If she calls, do what you can. She's something special.'" Collins' eyes lighted. "I always figured Madrid had gypsy blood in him. Perhaps he reads tea leaves. Anyhow, he feels things before they happen and he's usually right." He looked down into her upturned face. "You are something special."

She could feel the hot rush of tears start and held them back with a tremulous effort. That these two men, strangers to her, should have cared enough overwhelmed her.

"I sensed something about him." She spoke reflectively. "There was this baffling contradiction. It was as though I sat with two men who looked and sounded alike but were completely different. One was cold, driven, impersonal. The other? I was never quite sure about him. He had a gentleness."

Collins regarded her with surprise. "I think you and I are the only two persons in the world who would describe Sol Madrid as *gentle*. But he is. He is, also, the big cat, the hunter, the jungle stalker of infinite patience. He never gives up. There isn't a rule in the book he wouldn't break to corner a man he was after."

"That night—the only time I was with him—he said he was going to Mexico. Is he still there?"

"He has his paw on a rabbit but the claws aren't out. He's waiting to see what will come sniffing around. The Bureau has left him pretty well on his own and he hasn't passed on much information. The rabbit is your friend Harvey Mitchell."

In the early days of her recovery, when he had first come to see her, she had told Collins everything. The words spilled from her compulsively. It was as though by speaking of everything that came to mind she was purging herself of old memories, fears and uncertainties. She had started with her early background and carried the story through her relationship with Villanova, sparing herself nothing.

"Does he know about me? What happened?"

"No." Collins was grave. "You really aren't official business. I don't know whose business you are. Mine, I guess."

She smiled now and realized with a start she had been sitting idly at the table allowing her thoughts to wander while the work of cataloguing the new books went unattended. With an effort she put both Collins and Madrid out of her mind and rolled a file card into the typewriter.

In the hotel room high above downtown Los Angeles, Harvey Mitchell stood looking out at the bewildering complex of the freeways. On them the automobiles rushed like frantic beetles, diving on and off the ramps, swerving, curling through the interchange of lanes with what seemed to be an unbelievable recklessness and missing complete disaster by inches. Mitchell was not really aware of what he watched. It was all unreal, the fragment of a disordered dream. Behind him his breakfast, save for the coffee, remained untouched. At the table a man in his late thirties, a United States marshal, ate complacently of the bacon, eggs, cottage fried potatoes and hot rolls. He was, in Mitchell's eyes, obnoxiously healthy and cheerfully convivial. In one hand he held a copy of the Los Angeles *Times* and read as he chewed contentedly. Now and then he glanced over at Mitchell's spiritless back.

"You ought to eat something, Mr. Mitchell." The suggestion was made without any real interest.

"I'm not hungry."

They occupied a suite of two bedrooms with the connecting door open. As Madrid had promised, his departure from Hermosillo was without incident. A plane of the Mexican Government had flown him to the Tijuana airport. A motorcycle escort sped and protected his car to the border. There two American agents accompanied him in an unmarked limousine to Los Angeles. They had gone directly to these rooms where Madrid and the marshal waited.

There was no spirit left in Harvey Mitchell. He moved and spoke with a heavy weariness. Everything had been for nothing. The dream had been only a dream after all. He listened without expression when Madrid had detailed the measures taken for his safety. The United States marshal would be with him at all times. Every person already occupying rooms or coming to this floor had been or would be carefully screened. No word of his presence in Los Angeles would be leaked. Tomorrow a stenographer would take down a detailed deposition, everything he could answer in reply to the Bureau's questions concerning the Chicago *borgata* of *Cosa Nostra*. Later he would be called to testify before a federal grand jury.

Madrid had recited these things with calm preciseness. Not by the slightest shade of expression did he betray the satisfaction he felt. By this incalculable stroke of luck, the one in a million chance of Dano Villanova's accountant defecting and then falling into its hands, the Government was moving toward the strangulation of at least part of a many-bodied monster. Sol did not delude himself. The indictments which the grand jury must certainly return would not erase the dark shadow of *Cosa Nostra*. Actually, they would only lop off one of the tentacles of the octopus. But they would also shake the power and send a wave of fear and apprehension throughout its nervous system. Names would be named, the false faces of respectability torn away, the dummy corporations exposed, the interlocking units of vice and corruption spread out in the open for all to see. The Government, Sol knew, at times seemed to move with a ponderous ineptitude. The results were often obscured by the time it took to achieve them. But a Luciano was deported, a Costello convicted. A Bugsy Siegal was murdered by his own because pressure had driven him to rashness and he was no longer considered a good risk by his superiors. A Cohen was convicted of income tax fraud, a labor leader went to jail for misuse of funds. The punishment did not always fit the crime and sometimes appeared to have no relation to it. The ways of justice had to be devious. Sol had no illusions. Harvey Mitchell was a rare prize. His testimony would unlock many doors and lead law enforcement officers into obscure and unexplored back alleys of crime. It would throw a net of strangulation over the

Chicago *borgata* but it would not cover, in this single cast, all those who operated beyond its perimeter. The contest between good and evil was as old as man and it could never really end. There was no ultimate and complete victory to be achieved by either side. Sol knew this. Every cop on a neighborhood beat, the FBI and a county deputy sheriff knew it. Crime was the world's fever. It could be reduced locally now and then but never fully cured. So Madrid did not indulge himself in any specious triumph. Reviewing what had been accomplished, he experienced a familiar weariness. Tomorrow, the day after, next week, the endless pursuit would go on. It was, he thought with grim humor, a theatrical trick which took place on a continuous treadmill.

"You going to eat your bacon, Mr. Mitchell?" The young marshal had a healthy appetite and this assignment was an unexpected stroke of good luck. "It's getting cold."

"No. Help yourself if you want it."

"Something I can get you?" There was the sound of a modulated chuckle. "Mr. Madrid said you could have anything you wanted. But I guess that doesn't include dames and liquor. It sort of limits our diversions." He transferred the four slices of bacon from Harvey's plate to his own.

Mitchell experienced a wave of nausea. His ineptitude, the dismal defeat, the recognition of his puny capacity for mastery were all bad enough. But to be locked in with a pink-cheeked buffoon made him want to scream against the outrage of misfortune. They had him boxed in. There was no escape. Not for one moment did he question Madrid's threat. If he refused to testify, Madrid would put the finger on him for Carlo Scarpi or someone else. Of this he was certain. Madrid would have no scruples. He meant exactly what he had said back in Hermosillo. So, he would give his testimony to a federal grand jury. Villanova and some others might possibly go to jail, but even this had a question mark. There would be elaborate legal maneuvers; months, and possibly years, would pass. What of Harvey Mitchell all this time? Protective custody. He felt himself on the verge of hysterical laughter. They couldn't possibly protect him. He stood here, a man marked for execution. He was already dead but no one mourned. No one gave a damn. Harvey Mitchell? Who was he? Oh yes! Something to do with that *Cosa Nostra* investigation. Wonder whatever happened to him? Mitchell vomited suddenly and the filth spilled upon the carpet.

Madrid and Eddie Collins had breakfast in the oak-paneled men's grill. They lingered over their coffee and cigarettes with the easy companionship of old friends.

"The Old Man never says much," Collins smiled, "but he's pretty set up over this Mitchell thing. You might even get a District out of it."

Sol shook his head. "All I want is for you and the Bureau to keep Harvey alive and talkative."

"The Old Man was on the phone to Colonel Ortega last night. He's sending you back to Hermosillo to finish the job there."

"It figures." Madrid was glumly resigned. "I'd like to sit by the stove and warm my hands for awhile though." He grinned quickly. "I'm a fast operator down there. This Batuc and Vargas still can't figure how I have the fix-in at so many places on the border. It sure marks you and the Customs men lousy." He lit a fresh cigarette. "After awhile you forget who you really are. This Lieutenant Mendoza. He actually believes he is someone called Jalisco, a pimp and petty thief, a guide for a stray tourist. He's one hell of a man to work with."

"So are you, my *gitano* friend." Collins turned a lump of sugar slowly between his fingers, staring at it thoughtfully. "Before you went to Mexico you gave me the name of a girl. Remember?"

Sol looked up with quick interest. "Yes, sure. Stacey Woodward. Villanova's girl. She sort of got to me. I'm damned if I know why. It was a strange evening. What about her?"

"She made a call one night." Collins put aside the sugar he had been toying with. "I don't know what made you think she would but she did. She was in big trouble and needed help."

"So?" Madrid waited.

Carefully, omitting nothing but making the sentences as terse and sharply factual as he would in a written report, Collins told Madrid everything he knew of what happened to Stacey Woodward. As he talked Sol's face darkened with a savage anger.

"The bastards. The dirty bastards." His words came with a softly dangerous intensity.

"She's at Corona now," Collins finished. "I've," he hesitated, "well, I've seen her. She's all right. They'll give her probation. She's not worried about getting out."

"You never got a line on the house where they kept her?"

"How?" Collins made a gesture of helplessness. "She just thinks it's in the Valley somewhere. A dog used to bark at night. What the hell does that mean? There are thousands of dogs on thousands of farms in the Valley. Every time I see her I make her talk about it, hoping she'll remember something."

Sol glanced across the table. "Every time you see her?" The question had an inescapable implication.

"All right." Collins was actually embarrassed. "So I've been driving out once a week, sometimes twice a week when I get time. Anything wrong with that?"

"Why should there be anything wrong with it?" Madrid laid some bills and change on the check and stood up. "Let's get back to the shop."

"You act like you were sore or something."

"Why should I be sore?"

"How the hell do I know?" They were outside now and Collins had to raise his voice above the traffic sounds.

"What are you yelling for?"

"I'm not yelling at you, Spik bastard." He all but glared at Madrid. "If there was something between you two you should have said so."

"There isn't anything between us. I saw her once."

"All right." They worked their way along the crowded sidewalk. "I thought I'd go out again on Sunday. I usually do. She's asked about you. Maybe you want to come along?"

"I'll probably be on my way back to Mexico by Sunday."

"No one's pushing. The Old Man will give you about anything you want right now. Take some time off. A week or so won't make any difference in the setup down there."

"Maybe." Madrid's hand went to Collins' shoulder, steering him into the Federal Building's entrance. His eyes grew bright with amusement. "Jesus, but you're a lousy actor. Don't ever try to go underground. They'd tag you in five minutes. If you've got a big thing going for Woodward say so."

Collins looked back and his face broke into a wide smile.

"Me Pancho. You Cisco Kid. Ho Kay?"

They walked through the Bureau's central room, down a corridor with partitioned rooms and into Collins' office. Madrid dropped into the one comfortable chair, deep and upholstered in worn leather. He lit a cigarette and Collins settled himself behind a desk. He riffled through some papers and finally selected one, tossing it over toward Madrid.

"I forgot to tell you about this. A routine memo from the Beverly Hills Police Department. Villanova is in town."

Madrid jerked upright, reached for the paper and read it carefully. Then he replaced it on the desk.

"I might," he said carefully, "just take a little time off at that. I haven't checked in any place yet. The Beverly Hills Hotel sounds good."

The telephone rang. Collins picked up the instrument.

"Collins speaking."

He listened without comment for a minute and then slowly, carefully, put the receiver back on its cradle. He stared at it and then lifted his glance to meet Madrid's eyes.

"Your pigeon, Mitchell, just went out a twelfth-story window. No one told him he couldn't fly."

Without a word Madrid mashed the cigarette out on the floor with his shoe, grinding his heel into it. He arose and his features had hardened into a cold mask. He crossed the room and then, as an afterthought, turned.

"About that time off. Tell the Old Man I'm taking it. Right now I'm going out and get just about as drunk as one man can get."

The door closed with a sharp, nicking sound behind him.

14

THE curtains of bright chintz which framed the windows, the amber sheen of bamboo furniture and the linoleum with its polished squares of color didn't quite overcome the faintly antiseptic atmosphere of a sanitarium. The reception room of the Center, despite all efforts, remained stiffly formal. There was no real invitation to linger here. The place held no echo of laughter.

Standing by a center table with its neat stacks of magazines, Sol watched her as she crossed toward him with an eager stride. She walks, he thought, in the beauty of dignity. What might have destroyed a lesser person had left no visible scar. There was a pride of carriage and he was strangely moved by it. Nearing him, her steps slowed and the final yard or so was covered almost hesitantly. Her bright and vivid smile faded to the hopeful expression of a child who wasn't certain of its welcome. The hands which had been extended still reached for his but the gesture now was tentative, shy.

"Hello, Sol Madrid." The words were husky with emotion. "I hoped you'd come someday."

He took her hands, covering them with his own. The faintest trembling betrayed a nervousness and then the fingers tightened and linked with his in a return of confidence. For a second it seemed as though she tried to strain upward to reach his cheek with her lips. She waited, almost poised on the tips of her toes, and then relaxed.

"Should we sit down?"

He looked about him with obvious distaste. It was a cheerless place, without warmth. His reluctance displayed itself in a small frown.

"It's the best we have." She led him to the couch. "As it is you're stretching things with the Superintendent. This isn't a visitor's hour or even day."

She sat, tucking one leg beneath her. Neither seemed to be aware that one hand still held his. With his free one he worked a package of cigarettes out from a jacket pocket and offered her one. She shook her head, freed his hand so he could light one for himself, and then retook it.

"You've had it rough?"

"Yes, I've had it rough. So has everyone else here. It could have been worse. Many times I've wondered what prompted you to give me Eddie's," she faltered, "Mr. Collins' name and telephone number."

He smiled a little for the first time. "I guess you can call him Eddie."

"Yes." Her eyes brightened and there was amusement behind them. "I guess I can call him Eddie. Why did you do it?"

"A hunch. It isn't easy to explain. I get a feeling about things sometimes."

"Eddie says your mother ran a gypsy tearoom and you read tea leaves in a cup."

"No," he was solemn, "I burn chicken feathers in a graveyard at midnight. Through the smoke I see the future."

Watching the all but imperceptible play of mood over Madrid's face she had a desire to trace her fingers across the lithic features as a blind person might seek to feel and identify what could not be seen. How, she wondered hopelessly, to tell this man of the gratitude filling her heart? Words would not do it. She could only hope he would somehow understand.

"You look tired—drawn."

"It's a hangover. I went on a blast. It was pretty stupid. Kid stuff. I brought Mitchell back from Mexico. With him I could have torn Villanova and the Chicago family apart. The damn fool committed suicide before I was able to get him before a grand jury. By the way, Villanova is in Beverly Hills." He watched her.

"I guess I'm a disappointment to him. It didn't work out the way he planned. He wanted to see me crawling. All that trouble for nothing. Poor Dano." She spoke the name with grim humor. "He gets upset when something fails. I'll say this for him though. He really had it set up."

"You've been all right here? They try."

"Yes, I've been all right. Do you mind if I do something?" She didn't wait for a reply but laid her hand against his cheek, held it there with infinite tenderness for a moment and then took it away without embarrassment. "After," she continued evenly, "after I was able to think at all beyond myself, I thought of you often. I tried to imagine where you were, what you were doing. And," now she looked up at him, mystified by what she was about to say, "I could never really see you in my mind. Always, and this is the strange thing, you were a starkly drawn figure, lonely on a great, empty plain. I know"—she rushed the words—"this doesn't make sense. I wanted to cry for you. I'm not sure why I feel the need to say what I have."

He studied the gray ash on his cigarette, perplexed by what she had said. It was a feeling he experienced many times; a loneliness of unreality. How could she possibly be this intuitive, this sensitive? For they were little more than strangers. He reached behind him and put the cigarette out in a tray.

"In my trade you walk alone much of the time. It has to be that way. The really good men at the job have few friends and usually no family. I don't know how you could know that. Now," he switched manner and voice abruptly, "I want you to start from the beginning and tell me everything as it happened."

"Oh!" There was a weary dismay in the protest. "I've gone over it all with Eddie Collins dozens of times."

"All right. Just the same, I want you to tell it to me."

She sighed. "I'll take a cigarette then."

He lit one for her and then settled back, eyes half-closed. She spoke slowly but without hesitation, beginning with the assault on the street in Westwood and through it all until the night when, in the final torment of desperation, she had called Eddie Collins. He listened without comment until she finished.

"At the house—what did you wear? Did they go to Westwood for your clothes? That would have been the sensible thing; to pay your bill, check you out with some story. The management must have eventually notified the police you had disappeared. It would be normal procedure."

"No." She was mystified by his questions. "For the first few days I wore what I had. It was a new," she said this ruefully, "black, lightweight knit. I was wearing it for the first time. After that I wore a robe they gave me. And after that I don't know. I didn't care. Maybe I walked around naked. It didn't make any difference. You can understand that."

"But," he stared at the floor with a moody concentration, "when you were really hooked and they let you go? The night they dropped you off on 101 near Santa Monica or Malibu. What did you have on?"

"My own clothes, of course." There was an edge of impatience. "Oh, they fixed me up!" The tone was suddenly bitter. "I was supposed to hustle any man I could for the money I had to have. The woman did my hair and nails. My stockings had been torn. They bought me new ones. My dress was freshly cleaned and blocked."

"What!" He sat upright.

"I said," she was startled, "I said my dress had been cleaned and blocked. Shaped. They do that with knits."

"Was this something anyone at the house could have done?"

"Of course not." Her smile was patient, indulgent. "It would have to be done at a cleaner's, professionally."

For the first time he really smiled. The expression broke across his face as sun moving upon a shadow. He was a man, baffled by a puzzle, who came unexpectedly upon the missing piece.

"Did I say something?" Her surprise was complete.

"I think maybe you said something. Where is it? The dress? The knit?"

"Here. With my other things. Eddie brought them from West-wood. I don't know what he told the management."

"Go and get it. The dress."

She stared uncomprehendingly at him for a moment, shrugged and left. He stretched his legs before him, slouching comfortably into a corner of the couch. Relaxed. When she came back, the black knit was over one arm. She handed it to him without comment and then regarded him quizzically.

"You're being pretty damn smug about something."

He grinned. "If they had it cleaned then there is a cleaner's mark on it somewhere, the label maybe, in invisible ink. I'll take it to the FBI. When the laboratory boys finish we'll be able to trace it down to the town, the cleaner's. And when we have those things we'll be getting close to whoever brought it in. After that it won't be much of a job to locate the house and the people."

"Poor Eddie."

It wasn't at all what he had expected her to say and his eyebrows lifted in question marks.

"Poor Eddie." There was unhappy sympathy in the statement. "He tried so hard. Every time he came I had to go over it for him. 'Tell me something you haven't remembered before,' he'd always say it. 'Think hard.' I wanted to give him something. It just never came."

"Don't worry about Eddie." He was reassuring. "He'll understand. He's the best man I know for the job he's in. This is a little different. It happens that way sometimes. You follow along a thread, looking for the knot but it isn't there. You wonder why. You keep telling yourself it has to be here. Then, someone else comes along and the touch is new, the fingers different; a little more sensitive, maybe. They feel the knot which has been slipping past you. There isn't anything occult about it." He stood up, folding the dress into a square. "I'd like to think I'll always be this lucky."

"Or smart." Her eyes were shining.

He winked. "It sounds better when you say it."

They walked together from the reception room and out into the foyer. A young woman at a desk looked up and smiled briefly at Madrid. Then she went back to checking some records in their manila envelopes. Just outside the doorway they halted. She reached for his hand and her fingers clung almost desperately.

"I won't see you again, will I, Sol Madrid." It should have been a question but it wasn't.

"No." He didn't like the way it sounded but there was no other answer. "No, I guess not."

"I didn't think so." There was what seemed to be an intolerably long silence. "Damn it, I won't cry. You can't make me." She was miserably defiant.

"Here." He didn't look at her but took a handkerchief from his pocket. "Blow your nose."

She did.

He put his arm about her shoulders and she pressed into his side, suddenly seeming small, frail, vulnerable, a forlorn waif.

"You'll be all right now. Eddie will take things over from here on in."

"Yes, I'll be all right."

"I have to go back to Mexico. You understand?"

"No." The word was barely audible.

"There'll always be a Mexico somewhere. It may be called something else. That's the only difference."

"You'll take care of yourself, please?"

"Sure."

She turned away abruptly, hurrying back through the double doors. He stood for a moment, staring straight ahead. Then he went down the steps slowly and toward his car where it was parked in the driveway.

In oatmeal-colored shorts, sandals on his feet, chest bare to the warm day, eyes hidden behind dark glasses, Dano Villanova studied the cards in his hand. The girl, aware of the fact she was annoying him, leaned over the back of his chair. She glanced across at the man named George. He was making an expert, hungry and greedy-eyed appraisal of her breasts beneath the crimson bandeau. She puckered her mouth into an expression of contemptuous indifference. Let the jerk look. She was sick of George and wondered if he was a fairy. He dressed like one. Corduroy jacket, pink slacks, alligator pumps with a strap and large brass buckle. If he wasn't a fairy he was a pimp. She spoke the ugly word to herself with satisfaction. Always sucking up to Dano. Running over to the hotel every day to play gin rummy. A little dog jumping eagerly when Dano whistled. She was sick of George. Maybe if he wasn't around all the time Dano would take her out someplace. For the lack of something better to do she reached past Dano's shoulder now and placed a carmined fingernail on the ten of clubs.

"You're nuts." Dano shoved her hand away. "He's got to be wanting that. What the hell do you know about the game?"

"I can count, can't I?"

"Up to five, maybe. Go away before I smack you."

"Boom! Boom! Big Gun."

She pulled back and dropped petulantly into a reclining chair within the shade of the huge colored umbrella sheltering the table. For awhile she admired her long legs and then idly glanced around the pool. There were couples and groups at tables, stretched out on pads, splashing in the water. All the men had bellies, soft, round, nasty pods with black hair on them. Their navels looked like eyeless sockets. They made her a little sick at her stomach.

"Gin." It was George's fluting voice. Triumphant.

"I told you to play the ten." She spoke to the cloudless sky with wide-eyed innocence.

"I told you to play the ten. I told you to play the ten." Villanova parroted her words with dangerous anger. "Whoever said I should listen to a goddamned linthead? Add it up, George. We quit now."

"Let it go. We'll carry the score over until tomorrow." George pushed back his chair and stood up.

She half turned on her side to look at him. "What do you do at night, George? You got a girl or something?"

"Sometimes."

"Maybe you could find me one. Huh?"

"A real wise broad." Dano snorted.

"Look . . ." George hesitated. Dano didn't like suggestions. "How about our going down to Caliente Sunday for the races? I got a connection. We get a box upstairs in the new part of the Turf Club. Have lunch. Make some bets. Have a few drinks. Pass the day."

She sat up in the chair. "Please, Dano." She was prettily eager. "We never do anything but sit around this damned hotel. Sunday's an awful time anyhow. Church bells and everything. Please. We have the new Continental you rented. It hasn't been out of the parking lot. Can't we go, honey? Please. I'll do anything you say."

"Hell! You do that anyhow."

"Yes," she stuck the tip of her tongue out at him, "but better this time, honey." The gesture was mockingly obscene.

"Broads." Dano yielded a little. "Always got to be doing something." He nodded at George. "OK, Georgie. Get us the box for Sunday."

"Sure." George was pleased. "Maybe we eat in Tijuana. I know a place. Venison steaks even out of season. We take in a little jai alai if you like and get some laughs in the strip joints. I'll be over tomorrow and give you a chance to get your money back. Take care."

Villanova watched him as he walked away. Then he turned to the girl.

"I think the son of a bitch cheats but I don't know how. He can't be smart enough to win all the time."

"Why do you keep him around? He gives me the creeps. He gets a wet mouth every time he looks at me."

Dano yawned. "The world is filled with little Georgies. They run their ass off trying to keep up with someone and never quite make it. So let his tongue hang out when he looks at you. What's the difference? He ain't going to get it."

"Isn't." This primly.

"Besides being wise you're getting educated too, huh?" Surprisingly he was in a good humor. He took one of the padded deck chairs beside her. "When you see a waiter, order me a gin tonic."

The corner room in the hotel's west wing was brightly decorated with pastel green walls and vivid splashes of color on the draperies. Seated in front of the windows overlooking the hotel's carefully cultivated gardens, the slender, silvered trunks of crested palms and geometrically designed plots of flowers, a woman rocked placidly in a chair. She was well past middle age and with a heavy, sagging body. But her eyes behind gold-rimmed spectacles were sharply inquisitive. She knitted with a slow patience but her gaze, for the most part, was held by the scene below. The pool, tables and bungalows;

the waiters and white-coated busboys; the guests drinking, talking, swimming, or just lying in the sun.

"My, but they all seem to be having such a nice time, Mr. Sammis."

She spoke without turning to a man lying on a studio couch. The day was warm but he wore a vest of gray wool that matched the trousers of his suit. His plain white shirt was fully buttoned and a tie neatly knotted in the collar. On the floor beside him were scattered half-a-dozen magazines. He held one in both hands, studying the photographs avidly. They were variously titled: *Sin, Siren, Playgirls, Artists' Models, Studio Secrets.* And there were page after page of naked, incredibly breasted girls in various and provocative poses. He was in his late fifties, completely undistinguished in appearance; a small-town merchant or pharmacist perhaps, enjoying the rare experience of a vacation in California.

"Wherever do you suppose they get the girls to pose for those magazines, Mr. Sammis?" She rocked contentedly and the needles worked in and out of the wool with a steady rhythm. "My goodness, I've never seen anything like it. The tits on them." The gutter noun was spoken without emphasis. "I wonder if their parents ever see those magazines? We'll have to go downtown to that place on Hollywood Boulevard near Gower Street and get you some more. You do enjoy them so."

Harry Sammis licked a finger and turned a page. He was barely aware of his wife's comments. There was a knock on the door. Reluctantly he diverted his eyes toward it.

"Come in."

"Well!" There was genuine pleasure on the woman's face. "It's Georgie. I saw you a little while ago down by the pool playing cards." She put aside her knitting and beamed upon him.

George shut the door carefully. He took a cigarette from a flat gold case and lit it.

"Well, Georgie?" Mr. Sammis dropped his magazine and struggled into a sitting position. "How is everything?"

George ignored the man and the question. He spoke to the woman.

"Is he still there?"

"Oh yes! He's lying in a chair beside the blond girl. They don't move around much, do they?"

"Now listen, both of you." George was crisp. "This is the way it is. I've talked him into going down to Tijuana and Caliente on Sunday. That's the best I could do."

"My goodness, Georgie, that isn't very much," the woman rebuked him gently.

"What the hell am I supposed to do?" George was edgy. "Stand him against a wall for you?"

"It would be nice, Georgie. But," she admitted regretfully, "I guess you couldn't do that. This has all been very difficult for Mr. Sammis. I mean, there he is in that bungalow right across from us but he never gives Mr. Sammis a chance; like coming out at night for a breath of fresh air. Mr. Sammis could do it very well then right from this window. With that new silencer he uses it wouldn't sound much more than like someone cracking a peanut. Or," she continued chattily, "if he'd sit in the bungalow parlor without those shades down all the time so a person could see him. He never does. Mr. Sammis is very annoyed with him. Mr. Sammis says he must spend all of his time in bed with that blond girl."

"I'll tell Villanova how tough he's making it." George's sarcasm was wasted.

Mrs. Sammis picked up her knitting. "You remember how nice Bugsy Siegal fixed it for everyone? There was a gentleman who didn't cause trouble for people. He sat on a couch right in front of a window with a floor lamp behind him. A little boy could have done it with a B-B gun. I must say Mr. Sammis has been very patient with this Mr. Villanova. He doesn't seem to understand Mr. Sammis has other contracts. Right now we ought to be in Philadelphia attending to one. Although I must say, I do like California."

"What about this Caliente, Georgie?" Mr. Sammis spoke for the first time since George's arrival.

"I don't know." George shook his head. "We go to the races but I never heard of a hit being made in a Turf Club. It's a problem. Anyhow, we go to the races. Then, afterwards, we maybe eat and take in some of the joints. I've got it fixed with a broad from Hollywood. She'll make like I picked her up at the track and join the party. It gives me an excuse to duck out with her sometime during the evening. Like we're going to a motel. This, Villanova would understand. Anyhow, it's going to leave Villanova and the blonde to come back to L.A. alone. If it's late enough and not much traffic, maybe you can make a hit from your car somewhere on the freeway. I don't know about those things. He's going to be driving a yellow Lincoln Continental. Maybe it would be better if you stayed here or got back ahead of them and do it as he goes into the bungalow. Anyhow, here are a couple of passes to the Turf Club." He dropped two tickets on a table. "You'll see us there. After that it's all up to you. I promised to get him out of the hotel. That I did. It wasn't easy. He's got something on his mind. Like they say, the *modus operandi* is your problem so you'd better *operandi*. Chicago wants him hit real fast and it can't be a hospital case. It's D.O.A. or nothing. Now, I got to go."

"You're a good young man, Georgie," the woman said approvingly. "You've been helpful. Mr. Sammis will think of something."

George left, closing the door behind him. Mrs. Sammis frowned over her knitting. Sometimes when she talked she dropped a stitch.

"If we go to the racetrack, Mr. Sammis," she resumed her rocking, "I want you to promise me you won't make any bets on the horses. After all, it will be Sunday."

In Eddie Collins' office Madrid had twisted himself into the leather chair. He was studying a memo from the Federal Bureau of Investigation's laboratory.

"So. It gets narrowed down to a place called Sunland and then the Elite Cleaners there."

"That's it." Collins was pleased.

"Maybe." Sol was not too confident. "The house may only have been a rental for just this one thing. They may have blown by now."

"No." Collins handed him a yellow slip. "This was on the teletype from the sheriff's office. The man Oscar Jensen owns the place. He grows some oranges and markets them to a juice-canning plant. One of the other two, a punk named Buddy Wells, is Jensen's nephew and shacks there with a girl who calls herself Faye Carter. The woman, Edna Kleemer, is a practical not a registered nurse and has a part-time job in a clinic at Tijunga. She goes in three times a week. They are all quiet and have never been in trouble. The best we can figure is that it is all a front for something. Maybe they use the place as a drop for H smuggled over from Tijuana or Mexicali and brought to the Valley. They probably cut it there for distribution."

"There would have to be a connection," Sol agreed. "Anyhow, it's all dropped into your lap now, Eddie."

"That's where I want it." The eyes were slate-cold. "We can make enough charges against them to pull in every law enforcement agency in the country. Assault. Abduction. Forcible detention. Narcotics. There's something for everyone from the Bureau to the FBI, the county sheriff and local police. There will be so many badges in on it Sunland will look like a convention town."

Madrid seemed not to hear. "I want Villanova, Eddie. He's a taste in my mouth, vomit in my throat. I have to have him. He's chewing me up inside. Understand?"

"We'll get him." Collins was reassuring. Madrid's intensity was frightening. "When we pull in the four they'll squeal and put the finger on him, anything for an out and a deal. They'll name him for us."

"I wish I could be sure. I'm not. Villanova is too smart to have set this up himself. It was done through, maybe, half-a-dozen in-be-tweens, each one covering for the other so there was no direct link back to anyone in Chicago. Villanova's name was probably never mentioned."

"Here's something else." Collins picked up another memo, this one on pink paper. "Who do you think is in town?" He didn't wait for Sol to reply. "At the Statler-Hilton, Mr. Joe Vito. At the Beverly Wilshire, Mr. Angie Weiss. At the Beverly Hilton, Mr. Al Danziger. How do you like that? It sounds like a meeting of the Rod and Gun Club."

"Nobody at the Beverly Hills?" Madrid was surprised.

"No. At least, no one anyone knows. We've checked out every guest. Nothing turned up."

"That's a twist." Madrid scowled his perplexity. "There's only one pigeon big enough to bring out this kind of shoot. Villanova."

"The *Capo* himself?" Collins was incredulous.

"Well, who else? It has to be that way."

Collins leaned back and stared at the ceiling. He whistled softly, a tuneless sound.

"I guess so," he admitted finally.

"Someone has to be at the Beverly Hills. Someone who has been covered so well all these years we never heard of him. If Villanova isn't being capped at the hotel then it doesn't add up. It's wrong somewhere."

"You'd better get out your tea leaves."

Madrid half smiled. "This is a new angle. I've just been sort of lying around, keeping an eye on the store. Villanova hasn't left the hotel grounds since he checked in. My tea leaves tell me he's waiting for someone to bring him something. Probably the word on where Stacey Woodward is. This is what he came out for. It's driving him nuts. He's got to see her in the dirt. Without that, everything he did was for nothing. I have the doorman and the boys in the parking lot fixed to let me know if and when he orders his car brought around. Then, where he goes I go. I'm not worried about Woodward. He can't get to her but I want to know *why* he moves if he does."

"I know he's eating you out, Sol." Collins was serious. "Don't try and do it by yourself. Let's get him by the book. That will stick and you'll be clean. The other way"—he shook his head—"you can't do it, believe me."

"When are you going to move in on the place in the Valley?" Madrid ignored the warning.

"Sunday." Collins realized what he said had in no way deflected Madrid from what had become a consuming purpose. The man, he thought, would take Villanova with his bare hands rather than let him get away. "Sunday," he repeated. "It seems like the best time. They all ought to be at home. I've arranged to take Stacey out of the Center under custody for the day. We'll need her along."

"It's going to be rough as hell's cobbles on her, going back there."

"Don't you suppose I've thought of that?" Collins was dangerously close to being angry. "She has to make the complaint and identification. Otherwise, what do we have? Nothing."

"You could take them in on suspicion." Madrid wanted to spare Stacey Woodward the horror which must come when she walked again into that house. "Disturbing the peace. Any damn thing."

"They'd be out on bail in an hour, jump it and scatter. The bond money wouldn't mean a damn thing. You know it."

"I suppose so." Madrid stood up. He took an envelope from his inside coat pocket and dropped it on Collins' desk.

"This is dated as of yesterday. It keeps the Bureau clean if you should need it."

Collins didn't have to ask. He knew what the envelope contained. It was an out for the Department for whatever Sol intended to do. Taking a key he unlocked a compartment of a steel cabinet, filed the envelope under *M* and relocked the drawer. At another time and only if it became absolutely necessary would he read it.

"It's Friday. I won't be seeing you again for awhile, Eddie." Sol put out his hand. "I talked to the Old Man. He said to use my own judgment. I'll go back to Mexico Sunday, probably. There's a man almost as good as you are, waiting for me. We have something to do."

"I'd feel a damn sight easier in my mind if you left today; right now, from here."

"Why should I give up a good thing until I have to? I have a room with a view at the Beverly Hills, an expense account. Excitement. Things going on all the time. Take care of yourself."

Collins dropped back in his chair and watched the tall figure as it left the room and became a silhouette behind the frosted-glass partition. There was an optical distortion of line. In this moment Sol Madrid appeared to grow taller, roughly sinister, a dark and avenging shade bent upon destruction.

15

T HE telephone rang with a muted chime. Madrid pushed aside the scattered pages of the Sunday paper and reached for the instrument. He listened intently for a moment.

"All right. Thanks. Now. Do something for me. Get my car out of the lot and bring it up but not to the entrance. Leave it about halfway down the driveway."

He smiled a little as he hung up. The parking attendant could not keep the excitement from his voice. He was involved in some mysterious intrigue which the hotel's management would have frowned upon. He couldn't resist being a part of it, job or no job.

Madrid slipped into his coat, picked up the single bag. It was already packed. He looked around the room for anything he might have forgotten, and left.

On the way down in the elevator he tried to give himself a logical excuse for this consuming obsession with Villanova's movements. There was none. It was out of his hands. What happened to Villanova depended upon what Eddie Collins found today in the Valley. If the persons in the house there named him, then perhaps a charge of conspiracy might be made to stick. But, and Madrid found a sardonic humor in the idea, there were too many guns in town.

For one reason or another the Chicago "family" had decided Villanova was a liability. It was very possible the *Capo* might not last out the week, or even the day. This being so, then his chasing him around town didn't make much sense. Cops and robbers stuff. Still, he was unable to rid himself of this fixity of purpose. Villanova lived with him now. They were chained together. He had to know why, after days of not venturing beyond the hotel's grounds, the man was going out. It would probably end in nothing. Whatever happened today he would leave for Mexico in the evening. The rest would have to be up to Collins.

At the porter's desk in the lobby he asked the man to call American Airlines and cancel his reservation for an afternoon flight to El Paso. This done he paid his bill, turned the bag over to a bellboy and walked out into the warm light of a perfect California day.

They were already there. Villanova, the girl and George Smythe. Curiosity alone had prompted Madrid to have this Smythe checked out by the Bureau. He was a half-time agent for television. There was nothing on him, no record. His clients were principally girls who did bit parts and laid producers for the dubious privilege of a minute or two on the screen. Sol nodded to the doorman, who touched a finger to his cap in a returning salute. Followed by the boy, Madrid strode down the driveway to where his car was parked. It was a Ford rental. There was nothing to distinguish it from the thousands of the same year and make which would be out on the roads today. He tipped the boy, slid in behind the wheel, started the motor and let it idle while he waited.

The yellow Continental went past with a velvet whisper, halting at the hotel's canopied entrance. He watched as the trio took their places in the front seat with Villanova driving. As the Lincoln moved away he allowed it to take the curve of the slope before pulling out of his place. Villanova turned east on Sunset Boulevard. Madrid deliberately slowed for two cars to get in between the Continental and him. Then he settled down to following, wondering where the trail would end and why he pursued it.

Dano, apparently, was in no hurry. He maintained an even thirty-five miles an hour down Sunset. Keeping him in sight was no problem. They passed Doheney, Fairfax, Highland, Vine and Gower.

Then, at the downtown ramp of the Hollywood Freeway, Villanova turned and stepped up his speed to the legal 65 miles per hour. He stayed in the left-hand, express lane and Madrid was forced to jockey, cutting off cars determined to get in between him and the yellow convertible. Freeway drivers in California are of a particular breed. Any car's length of space becomes an immediate challenge. They must fill it. So traffic becomes bumper-to-bumper even though there is no need for it.

At the maze of turnoffs with ramps to the downtown business section, the diverging lanes leading to Pasadena, Ramona and Santa Anna, the convertible began edging toward the right-hand side. This is a maneuver only slightly less dangerous than diving into a swimming pool from which the water has been drained. Villanova took the Santa Anna Freeway. There were, Sol knew, several alternatives for the yellow vehicle. Villanova could eventually cut off toward Corona or, in the other direction, head for Long Beach, Balboa or any of the shore towns. If he stayed on the Santa Anna it must eventually lead him into San Diego. This was Sol's hunch. Why he was certain he could not say. San Diego and then down to Tijuana. The *Capo* was taking his girl friend and Georgie Smythe to the races at Caliente. A pleasant afternoon at the track.

So, Tijuana. Madrid whistled softly. Out of nowhere now came something. At first it was only the electric flash of an idea and as quickly dismissed. But it returned. He examined it with disbelief and it began to crystallize. Why not? He knew, of course, why not. The integrity of many persons, of the Bureau, was involved. He gave little thought to himself. Villanova. The son of a bitch deserved it. Carefully, exactly now, he began to lay it out in individual steps. It was so simple it had to work. Five to twenty years. That was what they handed out for the smuggling of narcotics across the border. Most persons didn't get the maximum. Villanova wouldn't. His lawyers would appeal, one legal trick after another. Time would pass but eventually it would stick. The *Capo* in a federal prison. Nothing like that had ever happened before. The top men just didn't go to jail. But this one would. He would scream and curse, yelling "Frame." But the evidence was there. Suddenly Madrid began to laugh with the first honest pleasure he had felt in a long time. This could be the ultimate, ironic jest. For ten years Sol Madrid had been after Villanova. Today he would get him.

Wedging himself into a corner of the seat he drove with an easy competency. There was no real problem now. Simply a matter of following a hunch and keeping the yellow car in sight.

In the rear seat of one of the Bureau's cars Stacey Woodward held Eddie Collins' hand in such a grip that her fingers hurt.

"There's nothing for you to be afraid of." He was acutely aware of her mounting panic.

"I'm not frightened." Fear wasn't the word. It was the horror of a person who, awakening from a nightmare, finds herself slipping back into the same dream. "Would you give me another cigarette, please?"

Collins lit one and passed it. She took it with a grateful smile and leaned against him. He put his arm about her with reassuring pressure.

Ahead of them an unmarked car of the FBI with two men in it drove at a steady pace. At a county substation of the sheriff's office they would pick up two more cars. Everything had been well arranged in advance. Warrants issued, instructions given and accepted. Collins didn't really expect trouble. These were no desperate killers holed-up who might be expected to try and shoot it out with the law. It was a pleasant, quiet Sunday morning. The air was fresh and filled with the scent of warm earth. He and this beautiful girl beside him could be bent upon nothing more serious than a drive in the Valley with lunch at some pleasant place ahead. Of course, the Bureau agent driving them would have been an unnecessary companion. He half grinned to himself. Maybe they should have double-dated.

Stacey held tightly to herself. Everything was so sharply inked on her mind. As the distance closed she wondered if she would be able to walk again into that house. How clearly it came back. The woman, that incredibly horrible woman. The way she would sit in an old-fashioned rocking chair. Swaying back and forth, taking a slyly sadistic pleasure in watching the unbearable torture creeping upon her. She waited for the plea, the groveling, the half-screamed cry for release. The man and the young couple. From what dark pit had their contempt and venom sprung? Never had there been a trace of compassion in their manner or on their faces. They, also, used to study her with the bright intentness of vicious animals. Sometimes, and this was part of the insanity once possessing her, she actually thought she could feel their teeth. They sought her flesh with the sharpness of bats. Thinking of them now she was amazed to realize she felt no hatred but only a loathing. Hatred, like the memory of pain, dissolved with time. She wanted to hate and couldn't.

"Don't keep thinking about it." Collins seemed to know the inky tracery of her mind.

"I try not to." She turned to him, hoping to find a momentary escape from the ordeal lying ahead. "Has Sol Madrid left for Mexico?"

"He was going this morning."

"It's strange you should say it that way." She was puzzled. "Why 'was going'?"

"Because I'm not sure he did or even intended to." He leaned forward to press out a cigarette in the ashtray. "I've been wondering about him. You know," his arm tightened as though they shared a secret, "he gets to you, doesn't he?"

"Yes." She didn't hesitate. "Sol Madrid gets to you. I wonder," the pause was involuntary, "if anyone ever gets to him?"

"You did." It was simply stated.

"Oh?" There was an abrupt wistfulness about her. "I don't think so. But, Eddie," her fingers relaxed and slid more comfortably into his, "he got to me. You know that."

"Yes. I know."

"I'm glad." She seemed relieved. "I wanted you to understand. If he didn't go to Mexico, where is he?"

"I don't know. He gave me an envelope. I have an idea the letter inside is his resignation from the Bureau. He didn't want it involved in anything he might do. I think he will kill Villanova if he gets a chance."

"Dano isn't worth it." She wasn't shocked by what Collins said. "It would be the real tragedy."

At the county sheriff's substation they swung into a graveled driveway before the neat brick building. Two cars waited and a young deputy went first to the FBI men and then came to Collins. He touched his hat.

"Mr. Collins, I'm Deputy Barker. The house is about two miles up the highway and then a mile or so on a dirt road. The people you want are in. We've had the place under observation. If it's all right with you, we will have one of our cars go in and around to the back. My partner and I with you and the FBI will cover the front." His handsome young face lighted. "We're setting up a big operation for only four persons in a farmhouse."

"These are four sort of special persons, Sheriff. I wouldn't want to lose any one of them."

"We don't lose many." The smile broke fully. "Why, every now and then we get a traffic violator or recover a stolen car." His manner changed. "We're ready if you are." He glanced with polite inquiry at Stacey.

"This is Miss Woodward. We wanted her to make a spot identification."

"Good. Well, let's go." He saluted and turned away.

And now the full, dreadful memory of the night and the time following took possession of Stacey Woodward. The cars left the highway, bouncing and slewing over the badly kept dirt road. That first evening as she lay, trussed and gagged, on the floor matting the distance had seemed interminable. Now it was only a few minutes. She began to tremble. Old fears crept up on her. She could not control the spasm.

The restraining arm of Collins tightened. "Do you recognize anything?"

"I was covered with a blanket until we were in the driveway. I never really saw the house." The words were faint. "But, the barn there and the orange grove behind it. Yes."

"Good girl." He sought to comfort her with his approval. "Hang on to me if you want to."

There was no wailing of sirens, no excitement. The three cars were braked to a halt before a set of low steps and a narrow porch. Save for the insignia on the doors of the sheriff's patrol there was nothing to mark this as more than a visit by friends upon a quietly rural home.

For a moment Stacey didn't believe she could find the strength, the will, the courage to get out. That which had seemed a delirium was becoming a reality.

"You all right?" Collins helped her.

"I'm all right." She forced herself to walk.

Jensen, the grower of oranges, answered the door. He stared uncomprehendingly at the deputy sheriff, the two FBI men, Collins and the girl. For a second there was a betraying flicker in his eyes but his features were a stolid mask.

"Yes, sir?"

"I have a warrant." Deputy Barker produced it.

"Well," there was a humble awe in the word, "I sure don't know what you would need a warrant for, Sheriff. We're law-abidin', peaceful people. Anyone around here can tell you the same." Jensen seemed completely bewildered as he backed inside. "You don't have to have no legal paper. Come in if you like."

The scene in the parlor was one of serene domesticity. These were hard-working country people taking their Sunday's rest at home. The television set was tuned to an old motion picture. A young man was sprawled on an overstuffed couch, a can of beer in his hand. Seated on the floor beside him was a girl in a flowered, print dress. They both looked up with annoyance at the intrusion. Then the man straightened, put the beer at his feet. There was a wariness here and he was not clever enough to conceal it. The girl looked up at him for guidance. A heavy-breasted but otherwise masculine-appearing woman swayed placidly in a rocker with a cushioned headrest. She put down a copy of *Life* and stared with pleased inquiry. Jensen answered her silent question.

"The sheriff and these folks wanted to come in. I said why not?"

"Well, my goodness, why not? It does seem funny, though, policemen on a Sunday."

"I think I'll get another beer." The young man rose and yawned. "Anyone else?"

"You can get along without the beer." One of the FBI men, Hawkins, stood before him. He turned to Stacey. "Are these the people, Miss Woodward?"

"Yes."

"You're certain?"

"Of course I'm certain." Anger flooded her at this unabashed, hypocritical display of innocence. "Those two," she pointed to the sullen young man and defiant girl, "forced me into a car in West-wood and brought me here. That woman," a fury began to display itself, "drugged me while the others held me down for the first couple of times. After that . . ." She couldn't finish.

"My goodness, dearie," there was unhappy disapproval and even a rebuke in the words, "whatever in the world are you talking about? I never saw you before in my life. Drugs." She shuddered at the thought. "You just know there must be a mistake." She appealed to everyone in the room.

"There's no mistake. Do you think I could ever forget any of you? Everything you are saying is a lie." The sound of that hateful voice infuriated her.

"Sheriff," the woman looked to the officer with an injured expression, "do I have to stand for being called a liar by a girl I never saw before? It ain't right."

"Stacey." Collins spoke before the sheriff could answer. "Turn around. Face away from them. Now, I want you to tell me about this house." He gave her a moment. "Where is the kitchen?"

She had to force herself to think, for the days spent here had an unreality.

"The dining room is there." She pointed without turning. "From it is a short hall. It has cabinets for dishes and things. It leads to the kitchen. A door opens from the kitchen to a back porch. They brought me in that way."

"Where's the bathroom?"

"Upstairs, at the head of the steps." She shut her eyes, trying to visualize everything. "But there's a toilet under the stairs. Oh! I remember something else. There's a hot-water heater in the kitchen. It's white but sort of chipped and rusty." She reached her hand out to touch Collins. "It's so hard to remember. You understand. I wasn't normal."

At each reply to a question the FBI men left the room to check on the answer. The deputy sheriff stood with one hand near his revolver.

"Where were you kept?"

"My room, you mean? It's on this floor, back of the parlor here. There's a single, old-fashioned iron bed and a rocking chair. She used to sit and watch me. There are three windows in it—two on the right as you go in, the other at the back. You can't see anything from them but the barn and a part of the grove. Wait a minute! From the back window you can see sort of a shack, a lean-to, I guess. There was a piece of machinery under it. It had prongs, a cultivator I believe they call it."

"Dearie, you're just out of your dear, sweet little mind." There was less assurance in the speech now. "I don't have any idea how you know these things. Maybe," she brightened, "you lived here as a child. It's a very old house."

"Anything else, Stacey?" Collins was quietly triumphant.

"Give me a cigarette and a minute to think." When it was lit and handed to her, she inhaled deeply. A frown was about her eyes. Then it cleared. "Yes. Somewhere out in back there is a chicken yard. I used to hear them and the rooster."

"Dearie"—she was patience itself—"all farms have chicken yards."

Stacey ignored her. "In the entrance hall there is a closet. The man keeps a shotgun there. He got it one night because he thought there was someone or an animal in the henhouse. The chickens were squawking, making an awful racket. He ran outside. The noise quieted. Then he came back and sat with the gun across his lap for awhile before putting it away."

One of the Federal men went to the hall closet and returned with a double-barreled shotgun. He broke it at the breech, taking out the shells.

Collins turned to the deputy sheriff. "Are you satisfied? I am."

"I tell you I didn't have nothin' to do with this." Jensen shouted his defense before anyone else could speak. "These people here just hired my house. I don't know what they did to the girl. 'Course I saw her here but I thought she was a friend, a guest like."

"You're a goddamned lying bastard." The young man leaped for him.

Collins' foot went out. The man tripped over it and his body slammed heavily to the floor. Then they all began to yell accusations and imprecations at one another. Each was eager to protest his innocence first. The woman's voice rose shrilly and her words were a combination of obscenities and pious declarations. The others had all been in it. She alone was guiltless. She was a practical nurse brought in to take care of the girl and had treated her because she was sick; a poor little thing. She was only doing her duty; the bound duty of a good woman dedicated to helping others. Jensen started for her, his face twisted into a fury. One of the Federal men shoved him roughly back against the wall. Only the young girl said nothing. She sat, head bowed, crying silently to herself.

Then the confusion died. The words trickled away. The miserable spectacle ended. It was as though a snarling pack of dogs began to slink off, each hoping to find safety by itself. Stacey turned from them with revulsion, remembering their leering confidence.

The deputy called his partner in. The four were handcuffed in pairs and led out. Jensen mumbled about wanting a lawyer. The woman babbled incoherently and the young man cursed steadily in a monotone of filth.

For a few moments Stacey and Collins stood together in the now silent room. Through the sleazy curtains they watched the patrol cars and the one with the FBI men in it drive away. Neither was quite sure why but this was suddenly an awkward moment. There was a constraint which had not existed between them before.

"Well," Collins attempted to make it sound cheerful, "I guess we can start back."

They both understood what this meant. Corona and the Center. The months until her application for parole could come before the Board. For awhile, this morning, it had been possible to forget Corona.

"I haven't read the book," Collins continued. "And it is probably against all regulations. But if you'd like to, we could stop off somewhere and have a drink. After all," he took her hand, "you're in my protective custody."

She smiled then. "I like the sound of that. I like it very much."

The Sunday traffic was funneling through the inadequate lanes at the border. Three cars ahead, where he had kept it, the yellow convertible barely slowed for the Mexican Customs and Immigration officers, whose presence here was a token gesture only. So certain was Madrid of Villanova's destination that following him now seemed useless.

There are a couple of ways to get to the track at Caliente. One is by a narrow but not too heavily traveled back road. The other is across a bridge and then down the raucous, tawdry Avenida de Revolución. Tijuana's main thoroughfare. The experienced horse-players take the former. The tourists bet themselves against slashing buses, sauntering pedestrians, other tourists and the taxis with their seemingly lunatic drivers who become maddened by the sight of an undented fender on a visiting car. Villanova chose to go through the town and Madrid resignedly stayed with him. There was one more thing he needed to know and this was the easiest way of finding it out.

Most border towns have a noisy similarity. Tijuana, though, must have the distinction of being the gaudiest and loudest. This is probably due to the hundreds of sailors from the San Diego Naval Base who crowd into it every weekend. Strip joints are wall to wall, each with its bar, musicians, its girls, its steerers, procurers and "performers." There are open markets and stalls. Shop after shop advertise English woolens and French perfumes duty free, leather goods, baskets, Hong Kong silk. At every intersection there are handcarts vending tacos with, undoubtedly, the highest bacteria count of any food in the world. Spacing these are the photographers with their old-fashioned box cameras and dispirited burros which, for some reason, are dismally painted with alternating stripes of white and black to resemble zebras. No one has ever quite figured out why this outlandish creation appeals so to the tourist. But they mount the sagging backs eagerly, put on a serape and sombrero loaned by the photographers, and have their pictures taken for the folks back home who have never been fortunate enough to visit Mexico. La Avenida de Revolución is the heart of the town. It runs straight through, past the Fronton Palace, for *jai alai,* the old bull ring and to the Caliente track some three or four miles distant.

The parking lot at Caliente covers several acres. Sol loafed along, watching as Villanova sought a space. Those near the Clubhouse were already filled and the convertible cruised slowly until Villanova was able to wedge in between a couple of cars. Then he, the girl and Georgie Smythe left and walked toward the Turf Club. Sol continued on past, as though hunting for a slot of his own. Then he made a wide turn taking him out of the lot, and headed back for Tijuana.

CLUB PARAISO. That is what the neon sign proclaimed and the figure of a naked girl, outlined in neon tubing, suggested untold delights. A doorman in shabby uniform gesticulated invitingly at Madrid and made a suggestive motion with thumb between two fingers. Just inside the door, enhanced by the pink lighting of this cavern of paradise, five or six girls in tight, startlingly colored dresses of rayon moved as a group toward Sol. They tried to take his arms, pressing against him.

"You come wit' me, mister. It is a good time to have."

They spoke the border *pochismo,* a bastard combination of English and Spanish, but their profession required no linguistic accomplishments. Madrid shook his head with a friendly indifference. They dropped back, taking no offense. It was catch-as-catch-can. Sometimes one had luck; sometimes none.

At the bar, Sol ordered a Scotch and bottled water, drank it slowly and pretended an interest in the floor show. This, at the moment, was provided by a girl who slithered, bumped and ground her pelvis without grace or animation. Sailors, seated at ringside tables, whistled and stretched out to pull away the scanty G-string. Somehow, she managed to stay just out of reach. In the booths the girls deliberately let fall a shoulder strap and their companions openly fondled the brown breasts with their flowering nipples of purple. The air was foul with tobacco smoke, perspiration and cheap perfume.

The girl wore a white sheath dress covered with sequins catching the light. It was soiled about the low neckline and there was a smudge below her belly where many hands had played. She moved close to Madrid and cocked a knee out, her leg touching his.

"You buy me drink?"

"Why not?" He was uninterested.

She ordered an anise, a sickening combination of sugar water lightly flavored with anisette and containing no alcohol. Madrid dropped a dollar on the bar. The attendant rang it up on the register and handed the girl a plastic chip. At the end of the day and night she turned these in for a quarter apiece. There was no subtlety attached to the transaction. Madrid had often marveled at the quantities of anise these girls could drink in the course of an hour or so.

"You come for good time? I speak the English."

"I speak the Spanish."

"So?" She shrugged. "Wot th' hell, huh?" She pushed away the dark hair falling about her face. As the girls went she was fairly pretty. "You buy 'nother drink?"

"We'll find a booth."

"Sure." This was the normal routine. "My name Cola. Like Coca-Cola. *Venga.*" This for the bartender's ears.

She led him to a darkened corner with its partly concealed booth and signaled a waiter. Madrid ordered another Scotch. The whisky in these places was usually good. There was no reason for it not to be. Tijuana was a free port and the Scotch came in without duty. The girl repeated with the anise.

"You never say your name."

"It doesn't make any difference."

He said nothing more until the waiter had brought their drinks, taken his two dollars with a tip and left.

"I want to make a buy."

Cola put her tongue to the anise. She was a whore and an informer. When he had been stationed in Los Angeles and San Diego before, he had used her often. She knew nothing about him save that he paid well for information and could be trusted.

"'Ow big this buy?"

"Three ounces."

She frowned doubtfully. It was part of an act in an effort to make the task seem really difficult and her part in it more important.

"It hard to get now, sometime."

"Cajo!"

She laughed moderately at the obscenity. This was the kind of reply she had expected.

"Three 'unnered an' feefty an *onza.* Feefty more dollar for me."

"How soon?"

"Now." She lifted a shoulder. *"Ahorita. Vamos!"*

They left the table. Passing the bar she nodded to the bartender. He understood. She was going out with the tourist for a quick trick in one of the cheap hotels which catered to the girls. He would expect two dollars of her ten-dollar fee because she hadn't been able to make him drink much.

In Madrid's car she spoke without looking at him.

"Calle Hidalgo. You know where?"

He inclined his head. The street ran parallel to the *avenida* a couple of blocks back. It was not a place of tourists. Here were the small shops, the bakeries and stores of the Mexicans.

"You give me money now."

He had drawn twenty-five hundred dollars expense money in Los Angeles. Now he took out his wallet, counted one thousand and fifty for the heroin and added two twenties and a ten for the girl. Her eyes grew foxily sharp at the sight of so much money. Then she sighed. This was not a man one could make a fool of.

"It has to be good. Understand? The best. Nothing else."

"Am I crazy to lie with you? It is best."

He drove to Hidalgo and she pointed out a small drugstore, motioning to a place at the curb just beyond where he could park.

"I want a small roll of tape. *Pegajoso.* You understand?"

She nodded but her expression revealed her astonishment as she took the coin, a fifty-cent piece.

Madrid lit a cigarette and waited. Everything had gone well. Now each step was important. The girl wasn't long away. She came back unhurriedly, completely indifferent to the fact she was wearing an evening dress in the middle of the day and ignoring a couple of inviting whistles. In the seat again her hand slid beneath him and left a packet there.

"Bien suerte." She wished him luck softly.

Now there was no hurry. He dropped her off at the club and then drove to the parking lot behind the Caesar Hotel. At the small office of Aeronaves de Mexico a pert young girl told him he could get a flight out of Tijuana for Juarez at six o'clock. He made and paid for a reservation. Then, getting several dollars in change from the cashier, he went to a telephone booth.

The first call was to the car rental agency in Los Angeles. He gave his name and the number of his credit card and explained he would have to leave the car in Tijuana. It would be in the Caesar Hotel lot and the keys at the desk. Whatever expense there was in having it picked up here should be put on his bill.

The second call took no more than a minute or so. He again dialed the operator and gave her a number in the United States, at the border.

The voice came crisply. "United States Customs. Haney speaking."

"Listen carefully and write down what I say."

"Who is this?"

"The hell with that. A yellow Lincoln Continental convertible. California license KRE 935. It will be coming back over this afternoon. Check it." He hung up.

Only a couple of more things. He left the car keys in an envelope with an assistant manager, explaining the car would be picked up. Then he went outside to the cabstand and took a taxi.

"Caliente."

On the way to the track he took the packet from his inside coat pocket and examined it. The weight felt right. He had done business too many times with Cola not to be certain she would have made sure of its contents. The powder was in a heavy plastic envelope and tightly sealed. The roll of adhesive tape was half an inch wide. It would do very well.

At Caliente he had the taxi driver let him out near the center of the parking area. He paid the man and watched him drive away. Then he walked along the lines of cars until he came to Villanova's car. There was no one around. The parking attendants were gathered about the Clubhouse entrance.

Within the space behind the convertible's rear bumper he carefully and securely taped the package of heroin into place. He used the entire roll. There was no chance of its being jolted loose. Then he stepped back and looked at the bumper from all angles. The envelope could not be seen. He laughed quietly. How often had the amateur smugglers used just such a hiding place? They were always so certain they were being clever. No one would think of looking at the bumpers. Yet they were one of the first places the Customs men searched. He had no worry the envelope would pass inspection.

He glanced at his watch. It was still early afternoon. Why not? He strolled across the lot, bought a *Racing Form* from a boy near the gate and was handed a Clubhouse admission ticket with the paper. No one ever paid to go to the races at Caliente. The management figured its take at the Mutuel windows more than offset an admission fee.

Inside he bought a program, walked up the ramp and looked at the tote board. The fifth race was just coming up. He went on inside, found a place at the crowded bar and ordered a tequila with the salt and limes. The taste of Scotch was pallid in his mouth. As a matter of fact, there was no flavor at all now in this day. Where was the satisfaction he should have felt; the elation of knowing he had nailed Villanova? Somehow it was missing and this disturbed him. There was an emptiness. It would have been different if he could have held on to Harvey Mitchell. With him he might have cracked the Chicago *borgata* wide open, exposing it for the rotten egg it was. With Chicago, much of the secrecy of *Cosa Nostra* itself would have been revealed. This way? Well, he had Villanova but the triumph was hollow. Angrily he thought this was a hell of a time to develop a conscience or scruples.

Shaking off the heaviness he leafed through the program. A tiny smile drew wrinkles at his eyes. What was it young Blakely at the border narcotics station had said? The fifth horse in the fifth race. How, he mused sarcastically, could anyone go wrong with a system like that? He had a second tequila and the lime bit with a pleasant nibble at his tongue.

Turning away from the bar he went to the $50 window. Almost ashamed to ask for the tickets he put down one hundred dollars.

"Dos en numero cinco."

Impassively the man punched out two of the colored slips, each bearing the numbers 5 and $50. Sol dropped them in his pocket. He was getting smarter all the time. The fifth horse in the fifth race for $100. That, sure as hell, wasn't what the Bureau advanced expense money to its agents for. Well, what he had done only a short time ago wasn't exactly government policy either. There was no point in playing it cozy now.

He wedged himself in again at the bar and ordered a third tequila. They were beginning to make themselves felt. He heard the bugle for the parade of horses to the post and stood, brooding over his drink. Finally, he went outside. The program was thrust in his coat pocket. He didn't even know the name of the horse.

The Clubhouse tables were filled with people eating, drinking, talking. Along the top aisle, standing, was the crowd of eagerly apprehensive bettors. They were concentrating on their *Forms,* the tip

sheets and newspaper selections; touting themselves off original wa-
gers in these last few minutes, frantically trying to figure out a hedge
bet to cover the one they were now certain would lose.

Sol glanced across the track to the totalizer board. Here the
electric computers constantly flashed the changing odds. Number Five was paying eighteen to one. Only two other horses were at
longer odds. He thought grimly they all, probably, pulled milk wag-
ons during weekdays. It was a six-furlong race. He turned away in
disgust and went back to the bar. Sometime, if he was still in the
service and had a chance, he'd tell Blakely what he thought of his
system.

There was plenty of room at the bar now. Everyone, save for a
couple of haggard sportsmen who looked as though they no longer
cared, was outside to watch and yell. They didn't, Madrid thought,
come here for fun or the pleasure of watching beautiful animals run.
They only hoped desperately to make a few bucks. He had another
tequila. Hell. I might as well be really drunk. Dimly he heard the
call of the start over the loudspeakers. Then, the mounting screams
of frenzy as yells of encouragement for the favored animals rose.
The roar increased to one final, full-throated sound and then died
abruptly as the race ended. Singly, in pairs and groups the players
drifted back. Those who held winning tickets hurried to the payoff
windows to stand in line. The losers tore up their coupons, scatter-
ing the pieces as they walked.

A man moved in beside Madrid. He ordered a bourbon and
gulped it down straight.

"I'll be a son of a bitch." He spoke to no one in particular. "I'll
just be a son of a bitch." The idea of his unusual parentage seemed
to give him a particularly gloomy satisfaction. He repeated it.

"What won?" Madrid sucked on a lime quarter. He really had no
interest.

"A donkey. A dog. A thing called Mistress Nell. I'd give it a head
start and beat it by six lengths myself." He ordered another bourbon,
drank it as quickly and looked at Madrid for the first time. "I'll tell
you one thing, friend. You never see one of those horses trying to
hustle a dollar or two to get back home after the races. Which, I
guess," he crooked a finger for more whisky, "proves horses are
smarter than people."

The flight from Tijuana is a short one. No meal was served but it was possible to get a sandwich and a drink. There were only a few passengers on the plane. Leaning back in his seat, Madrid was mildly astonished to realize he hadn't actually been surprised. For a moment back there he had been tempted not to look at the program but just go to the cashier's window and put down his tickets. When he did look it was there as he knew it must be.

5   MISTRESS NELL

On the one-hundred-dollar bet he had collected $1,900. He could feel the bulge of his wallet against the cushion. At least he was square with the United States Treasury Department and the Federal Bureau of Narcotics. The expense money could be accounted for. He could quit clean. Maybe, and the notion amused him, my mother was a gypsy after all.

They were coming into Juarez. The NO SMOKING and FASTEN SEAT BELTS sign went on. He would have to lay over in the Mexican town until morning. Then there was a flight to Chihuahua and from there the hop to Sonora and Hermosillo. He wasn't quite sure why he was coming back. It was a promise made to a man he respected, Lieutenant Mendoza. A job had been started and ought to be finished. The setup was too carefully arranged. It had been planned too well.

He thought about Villanova. If it only could have been done a little better. That was his real regret. There would, he knew, be some curious speculation among the Customs men at the border. The Old Man might wonder but Collins would know. Eddie was too smart, too long at the business, to believe Dano Villanova was fool enough to try and bring in three ounces of heroin taped to the bumper. Hell! If Villanova wanted the powder all he would have to do was make a telephone call from his bungalow at the Beverly Hills and have a kilo delivered to the door.

The plane came down at Hermosillo. In addition to Madrid there were only five passengers. One was a Mexican. The other four were obviously tourists, middle-aged, loaded down with cameras, making a package tour of Mexico.

Carrying his light bag Sol walked across the cement ramp toward the small terminal.

Holding the ridiculous, stiff straw hat with its brightly colored band to his chest, Jalisco trotted beside the tourists, offering his services as a guide. They were sophisticatedly suspicious of strange Mexicans who tried to attach themselves. They couldn't be trusted. The tour agency had warned them to leave such matters to its representatives at the designated hotels. Then they would not be overcharged.

Jalisco turned away with an expression of melancholy. He waited until Madrid approached, then bowed with a flowing courtesy and smiling humility.

"Could I be of service again to the gentleman? I am, you remember, Jalisco. Very dependable. Your bag, perhaps, gentleman?" He took it from Madrid's hand.

"Would you know of a good place to have a drink and where there might be some almost virgins?" Madrid held back a smile with an effort.

"*Señor*," they were approaching the single remaining taxi, "the number of almost virgins increases daily."

He waited until Madrid was seated, closed the door and then climbed into the front seat with the driver. He turned.

"Since the *señor* has been in Hermosillo before he would, undoubtedly, like to go to the Hotel Monique?"

"That's fine."

With a lordly wave of his hand Jalisco gave the instructions to the driver and then settled back with a fine air of dignified propriety.

"I am," he told the driver, "a very special companion and guide of the *señor*. We were even in jail once together."

There was no question but that this implied a rare distinction on the American's part.

At the Monique, Sol registered. Jalisco stood at one side.

"I will be here in the lobby, *señor,* should you wish my services later. *Bienvenido* to Hermosillo." Again he clasped hat to chest. "It is with great pleasure I see you once more."

In his room, Madrid began to strip off his clothing for a shower. The telephone rang.

"Los Angeles, California, is calling, *señor.*" The operator was a little impressed.

Sol waited while a variety of voices passed across the wire. Well, here it was. He had been an idiot to think he could get away with it.

"Señor Madrid?" The voice was slightly mocking.

"Yes."

"This is a friend in Los Angeles." There was no mistaking Eddie Collins. "A funny thing happened Sunday after the races at Caliente. A man was picked up at the border carrying three ounces of the powder. It was taped to the bumper." Complete incredulity was in the inflection. "Now, wouldn't you think he'd know better than to do such a fool thing?" There was a slight pause. "He was arraigned before a United States Commissioner. Then another funny thing happened. He was screaming for his lawyers and bail until someone told him of the boys who were in town. We couldn't keep him out of jail after that. He begged to be locked up and that's exactly what they did. How do you like that?"

Sol said nothing but Collins seemed undisturbed by the silence.

"No one around here can figure how he could have been so stupid, but I guess those things happen sometimes," Collins continued on an even, conversational tone. "Another thing." This suddenly occurred to him. "I was cleaning out some of my files and I'll be damned if the janitor or one of the wool-headed secretaries we have around here didn't throw a lot of stuff into a wastepaper basket and it was burned by mistake. There could have been something important like a letter or something. You know how those things are? The whole thing makes you wonder how the Government manages to get along with all the carelessness and inefficiency. Well. Like they say in your country. *Hasta la vista y bien suerte.*" The connection was abruptly broken.

For a moment Madrid stood, holding the instrument in his hand. Then gently, carefully, as though fearful of breaking a spell, he replaced it and finished undressing.